WINTER BREAKS

JOSEPH CONNOLLY

Quercus

First published in Great Britain in 1999
by Faber and Faber Limited

This paperback edition published in 2014 by

Quercus Editions Ltd
55 Baker Street
7th Floor, South Block
London
W1U 8EW

A CIP catalogue record for this book is available
from the British Library

ISBN 978 1 78206 706 1
EBOOK ISBN 978 1 78206 716 0

10 9 8 7 6 5 4 3 2 1

Printed and bound in Great Britain by Clays Ltd, St Ives plc

To Finn, at the very beginning . . .

PART ONE

Cold Snaps

CHAPTER ONE

Every single day of my life, now, I give up the drink: from that time of night when, quite stunned, I fall off the world, right up until the moment morning hits and takes me. The drink is spiking and enhancing everything I do. Which has become less, and then even less; it all diminishes very near tangibly, and I just watch it go. What are you up to, people say: what is it, in fact, that you do? I am up to nothing at all in the whole wide world, and what I do is little. What I do is drink.

Having moodily and once more thought all that (he edited it frequently – constantly refining, getting it right), John Powers swivelled round and very nearly focused on close to where he could almost have sworn his Lulu's voice had come from.

'Don't,' he just about muttered. 'Please don't leave me, Lulu. I'll improve, I swear. I'll get help.'

'Oh John . . .' was all Lulu could sigh.

'*You* could help me, Lulu,' John was now imploring. And then quite flatly: 'You're the only one who ever could.'

'Get up, John. Let me help you up.'

John raised a dead bent arm, and Lulu half dragged and lifted him up from the latest piece of furniture into which he had careered and collapsed, this time snapping some brittle bit of it – don't know what until I get him up and out of here.

'Lulu . . .?' John pursued, once he was slumped like a sack of something into the nearest sofa.

'John,' cut in Lulu – sharply, quite sharply (it was, maybe

sadly, the only way, these days). 'We've been over all this, haven't we? Hm? We've *said* all this, no? Now just leave it.'

But John couldn't think of Lulu leaving it – couldn't drag himself round to think of Lulu leaving him. Even now the bulbous pouches beneath bloated and bee-stung eyes creased up and flinched away from the recurrent lick of this terrible inevitability. But she was right about one thing: they *had* been over it, hadn't they? Hm? They'd *said* all this, no? But now, dearest Lulu, I just can't leave it – so *you* go, *you* drift, you carry on falling back into shadows as you do, and leave me to trudge through it all on my own – just this one more time before the next time (which won't at all be long in coming).

It was only last summer. How could one summer – one holiday – just one more stupid summer thing amid a life-time of others: how could just that have done it to me? Who, in fact, was to *blame* for this? Not myself, surely? No no – not a bit. It was Lulu: she betrayed me. She is a lustful and wayward harlot and I loathe her with depth and a bright white clarity, while I love her more than anything else I have ever touched or seen.

'Can I have some ice-cream?' asked John. 'Lulu? Are you still here?'

Lulu was intimidated by the new child that had been born within John since just last summer; but if she were not careful, she could respond to it, too, which chilled her. She simply had to be away from him.

'You spilt it last time,' she said softly. 'Didn't you? Made an awful mess.'

'This time will be different,' whispered John, his eyes flicking up and scanning any vista that might take in his Lulu. '*Please* believe me . . .'

By the time Lulu got back from the kitchen with a sundae bowl brimming with Melba, John was deeply asleep – mouth both askew and ajar, like a quickly rigged-up trap that no one was falling for. Lulu sighed and shook her head, not with affection and maybe neither in indulgence nor sorrow, but simply because the scene now touched her as requiring it. Kneeling, she spooned the peachy cream out of the bowl and around John's gaping and chasmic mouth – two more scooplets she dropped on to the crotch of his trousers, before placing the bowl sideways on the floor and then cracking it beneath her heel. Guilty awakenings, she had found, made her life more tolerable; and until she could truly bulldoze this madman out of her life just once and for all, Lulu needed all the help she could lay her hands on.

She glanced briefly at her face in the mirror in the hall. She must be beautiful, she supposed: so many people kept on saying so – and maybe none more often than Lizzie. Lulu opened her full and lipsticky mouth into a distended oval and softly applied the pad of a middle finger to one taut corner and then to the next – for no reason at all except that here was a part of the ritual of leaving, and leaving was both huge and wonderfully looming. *How lovely to be away from the awfulness of John and on my way to the bliss of Lizzie. Whom I love so very much – more and more with each day's passing. For what woman, in fact, actually needs a man, hm? I mean to say – will someone please tell her what precisely it is they are meant to be for? At base, they're nothing but trouble, aren't they? Well, aren't they?* Lulu thought so; and some day soon, she hoped and dreamed, Lizzie would finally think so too.

❋

'Duh-duh-duh-duh-duh-duh-duh!' juddered Lulu in the porch, as Elizabeth swung wide the front door; her nose – redly kissable, due to the cold – was moving in time to this stuttered exaggeration. 'God, Lizzie – it's absolutely f-f-freezing!'

'Oh God come in come in come in,' urged Elizabeth, one hand on Lulu's shoulder, now, and hauling her into the heat of the hall. With the door firmly shut behind them – and

Lulu still well into her colossal show of shivering – Elizabeth dabbed her lips against Lulu's nose (still pinkly kissable, due to the cold – and now alive with tingling, if Elizabeth's wide, warm mouth had a say in the matter).

Many scarves and layers (one pashmina, the rest just cashmere) were gradually and really quite teasingly discarded ('Oh I can't help it – I just seem to *feel* the cold more than other people – brr!') and a cup of fresh-roast Kenyan was eagerly clutched (not so good a hand-warmer as a mug might be, true, but Elizabeth – Lizzie to Lulu – could never abide mugs in any shape or form, as simply anyone at all could have told you). The coffee was still too piping to even be sipped at, so Lulu thought OK, then, let's get going – and launched straight in:

'So. What's for today, Lizzie?'

'A Mrs *Bramley*, I'm pretty sure she said her name was. Sounded rather odd on the phone.'

'Oh God – they're *all* odd,' laughed Lulu. 'Bats, most of them. I still think it's absolutely amazing these women actually *pay* us to do all this junk. I mean – what's *wrong* with them all?'

Elizabeth shrugged. 'Don't knock it,' she said. And smiled.

Yes: it was the last thing in the world that Elizabeth would have imagined, but here she was, for the first time in her life, actually earning money – was even rather enjoying the process. Wasn't *necessary*, of course – it wasn't a case of that, no; her husband Howard took good care of that side of things – estate agent, did she mention? Well – I say estate agent: just happens to own maybe not the largest but certainly the most prestigious firm in the area, and I don't have to tell you what has happened just lately to house prices in this part of London – I don't really think I need to spell it out. Dear Howard. Oh now where was I? Got completely sidetracked, there; it was something Lulu said, and . . . oh yes yes yes – all these rather silly women who don't seem to be able to look after themselves. Elizabeth had had no idea that such women *existed*, but my God – every single job they got seemed to lead to about half a dozen more purely on the strength of recommendation. Extraordinary. But yes: don't knock it, as she says.

It had all started ('Isn't it *always* the way?') completely by accident. God – even Lulu *being* here was an utter and total fluke: if just last summer they hadn't happened to be booked into that same seaside hotel, they never would even have *met*. Seems impossible, now, that I haven't known Lulu for every single day of my entire life on earth, but there it is – that is the truth of the matter. Only a few months: where are we now? Oh Lord, nearly Christmas – *please* don't remind me. So the holiday was in August, so . . . yep, four and a bit months: that's all it is. Amazing. And just think! If I hadn't offered her that one glass of champagne in the bar of . . . oh God – do you know, in just this short time I've already forgotten the name of the . . . *Excelsior*, that's it: Excelsior, of course. Nice hotel. Lovely, actually.

Anyway. That evening, yes. Dotty had gone off, can't quite remember why – something to do with the baby, probably; Melody had gone, of course – that absolutely *ghastly* man she'd picked up. Could've told her, poor thing, where all *that* was headed, but God – you know Melody: once she's got a man in her sights . . . anyway. Now what was I . . .? Oh yes. And there was dear sweet Lulu, all on her own, looking so lovely and *so* gorgeously dressed, just as she always does . . . had had the most *beastly* evening (this I found out *much* later) with that quite appalling madman husband of hers. John. I tell you – he is *so* jealous, *so* mad – really quite insane. And just think – if I'd only left earlier, or gone to another bar, or something, we never would've . . . *and*, of course, if she hadn't had this terrible row with John. If it hadn't been for that, he never would've even let her out of his sight and Lulu and I never would've . . . *and* she started calling me 'Lizzie' right from the word go. Can't think why. It's not as if I *asked* her to, or anything; no one else ever has. But I love it. Although it's just for Lulu, now; wouldn't like anyone *else* calling me Lizzie, not now. Dotty tried it for a while, but I had to put a stop to that. Poor Dotty. But I can't think of Dotty just now – there's work to be done. Yes . . . No – Lizzie is just for Lulu. As I say.

'So,' said Lulu. She loved saying *so*, like this – sounded so businesslike: *so-o-o* businesslike. And no, since we're delving – Lulu hadn't worked for ages either, mainly because *John*, of course, became too paranoid about her actually exchanging a Good Morning with some *man* or other, felt quite convinced that should such a thing just once occur, then this *man* would be instantly transformed into a rapist or (worse, much worse) a lover. And he always pronounced the word '*man*' like that – with an emphasis tinged by terror, as if for all he knew it could easily be some pernicious and disfiguring disease – which quite possibly, given the mental state of him, is just how he perceived it. And has Lulu told you that John is still quite unshakeable in his belief that last summer at the Excelsior (where I met my blissy Lizzie – so at least *some* good came out of that ghastly time) I had actually had some sort of *affair* with someone? And the joke is – well, *joke*: I say joke, but I didn't think of it as a joke at the *time* (Christ, he nearly broke me) but thanks to Lizzie I can see the funny side of it now . . . no, the joke is that the man I was supposedly screwing – all he did was give me an Extra Strong Mint that I didn't even want! Believe it? Well that's John for you. Mental. And even this crazy job I do with Lizzie – Oh No You're Not, he goes. I'm not having you going into people's houses all on your own: on and on. But they're all *women*, I said to him: *women*, Johnny. *Ah*, he comes back – but they've got *husbands*, haven't they? *Sons*?! OK – he stopped short of grandfathers and servants, but Jesus. Anyway – couldn't give a shit about what he thinks now. This divorce, believe me, just cannot come soon enough. Every *hour* with that man is just . . . oh.

Anyway. The laugh is – I actually *prefer* women. Hate men. Hate them. Enough of all that. Now: to work.

'So,' said Lulu, one more time. 'What's Mrs Bramley after? What – Bramley like the apple?'

'*Think* she said Bramley,' said Elizabeth. And then – with mock consternation – 'God! Can't have been Granny *Smith*, can it?'

Lulu laughed. 'Crazy, Lizzie! Mm – I really do love this coffee – do you still get it from – ?'

'Mm. They're very good. Anyway – Granny Bramley, or whatever her name is –'

'Cox's Pippin! Sorry, Lizzie.'

Elizabeth put on her silly stern voice, now – which Lulu rather loved. '*Quite* enough apple jokes – *thank* you, Mrs Powers.'

'Won't *be* Mrs Powers for much longer. Bliss. Anyway – what's the silly woman want? I'm really hot, now. Think I'll take this jumper off.'

'Usual,' said Elizabeth. 'Wardrobe. Oh – and flowers.'

And that is what Lulu and Elizabeth did: they told other women what in their wardrobe they should get rid of ('God!' Lulu had laughed out loud, one time. 'Some of the stuff you see there – quite incredible anyone could actually have bought them in the first place! Amazing such things could be *made*!'). And then they advised them on what to get. Sometimes even went along with them to the shops, if you can believe it – which was actually fine by Elizabeth and Lulu as most of their waking hours were spent on buying clothes anyway. ('And that's the bloody trouble!' Elizabeth had once wailed in bogus despair. 'Every time we take them to Harvey Nicks, we end up spending more than they do!') And some of these women (grief – all this, you know, had only started because a friend of Lulu had asked her opinion on some dress, outfit, costume – something – and now it was a fully-fledged business!) – yes, some of them wanted to know how to hang pictures – arrange

9

flowers (our Mrs Bramley, if such she be called, being the latest case in point). An odd mixture of women, Lulu had mused: they're either striving to do just *everything* in their lives (kids, career, entertaining and wifey – the whole damn bit) or else seem confounded by simply anything at all. Elizabeth – now that her daughter Katie was all grown up (seventeen! Still can't believe it) – had once believed that she had maybe been in danger of becoming one of these (Howard earned money, Elizabeth got shot of it) but she had always assumed that her very obvious talents – home-making, cooking, arranging, dressing – were just *normal*; had no idea they could actually be *marketed*. But well, she had concluded: there you go. (Well yes all right – I *do* know I'm good at all those things: known that for ages. I suppose I shouldn't say it, but there – I've done it now.)

'And –' added Elizabeth.

'Don't tell me! She needs her laces tied. God, Lizzie – don't you ever feel like laughing when you're with these people?'

'Not when they write the cheque,' smiled Elizabeth. 'Actually,' she amended, 'maybe that's *exactly* when. Anyway – oh God's sake *listen*, Lulu: you're practically meant to *be* there by now. She wants Christmas decorations. Tree. Mantelpiece. And something on the door.'

'Oh right,' agreed Lulu. 'I suppose we'll be getting quite a lot of that, now. I'm really looking forward to Christmas, this year. Well – the bit that's here, anyway.'

Yes indeed, thought Elizabeth: you just wait, everyone. My Christmas party – well, the whole weekend, really: you just wait. It'll be the best ever. And simply *everyone's* coming – I'm just bursting to tell you. There'll be – well, Howard, of course (if he's quite recovered from Paris – we're going to Paris, you know: just a little winter break – God knows I need one – and Howard, poor Howard, he hasn't even *had* a holiday this year. Didn't come to the seaside last August because he had to *work*, poor lamb). So anyway – *Howard*, and Lulu and oh God I *suppose* bloody John will have to come too, but I do hope not. Brian and Dotty, of course (God, *they'll* need it, that's for sure: how can they *bear* being cooped up in a caravan? – *three* of them, with Colin). Colin is their son, about fifteen – maybe more, now. Talking of Colin . . . actually no, I can't tell you, because I'm rather ashamed of myself. Well – a bit. Oh look – it's all terribly complicated and maybe not very interesting but last summer Brian and Dotty and Colin and me and Melody – she's a friend, don't think you know her – all went to the same seaside resort (where I met Lulu, as you know) – wasn't really a coincidence, but it wasn't planned either – and, well . . . Colin and I got a wee bit carried away one night, and . . . oh look I *know* it's dreadful, I *know* it is – how do you think I feel? I mean – he's a child and Dotty's my *friend*, for God's sake: lives next door. Well *doesn't* any more, poor thing – now lives in a caravan, if you can possibly believe it, which is as we speak, parked in *my* driveway! Long story – ask Howard: don't ask Brian, as he'll never stop telling you. Seems they're completely broke, which just must be simply too ghastly. Anyway – daresay Dotty will tell you more. *And*, poor Dotty – she keeps asking Lulu and me to be part of our, you know, *venture*, but the really awful thing is that Dotty is just simply dreadful at anything at all like that, you only have to look at her. But you can't *say* that, can you? You can't just tell people to their faces.

So anyway – *they'll* be coming; and our new neighbours, Cyril and Edna – the ones in Brian and Dotty's old house: quite nice, I think. Not sure yet. They've torn the place to pieces – ripped out absolutely everything. Anyway, they'll be there. And my darling and virginal daughter Katie (ho ho) is apparently importing some American man she met in Chicago last summer. I wanted her to come to the seaside with us – but no. Had to be little Miss Independent, didn't she? And look where it got her. Enough about that. And Mummy's coming. She does every Christmas, since Daddy died. Just a teensy bit of a handful, but it's probably not her fault.

Melody, of course. Did I mention Melody? With, I suppose, whatever awful man she currently has in tow. Will she bring Dawn? (Dawn is her baby – screams the place down.) Have to, really. But look, don't worry – you'll meet them all, in time. It's been something of a *strange* year for a lot of us, in many ways – yes, I suppose it has. Anyway – I can, I think, promise everyone it'll be quite a Christmas: truly one to remember. You just wait.

❋

'What on earth are you talking about, "cold *snap*"?!' snapped Dotty. 'This isn't a cold *snap*, Brian – it's bloody *arctic*. It's like the bloody North Pole. Maybe it's not so bad for people who actually live in a *house*, with walls and a roof and proper bloody heating, but if you happen to be trapped in a glorified tin can in the middle of someone else's bloody front garden – !'

'I don't find it that cold,' said Brian, mildly, shifting his practically gelid buttocks on the narrow bench that formed the main bulk of the seating in this admittedly none-too-spacious and effectively immobile home.

'That's because you're wearing all of your *clothes*, Brian – absolutely every single rag you possess.'

In what you might suppose must be termed the caravan's kitchenette, Dotty was creating far more clatter than was remotely necessary, but along with most of whatever she had to say, Brian barely heard any of it any more – it was just the way Dotty was, nowadays: nowadays, Dotty was ratty on a permanent basis. And who could actually blame her? Can't, can it, be a whole load of fun, being married to me – no, I don't for a moment suppose it can. Poor Dotty. Just take one look at what I've inflicted on her and Colin – never mind grossing it all up over the, Christ, ages they've been stuck with me – let's just take this one year alone: I've hoiked Colin out of school and shoved him into the local comprehensive, which he hates (maybe not quite so much this term as last – the boy's growing up, but Christ: what into? You know how it is in these London schools). And then, last summer, instead of taking everyone to the luxurious five-star hotel on the coast that Dotty had more or less pleaded for – she had wanted everything, every detail of the holiday to be just like Elizabeth's: God knows why (women for you) – I rented a bloody little caravan amid a sea of other caravans clinging to a windswept cliffside – though maybe not quite so poky as the one we now live in on a (Jesus, can it really be?) permanent basis.

And how does it come about, people would be entitled to inquire – how in fact has it come to pass that a family of three now do their terrible best to live in a caravan parked on their friends' and former neighbours' carriage driveway? Oh Christ because I lost bloody *everything*, didn't I? I still don't understand quite why or how – thought I was a pretty fair little businessman until everything, um – do they say belly-flopped, is that right? The phrase? *Flopped,* anyway – no bones about it. Carpets – that was my game; kept expanding, and so did the bloody recession. Didn't take long. All I had left was the house, and that's now history. One of the most painful bits of this whole thing is actually having to witness the ritual destruction of, oh – I can't tell you just how much hard work I put into that accursed house, all down the years. I'm really into DIY, you know – quite the little handyman, though I do say it myself. One of the first things Mister Cyril Davies ripped out – sorry, *Doctor* bloody Davies: the man's a psychiatrist and, like most of his breed, barmy – totally nuts. Anyway, like I was saying, one of the first things to go (and don't even think about getting me on to how much he *paid* for the bloody house – songs don't remotely come into it: snips don't even enter) . . . yeah, practically the very first thing I see heaved into a skip is a pair of very tasteful blockboard units I constructed especially to house my collection of manhole covers. Now granted, not everyone is fortunate enough to possess such a treasure-trove (I have arranged them outside the caravan, pro tem – as a sort of cross between a pathway and stepping stones, but the threat of theft troubles me greatly, and is with me always); but still, those units would have done sterling service as, say . . . well, just about anything, really: you just need a bit of imagination. I thought of trying to squeeze them into the caravan, but Dotty said that if I even so much as attempted such a thing, she'd nail my head to the wall.

Talking of whom – hang on: Dotty is just now becoming shrill. What's she say?

'I *said*, Christ curse you,' sang out Dotty, eyes ablaze and hair awry as it always bloody was these days because it kept on catching in just anything at *all* in this fucking little box, God help her, 'that you're getting bloody chips of wood all over the bloody *floor* and I've just this morning *cleaned* the bloody floor and why can't you put newspapers down and why in God's name are you chopping up bits of wood *anyway* and Christ I'd just really love to *kill* you, Brian!'

Brian nodded. 'Point taken,' he said, as loudly as he dared.

I'm not, he thought, 'chopping up bits of wood'; I am, if you really want to know, Dotty, creating model boats; schooners, fairly sure, but I haven't yet worked out about sails and rigging and all the rest of it. Maybe (walk before you run, right?) I'll settle for canoes. Anyway – my thinking goes like this: got to get money, right? Right – believe it. OK – Dotty's got a part-time job, now (some sort of office work in a department store – hates it, of course; of course), but that goes nowhere. And me? I can't get any sort of a job at all. Not for want of trying. Mind you, I don't really blame them, these employers, for not all rushing to take me on: not as if I can *do* anything, or anything. Put an ad in the local rag, one time: odd bits about the house –

14

decorating, you name it. Didn't work. Only got two calls. First woman, she won't even let me through the door because she says I've got funny eyes. And the second could hardly be termed a blinding success; how was I to know the wall was bloody load-bearing? Bloody isn't now.

So is it any wonder that I really need to kill myself? And here, believe me, is no idle banter. I'm an old hand at the suicide game, Christ yes; never actually pulled it off, it's true to say, but Jesus (like job-hunting), it's not for the want of trying. And that's *another* thing I've done this year – at the seaside, in point of fact: right slap-bang in the middle of our so-called holiday I decided to jump off a cliff. Well – it was handy. In the past I've tried gas ovens, pills – toyed with electrocution and disembowelling. Suffice it to say, none of them worked. And nor did the bloody cliff – mud at the bottom, you see: not the sharp and fang-like rocks I'd been hoping for. Every summer and every bloody Christmas (I can't – I know I should, I know, but I can't even *think* about Christmas) things just, oh – get on top of me and I just go Right Mate – Owe-Yew-Tee spells Out. Yes. And I don't even seem able to do *that*. Poor Dotty. Poor Colin. They really don't deserve it.

Anyway, until the fog that surrounds me thickens up and turns even blacker, I am making what very well might turn out to be canoes (this one looks like a barge, if the truth be known – maybe if I just ease a leeedle bit off the prow with the shaver . . . no, that's buggered up the other side now, oh Christ); and then I can give them a lick of Humbrol (red, blue, yellow – let's not stint) and maybe sell them to, um . . . whoever buys such things. Oh God. I know. It's hopeless, isn't it? Tragic. Yes it is – but I just have to keep on *trying*, don't I? Right up until I just can't try any more.

CHAPTER TWO

'Howard? Is that you?' called Elizabeth from upstairs, somewhere.

You know it's funny, thought Howard – not for the first time – how the rituals of two people living together become, after time, so defined and immutable. I mean – just take that: every single evening I come back from the office round about now and drop my briefcase noisily to the floor (the reason why, says Elizabeth, it looks so terribly scruffy – why on *earth*, Howard, don't you go to Tanner Krolle and get yourself a really smart *new* one? Because I happen to like this one, Elizabeth – I'm scruffy too and it suits me. Tanner *who*?). I next yawn with all the sound effects you would decently expect – and so extravagantly that sometimes I feel my jaw will clickingly set into a permanent rictus of large amazement – and then by way of a rousing finale I hurl my vast fob of keys – damn bloody keys, bane of my life – into a brass sort of bowl thing on the table just west of the drawing room. And what happens then? What happens then is that Elizabeth, from wherever in the house she is currently wafting, requires to be informed (please tell me, Howard) whether or not it's *me*. And to this quest for affirmation I invariably respond as I do right now:

'It's me,' Howard exhaled. And then he sighed in the very same tone.

Elizabeth was coming down the stairs and patting her hair, rather in the way that American women on television seem inclined to pat theirs. New dress? Could be. Maybe say something.

'Good day?' she asked, very nearly kissing his averted cheek.

'Usual,' smiled Howard. 'Nice, thing – dress.'

'Oh *darling* I'm so glad you like it. It's new.'

'I know. Lovely.'

All this too was pretty much par for the course – but will Howard, one wonders, be changing the next bit at all? The bit where he ambles into the back room and pours himself a very large Scotch from the chunky decanter in the mahogany tantalus and then adds just a bit more before the Malvern goes in. In the light of what has just recently occurred, maybe he will in some way vary the procedure?

It seems not. This is what Howard has now done; there is some small possibility that the whisky is maybe just a shade shy of the usual big-hearted measure, but more by accident than design, it seems. Yes, this is so – because Howard now is actually thinking Oh Sod And Fuck It – I *like* whisky, like it: it's what I like and it's what I do so fuck them. These doctors – what do they know? Some of them look no more than schoolkids.

Contrary to his response to Elizabeth, today hadn't, in fact, been usual for Howard; indeed, his days were very seldom that (what with one thing and another). The one trouble with being the boss – owning the thing – was that there was really no reason at all, most days, why you shouldn't do exactly as you bloody well please, and some-times the things that came close to pleasing Howard could by no stretch of the imagination be seen to be 'usual'. Not that today had been fun – no, not a bit. Necessary evil – can't put it off any longer, get it done, bite the bullet: that had been the scenario. Well all it was was a *medical*, God's sake – nothing really to get worked up about. Had one every two years-ish. Should maybe now be annual, who was to say? And I mean OK, it was that rather swish BUPA clinic, Gray's Inn Road, don't know if you know it – as decent as any such place can feasibly be – but, well . . .

17

difficult for Howard to actually *express* in just so many words, but he didn't at all care to do anything that wasn't, so to say – *contextual*. Like undressing. You undress for a bath. Or a swim. Or, um – well yes: obviously that. But to lie on a hard little couch affair and have sort of Vaseline smeared over your nipples and other pink and shyly crouching parts so that a veritable vermicelli of rather too cool and insinuating wires can be criss-crossed here and then plugged in there? I don't think so. And there was the very business of lying there – just pegged out like that, more in the manner of haddock on a slab than any seriously *human* posture, while some little girl in her brand-new I'm A Nursy-Wursy outfit says to you 'Little Prick' and then shoves a fucking great needle in your arm and unsmilingly sets about siphoning off your bloody blood. Never stared at a pale grey wall for so bloody long in my life.

I mean it wasn't *all* bad: urine sample, say – Howard had not the slightest problem there (piece of piss, in point of fact) – but all that listening out for tiny sounds and peering at impossibly distant and fuzzy lettering – joke, right? And then you get a final pummelling from a quasi grown-up doctor at the end (replete with many of the invasions you care not to dwell on) who in this case comes up with all of this liver nonsense. Shade concerned about Howard's liver, he said he was. You have put on your questionnaire, says the healer (amazing he can read), that you 'occasionally enjoy a glass or two of wine with your dinner . . .?' And leaving the neon irony of his inverted commas to glimmer and fizz in the air, he just started staring at Howard – which was a pretty bloody impudent thing to do, if you want the truth . . . but yes, OK: Howard took the point – even smirked a bit, because what Howard *habitually* enjoyed with his dinner (and, increasingly often, lunch; sometimes, let's face it, bloody breakfast) was a frankly massive Scotch. Followed by at least another. But it is true that he didn't always have a whisky *after* the meal, it has to be said; sometimes it was a fucking great slug of old Armagnac. And wine? Oh *Christ* yes – wine: could be a couple of bottles, if he wasn't really in the mood.

So yeah: took the point. But after so distressing and disorienting an experience, Howard bloody well *needed* a drink, now – didn't he? You surely wouldn't, I hope, deny him? (Elizabeth might, if she had an inkling – but she wouldn't ever: Howard would make sure of that.)

'You've only just missed, oh – everyone, really,' said Elizabeth, flopping down into a damn big sofa. 'Well actually Lulu left hours ago – but Peter's only just gone.' The strangest thing: this very afternoon, Peter said so sweetly would I mind calling him *Zoo-Zoo*! But then he is strange, Peter – though very lovely as well. It actually quite suits him, Zoo-Zoo. Rather like it. 'And so has Nelligan. Oh God – I don't know if that kitchen's *ever* going to be finished – everything's so – ! I sometimes wish I'd left it as it was.'

You are not alone, thought Howard. Our kitchen before was truly beautiful – you just had to ask anyone. But ah! Well do I know the workings of my Elizabeth's mind. Cyril and Edna Davies next door were busy replacing just everything, right? (Well – in their case you can understand it: God, it was a tip, that place, when Brian and Dotty were there.) But Elizabeth's kitchen had been just perfect; everyone was amazed when they saw it in the street. And the cost of the new one (*if*, as Elizabeth says, it ever does get finished)? Please – don't ask. If he does not already possess an array of such things, Mister Nelligan will be able soon to buy a sultan's palace in some rich and balmy spot – maybe even run to off-street parking and a self-contained granny flat – and why don't we throw in a scented harem while we're about it, hey? It wouldn't be so bad if Elizabeth didn't complain about the *mess* every day: it's *her* bloody mess, and Howard has to live with it. And oh God, there's Paris at any minute – *that* she arranged even before the kitchen had so much as wandered into her mind. Then Christmas.

Elizabeth is having the world over for Christmas, this year, she was telling me. Not a single word (as per) about where all the bloody money was supposed to come from – thank God the property market's in one of its seemingly unstoppable upswings just at the moment, that's all I can say. 'Oh but Howard,' Elizabeth had piped up only the other night (Howard had been groaning at the hugeness of some or other totally unnecessary and frankly quite silly bill), 'don't forget that *I'm* a little earner now!' Pleased as Punch (or Judy) she'd been. M'yes, was all Howard could think to that (wouldn't say it) – but you spend it all, don't you? Every penny you bring in goes on yet *more* bloody clothes. I tell you – sometimes, I feel bloody sure, Elizabeth just goes to the shops simply to check on the outside unlikelihood of their having any little thing she might be lacking; and if so, she gets it. And Katie – Katie was just the same: worse, if anything. Oh look – so long as it made them happy; leave Howard in peace to do *his* thing, right? Which was what, exactly, these days?

'Peter was a complete *dream* about the house today,' Elizabeth was now trilling. 'It's difficult to remember, sometimes, how on earth I ever managed without him.'

Howard nodded, quite slowly, thinking Now what exactly is it that I feel about this? Can't at all decide. Because Peter, once – and not too bloody long ago – had in fact been it: Howard's thing. Except that he had called him not Peter, but Zoo-Zoo. Even Howard had to smile at that, now; not, maybe, smile – but glancingly elongate half his face into some sort of rueful reflection. The Zoo-Zoo episode simply must have been the most extraordinary in his life, and yet at the time (is this not often the way?) it had seemed the most natural thing in the world. Yes indeed; I well think, thought Howard, that I might now take advantage of the fact that Elizabeth has embarked upon her no doubt customarily interminable summation of the doings of the man who is Nelligan, following which she will segue seamlessly into the cast list of just who it is who is coming to dinner (there always seemed to be someone, just lately: Brian and Dotty, largely – I think because Elizabeth really feels she *ought*) and, I feel sure, not only an itemization of said dinner's courses, but also the provenance of each and every one of their ingredients, plus the method and timing of their cooking, not to say preparation. This being the case – and Elizabeth is well into it (she'd already changed up into second) – I think I will use the time available to chivvy and freshen this now rather weary whisky and sit back and dwell for some little time on this erstwhile Zoo-Zoo thing of mine (all the while, but of course, remaining punctilious in my judicious supply and alteration of an Identikit's worth of eyebrow liftings, lip purses, indulgent half-smiles, eye widening and even the odd lobe-tug whenever my whirring antennae, tuned to pinpoint precision as a result of years of subliminal twiddling, automatically prompted whichever touch of mumming was required to encourage Elizabeth to go on, quite unfazed, while I go off somewhere else entirely).

Peter – or Zoo-Zoo, yes: still think of him as Zoo-Zoo – is the sixteen-or-so-year-old son of one of the cleaners at the office, if you can believe any such thing. Amazing. Sometimes I can hardly come to credit it myself. Mostly Filipino, pretty sure. Well the *cleaners*, needless to say, have pushed off, now (where does one actually get decent cleaners who hang around longer than half an hour, these days? If you ever find out, Howard would dearly love to know). But Zoo-Zoo, of course, lingered on. The joke is, I'm not actually a, um – you know: *like* that. Christ – the women I've had *since* Elizabeth, never mind before . . . Melody, most notably, I suppose; still fond of Melody, although Christ: bit of a handful – never knows really what she wants, quite what she's after. Seems desperate for just anyone who'll pick up the bills, since Dawn was born – and I suppose you can't blame her for that. The father was off like a shot; not

21

unheard-of. So yes anyway, as I say . . . um . . . oh Christ: my mind. I do this more and more, you know. I'm talking about one thing, and then some other damn thing flashes up and *occurs* to me and I'm buggered if I can . . . just goes completely out of my head. As, I very much regret to say, it has done right now. Never mind. Leave it. Think of something else and it'll – oh Zoo-Zoo! Yes yes – Zoo-Zoo, of course of course: got it now. Zoo-Zoo, yes.

'You don't *mind*, do you, Howard?' is what was breaking through now; an ultra-sense, as ever, alerted him to this more direct form of comment. 'You don't *mind* that they're coming over?'

Some people were coming over, it would very much seem: well, no great shocks there. 'Mind?' said Howard, at his most benign and rhetorical. 'No of course I don't mind. Why should I mind?'

Elizabeth said 'Sweet, Howard,' before immediately returning to the burning issue. Howard unclenched his sweetness, lulled by the resumption of this really rather comforting wash of more all-embracing guff.

Zoo-Zoo: yes. Very beautiful – just happened to be, um, a boy: that's all. Everything was fine right up until that seaside holiday – August, must it have been? Think so: early on in the month. I managed to get out of that, thank Jesus – it had all gone rather nicely. Melody was round for dinner (just a couple of days before the off, seem to recall) and it turns out she's broke, as usual, and so of course Elizabeth comes up with one of her famous and oh-so-generous schemes: why don't you, Melody, share our suite with us: *mustn't* she, Howard? That was my cue to put on my Mm, yes, absolutely, but-of-bloody-*course* look – while all the time thinking *Ohhh* no *ohhh* no – got to think of something quick. Ha! And when Melody announced that she'd have to bring Dawn as well (Christ – you should have seen Elizabeth's face when she dropped on her *that* particular bombshell: Jesus, the lungs on that kid – I'm not joking) well then I just *knew* I needed a lifebelt, and fast. So I ran up some cock-and-bull nonsense about urgent business at work, didn't feel happy about leaving the house (quite good, that one, because of course Brian and Dotty weren't going to be here either – they still owned next door, then) and *look*, Melody: *look*, Elizabeth – it's simple, isn't it? Staring us in the face: Melody goes with you, and I stay behind and then everyone's happy!

Zoo-Zoo was happy, anyway: what a week we had. And then . . . I don't really know what happened then, but after the garden party (I know: only Elizabeth could come back from a holiday and get me to hire a bloody great marquee so she could have what actually turned out to be a pretty disastrous party for just about everyone she'd ever met in her life) . . . and, er . . . sorry, sorry – here I go again. Losing the drift – let's just recap . . . holiday, party . . . oh yeh, Zoo-Zoo (Christ, my mind). Yes. Zoo-Zoo and Elizabeth had never actually met before (well – you see how it was) but my God, they took to each other like, um – oh Christ, what is it, that thing? That thing that takes to something like, er, something else? Some other thing. Water to a duck's back, is it? Oh Christ, anyway – you get the, you know – *idea*. And since then, well . . . Zoo-Zoo came into the office less and less: always seemed to be helping Elizabeth at home, instead. Became a sort of au pair, I suppose. It was never really the same after that. Well – let us face facts when they present themselves, why don't we? Wasn't *remotely* the same . . . no, quite different: *over*, really. But anyway, by then I'd already started my thing with Laa-Laa: Laa-Laa is now my thing. Which is, I think, how we got into all this, round about a thousand years ago – and Elizabeth is *still* just chuntering on about whatever on earth (you wouldn't really think it possible, would you? But look – this all seems like rather good timing to me, because she's just now about to get off the general sort of stuff and hit me with a particular, pretty sure: certainly she's got that look in her eye).

'So I *think* I've filled you in on everything,' said Elizabeth, clearly very satisfied with both the breadth and concision of the bulletins, together with the colour of the coverage in all the larger senses. 'Ooh – and you'll never *guess* who phoned!'

Well no – he wouldn't, would he? Otherwise she wouldn't have said it, would she? So Howard now had to go along with this one, too.

'Who?' he said. Round One.

'You'll never guess!'

'Well who?' repeated Howard. Round Two.

'I couldn't believe it when he said who he was. I never *dreamed* we'd ever hear from him again. Not after all that *awfulness* . . .'

And now Howard was even intrigued. Normally when Elizabeth did all this it turned out to be someone who Howard might very well have guessed – Elizabeth's mother, Melody, Lulu . . . not Dotty any more, alas: Dotty just banged on the bloody door, nowadays.

'Well who *was* it?' prodded Howard. Round Three. (It's bloody irritating, this.)

Elizabeth hugged her knowledge to her. 'Tell you?' she teased.

Howard knocked back the last of his Scotch: oh God – I sometimes get so *tired*.

'*Yes*, tell me – who *was* it, God's sake?' Round Fucking Four, by Christ.

Elizabeth's eyes were bright – the message seems to be *Well* – I don't know *what* you're going to make of this!

'Norman!' she at last let out.

Howard nearly gaped at her. KO, really: points don't make it.

'Norman!' he barked. 'What . . . Norman as in, what – Norman bloody *Furnish*, Norman?!'

Elizabeth nodded. 'Just about an hour ago.'

'Well what the fuck does that little sod want? Bloody

24

nerve of him – he's lucky he's not behind bars, is Mister Norman bloody Furnish!'

'He sounded quite *normal*,' advised Elizabeth, fairly cautiously. 'Howard, I really must get the vegetables on.'

'Normal!' rasped out Howard. 'There's nothing *normal* about Norman – the man's a complete and utter lunatic, not to say a bloody crook. What the hell did he want?' And even while Elizabeth was replying, Howard was muttering with quite a degree of venom: '*Nerve . . . bloody nerve . . .*'

'Well he was actually after Katie – '

And Elizabeth put her hands up now – a quasi flinch – and wondered whether it would have been wiser (yes, I think so – Howard's getting that flush he gets, look) not to have mentioned it at all. In point of fact, Howard was not just flushed, but standing up and striding – outrage and whisky working on him now so that his face looked wholly empowered by anger and practically cooked.

'*Katie!*' he bawled. 'He's actually got the nerve . . . he's got the thing, what is it – *gall* to phone Katie after all that nonsense last summer! I'll bloody kill him.'

'He said,' said Elizabeth quietly, 'he had something to give her – or show her, or something. Oh don't get all worked up, Howard – just learn to *ignore*. Look, darling, I simply must get going on dinner because you know how Brian and Dotty are always bang on time, these days . . .'

'*Kill* him,' concluded Howard, as the doorbell sounded.

'That'll be Melody, darling – would you . . .? I really *must . . .*'

'Melody?' queried Howard – not all that mollified, dear God no. 'Didn't know Melody was coming.'

Elizabeth sighed with huge and near-maternal well-I-simply-give-up and put-upon despair. 'I've just spent the best part of half an hour *telling* you, Howard.'

Howard was well on his way to the front door, and swigging whisky as he went.

'Oh yes of course,' he bluffed. 'My mind. Hello Melody,

my dear – welcome, welcome. Ah – you've brought little Dawn. Lovely.'

'I don't even suppose,' admonished Elizabeth, ' – Hello, Melody – do help yourself to a . . . ello ickle Dawn, ooza prippy ickle thing? . . . drink of something. Howard – do you at all recall what I said we are having for dinner? Did you hear that much? Honestly, Melody – this man of mine.'

'Of course I did,' harrumphed Howard. Oh Christ. 'Here, Melody – white wine, yes?'

'Lovely, Howard,' smiled Melody. 'Oh Dawn *please* . . . oh God *please* don't start crying now we've just arrived . . .!'

But Dawn didn't get the picture. As Howard averted his hunched-shouldered back and poured more whisky, Melody's eyes flicked up in supplication to any god or devil who happened to be glancing, while knowing that even mercy had no chance in the face of this. Elizabeth braced herself against the really quite unworldly and appallingly familiar shrieking that so little a thing could effortlessly generate, while more or less shouting out:

'Never mind – Dotty will be here soon! Dotty will quieten her down! And for anyone who's interested – it's lovely and tender calves' liver for the main thing, and a pretty scrumptious pudding! OK?!'

Melody mimed back by way of a much-used facial blend of gratitude and damn near tattered anguish, while Howard thought Hm – liver, eh, as he sipped at Scotch: can't be bad. Well can it?

❈

Lulu well knew the feeling of deadness that overcame her whenever she put the key into her own front door. And yet it had been quite a happy home, before John went mad (so yes, I suppose, not really for long). Every day now, though, brought Lulu closer and closer to the end of all this, and it was just that thought – that thought alone – which lent her the determination to each day return: the simple and so alluring dream of one morning leaving, and then not having to do that other thing: come back.

It *was* Mrs Bramley – that really was her name – and my God! Even Lulu had been genuinely shocked by so much self-indulgence. Gorgeous house in Hampstead – lost count of the number of rooms, and yet she lived all alone, this woman, and . . . hang on, though, thought Lulu now – maybe if I just go very quietly upstairs to ring Lizzie then just possibly I can sidestep the beastliness of seeing bloody John again . . . yes, yes, I might just make it – tiptoe past the living room (don't suppose he's left any drink, the pig – quite do with a drink now, actually) and then I can quickly –

'Lulu? My drain-gel – darling *angel*, is what I mean, what I'm meaning, Lulu – is that you, Lulu? Is that you?'

And even now, Lulu cowered and froze in the bright-lit hall as might a heart-stopped child well back into the dark of an understairs cupboard – and Sh! Yes Shh! If I can just close my eyes really tightly and never ever draw breath again then maybe even now I can escape not just discovery but the damage of intrusion . . .

'Lulu!' gasped John, his eyes glassy, bulbous and out of sync, but still suffused by a wash of quite infantile relief that he felt must surely be love. He slumped against the door-jamb and held out an arm (one was all he dared) and his face did its best to beckon – but surely, thought Lulu (oh hell, oh hell – the game is both up and lost), he did not, could not, actually expect her now to *go* to him?

So she did not. She turned away, having eyed him with real displeasure, tinged with mandatory contempt, while saying quite flatly:

'You've got ice-cream all over you, John.'

Guilt sprang into one of John's eyes – the one which largely could be left to just about cope with the business of focusing – while a hand went to cover the caked-on glaze of his mouth and chin; of the state of his clothes, he was more than likely oblivious.

27

'Yes,' admitted John, quietly. 'I'm – uh – sorry about that, Lulu, I'll – um – clear it up. Clear it up, yes. Soon.'

I will also – um – continue to talk quietly, John thought, because otherwise she'll rush upstairs and, yes, ring Lizzie and I desperately need her to stay down here with me and I can't, mustn't, make a lunge for her because then she'll *truly* rush upstairs and, yes, ring Lizzie but by then anyway I will have fallen over again because I am so brim-filled with drink that I can barely remember the genesis of this very thought or train of events – how even it occurred to occur to me. And John was staring quite obliquely at the angled form of Lulu's lovely ankles making fast for the staircase even before he realized that he had fallen over again – but yes, here was a duller ache hovering maybe just inches over his could-easily-be right temple, a puffed-up cloud unleashing a drizzle of pain that might well get a good deal heavier as the evening wore on; and here once more was the rasp of carpet against his prickled cheek, and again that deep-down smell of pile.

John rocked himself over on to his back as the clatter of Lulu receded, and the functioning part of his brain idled him back into the rut of wondering just how even some small part of all this could ever have happened. Lulu says that my insane jealousy finally turned and once and for all rendered me truly insane – but I do not choose to see it like this, for here is a lie of convenience, all of Lulu's making. I was not so much jealous as deeply suspicious of every little thing that Lulu might ever do or think or say: this simply is *caution* – all I did was guard, protect us both against . . . possibilities. And then last summer, I was seen to be right. I find it hard, now, to quite recall detail (Christ – I find it hard, now, to quite recall my fucking name) but in not maybe exactly this order my Lulu seduced (was seduced by? Hardly matters – a screw is a screw) some vile *man* in a lift in that hotel, whatever the name of that hotel might be – and that man hit me. And then again she did this, and once

28

more I ended up beaten. This may have happened yet again
– oh look, it's all in my notebooks, somewhere. This *man*
even followed my Lulu – tracked her down to Howard and
Lizzie's summer thing – garden party – and on that
occasion, while I attempted only to shield my wife and
myself from public shame and dishonour, I do believe he
practically murdered me. Now whichever way you cut it,
this can't be right, can it? I mean – I'm not *wrong*, am I? So
all this just can't be right, can it? So much, at least, is
rational. Clear too is the fact that I love my Lulu dearly. God
I could die for my love of that woman: kill, if I had to. So I
try to help: you need *help*, I said to her – maybe you should
be *talking* to someone. Even had a word with that new
neighbour of Howard and Lizzie's – what was his name?
Eric? Cyril? Bruce? Nebuchadnezzar? (Needn't be any of
those.) The psychiatrist, anyway – but she practically ran a
mile (if not amok); said to me later – was quite convinced –
that Cyril (yes, I think it's Cyril) had actually made a *pass* at
her – slap in the middle of Lizzie's marquee! Well – I think
you see the gravity of the problem. And then she seems to
just forget everything – everything she's ever said to me on
these terrible matters, all the awful, wide-eyed, so-bloody-
what and throwaway admissions of her tawdry and quite
shocking behaviour seem simply to evanesce: vanish into
vapour.

So imagine, will you, my delight when one bright
morning not that long ago (I was slaving over some ghastly
thousand-word piece for the magazine – thinking I ought to
be getting on with this novel of mine, but quite keen for an
excuse to abandon them both, if I'm completely honest here)
Lulu came into my study – a thing she rarely (come to think
of it, never) does these days and says *John*: I've made an
appointment with a very eminent analyst – top in his field:
would you mind driving? My heart was guilty of swelling –
I swam among warm seas of pride for her: the confrontation
is half the battle, I said – acknowledge your problem, and

you are close to conquering it – everyone says that (this is known by simply everybody). And even this, you know, was later turned against me: Why then, Johnny, can't you go to an AA meeting and stand up proudly and say My name is John Powers and I am an alcoholic? What's the problem *there*, then, John? Well many, I might have replied – had she stopped to listen, and had I myself not been just slightly the worse for wear: firstly, of course, I am *not* an alcoholic, plain as day. I *drink*, granted – Christ, I'd be the last to, you know, *deny* that or anything (difficult, given the circumstances) but here is simply a temporary expedient: a *defence*, Lulu – a *defence*, can't you see it, against all the pain you put me through. I wrap myself up in this liquid warmth – I am *swaddled* in drink because I cannot bear it when you say you are leaving me (and here, I know, is partly why you are going). And another reason I couldn't go to such a meeting is, quite simply, that they are not *me*: I don't get on in groups, and I don't suppose I ever shall. And yes I *do* know what they are like, *actually*, because I once attended a *Gamblers* Anonymous evening, as it happens (and that I only went to for a bet).

So let's just cut back to the point of this: I drove her down to Harley Street (took me just about forever to find a bloody meter) and I turned to her brightly, my face maybe even alight with encouragement, beaming at her the promise that soon, hereafter, our lives would surpass all the joy of before. So *tell* me, Lulu, I said: shall I wait for you here in the car, or would you like me to walk you in and hold your hand? Turns out the bloody appointment's for me! I mean Christ – if that isn't proof the woman's mental just you bloody tell me what is! *Me*, I said – what do you mean *me* – you're the one who's fucking bats, what the hell have *I* got to do with it?! *Me*, she goes: *me*! There's nothing wrong with *me*, for Christ's sake, John – it's *you* who needs help, Johnny – *you're* the bloody crazy one. So you can see – a fairly fundamental communication problem, here. We were squabbling for so bloody long in the car (I swear it was practically rocking on its springs) that what with that and the time it had taken me to find the parking space the bloody hour's appointment was shot to hell anyway so all we could do was drive back home, each of us now mortally convinced that the other was madder than ever.

And yes, it got worse and worse – day by day – until Lulu finally upped and said to me (cold, and quite point-blank) I'm sorry but it's no good, Johnny, it's just no good any more: I thought maybe I might have been able to go on with all this but I know, just know now – that I can't. And I laughed. No – I didn't think it was *funny*, of course not: just one more of my defences that don't bloody work. But I could see what was coming (smelled it in the air) and all I could think was no *please* don't no *please* don't no *please* don't no *please* don't . . . and then she just did: said she was leaving me. All over, Johnny. All gone, John. It's just no good (and by that she meant it was *bad*). So I did what any man in my position would do: drank myself to the brink of the insanity which she believed already and long was clutching and which would never, she thought, let up on me.

So here, then, is what happened – but how I'm still not sure. Which brings us to the here and now – slumped, I am, against the wall of the hall, while Lulu is upstairs and ringing Lizzie, pretty sure. Soon find out: reach out for the cordless (where is the – gah! – bloody thing) then lift the receiver, and now let's just see what we hear:

' – the pictures and did the flowers, but my *God*, Lizzie, this one, I tell you – weirder than ever – '

Yup, thought John, replacing the handset as deftly as may be expected of a man near palsied by the first tremors of withdrawal that the evening had to offer him. Once, I would have listened in; but now I have heard simply everything there is. I think I need a drink.

'Did you get that?' husked Lulu, from behind the locked door of the bedroom that was these days truly hers and hers alone. 'It clicked. John again. *Christ*, Lizzie – I thought he'd stopped doing all that: listening in all the bloody time.'

'Oh don't let it get to you,' placated Elizabeth (bit bored with the subject by now, quite frankly). 'Not as if we're trading state secrets. Anyway, he's put it down now, so forget him. Tell me about Dame Bramley quickly, and then I really must get going on dinner. Howard's due soon, and I like to have everything . . . well, you know just how I like to do things.'

But Lulu was still in a mind to linger, here.

'I *know*, Lizzie, but Christ – if you can't even use the bloody phone in your own bloody house . . .'

'Well you'll be in *my* house soon, won't you? And then you can use the phone any time you like!'

'I'll only be ringing you in Paris!' laughed Lulu – straight away bucked up by this reminder: that will be fun – yes, that will be really good. Indeed, it had been Lulu who had maybe prompted the idea in the first place, by pointing out the problem:

'Well what on earth am I going to *do*, then?' Elizabeth had wailed, when first this collision of all her well-laid plans had suddenly become plain. 'I can't leave Nelligan all alone in the house – I mean, I *think* he's trustworthy, think so, but you never *really* know with these sorts of people, do you? Katie's hopeless. And it would be just *too* heartbreaking to cancel Paris now everything's arranged – and Howard, poor lamb, he's *so* looking forward!'

The poor lamb had actually overheard that last bit, as he idled through to the back room (smallish Scotch and water might just hit the spot) and it was all he could do to cover the cower. He was actually – for various, but not at all complex, reasons – quite dreading Paris, but even he knew

32

that there was no way at all he could wriggle out of *two* of Elizabeth's wheezes – certainly not in the selfsame year, anyway: that much was for sure.

'I *mean*,' went on Elizabeth, plaintively (and Lulu's mind was already clicking away – maybe, she thought later, Lizzie's broader intention?), '*Dotty* has offered to keep an eye on things, poor Dotty – but, well, much as I love her dearly, she's not, is she, the sort of person who's *meant* to look after houses, I mean is she? What I mean to say is – *marvellous* with kiddies: we've all seen her work her magic with Dawn . . . but . . . well: we remember what *Dotty's* house was like, poor Dotty. Don't we? Hm? Even the caravan looks like the inside of a wheelie bin, but God – I suppose there's only so much you can do in a ghastly contraption like that. Poor Dotty. But you do see my *point*?'

So Lulu, but of course, had made her offer (oh what bliss to be away from John – maybe *this* had been Lizzie's broader intention? God she's so lovely – I love her so much) and Elizabeth had minced no words in seizing on it immediately. (Elizabeth's problems, such as they were, were never allowed to furrow her brow for very long at all – people could generally be depended upon to rally round. Yes, the horizon was usually as bright as a button within minutes of a raincloud having had the temerity to even hover, let alone lurk.)

And it was more or less true that it *would* only be Lizzie that Lulu would call – who else, actually, would she be inclined to? Even today – as soon as she had got in from having sorted out Mrs Bramley's existence on earth, Lulu's one big thought had been to tell all to Elizabeth: thank God John had fallen flat on his face in the hall, when he did – otherwise there would have been no time (for Lulu was well aware that when the hour was looming for Howard to come home, Elizabeth would start to busy herself with making sure she had everything . . . well, Lulu knew just how she liked to do things).

33

So now Lulu quickly hit her with the Bramley thing: at first, the whole business had gone much in the way it generally tends to – you admire their fabulous home, and so forth and so on, and then rapidly graduate to the clothes (and this is where all the tight-faced diplomacy comes in – you can't replicate the sounds of impending vomit, and nor must you laugh out loud). All the while, Mrs Bramley had conducted Lulu from this room to that in as near to silence as you ever really get; it was only when the tea was chinkingly set and poured that she opened out in a manner a good deal larger than Lulu might have expected. It turns out that Mrs Bramley (what must she be? Sixties? Early sixties? Something like that) had been very recently widowed. Already her hair was newly cut short (reasonably effective, thought Lulu) and now was the time for a more encompassing makeover – clothes, furnishings, all of that. And her late husband had always attended to the Christmas decorations, she said – and she for one just *loved* Christmas decorations but – in common with much else, it quickly transpired – hadn't a single *clue*.

'Call me Naomi,' invited Mrs Bramley, then, proffering a wedge of Dundee cake, 'It isn't my name, but call me it anyway.'

Lulu looked up and sort of smiled.

'I suspect,' went on 'Naomi', stirring, stirring – my God, thought Lulu, is she ever going to pack in stirring that tea! – 'that my marriage was relatively usual. Mercifully brief. He was blind, you see.'

'Ah!' acknowledged Lulu (thinking Jesus – and *he* did the Christmas decorations?). 'I see . . . I didn't know . . .'

Mrs Bramley eyed her sharply. 'Well you wouldn't,' she said, with a touch of severity. 'How could you? You do see?'

Lulu nodded. 'Yes,' she said.

Mrs Bramley nodded too. 'Well he didn't. Anyway, one day – quite out of the blue – he blundered into a Turkish Bath. Asthmatic – couldn't catch his breath.'

'How awful,' commented Lulu. 'And that's how he – ?'

'Oh no. It was only a mild sort of attack. Had his Ventolin, and everything. It's just that he fell into a pool there. Couldn't swim. Didn't *see* it, you see.'

'Ghastly,' said Lulu.

'Not *too* ghastly. They pulled him out. He was fine. *Wet*, of course . . .'

'Of course,' whispered Lulu automatically, becoming quite entranced by this, and already rehearsing her re-enactment to Lizzie. 'So . . . ?'

'So later he was hit by a car. Didn't hear it coming. He was always rather deaf – did I say? Not later the same *day*, naturally: that would be ridiculous.'

Lulu now nodded with energy – her eyes as wide as wide, and her face encased in starch. 'Right,' she said.

'Was convalescing in the country for ages. Will you take cake? A sliver? No? And then he fell out of a window. The first time it didn't matter at all because it was on the ground floor and the sole casualty, I'm told, were the tulips there. But then he just would do it *again*, of course, and this time he found himself in the attic. But,' added on Mrs Bramley, with drama – 'not for long!'

And this came out of Lulu before she was aware of even having thought it: 'Couldn't fly?'

Mrs Bramley looked at Lulu, as if undecided – though maybe more about Lulu's demeanour than on any sort of avian proficiency her late husband may or may not have commanded.

'Indeed . . . not,' she said slowly. 'It wasn't the fall that killed him. There was all this, what do they call it at the bottom – *dung*, for want of a better term. So much of it, I am informed, that it took them ages to actually find him. It was, I believe the expression is, very deep doo-doos indeed. I'm not boring you?'

Lulu felt sure that she was shaking her head.

'He always did have a very low boredom threshold,'

concluded Mrs Bramley. 'It was tedium, I think, that did for him in the end.'

'So . . .' tried Lulu, slowly, setting down her cup with care. 'What . . . he actually, died in the – ?'

'Dung, quite. They dug him out, of course. And then we buried him. Somewhere else.'

'I see. Yes. Well. I am so sorry.'

And suddenly the air was filled with kindergarten laughter that couldn't have, surely (surely not), escaped the box-like mouth of Mrs Bramley?

'Oh don't be!' she trilled. 'It was a blessed release. Well for *me*, anyway: couldn't *stand* the man – can't think why we've wasted so much time talking about him. His name was Gilbert. Still *is*, of course, if you believe in all that sort of thing. Odd to think of him as an angel.'

Lulu nodded. 'Flying at last.'

Mrs Bramley was smiling thinly. 'But rather too late for any of us. According to the hospital people, his last words were . . .'

'Mm?' prompted Lulu, intrigued.

' . . . indecipherable. Are you really *sure* you won't take cake?'

And Elizabeth had howled when Lulu regaled her with the best bits. 'Delicious! The Tale of Mrs Bramley.'

'*Golden* delicious!' burst out Lulu – her love for Lizzie, as ever, surging when the two of them laughed in unison.

'Look, Lulu,' said Elizabeth, now, 'I've just heard Howard drop that ghastly bag of his in the hall – I really must dash. See you in the morning, yes? Tennish?'

'Tennish,' agreed Lulu, hearing faintly Elizabeth's call of 'Howard? Is that you?' before she replaced the receiver.

How lovely, thought Lulu, to be Howard. Maybe one day soon I will be.

CHAPTER THREE

Elizabeth had ordained that this was to be one of her very most *casual* evenings, which in truth meant that her hospitality was quite as really big-hearted and lavish as ever: all sorts of good things were on offer (God look, ogled Melody – Beef Wellington: how utterly yum) except that now people found themselves craning and twisting rather awkwardly and sometimes – no two ways about it – even sideways at various points along the damn big sofas. Colin had elected for the was-it-maybe-Persian-or-something rug, soft and lustrous and glowing warmly in front of the fire that surely did echo one of the smugger advertisements for the traditional Jaffa-coloured lickety-flame and flickery set-ups (a married pair of fools alongside, beaming at you hints of all the advantages a concealed back boiler surely did afford).

So there they all were, each striving for level best in the pretty tricky business of perching big plates on bony and tightly compressed knees, while bearing in mind too that the slightest inadvertent shifting of just one pinned-and-needled foot would have their really rather quaffable, though generic, Côtes-du-Rhône splattering just everywhere. Far less trouble round the dining table in the room next door, of course (where there was also negative risk of unsightly staining to Elizabeth's plush and softer furnishings) – but this way was the very most *casual*, yes? And after all – it was only friends, so let's just relax and enjoy ourselves, why don't we?

'Honestly, Elizabeth,' said Dotty now – a couple of crumbs at the side of her mouth quickly tidied up with just one pinky – 'I don't know how on earth you've managed to *do* all this! I mean, I had a peek in the kitchen before and it's all still just – '

'Oh *don't*, Dotty,' interjected Elizabeth. ' "Kitchen" is an absolutely taboo word round here – and God, don't get Howard on to it. I just don't know why I started on it. Colin – have some more gratin, yes? Bit more?'

No, thought Dotty, as Colin helped himself to another scoop (smiling pleasantly, yes – but not really at and into Elizabeth, as he used to just always: felt a bit funny about her, now). No, thought Dotty, as she gazed with sheer love at baby Dawn – asleep again now, and close by her side – no, nor do I, Elizabeth, and nor does anyone else: your kitchen was a showpiece, divine in every way, and larger and lusher than the entire space in which Colin and I and the oaf who is Brian now spend each of our waking days – so no, Elizabeth, no: I don't either.

'I think when Mister Nelligan is finally done,' intoned Howard – heavy, resigned, I suppose it could have sounded – but really only rather indulgent for the benefit of the assembly, 'that I am contracted to present to him the free-hold of the house. Only *part* payment, of course.'

'Oh Howard!' laughed Elizabeth. 'Not *that* bad . . .' And she trained her wide and *yes*-I'm-spoiled and *yes*-I'm-naughty eyes on anyone who had time mid-gobble for a quick glance upwards. 'Honestly!' she said. (Maybe, actually, one shouldn't bring up freeholds – not when Brian and Dotty were here.)

Howard wagged his head, which went with his half-smile, while thinking Right, had enough of that – what damn-fool thing now shall I say to just who, exactly? Be nice if occasionally I could have an evening in alone – he thought that too, because if he couldn't be with Laa-Laa, then alone is what Howard would always choose to be.

'What are you up to these days, Brian?' is what he now

38

thought he'd settle for, following absolutely no consideration at all on the matter. 'How are you filling your time?'

Brian's mouth was well on the way to becoming ajar, but Dotty could always leave him standing in the conversation stakes and it was her voice, now, that ringingly filled the room:

'Oh God don't *ask*,' is what she said (Brian now reflecting more resignedly than with any form of irritation Well Yes, Dotty, but he *has* asked, hasn't he? That's what Howard is doing, asking – and moreover, he's asking *me*). 'I'm clearing up after him all day long. The latest scheme to make us all millionaires is apparently the manufacture of miniature *clogs*.'

Katie laughed out loud: Christ – all these people, every single one of them, even Dad: they don't really have a clue, do they? I suppose this is what comes of being old. But Jesus – Brian and Dotty, they really were the fucking limit. He used to collect 'manhole covers', he was once bloody endlessly telling me (probably still does, silly old fart), and meanwhile Dotty had been busy filling up their house with all the sorts of ghastly little shitty knick-knacks you don't really even want to win at a funfair. Christ – they live in a caravan in our bloody driveway – completely bust, apparently – and now here was Brian making –

'Miniature *clogs*?!' sang out Melody. 'God, Brian – that's pretty weird, isn't it? Even for you.'

Which Dotty didn't like for a minute – no, not one bit. Why don't you find a husband of your *own* to criticize, Melody? Hm? Would help, maybe, if you could even look after your very own sweet and, yes, just achingly adorable baby. What sort of woman, in fact, Melody, *are* you? Hm? Maybe Dotty's *look* would say it all – but no, didn't, because Melody was wide-eyed in Brian's direction, waiting for his latest moronic response; Katie too was playing along for the hell of it, while Colin reddened and cringed as he habitually did whenever his mother or – far more particularly – his father was ever on the point of saying just anything at all. Why couldn't they be normal, or sane – or even *solvent*? Why couldn't Colin's father be like Carol's father? He was really fab; God, Carol – can't wait to see you again. It won't be long. Just two days, now. Can't wait.

'Well actually,' started Brian, slowly – as if every sixth word were a live round in the chamber, and could spell the end of him, 'what I am making are not . . . in fact, Dotty, they are not miniature *clogs*, as you seem to think; they are, um, yachts.'

'Yachts!' shot back Dotty, her quick and bright-eyed scan of the room intended to make clear to everyone that if they had with forethought come armed with rotting cauliflowers and past-it turnips, then now might well be the time to hurl them. '*Yachts*?!' she threw in, for sheer and cruel good measure.

Oh Christ, thought Colin – please don't talk about *yachts*: Carol's dad is a yachtsman – terrific. Just once last summer I went out on their boat and . . . oh God, I'm blushing again just at the memory – I can feel it in my ears. I never thought anyone could be that sick and actually *live*. Sorry, Carol. But at least I'm seeing you soon. Can't wait.

'Or,' qualified Brian, 'maybe schooners.' I don't know why everyone seems to think this is so *funny*, thought Brian now. Then he said: 'And nor am I ruling out canoes.'

Howard nodded. 'But Brian – what, um . . .?'

What was on his mind was Christ Almighty, Brian – aren't you going to make *any* sort of an effort to get a proper job, get a proper home? I mean, what – you're going to be living in my bloody front garden for *ever*, are you? What in Christ's name are you fucking about with little wooden *boats* for? But 'what, um . . .?' is the farthest he got with it; Katie, though, thought there could well be some mileage in more:

'But *why*, Brian?' she probed. 'Mm – this pudding thing is actually gorgeous – anyone want?'

'Well –' tried Brian.

'Pass it *round*,' said Elizabeth. 'God's *sake*, Katie.'

'I'll have some,' volunteered Colin.

'Well –' tried Brian.

'Well can you come and get it, Colin?' said Katie. 'Only I'm sort of juggling everything, here. But Brian – you don't expect to *sell* them, or anything – do you?' Christ it was hysterical – thank God all men aren't as stupid as this. 'Do they *float*?'

'Well –' tried Brian.

'Is there cream?' asked Colin. Didn't want cream, not really – it's just that he was now crimson as a result of all this (why can't Dad see what a joke he is and just bloody shut his mouth? Why does he have to *respond*?) – and so maybe if I just go on prattling then he might maybe stop: *please*, yes?

'*Well*,' insisted Brian, now, 'that's a very interesting question, Katie. I am actually making them because – well, as you know, I haven't got much . . . well, there's very little *space*, these days, and uh – so I can't do, you know – the sort of thing I used to: large scale.'

'Thank Christ,' muttered Dotty.

'As to *selling* them – no. No, not at all.' And yes – of *course* that had been the intention, but there was a limit as to how much ridicule Brian could reasonably get down over the course of just the one evening, so what he was going for now, was: 'I actually thought I'd, you know – finish them nicely, paint them up and all the rest of it and, um, maybe give them to some children's charity or other.'

Yes, thought Brian – a charity might accept them for bloody nothing, just maybe. And he also thought Yes Yes Yes But What About *Money*, at just about the same time as nearly everyone else did too. But there was the threat of contagion in the air, now: no one wished to be nearly so close to this degree of desperation – a sickness at heart on this sort of scale.

'As to the other thing, I don't,' tacked on Brian, more or less wretchedly, 'actually know if they float.'

No, he thought – I've no idea; but if they have been imbued with anything of their maker, a transference – if some force or other has caused infection deep within the very grain of their rickety and maybe not-at-all-shipshape hulls and decking – well in that case, they will simply be seen to be as seaworthy as a Chieftain tank, and sink: like deadweight does.

❋

Melody, later, was fooling with coffee – slowly trickling in the demerara, some few grains fizzingly missing the demitasse and spattering into the tiny saucer; then she'd let an espresso spoonful idly plip-plop back before stirring it again this way, agitating the sort of wasn't-really-froth and then chivvying it back in the other direction. I always do this, it dimly occurred to her, as the undulating hum of various muted grudges and disagreements surged and then receded around her; always do everything except bloody well drink the fucking stuff, which is all it is for, after all.

Just take one look at Dotty, thought Melody now. And her lips tightened at the truth that whenever she thought that, it was never at all what she actually meant. No – what she was really saying, here, was: take one look at *Dawn*. Look at Dawn, my baby – will you look at Dawn with Dotty, and then just think (claw back the memory of all the red-faced and bawling anguish) of whenever Dawn – my baby – is solely stuck with me, her so-called parent. It just is not, is it, meant to be. And yet I tried to give her up – *yearned* to give her up, if I'm being totally honest (and no, not any longer – it doesn't even remotely hurt to say it) – and Dotty, my God – never seen anyone so keen to take on a baby in my life. So why didn't I go through with it and just let Dotty *have* the bloody thing? Don't know. Something deep inside me. And no – *please* don't bang on for Christ's sake for even so much as a second about any sort of mother's fucking instinct because I just don't have any of that. I am not a mother, and never was; it just so happens I have a little child, is all. And after Miles, there was no real point in getting rid of her. No point.

Melody realized that she had been so purposely peering at Dotty (so purposely peering at Dawn) only when she jerked away her gaze as Dotty looked up sharply and then obliquely at that funny husband of hers, who seemed on the verge of tentative speech:

'Get you anything, Dotty?' Brian offered, pleasantly enough.

Dotty held his look, though a hard and not elastic enough ache was tugging back her eyes to where they most loved to linger.

'You never have,' she said tightly. 'So why bother now?'

'Colin?' pursued Brian (for this treatment, Melody surmised, could hardly be anything like a revelation to him). 'Get you something? Drink? Or are you OK?'

But Colin was tapping at a hand-held video game and hadn't heard and wasn't looking. For Dotty, I feel sure (and this was the way Melody now was thinking), these two barely exist. She seems to come alive only whenever she can be with Dawn. And me? What about me? Who do I live for? Hm? Now that Miles is a memory. The vilest man who ever breathed, and still I love him deeply. What the hell is wrong with me – what the hell is *wrong* with me, wondered Melody yet again, while glugging more wine and giving in to her eyelids' urging for a heavily indulgent quasi-droop – sardonic if small acknowledgement that here, indeed, were the very words that Miles had hurled and hurled at her, when finally on that terrible day she could stand no more and had tracked him down.

'Jesus Christ Al-fucking-*Mighty*, woman!' he had roared at her (and God, oh God – they weren't even alone). 'What the hell is wrong with you? What the hell is *wrong* with you – huh?!'

I'm not really sure, thought Melody now, that I want to go over it all again. It's not as if I don't know every word and scene by heart. (Suddenly a swish of air, and now there is a shadow – who is standing over me? Oh – Howard: only Howard. I wish I had a Howard.)

'All right, Melody?' he said. And then he tugged on whisky.

He always did say just that sort of thing – questions that really aren't at all questions, are they, to which no answers can ever exist. Melody smiled the smile of sly contentment, something close to muted rapture, that little things like this seemed so often to require ('Katie!' she heard Elizabeth admonishing from somewhere around, 'don't keep hogging the bittermints, God's sake – pass them *round*'). Howard looks after Elizabeth so terribly well, but he never did me – not when we were together. Why not, I asked him. He said: it doesn't work like that. Why not, I asked him. He said, it just doesn't. I tend to get this sort of thing from men (it must be something deep inside me); they look me up, they call me up, they build me up, they knock me up and then they (yeah) – they put me down. It must be something not that deep inside me.

Take the most recent case in point: Miles McInerney. Now Miles . . . actually, before I trek through this lot again, I could quite go for – I'd quite like another glass of . . . ow ow *ow*: Christ, I've been squatting here so long my foot's gone to – God, it's such a funny feeling, that, when your foot goes to . . . it feels so heavy and deformed and not really quite yours.

'My *God*, Melody!' hooted Elizabeth. 'You're limping! You're limping!' And then – her voice now coated in lavish concern, quite as thickly as might be a wriggle of her favourite candied orange, when newly robed in bitter chocolate – 'Howard! Howard! Melody is – !'

'It's just,' protested Melody, chucking in a half-laugh, 'it's only that my foot's gone to . . . it's better now: I'm *feeling* it again! Oh Jesus, Elizabeth – I've knocked over the – '

'I get that, sometimes,' Brian almost moaned.

'How can you tell?' shot out Dotty. 'You're in a coma from the brain downwards.'

'Oh *Dotty*!' cajoled Elizabeth. God – that Dotty; mind you – with Brian, could you blame her? It's only *tomato* you've knocked over, Melody – not to worry. Peter – Zoo-Zoo – is very good on carpets.

'Always was,' concluded Dotty.

'It *is* a funny feeling,' whispered Brian, thinking Please don't add any more to that, anyone: I feel so bad as it is.

'Here, Melody,' offered Katie (Christ I'm bored – think I'll go to bed quite soon). 'What do you want? Wine? Yeh? I'll get.'

Melody half slumped back down to her corner, and Katie brought over a brimming Chardonnay – in a *tumbler*, much to Elizabeth's considerable pain.

'We haven't talked for – ' pitched in Katie (and then she was nodding along as soon as Melody started it up).

'I know,' agreed Melody. 'Simply ages.'

'How is, you know . . .' tiptoed Katie. 'Everything?'

Melody's nodding was slower, now.

'Same,' she said. 'More or less the same.'

Yes, she thought – that just about rounded up the shocking vacuum that formed the sum total of Melody's existence on earth. What Katie meant, of course (what she was pawing around), was, well – had Melody managed to hook another bloke since the fallout of the Miles fiasco? Well no, no she hadn't – not in the sense that Katie meant, no. And yes I suppose *fiasco* was a good enough word for the whole affair – but not at the beginning, it hadn't been: God no, Christ. But then, they never are that, are they? Not at the beginning, they aren't. But the beginning, oh dear, had been so terribly and cruelly close to the end: she had barely known the man a week. A week. How could Melody have decided to give up her baby (she had lied about the very existence of Dawn – Miles, she could tell, wasn't at all big on babies) and then to marry him all in the space of a single week? Well it hadn't actually taken a week: Melody was pretty well committed to the thing from just about the first time they had drunkenly fucked in his suite at the utterly divine Excelsior Hotel – could it really only be, what – four or so months ago? Could indeed, could indeed. And now the memories flooded and covered her:

It had been the perfect summer for falling in love. (Had it? Was this honest? Or was I only a well-placed dupe, just aching to be conned? You! Hey you! Yeah – you over there: you know who I'm talking about. Come on over and make a fucking fool of me, why don't you?) And Melody knows that this is irrelevant (wholly beside the point) but just that mention of summer, there, has her swimmy-eyed and yearning to have back the feeling of sun on her shoulders, fingering her warmly and lighting up each now golden hair, so downy against the ever-deepening, oil-soft tanning (winter just wasn't the same: winter can never do anything). But that summer with a man had been everything to Melody – surely this just had to be all? And now what I am is on my own and in the cold – and trembling, I think, from not just cold alone.

Miles was a salesman; hey – not *just* a salesman, baby, he had kept on saying, but *the* salesman bar none – numero uno (you better believe it). He certainly sold himself: I was sold, for one (but then what was I, if not on the market?). We did all the things you do – bliss for me because normally I can't do bloody anything, not with Dawn and never ever having any bloody money. But Dotty had Dawn (I said she was hers – that's what I told him; he believed it and God, I so much wanted to too) and Miles – he just signed for everything! Champagne, clubs – fabulous food ... but mostly it was bed. And floors and walls and cupboards;

once even on the verandah. He said he loved me. Are you sure, Miles – are you sure? Cos I've had these summer things – I've done all these and I don't want it any more. *Sure* I'm sure, he said (he had a way, a soothing manner – I just felt all wrapped up in his easy capability; that's when, maybe, I fell). And then I said God, Miles – I'd really like to ... I mean, what I mean is, I don't ever want you to go, now, Miles – don't ever want you to leave me ...? And he said – well, you know what he said, I expect; perhaps most people have been here before, have they maybe? Done all this? Anyway – *leave* you, he says: *leave* you? Nah. Never. Not me, girl. And then I go and say Yeh, OK – that's fine, Miles, but it's not, is it – *commitment*? So he bloody well knocks me down with this: Commitment? Commitment, he says – you want commitment, darling? And my eyes were sucking him in, but I may have nodded at him, then; yeah – I think I must have. So he says we'll get married. And I cried. And then we fucked. Which was great.

So after the holiday there was Elizabeth's summer party – there, right there, if you can believe it, through those french doors and in a marquee right in the middle of the lawn; all the floodlights show me now are black glass, hard frost and long and chilling shadows. After that we were going to make plans for the future. I waited ages: a week. Bit less. And then I rang him. I'd nicked a card from his wallet – otherwise I would've had nothing, nothing of him at all. Some girl said Hang on, I'll just put you through. And then I listened to tinkly music, just waiting for the second when Miles's big and manly voice would cut into all that with warmth and assurance and a huge and solid reason as to why he had been able to exist for a whole week (bit less) without reaching out to make contact. And then the girl came back and said Sorry, actually, but he's out of the office. And I said Yeah, fine, OK, right – would it be possible for you to get him to ring me? And the girl – who I kind of hated, by now – said Yeah surely: no problem.

I seem to have said as well as thought some parts of this, because Katie is nodding at me maybe impatiently; do you know, she's practically finished that box of bittermints all on her own.

'Yeh – I know all that bit,' said Katie (Christ Almighty, Melody – you've told and told me all *that* bit: Jesus). 'What I want to know is what happened when you actually went *round*. Here – this bottle's practically done: you might as well finish it off.'

'Yes,' said Melody slowly. 'I went round.' She sipped white wine and then thought oh to fuck with sipping and opened wide her mouth, the better to slop in half a bloody glassful.

'All right, Melody?' blustered Howard – swaying, could be, and glowing hotly. 'Katie? All right?'

Melody and Katie now snapped on and off seemingly synchronized yes-thanks-shove-off simpers – but already an eager Katie was back on the case:

'So-o-o . . .?' she egged on – her eyes maybe arched into sororial complicity, but certainly theatrically wide.

'Oh Colin . . .' sighed Dotty, 'are you ever going to be done with that accursed *machine*? You haven't said a word since we got here. Look at the food all around your *chair*, Brian – with you it's like living in a sty.'

Colin said 'What say?' just about at the same moment as Brian stumbled over some variation on his lifelong theme of apology, while Elizabeth batted air with both flat palms in her eagerness to convey to the company Oh God's *sake* – doesn't matter doesn't matter doesn't matter: *friends*, after all.

'So you went *round* . . .' urged Katie, now thinking Now look, OK – I *am* eager to know for actually various reasons but Christ there is a bloody limit, here; if she's not going to talk then fuck it – I'm off to bed.

But Melody, now, was shaking her head. I feel rather woozy, thank Christ, and it could be, maybe, just this wash of tiredness (possibly some deeper reluctance) but I suddenly, terribly, don't want to say to Katie one more word about it. Why should I? To diminish me even further? I don't really think there is scope for that. Never mind telling it – I wish to God it would leave my mind; I wish, whenever its clamour seemed distant – several chambers away (somewhere in my skull I never go) – that it would not beat down doors and break through walls and with huge and deafening derision once again uproariously confront me.

But I can't forget. I remember so well the eerie blend of girlish eagerness and heavy-footed dread that shook me like a cocktail as I stood there – cowed as a victim – in that massive glass and granite atrium: a polar waste with an Amazonic jungle at its centre.

'I wonder if I could see . . . could you please tell Mister Miles McInerney that I am here. I'm sorry I don't have a – '

'Do you have an appointment?' cut in the cold-eyed girl, tapping a fingernail and glancing anywhere that was nowhere close to Melody's face (Look Miss Whoeveryouare – I spend my day doing this, yeh? Some people I talk to are actually pretty important, OK? I mean, I'm like – *busy*, you know?).

'No,' said Melody, softly. 'I . . . no.'

The girl muttered into a mouthpiece what might have been some form of cabbalistic imprecation, nodding could be intently throughout the dead pause that followed. Now she looked at Melody, a swinish smile just barely restrained. Within each eye, only the pilot glimmered (no more light or heat were needed).

'Mr McInerney,' she said, 'no longer operates from this building.'

After a beat, Melody came up with 'I see . . . well could you tell me where – ?'

The girl now looked down, her hands and eyes rummaging through nonsense for no good reason at all. 'We have no more information, I'm afraid.'

49

No glint, now, in Melody's eyes, other than the light of alarm. 'I only want to know – '

'That's all the information we have.' And when the girl was satisfied that the knife was up to the hilt and down to the bone, she gave it just the most deft twist: 'Sorry.'

Melody sat in the park. Had she maybe seen a film, one time, where a verging-on-desolate girl sits mutely in a park, dimly aware of some kindly old woman (the sort that features in stair-lift ads) smugly feeding ducks – while not too far away a cared-for wife frolics with super-nourished children and possibly a kite or so? Maybe, maybe not; either way she very soon thought Oh fuck it, and went to the pub. And later on – no more than mid-afternoon – she went to the house. Miles's house. All she had had was a phone number – for the address it had taken her four separate goes to find not just a man at Directory Enquiries, but one who proved at last susceptible (Christ it took ages) to the full barrage of tears, pleas, intrigue and flirtation that Melody had so utterly brought to bear – for here, increasingly, was a situation beginning to burn, and all her instincts plucked at her to run, run (come away now from the danger of singeing), but still she went forward, dry-mouthed and woodenly, towards what she knew must end in roaring.

Even as she rang the bell Melody was thinking This is crazy, he won't yet be back from work. So she retreated a step or two and glanced upwards to the roof, back down again to ground level and a capacious bow window, its doughty and multi-paned frame seemingly steeped in gravy. Was what she was dealing with here one of those sort of Eighties Executive Homes? Melody rather thought it might be; I could be really happy here – it's really very nice: little front garden, jammed with busy lizzies – roll-up door on the garage, there. I could be really happy here. But I'm just not going to be, am I? Melody gave a sigh that elongated into shivering, and was going to ring again for form's sake when the front door surprised her by just about moving inwards – and now a small face peered up at her from within a six-inch chained-up crevice. Only then was she amazed to see three red and bobbing balloons tethered to a carriage lamp.

Melody had not at all expected to be saying Hello, I'm looking for, um, Mr McInerney, Miles, to a little boy of, oh Christ: not very good at this – five, six, seven (something?) – but this is how it surely went. He arched back his head and called out Mu-um! – but Mum, it seemed, was here already:

'Hell pew?' offered the woman, unfastening the chain and opening wider the door. She had a broad and giving face and seemed willing to smile, it looked like to Melody – and although blunt confusion was already giving way to an even duller sickness, a smile of sorts would be good, right now.

'It's Miles you want, is it?'

There was no more than mild enquiry there, but when Melody's face creased up – as sucked-in nostrils flinched away from all that they were smelling (when hot tears stung her bright cold cheeks) – then the woman gently took hold of the young boy's head and turning him inside she whispered You go off to your room now, Damien (Mummy will come up soon); and then to Melody, as if embracing a heavy inevitability: I think you had better come in.

'You haven't picked a very good day,' said the woman – leading Melody through to the back room and indicating with no more than a gesture a table in the adjoining conservatory piled high with a coloured and silly feast right out of the *Beano*: big white gooey cake, smaller ones that looked like footballs, Smarties, crisps and Coca-Cola – and even now through all of this Melody found herself only thinking Gosh how wonderful she managed to make those jelly moulds actually work: I can never get them to come out like that. 'I'm Sheila, by the way. And you are . . .?'

'I'm . . . my name is Melody. Is Miles – ?'

Sheila fell into an armchair, pulled out a Silk Cut from a

51

half-done packet and with a looked-like Dunhill snapped it alight. She cast an inviting arm over to the sofa as she sucked down deep the smoke.

'It's Damien's birthday,' she said, as if it had just occurred to her. 'Seven. And Mark's not much short of six, now. Getting old.' And then she looked at Melody closely, rather as one might when deciding whether or not a thing was actually worth the money. 'You're not his latest, though, are you, Melody? Nice name. His latest, I happen to know, is called Catherine. What did he promise you? The world?'

Melody merely gazed as Sheila winced away from maybe pain, though there was the spur of disgust in the way she combined now a shrug with snorting. Melody's face felt set and tautened – the tears had caked and for now, it seemed, there were no more. She grabbed at the resigned if unreal peace that fell, so aware that in not long (and for how long?) war would rage all through her.

'I feel . . .' probed Melody ' . . . so small. I feel, oh God – so bloody fucking *stupid*.' And then she turned eyes full on to Sheila. 'I *love* him,' she almost pleaded, as if not near even barely understanding – and oh Christ no, I'm bloody bloody *crying* again!

Yeh yeh, is what Sheila's vigorous nodding was putting across – heard it all before, haven't I darling?

'You grow out of it,' she said, quite flatly. 'Believe me. And before you start asking how I can stand it I don't bloody *know* how I can stand it, I just bloody do. If I could change it, I'd change it, but I can't.'

Melody now had to leave. 'I'm sorry, I – I hope the party goes . . .' And then she crumpled. 'Oh Christ oh Christ what a *shit*! Oh God that man is such a fucking *shit*.'

And just about in time with that last emphatic *shit*, the front door clicked open and then crashed home and a big deep voice familiar to just everyone around was bawling out like a ringmaster: 'OK OK OK! Where's that big grown-up birthday boy of mine, then – hey?!'

Sheila looked dead at Melody and said quite simply: 'Why don't you tell him yourself?' – just as Melody was surging and charged with a bursting need to Christ yes *do* that (and don't you try to bloody stop me).

Miles just stood there. For some seconds (looking back, Melody thought it could even have been weeks) it seemed as if the lower half of his face might well fall clean away, and his pink, dead and sausagey fingers were off-duty and loafing and in no state to catch it. Melody's breath was all stopped up as a result of the inner thud of a kick of love and yes even at that endless moment almost surely lust – though this was soon cripplingly twinned with the need to quickly kill him, and it was this compulsion that took her now. She felt certain that her mouth – though tight and grudging – was busy forming words, but her brain seemed surer there were none that sprang to mind. Melody knew she had truly connected when the wholly pleasing jarring shuddered up her arm from the impact around her wrist as she slammed the big white gooey cake hard into the bastard's groin – though how this thing came to be in her hand was something else again. Sheila was shocked, it sounded – yelps of outrage were in the air and Melody's time was running out. Miles's great booming protest erupted as he struggled with the force of a deep-down and sick-making swelling of agony from somewhere so profoundly within him as to make him yield and quite uglily faint, while clawing at dollops of obscenely creamy sponge, dropping in gobbets now – and flying too as Miles's wilder animation began to kick in and became quite energetic. Melody cracked a hasty fist across the fucker's jaw, while seemingly jabbing that great bloody nose at the identical moment. Arms were restraining her now, and Melody just had to be out of there while her own blood continued to thrill her; Miles made a lunge and slithered heavily in cake, his chin coming down hugely and badly on to the corner of a coffee table, this sending just everywhere a pile of jaunty and Disney goody-bags (enticingly bulging with kray-zee straws, rotgut, and sooper-bouncy balls).

And as Melody shouldered her way into the hall, all she saw was a quite curious Damien together with did-Sheila-say Mark, just lolling alongside. Their eyes were big with what could have been anything from terror to admiration – though Damien maybe didn't hear her wishing him a Very Happy Birthday because now the house trembled with his father's ravings:

'Jesus Christ Al-fucking-*Mighty*, woman! What the hell is wrong with you? What the hell is *wrong* with you – huh?! Oh Christ I hurt – I *hurt*, you bitch: I'm *hurting*!'

All this was greeted in different ways by the first filter of kiddies, clutching more tightly both wrapped-up Lego and parents' hands. One or two turned and fled; one lad (and don't ask why or how Melody could even begin to observe such a thing) – he seemed rapt and dead eager for more, but he was dragged out of the house more or less by his hair, his practically demented mother repeatedly muttering *Right*, that's it, that's enough, that's really *it*, this time. All Melody said in passing to a young maybe au pair who just seemed to stand there was He's such a shit, a shit – an absolute shit – to which the girl just lowered her eyes, could have even been in sorrow, and said so quietly Oh I know, I know, I know. Sheila was now screaming in the front room: She says you promised her a *ring*, you bastard, and Miles was roaring back Not a *ring* ring, you stupid bloody woman – I said I'd call, I said I'd *ring* her, is all, for Christ's sake, Jesus!

Melody slammed the door on all of it, and outside the air was summery and sweet. One stiff finger creamed off from her skirt a splattering of sponge; she sucked that now and smiled in a frankly fairly twisted way. Nice cake, she confided gaily, to a couple of hesitant newcomers. Glancing once more and finally at this family home she hoped she'd been a part of wrecking, Melody thought No, no no – I was

54

quite wrong about this house: no one could ever be happy here.

And now the blood-heat of this had carried Melody well into winter. Draining the last of her Chardonnay, now, she felt no – she didn't at all want to tell Katie anything whatever about just what had happened that time she went round. Katie just shrugged; she had merely been curious about Melody's version – she knew most of it, anyway, from Miles (who, when he called her the day after the summer party, had for some reason straight away started calling her Catherine).

❄

Anyway, thought Katie now – chin nestling warmly amid great puffy mounds of Badedas bubbles, her long and heavy limbs playing at being utterly spent as they came close to floating in this big deep hot and blissful bath – I was tired and, Jesus, bored to death. I wonder sometimes quite why they're all so terminally dull – I mean, leave out Brian and Dotty (puh-leese!): they're just mental. But even Daddy – sweetest thing in the world, of course (and fably generous, hee hee hee), but completely and utterly out of touch, for most of the time. Maybe the whisky, a bit. I'm so glad I don't work with him any more, though – God that was deadly. Can it just be his age? It can't just be age, though, can it? I mean, not everyone gets like that when they're older, do they? Well maybe they bloody well do cos I sure as hell can't think of anyone who hasn't. Melody's not that old, but she's boring too, now.

Which is maybe why I need blokes so much. They're great at the beginning when they're keen and all over you – mind you, they do go off pretty fast after that and then they become (let's hear it) Baw-aw-awring! Yeh. Actually, I think the only reason I'm looking forward to Christmas and seeing Rick again is because he's still fairly sort of fresh – you know? On account of living in Chicago. Only seen him

55

once since last summer (he came over for a short weekend – at the Ritz, if you wanna know, so pretty damn cool – and we more or less carried on what we'd been doing in America – fucking each other blind, eating a bit, drinking and scoring a lot, and then doing it all over again: he's pretty fit, Rick).

I can never turn on the tap with my toes; I saw that in a film once – one of those huge sky-blue Fifties bathrooms with millions of towels – American, obviously: in some parts of this bloody country they were probably still hauling out a tin tub and setting it in front of the stove. Maybe Doris Day. And anyway she or whoever it was did that, but I think you need pretty weird feet – or maybe American taps. Faucets. So I'll do it the hard way: done that now, so just slosh back and watch the steam rise (it doesn't actually matter about my hair, cos I'm getting it done in the morning – quite tempted to have it short again, but I don't know if I dare; maybe long is always favourite – sexier, huh?).

God it was a blast, that holiday – Christ it was so bloody crazy: sometimes I couldn't remember who I was supposed to be with! Look, OK – it sounds nuts I know but listen – I was meant to be going to Chicago, OK, with someone I was at school with called Ellie, except that Ellie doesn't actually exist on account of I made her up for my *parents'* sake cos they would've gone absolutely loopy if they'd known I was actually *really* going with the original creep from hell, Mister Norman fucking Furnish. Well . . . he worked for Daddy at the time and so it was sort of *convenient*; the sex (unbelievable if you look at him) was actually pretty good, OK, quite all right – and I like sex, yeah. But then I met Rick there, so Norman was out of the picture straight away: hiss-taw-ree. Which, I don't know, I suppose maybe *hurt* him or something, but what the hell – he isn't a kid.

And do you think the bastard will leave me alone? Sheesh. Ever since the holiday and Mummy's party he's on my case – you know? (Daddy sacked him pronto – not just the business with me, which I lied about anyway, but apparently he was nicking money from the company, if you can believe it; I wondered, sometimes, where all the loot was coming from – he always paid for everything cos I don't know about you lot but this is a cast-iron policy with me: the bloke pays – period.) Yeh, so anyway: Daddy gives him the boot, right, and that you'd think would be the end of him, yeah? But oh Christ no! Jesus, the number of sad little wanky letters I've had from him – and Mummy told me just now that today he'd actually gone and *rung* me. Keeps on about something he wants to give, show me, the twat – Christ knows what he's on about, and I for one could not give one single shit, believe it.

Do you ever get so it's so comfortable in the bath that you never actually want to, you know – leave it? But the bubbles are going all milky, now, and I'm looking pretty pruney myself so OK – where's the bloody towel?

And it hasn't been easy for me, this year, you know: first off I had to get an abortion, which was a bit of a drag – but they're pretty much nothing, these days. I had one when I was fifteen – about, um, nearly three years ago, now (Christ – seems longer) and that took bloody ages; but it's just in and out, these days. They cost a bit, but Daddy never knows what the hell he's paying for, half the time. Not quite sure if Norman was the father – needn't have been. Anyway, doesn't matter now, does it? Cos it's gone. Then I had to find some job – *anything* rather than Daddy's office; clothes shop, it turned out to be: no great surprise (most weeks I end up owing *them*). Rick says Hey baby – you come home and be my wife and you won't ever have to work again, my little honey. He is pretty loaded, to be fair – Ferrari, all that – but I don't know: just don't know. I think it was that word 'wife' that made me shudder. Really got to me, that. Getting away from Mum and Dad would be good, though, so . . . well, leave it and see what kicks.

Course, I've had a few blokes since then (well Jesus –

57

summer was bloody months ago): there's Miles, of course – he's OK (total shit, yeah? But OK) and David, briefly, and – oh yeh! *Howard*! Can you believe it? I thought it was really spooky he had the same name as Dad, but actually it was pretty funny and OK, in the end; I think maybe that was the only reason I had him cos quite frankly he was more than a bit of a jerk.

Mum has got this gorgeous sort of shiny wooden caskety box-type thing – where is it? It's usually . . . and you take the lid off, right, and there's this great big Hollywood kind of powder puff and you – *here* it is, great – splodge all this fabulous talc all over you and it's so decadent and so utterly divine – yum! Floris, it says here. OK, you end up looking like a vampire's victim, but afterwards you can smell and feel you all night long. I maybe ought to ring bloody Norman Furnish cos I don't want him all the time pestering me when Rick's around; mind you, thinking about it, that just might be the best idea cos then Rick will just bloody well kill him and people like Norman probably deserve all that they get cos every one of them is just so bloody bloody eternally baw-ring!

Glurk. All those choccy mints: feeling just a leedle bit *blur*.

Just picture this scene: the man is down on one knee and proffering to the suitably startled and very likely cringing young woman a maroon and plastic cuboid box, the lid cranked way back the better to display a fairly mingy ring (really rather puny) with some sort of stone in the middle, not so much twinkling as dully aglow with a sullen resentment – it just about peeped out from its bed of toning velveteen (looked a bit like coal, or maybe kerbstone). Is anyone fool enough to imagine that such a tableau could never in this day and age even begin to be glimpsed? Quite wrong – all this took place barely more than a month ago, when the two of them had just got back from Kentucky (the joint and not the state).

Charlene (the woman's name is Charlene) was unsure – is this guy having some sort of a gag? Not likely: in the ridiculously short space of time she had known him (are you ready for this? Days – just a few days, that's truly all it was) she surely had him down as not the gagging type. Oh God – all this was so-o-o . . .

She reached out to touch the thing (better show willing) and when she plucked it from the box the little furry spongey bit was hoiked out too and while she was disengaging the Christ-it-weighs-nothing-at-all, this ring, from that, she had to cope also with pretending not to have noticed the Argos Sixteen Day Money Back Guarantee that had fluttered to the floor – and the bloke now made a dive for it.

'Heavens, Simon,' she eventually managed. 'All this is

so-o-o . . . unexpected, yeah?' And then she thought she should address the funny ring itself (thin to the point of transparency it may have been, but it surely made up for all shortcomings of that order in terms of sheer circumference – it seemed to be built more on the lines of a midget's bangle: ample room for a couple of navvies' thumbs and some to spare, she would have said). 'It's . . .' was all that came out of her this time; couldn't quite run to the 'lovely' bit because, let's face it, it wasn't lovely in the least. How could she best describe it? 'Pukey' was the front runner so far.

'We could get it altered,' suggested Romeo, humbly (is it all right to get up now, I wonder – not quite sure of the etiquette here, but the old leg's giving me a bit of gyp, if I'm honest. Oh look – doesn't seem like it's going to take much longer: Charlene is shaking her head).

'Look, Simon,' she said – trying to sound kindly, doing her best not to be sick – 'this is terribly *sweet* of you and everything, and I'm very, um – you know, *touched* and all the rest of it – but God, Simon, we barely *know* each other – we've only just . . . I mean we haven't even . . .'

'I know.' Yes indeed. He knew.

'But really, Simon – I don't want a commitment, not now. I'm too young for all that . . . I'm sorry, Simon.'

She dropped the ring back into its plastic grave where it clicked and rattled (can't for the moment lay my hands on the little spongey bit) and a long and heartfelt nodding was all the reaction she got to that – along with just a touch of a grunt as the bent leg was now stretched out straight as if maybe the idea was a last-ditch effort at impressing young Charlene with a glimpse of the buccaneer within him by way of a spirited round of Cossack dancing.

She kissed his cheek, and became quite caring and nursey.

'All right? Hm? Simon?'

'Oh yes. I'll survive.' Time for a big sigh, now. 'Oh and um, by the way – it's *Norman*, actually.'

60

Yes indeed – here was just another day in the life of Norman Furnish: always seeking commitment and opening himself wide to yet another drubbing, but still so acutely relieved when one more time it all comes to nothing. But it was Katie he yearned for – Katie he dreamed of: still it was Katie at the centre of his being. Since he lost her (but I have had her, oh yes – at least there was always that: but if only I had her still or again) – since that time, nothing in Norman's life had seemed worth even bothering about. Christ Jesus – it's always so bloody *cold* in this grotty little room – I seem to put every bloody penny I get into that sodding little meter and still it's always like a fucking fridge in here – it's even worse than the last place, if you can possibly imagine that. At least then it was summer and it wasn't so ... oh God oh God – can't bear to think of summer, now – that's when I lost her to that American bastard. Who won't have lasted. And who, I wonder (all the time, all the time) – who can be having her now?

I mean it's not as if I even really *wanted* Charlene; well, granted, I wanted her in that she was a woman, OK, and I haven't had a woman since, well – I didn't even at that awful place in King's Cross when I ... oh Jesus, it was all so terrible, I just can't go in to that now: maybe later, maybe some day, but not now I can't – no way José. I mean – what I mean to say is: what exactly would I have done if Charlene had lost her mind and said Yes? Apart, that is, from answer to the fucking name of Simon for the rest of my days. I'll tell you what – (a) I would've felt great because oh wow this girl who I've known for the best part of twenty minutes does not in fact find me too wholly repulsive (that and the simple joy, now almost entirely forgotten, of someone – but anyone – saying a straightforward Yes when I ask for just anything at all; No is what people say: *no*). And (b) in no time at all I would've been baling out of the entire bloody caper. Just like I did when Melody had the baby; well Jesus – I'm no *father*, am I? I can't bloody look after *me*, let alone

some bloody little baby. She was better off on her own –
anyone's better off without me, let's face it; the last time I
saw her was at Howard's summer party (Mr Street's,
I should say now – because we certainly don't know one
another, not any more, that's for bloody sure) and she told
me she was in love and happy and going to get married to
someone called Miles, I think she said – and that Brian and
Dotty Morgan were going to adopt little Dawn in a totally
official sort of way. I suppose all that's happened, now. I
wouldn't know – I haven't seen any of them since that
blindingly hot and dreadful afternoon and nor, it seems
more or less certain, will I ever again. For all of that lot,
Norman bloody Furnish is very much persona non grata:
does not that come as one big shock? (Took the ring back to
Argos, did I say? Changed it for a Cosimax hot water bottle
– yes, yes, very ironic, I'm sure, but if you had to live in this
deep freeze, believe me you'd understand; it cost a fair bit
more than the ring.)

Ah but it was Katie I wanted, Katie I loved. And all these
women I've attempted to pick up in pubs – I hate them
before I even open my mouth because not one of them is
her. Anyway, it all got too expensive, all that – they only talk
back so long as the drinks keep coming and most of them
seem to be on triple vodkas, these days. They were a sorry
lot, anyway – the usual tale of bags to bitches. One or two I
even stretched to a curry – and *one* girl, one time (Christ
don't ask me her name – it was some name or other), even
managed to touch me for the price of a taxi home – *her*
home, she made it plain: where she was going alone. Great,
I thought afterwards as I trekked back through the fucking
slashing rain to my bloody awful little pit – now I'm even
paying to get smashed in the face. Which is what I think
finally made me sufficiently desperate and gave me the
courage (Jesus, I was shaking) to go with that tart in bloody
King's Cross (and no – I still can't bring myself to dwell on
that: like I say, another day, maybe). Because on the whole,

whether you like it or not, whores can be a good deal cheaper than women, in the long run (when you actually sit down and tot up all the figures). Anyway – now, if you can believe it, I've only gone and signed up with one of these *dating* agencies – and that cost me just about every single penny I had (waste of time anyway because she just won't, will she? Katie won't be on their books).

And talking of money: let's not bother, shall we – ay? I mean in my case, what's to say? Look – I never had much (goes without saying) but at least when I had the full-time job with Howard, Mr Street – and before I started selling quite literally everything I owned to keep up with Katie . . . and after I just, oh Christ, started helping myself . . . but it's really not *me*, you know, all that. I'm not *like* that – it was just Katie, Katie – just do anything in the *world* for Katie (wouldn't do a sod, now, for any-bloody-one else). All I've got left is a very part-time job – just some afternoons – with Bixby's (another estate agent, pretty local – at least at estate agents they don't expect you to be able to do anything) – and Jesus, I practically had to go down on my knees for that (and anyone so-called 'low-paid', believe me, hauls down a fucking sight more than I do). So in some sad attempt to cut my expenses – oh dear oh dear – I moved to an even more cramped and dark and nasty room than the last vile hole (Christ, if they get any smaller the bed's going to have to go up the wall and the sink'll be out on the landing, I'm not bloody kidding you).

I'm vaguely trying to build up a few possessions, but so far it's not much more than half a dozen Penguins and a bloody awful jacket: they said in the Help The Aged the bloke had just this week died, but prior to that had led a clean and blameless life, which is always nice to know. (Once – and Christ knows what's made me think of this, now – I was in a chain store, department store, and I saw this sign: Men's Sundries, it said – and it occurred to me no, no – I don't have any of those things either: before you stands a man who has not two sundries to rub together.) So I just sit here, most of the time: take today – as it's a weekday I had a good long lie-in; weekends I don't bother getting up at all – and from time to time I thaw out cheap gloop and swallow it and then I stare at my rented TV – that expense is truly vital, because without the TV I'd never get in any conversation at all: shouting at the newsreaders is sometimes good. I think I might as well watch some right now, actually – it doesn't matter too much what's on … what's on, in fact? Oh, it's something with a shirtsleeved policeman in it; this means, unless I've missed that bit, that any second now he'll tap on a frosted-glass door and stick his head round and some older, balder, fatter copper will look up from a single sheet of paper and the other one will say Any Chance Of A Quick Word, Guv? Yes … here it comes now. Yes, he's done that – and the older, balder, fatter merchant drops his paper and extends an arm and pipes up Surely, George – Pull Up A Pew. Oh God – I think I must be losing my mind. But it helps, you see, with the Katie thing; with the telly, sometimes as much as an hour can pass and I don't think of Katie at all.

I have written her another letter: I write one every week. This will be the last before I send her Christmas card – for that bright and mocking time will soon be here to crush me lower. I could maybe tonight go down to Trafalgar Square; perhaps in lieu of a bauble I could hang myself on the tree. *Christ* it's bloody cold in here – how can a garret the size of a packing case actually ever get to *be* this cold? The gaps in the window are hardly helping, even though I've stuffed most of the curtains into them and tried to seal the edges with the contents of a packet of I do believe filo pastry – abandoned by whatever poor wretch went mad in this room before I came along to lay my claim and taint it further. In this letter to Katie I have hinted more broadly than in the past as to the nature of the thing – this intimate part of how we used to be – that I have to show her, remind her of (but surely she can't have forgotten? Me it burns always). In the battle for Katie, I clutch to me just this single weapon – though God knows how to wield it. This letter I want her to read right now.

But thinking back – what I was saying earlier: all that about any sort of underhandedness not at all being me, not being part of my nature ... can it in fact quite strictly be true? If I am so high and pure, please tell me why I am contemplating the threat of blackmail? It can't really be – can it – for love alone?

This letter I want her to read right now. I think I'll take it round.

❉

'No really, honestly – we really *must* go now, Elizabeth – everything was so lovely, as always,' insisted Dotty.

'Oh *stay*, Dotty,' implored Elizabeth as she customarily did. Well look – it wasn't as if getting back could be posing any sort of a problem: step outside the front door, take four paces to the left and the first oversized tin can you come to, you're home and dry (if bleeding cold).

Brian was already standing and grinning half-heartedly if idly, longing to vanish, as ever (certainly keener to be ignored than derided) – because if Dotty said they were going then they were going, no two ways about it: and she surely seemed determined. Which she was, very – largely due to the fact that during the last ten or so minutes while the Armagnac had been going round and round (though more round Howard than anyone else, Dotty could hardly help observing) the twin dread subjects of winter breaks and Christmas shopping had ... well, Dotty might have said 'arisen', but this would suggest an altogether natural development, rather like daybreak – but emanating as such white-hot topics had from none other than Elizabeth, Dotty considered them to be far more the result of deft and careful architecture.

'I'm *so* looking forward to Paris,' is how it had gone. 'Aren't we, Howard? Hm? Say what you like about London but there's still something about shopping in Paris that's just . . . and it's so terribly easy to be extravagant at Christmas, isn't it?' And then the voice dropped at least a modicum. 'I don't suppose in the, um – the way things are, Dotty, that you'll be . . .?'

I know. On purpose, is it? Even after all these years, Dotty could never decide; considered herself to be a true friend of Elizabeth's (did, anyway, when Miss Absolutely-Fabulous *Lulu* wasn't around) and God knows Elizabeth had shown such kindness . . . and yet, and yet: there always lurked the hint of this *thing*.

And nor was Melody enjoying the thrust of the chat: yeh yeh, she was thinking – Christmas and I'm totally broke and I can't stop thinking about Miles and I'm stuck for the whole time with my bloody little noisy *kid*; wasn't noisy *now*, of course – looked more like a proof of the label for Heinz Stewed Prunes, so picture-perfect was she in her utter contentment to be safely next to Dotty. Which is a thought. I wonder if Dotty could be persuaded to . . .? Well of course she could, of course: and persuasion wouldn't even enter. But I don't know – do I want to? If I let her have her again I'll get used to it, won't I? And Dotty will get used to it and oh Christ oh Christ I just don't *know* any more: it just wears me out to even *think* about anything, these days – so yeh, I think I'll go too, now. I wonder if Howard is in any fit state to drop me off? He looks pretty gone, but then doesn't he always?

'Well actually,' rallied round Dotty (I might as well come clean about this latest wound – it'll only fester if I leave it gaping), 'we *are* going off for just a, you know – very short little sort of a break. Brian was telling me.'

Brian flinched at this mention of his name and thought oh dear God I believed I was finally and officially dead for the night, but now here I am this late in the play, shoved back in from the wings. Maybe I should've said nothing about any sort of break at all . . . it's just that I feel so horribly crushed by my own weight in guilt: I have to offer them *something*, don't I? Dotty and Colin? Hey? So I maybe foolishly offered them this. Didn't go *into* it, or anything (not too big on going into things, whenever I can help it, thanks very much); so I said the same as I said last summer – *surprise*: can't tell you more, just let it be a little surprise. Christ, you should have seen the expression on her face – starved and abused French aristocrats on their way to the scaffold in a fruit cart had maybe sported something on similar lines. And Jesus can you really *blame* her? You can't, can you? Not after just *everything*.

And that was very much the point when Dotty decided that they truly *had* to leave because Elizabeth would only go on and on about it, wouldn't she? And Dotty had no details to give her because quite frankly she dreaded even *knowing*. Last summer, Brian's 'surprise' had been a week in a caravan; now they lived in one shamingly similar so do please tell Dotty what form the jollities might possibly assume now just prior to the festive season? Each of them summarily interred in a shallow grave down Epping Forest way, maybe? Or could they perhaps queue up to be sealed within a hastily papered niche or cavity in the dank and dismal scullery of a modern-day and quietly-spoken Crippen? With Brian as your host and compère – Dotty is telling you, so please believe her – you wouldn't ever really get down to the what and the where and nor, increasingly, could you frankly stand to.

But all this stuff was news to Colin (Dotty had held back from breaking to her only child that his father was mooting a little winter getaway thickly clouded by the language of mystery, for fear the boy would kill himself). But now that he knew this awful truth, Colin felt suffused with an almost giddy delight because the fabulous scheme he had really only half-hopefully thrashed out that time with Carol (and

God there were problems – loads of pitfalls) must surely have a real chance of working, now – because there was absolutely no way on God's earth that Colin was ever again going to be a party to any prospect at all that was even remotely to do with his father – hear him? (All I want to do, right, is grow up, leave school and just *go*. But all I want in the meantime is Carol, OK – and soon I can see her and then we can fix it.)

And now, by way of a protracted and dilatory crab-like shuffle, everyone found themselves more or less in the hall and mounds of coats were bundled out from cupboards and Dotty went through one or two Brr-brr-back-out-into-the-Arctic type noises and Melody predictably came back with Oh God Dotty it's not as if you've got very far to *go*, or anything – though Dotty thought on the whole she could pass up on the humiliation of countering all that with the observation that it was not the ten-second journey to the caravan she was dreading so much as the bleak and practically polar conditions inside the fucking thing; sometimes, on a milder and merely frosty day, she half expected to tug open the door and find a full-scale blizzard raging within.

'So when exactly are you *going*, Dotty?' urged Elizabeth, as if eagerly egging on a wide-eyed and credulous infant to wrap up his very first lost and milky tooth in lovely crinkly silver paper and just *see* what a surprise he gets in the morning. Then she glanced at Brian – who looked now as if he had very recently passed away – and widened her eyes as her shoulders came up in some sort of evocation of girlish and pent-up excitement. What she was thinking was God oh God, Brian, what are you going to inflict on them this time?

'Well soon – very soon,' prattled back Dotty – grateful for Elizabeth's simulations of enthusiasm, and desperate to catch the throwaway thrill of it. 'When you go to Paris – I thought that was OK, with the house and everything, because – '

'Oh *yes*,' Elizabeth assured her, 'because Lulu – '

'Well I *know* you said Lulu was coming to stay,' cut in Dotty, while nodding absently. 'I think I had a scarf . . . long blue sort of thing.'

'All right, Melody?' blustered Howard.

'Are *you* all right, Howard? I mean I can always get a cab if – '

'Oh no *nonsense*,' broke in Elizabeth. 'Of *course* Howard will take you – won't you, Howard? Here it is, Dotty – goodness it's served you so well, hasn't it? This old scarf. Dior, isn't it?'

Howard nodded with energy: Yes I will – yes I was going to. Could actually have said all that for myself.

'I think so,' said Dotty. 'Think it is.'

'Oh no we're both wrong!' laughed Elizabeth, in a way that really had to be pleasant. 'It's Jonelle – "Machine Washable"; anyway – jolly warm, I should think. Let me wrap it round you.'

And as Elizabeth circled Dotty – trailing around the scarf as unselfconsciously as a Morris dancer at the Maypole – she sensed rather than saw young Colin intent on her. In the old days, she would have met such a gaze with a big, broad gash of a smile as she waited to be gratified by his more languorous but no less giving version. But heaven knows what he thinks of me these days, thought Elizabeth, who now chose to focus instead on his mother. It maybe wouldn't please Dotty, would it, were she ever to find out that during the nights and days when she struggled with the twin forces of loathing Brian and loving Dawn in the powder-blue holiday caravan, moaning in the wind on that seaside clifftop, Elizabeth had been wrestling no less vigorously with – no, not her conscience, but churned-up sheets in a bed as big as a field amid a scattered litter of green and clanking evidence of so much swilled and spilled champagne, while the warmth in Colin's long and golden limbs covered her and made her gasp before crying – and how many times since has she closed her eyes and caught her breath while trying again to feel the feeling of his slim and needle-hardness for the first time piercing? She had been ablaze for him, then, but now the memory merely burned her.

Elizabeth chanced a glance, but she saw that she had lost him: Colin was now looking across at the door – Howard seemed to be doing that too, and so were Dotty and Melody and everyone was utterly silent; even Brian was goggling over there, now, and a sudden clattering made Elizabeth start and pivot and give in to a quite involuntary recoil – and now she slightly shrieked with shock at what she saw there and as Melody whimpered briefly Elizabeth could hear Howard at first rumbling and then building up the outrage into What In Christ's Name . . .! What The Bloody . . .?! And maybe the owner of the long pale hand that wriggled bonily through the letterbox like an eerie and separate just-poached octopus could possibly have cottoned on to some of that too because the fingers were frozen now and inverted, like the imploring mitt of a boxed-in beggar.

Now Howard registered the envelope on the mat and he strode forward to scoop up that while heaving open the door in one and the same movement and there was quite a bit of yelping as Norman Furnish was dragged inwards and downwards and crashing to his knees as a good half of his face slammed into the panels and even now with the great bright lights of the hall and the sweeping gusts of sleeting wind swirling on in to the house, while everyone but Howard was agog and flustered, Norman still managed to be both inside the house and out, aware only that a good many of his joints were paining him, and also that this is not at all how it was meant to have gone. As Melody bawled out in relief and derision Oh Norman oh Christ *Norman*, you total fucking fool, so to some of the party he presented in profile a hunchbacked penitent placidly awaiting a damn good flogging, while one or two others in the already quite astoundingly icy hall saw only the reddening hand now revolved and outstretched as if in mid-hover over the keyboard of a glossy Steinway, and threatening to come down like Jesus into one mother of a chord.

'Get out of my bloody door, Furnish!' roared Howard – and he grasped at Norman's rigid hand and began to haul it in way up to the elbow – which was, thought Elizabeth as her eyes blinked briefly and rolled up to heaven, so utterly typical of Howard when he's had a few drinks and really isn't *thinking*. Norman was given to blurting out Glah! on more than one occasion, now, because at each great and brutal tug he received joint and urgent warnings from his hugely troubled shoulder (now on the point of being done with the whole business and *giving* Howard the arm, if he bloody wants it so much) and the muscles in his face and crunched-up bones beneath – now desperate to alert Norman to the truth that if they continued to be smashed sideways into this door for very much longer, then no more could they guarantee the retention of such as eyes and teeth, and nor might Norman ever speak again.

It was Melody, eventually, who batted away Howard and extracted Norman – as Howard drew back and simply glared.

'Go!' he roared. 'Get off my property, Furnish – if I ever see you at this house again I'll bloody *kill* you, hear me? And then I'll report you to the police.'

'Well,' said Brian, mildly, 'we'd really best be off . . .'

Dotty nodded to that (not even quite sure who the loony is – is he the one who used to work for Howard and stole money from him?) and she and Brian hustled away the few paces to their super little home on wheels, Colin tagging on with a face fit to burst – Christ Almighty how totally hilarious! All these people are *mental*, I tell you: Carol is the only *normal* person I know, apart from being lovely.

'Look, Howard,' tried Norman – 'Mr *Street*,' he added on right away and with much more than a touch of hurry up because Howard took one step towards him at that and he was a pretty big bloke, Howard – and Christ he reeked of Scotch.

Norman opened his mouth again, and then he closed it down. It was maybe not the ideal moment for talking it all over, and so focusing on nothing, he turned to go – and Jesus, my knees are really killing me and I've torn my trousers, now; good God, I haven't been in genuflection mode for so bloody long in my life – not even when I proposed to young Charlene, that time. And my face feels slatted, like a Venetian blind. It's just as well I don't play the violin, or anything, because with my hand like this, all that would be history – the bow would go just everywhere. And I'd only stooped down to the letterbox because it occurred to me that it would maybe be nice to glimpse for just a short while all the colour and warmth of Katie's house, and then to slowly suck in some sweet air that she herself had breathed, before she softly let it go. (And then I wondered where she might be: maybe having fun with a *person*.)

When Howard was completely sure the bloody sod had gone, he turned to Elizabeth and then to Melody. Christ Almighty, he said: Christ Almighty. Elizabeth took some glasses into the kitchen (oh God – the mess, the mess: I wish to God I'd never even *started* all this) along with Norman's letter to Katie – at least make sure she *gets* it anyway; Howard would only have torn it to pieces – or, maybe worse – opened and read it. Poor Norman. Though God knows what he wants with *Katie*: clearly the boy was in need of help.

Howard clicked home the seatbelt in the Jaguar, and Melody said Oh God I'm so sorry, Howard, I can never find the slot on this thing – it seems a bit – I think I may be sitting on it – ah no, OK, got it – right. Fine now.

Of which Howard had heard not a single word. 'Christ

Almighty,' was all he said. It maybe sounded as if he was utterly bemused, but he wasn't really even thinking 'Christ Almighty' – these recent and maddening events were no longer the issue. All he was thinking as he slid the very dark blue car away from the driveway and into the night was Laa-Laa, Laa-Laa – oh my darling, if I don't see you soon, I think I'll go nuts.

❄

'Well,' concluded Edna Davies, with some reluctance letting the heavy curtains slump back together and join again. 'I certainly couldn't *see* anything – what on earth was all that about, Cyril, do you think? Hm? Howard doing all the shouting, fairly sure. Unlike him, isn't it? Don't usually hear him *shouting*, or anything.'

'You never know,' said Cyril slowly, setting down his glass of pale fino sherry with considerable care on to the forest green and melamine drink mat bearing a dull gold fleur-de-lys at its heart; he succeeded in placing the copita perfectly centrally, so that the thin and faceted stem appeared to grow up and away from it, bloom-like, while the circular base remained precisely framed by equal measures of coaster, this brought up short by gilded and gently chamfered corners: as Cyril himself would tell you – it pleased him so to do. 'You never can tell with people such as Howard. Not by any means always quite what they seem. I have observed it before.'

'They never ask *us* to any of these supper things they always seem to be having,' Edna was near enough huffing. 'Maybe just as well if they all end like that one.' She now just about sat on a side-chair – although matching pairs of sofas abounded – adjacent to where Cyril presided within the deep and tobacco-coloured buttoning of what they both loved to call the Master's Chair. 'Perhaps they think we're not *good* enough for them, or something.'

And Cyril joined Edna now in her ironic and deeply

73

indulgent chuckle at that – the two cadences fusing into what might easily have passed for an outtake from some radio laughter track, when marginal notes had specified a good degree of avuncular and knowingly amused acknowledgement of a notion frankly too preposterous to even remotely or for a second be seriously entertained.

'I very much doubt it's *that*,' is how Cyril rounded it off. 'Takes time, Edna, to assimilate into a new area – all very tribal. They have to sniff around us for quite a good deal longer. Anyway, we're quite happy – just us here on our own, aren't we? Hm? And they *have* asked us round for Christmas, after all.'

Edna nodded concedingly. 'Yes – yes of *course* you're right, Cyril.' But in answer to your question, she was thinking, No – not really: not too happy at all to be just us here, on our own all the time – and yes I *know* it's ungrateful, I know it is, after all the money Cyril has spent on this lovely, lovely house (and God knows it's far from finished yet). I've always got lots to do – I know that too; it's just that there never seems to be anything that has to be done. People with children feel differently, I'm told – but it *would*, I suppose, have been disastrous for Cyril's career if we'd gone ahead and had them then. He always did have a practice at home (and God you should see his consulting room here! So utterly de luxe you wouldn't *believe*) – and I *can* see, yes, that when people come – you know, people with mental, um – oh I don't know what it is I should call them, never did – but Cyril's patients, clients, whatever they are . . . when people are *disturbed* in whichever way they are . . . well, they don't, do they – don't want to come to an *enervating* place with children and noise and upset and clamour? Of course they don't. They seek solace, and peace and the quieter, um – what was it again? Quieter *spaces*, I think he said, where they in their minds can wander. Something. Cyril has explained it all to me, very patiently – oh, many many times. And he was right – of course he was right. He never would have built up his reputation to such a degree that we could ever have even *thought* of affording a house such as this. With all these lovely things. So yes – I suppose he's right about that too: we *are* quite happy, just us here on our own. (*He* thinks so, anyway.)

'Oh Cyril!' she said now, suddenly. 'Did you see my message?'

Well quite possibly, is what Cyril was thinking. I've seen *a* message, haven't I? Dozens of them daily. She has this board, Edna (you might as well know now) – green baize affair criss-crossed with contrasting bias binding, stuck at the intersections with great brass studs. It is the size of something that could well serve to flash up the latest lowdown on departures from somewhere not much smaller than Waterloo. Every time we move, she gets an ever bigger board; this one she *commissioned*, if you please, from the can't-believe-his-luck joiner whom she has instructed, it surely seems to me, to encase just about everything except the glass in the windows. This obsession ranges from the perfectly admissible (radiators, plumbing) to the seriously, well – words do fail: and I'm meant to be versed in pinpointing and lending form to new strains of derangement. Such as? Such as this: light switches. Oh yes, oh yes – I am not joking. Each switch in the hall and main reception rooms is now nestling within a tiny little mahogany armoire, and fitted with a Dutch teardrop handle that would be perfectly serviceable to anyone under the age of about four, so bloody – Christ you wouldn't *believe* how fucking fiddly they are, cursed little things. God's *sake*, Edna (Cyril had tried this when only the first of them had been up and running): you go into a dark room, you want to just snap on the light, not be feeling around for some damn teensy wardrobe stuck halfway up the wall. I mean, God – it's not as if you can always lay your hands on the thing and there you are groping around and sending all the picture frames this way and that and you can't *see*, or anything,

75

because the lights aren't on because the switches (see?) are hidden in a bloody little cupboard. Christ – what with that and her new fascination for all things *trompe-l'oeil* . . . I just can't tell you how disconcerting all that can be in a house you haven't yet got the hang of: oh look, you think – a Mediterranean round-topped arch with an ajar and beckoning wrought-iron gate: what could be nicer? A handy short cut through to the kitchen, maybe. Only too late do you register the garlands of out-of-season flowers and the orange horizon and all the bloody *peacocks*, Christ help us, and again you're sent slamming face-first into a wall. Dear God – concealment and illusions – what can I tell you that already you do not see so clearly? I could fill a textbook with just the doings of Edna alone – and one day, who knows, I might just do it.

'What message was that?' said Cyril, quite neutrally. Was it the one I caught sight of after breakfast which read 'Cyril – did you get my message of earlier?' Was it that one? Or was it the one that said 'Cyril – ignore my second message: it doesn't matter any more.' Good God – once he had come across one of her interminable lists intended for *herself*; that had been headed 'Edna', and Cyril will never forget the concluding memorandum: 'Urgent – make out tomorrow's list *now*.'

'About your *stars*, Cyril. Didn't you see it? It said for you this week that although it would start off with some obstruction from colleagues or at home, by Thursday huge opportunities are coming your way.'

'Nice to know,' said Cyril. And that was another thing: the stars! Dear oh dear oh dear.

'But *I'm* not obstructing you am I, dear? Because you don't, do you, actually *have* any colleagues.'

'Not, er . . . not really, no.' And she can pick the bones of that for any meaning she likes.

'Do you want more sherry, Cyril? Another glass, yes? I'm quite tired – I think I might go up.'

'Reached my quota, thank you. I wonder if the house will ever be free of the smell of sawdust. Have you seen my glasses? I might just – '

'Oh Cyril – not *more* work! It's late.'

' – read a bit. That's all.'

'Do you know . . . I'm still not absolutely sure about that colour . . .'

'Nice colour,' said Cyril. Whatever it is, the colour's just fine: hardly anything here's the same shade from one week to the next.

'You don't think it's too . . .?'

'No. I think it's perfect. Is it Monday or Tuesday?'

'Monday. No Tuesday – yes it *is* Tuesday because I remember thinking yesterday oh my goodness, the start of another week. Is there anything special you want for Christmas, Cyril? It'll be upon us, you know, before you can say . . . oh and *Cyril*, the builders are coming round extra early tomorrow because I didn't want the noise to disturb your first appointment. Did I say what they're doing? I did, no? Yes? Urn?'

'Which one's he?'

'No, dear – *urn*, not . . . oh *you* remember – that wonderful overscaled urn that we're having in the hall, hm? It'll take four of them just to *budge* it, I reckon. Have you no thoughts at *all* on Christmas, Cyril? Have you got me a surprise?'

'If it's *overscaled*, Edna . . . that means, well – that it's too bloody *big*, doesn't it, so why – ?'

'It's what they *do*, Cyril – it's what they *all* do: you deliberately overscale somewhere like an entrance hall or a little walled garden, or something, so that it makes a dramatic *statement*, yes? We talked about it.'

'There's nothing I really want for Christmas. I actually thought I put them down here somewhere, my glasses, but I can't seem to . . .'

'They might be next door. There must be *something* you want, though Cyril – ooh, I must just leave a message for them or they'll be treading all over everything in their horrible muddy boots. If you *haven't* got me a surprise, Cyril, there are one or two things . . . shall I leave you a message about it? That's best, isn't it? Yes – I think so: leave you a message in the morning.'

'Fine. Fine. I'm actually just wondering if I'm hungry or not . . .'

'I could quickly make you a – '

'No – no, I don't think I really . . . it's not *hunger*, I'm just a bit . . . no, I won't sleep if I – '

'Sure? Or I could do you some – '

'No really not. Maybe just a drop more fino, and then I'll quickly skim over this bit about . . . have you *really* not seen my glasses, Edna?'

'I'll look. And think about Christmas, Cyril – I'm going in to the West End in a day or so, so I want to know. It *was* going to be tomorrow, but I don't think I can, now. I *must* get some more peppermint tea: quite taken to that. And conditioner we're out of, again. Goes nowhere. They forecast *snow* tomorrow, too – it's so very boring, winter.'

I just know, thought Cyril as Edna fluttered away, that the only thing I want for Christmas is the only thing I've wanted since first I became aware of its existence that stunningly hot and sunny day in Howard and Elizabeth's party marquee. Only just that week bought the house – funny week: weird. And then this evident psychotic came up to me – heard what I did, knew what I was – and asked me if I'd take a look at his wife (convinced she was a straitjacket case, if you can believe what I'm telling you). I looked – I took one look at Lulu Powers, and the vision has stayed with me every day since. What an utterly beautiful woman – truly, honestly: just for once, the big, real thing. She's often round to see Elizabeth next door (think they're in some sort of venture together) but so far I've completely failed to strike up any sort of rapport or even *conversation*, if I'm honest here: she's not at all giving, Mrs Powers, no not a bit

– but just think what a challenge she'd be. And then only the other day, Howard was telling me that Lulu is soon going to home-sit, sort of thing – anyway, *be* there – while he and Elizabeth go off to Paris. I tell you, what with the fixations of Edna, the bloody daily builders and the succession of nutters I'm expected to cope with, the breath-stopping breeze of Lulu in my life could truly blast away all the clogged-up filth and caked-on grime that weigh me down and make me grey. If only somehow I could clutch to me this one sweet thing.

'They were in the *hall*,' sighed Edna, wafting back in. 'You're *always* leaving them there, Cyril, and yet it's the last place you ever think of looking. I'm off up, now – you'll do the lights, yes? Don't read too long. And remember, Cyril – think about what you *want*. Promise? Yes?'

Cyril nodded, smiled and said I will, I will – of course I will: promise you faithfully.

❋

Men were flitting in and out of Lulu's mind, now, at the thought of Elizabeth going away – and men were seldom welcome there. John, of course, primarily; she had not yet told him about the arrangement – not just for the usual reason, the old reason, the reason that had confounded her thinking and dogged her being for so terribly long: not *just* because he would be struck silent, quiver, and then crank up into his big, bad boiling rage of jealousy and accuse her of concocting an entire and intricate panoply of evil invention, simply in order to cover the sin of her tracks. '*Lizzie*?!' he would roar with huge derision and thickly, delivery beaten in by the most recent and felling intake of hardcore booze. '*Lizzie's* house?! You're never going to bloody Lizzie's house – you're off somewhere, aren't you? Aren't you? *Aren't* you? Hm? With who? Who with? What's his *name*? Or are there more than one – a group, a group, yes? Some pre-orranged argy, is it? I mean . . . what I mean,

79

pre ... pre ... *Christ*, Lulu, you know *lust* what I mean ... just, I mean. How can you do it, Lulu? How can you? How can you bring yourself to *do* this to me – how is it that you cannot come to see just how much I *love* you?'

No – these days she could simply stride away from all of that; of course he would make an elaborate grab at her – at one of the many images of Lulu throbbing semi-opaquely before him – then fall heavily through blurred thin air and crack his head and end up somewhere in a dazed and barely muttering heap, one dead leg awry; other times he could abruptly cease, mid-tirade, a wincing expression of quick amazement dulling into sheer confusion just glancing across him before the knees gave way and he passed clean out.

No – John, now, she could handle; but what of Howard? Howard, yes – but oddly *not* Howard at all because of course Lulu didn't even *know* Howard, did she? No she didn't – not in any real sense, anyway; met him – how many times? No no – it wasn't Howard, no, but simply the space he took up. He was with Lizzie, yes? And increasingly (more and more, day by day) that is where Lulu so much wanted to be. And although she hoped when in the company of Lizzie she conveyed all of the pleasure it gave her (but none of the yearning for more), any joy she had felt at the prospect of being properly shot of John – even briefly – and being free to graze on and pry into Lizzie's secret places (touching her things, feeling her things) had recently and potently given way to dark, sick thoughts of only Lizzie and Howard, alone and at large. Which yes was lunatic on so many counts – apart from being uncomfortably close to the puerile compulsion of a driven third-former bursting with passion for the Head of House – this was also too near the crumbling outskirts of black and unguarded places: those where John held tenure, pacing and policing. With a shock, Lulu had come – not close, but maybe just within the faintest earshot of some of what John had for so long been screaming – and she backed away deftly from that, before turning and running headlong. And *mad* like John, too, all these thoughts – because what: did Lulu really think that Howard, after so many years, could easily become a silkily attentive and sexual demon, simply on account of inhaling Paris, along with Lizzie? Unthinkable. And how, in his place, might Lulu be? Maybe unthinkable also. And now all Lulu could feel about being free to graze on and pry into Lizzie's secret places (touching her things, feeling her things) was a tenderly aching sense of displacement, that could tug her deeper into mute desolation.

Actually, John doesn't seem quite so bad as usual, tonight, Lulu was idly thinking, as she slammed through the pages from back to front in some thick and shiny magazine: drinking only wine, and practically focused, looked like. She still started, though, when his voice was suddenly hanging there, coarsely – never quite the right pitch or volume, these days, but this was by no means as barked out and starkly brutal as it could be.

'So!' was the first sound – and John too was aware of the quite unintended harshness, even the pause that followed seeming strident (but he knew, John – he knew it well – that modulation was just one of the many things beyond his control). 'What are you, um – up to, Lulu? my darling. Hm? Can I pour you some . . .?'

Lulu looked at him: he was, he could see, being regarded. But there had been no threat or challenge in his voice that Lulu could detect – none of the customary sneering nor hint of his having interwoven the lure of thin and leafy saplings across a chasm of some imagined culpability into which Lulu was expected to crash and tumble.

'Up to, John? Up to in what sense? Do you mean what have I been doing at work, up to? Or are you mad and in the clouds again?'

John tried to keep on as brave a face as he had been able

to master – didn't think his eyes had flickered away from the hot lick of that barb. I have to try to pretend to be *fine*, you see – because otherwise I'll never know anything and nor – when the day comes for Lulu to leave me – will I have the means to track her down, or even the reason why.

'Well work, yes . . .' he replied with caution, raising an eyebrow, tipping the neck of the Rioja bottle sort of invitingly in Lulu's direction, and when she tossed away her perfectly cut and glossy hair, angling it back down and pouring more into the mug before him; oh bugger, slopped a bit, not much – don't think she's noticed. If Lulu thinks I'm drunk, she'll walk away and she never lets me follow, now. It was that thing with her hair that had done it – so cool, so dismissive, so shame-makingly erotic (oh God, oh God – she's so beautiful, so lovely – I'd die for my love of Lulu, kill if I had to; she's my wife – for a bit longer, anyway, she's my wife, still, and I cannot recall the last time I so much as touched her without being held off or brushed, smacked or shoved away – and they were the times when I was so far gone that her look alone had not been enough). 'But also I mean, well . . . Christmas, I suppose I mean. You mentioned, I think you mentioned Howard and Lizzie unless I'm . . . er . . . you sure you won't have any wine, Lulu? No? OK. Um . . . mistaken.' And that's about as far as I can go, thought John now – quite without warning, flooded by misery. New Year? Can't, can I? Think of that. Look at Lulu: that woman is so resolved. That woman, I tell you, is bent on resolutions.

Lulu had known it would come up some time, so maybe try to deflect it now, when John was possibly as sane and sober as he ever would be again (which is to say – yes – not very).

'*I* will be there for Christmas, yes John . . .'

John nodded. I know: I listened on the phone. And you're going to be there for days before when they go off to Paris. I know: I listened on the phone.

' . . . but,' resumed Lulu (kind but firm, was the intention, now), 'I don't really think it would be a good idea for you to – '

'Please . . .?' cut in John, his voice so soft that Lulu had to look up and be sure that he had spoken at all, the near-wet supplication in his eyes telling her yes, and touching her too.

'Look, John,' she said, turning away. 'You *know* the situation. In the new year, in January – I told you what I'm going to do and it's really no use – '

'*Please* . . .?' came back John with an urgency she knew; his voice was near to breaking and Lulu wished he was as drunk as usual so she wouldn't have to bear it. Now he could no longer hold her gaze, John concentrated hard on keeping steady his head – for while his renewed imploring still floated undisturbed in the air, there might remain at least some attendant hope?

Lulu was sighing, but not in pity (she was done with pity) and nor quite out of a more simple exasperation; John, she knew, could be very devious – apparently without pretence and guileless, yes, but behind the wide eyes there always lurked a pulsating agenda. Here is what I am smelling now: I have no money. What I earn with Lizzie I spend on, God – oh *Christ* knows what (why do I *do* that?) as soon as it arrives (damn, damn!). John – so very generous, before all this – now paid the bills and gave to Lulu nothing at all. Her solicitor was working on a handsome settlement, oh yes, but all that would take . . . and so until that heavenly moment (and here is what I'm smelling now) he knows I have no money.

'Because,' continued John, as carefully as careful (would love to have a mighty slug of wine right now but that would break what spell we have), 'if we *are* going round there, you know – for Christmas, you'll need to buy, well – all sorts of things, won't you, Lulu? And you haven't yet told me what you want for yourself . . .'

83

Yes, thought Lulu, as she turned again to face him – once more (and he knows it, he knows it: just look at him, he knows it) John is on the point of snatching away the round during the final seconds. OK – the *round*, John – conceded, but the match, believe me, has long been a foregone conclusion: the championship is in the bag, John, because now I am a heavyweight and soon – really soon – as well as being down you will very much be out.

❄

John was expecting Lulu to go up to bed pretty well immediately after this stilted but at least conclusive exchange; well, they were hardly going to round off the evening with easy chit-chat about the mutualities of this and that, followed by an amiable and dozy game of Scrabble over the Bournville cocoa. Were they? No. Did people, actually – couples – still really do such things? Outside of advertisements for Scrabble and Bournville cocoa? Or was it all arguments about money and in-laws against a backdrop of fizzing television presaging the big and resentful silence before the epilogue of locking doors? At least we didn't have to pointedly wrangle over money: she knows I know she has none. And let us thank God for that.

So when Lulu went up to bed pretty well immediately, John was barely aware. (She slides home the bolt, you know, these days: slides home the bolt. The first time I heard it – prostrate on the landing and baying, baying – I had thought it the very coldest sound, truly like a visceral piercing. But at least it means I am still a threat and still a force? Though so is the common cold.)

At last I can now stop drinking with care: it has been an agony, tonight, sticking to just the one magnum of Spanish, but of course I knew I had to be not just conscious but coherent. (A perfectly handy measure, the magnum – useful when you just fancy a little something but don't want to open a whole bloody case.) But as this little mission is as

84

near to accomplished as any of mine ever will be, now, it's time to make serious inroads into quite a few more. As well as, so the theory goes, maybe eat a bit of something. Needn't bother: the Screwpull is to hand – and I've got a fresh pack of Bensons here, somewhere (yes, started up that again – but it's always nice, of an evening, to have twenty good friends over: ho ho ho).

That quip – the cigarette gag that just flitted into and out of my mind: is it, you know – *funny*, or anything? Bit witty? Not, is it? Lame. It would help if I could still tell the bloody difference (it fogs and dulls you, the drink, there's no point in denying) because I am in fact meant to be a *writer*, you know, if anyone cares – and yes, OK, I can just about hold down all these crappy 'lifestyle' features (they kill me while affording a living) – but Christ, there *are* only half a dozen pieces you can ever write, and I have been fooling with variations of those for centuries. But if I have any hope at all of surviving the devastation that Lulu is all set to unleash (for she remains fully ready to lay me to waste) then it is in the form of the bloody *novel* I'm meant to be doing, surely. Should I not get straight and get sorted? Chuck the booze and chain me to a keyboard? I'll let you know in a magnum, or so. And (oh dear) there, I'm afraid, you have it: that is the state of me now.

God I need a woman. Odd how that thought just hits you from nowhere. I mean – Lulu, for preference (Jesus, I barely recall the soft and downy ins and outs of her) – but anything knockout would do for me, lately. If, through the haze, Tara could even begin to reach me. Now *that* was funny (. . . God, these bottles – they *look* big enough but Jesus, they go nowhere once you've got the corks out) – no, that was very funny indeed. Not funny as in Was the Bensons gag funny, no, but funny in that I was thinking of women in a depersonalized sense (as you do) and suddenly in my head there was the tame of Nara, name of Tara. Tara, I might say, is the editor of the monthly magazine that I more or less write

85

single-handed, it seems to me – and Christ she can be a bitch (she's really good at it). It's just that she knows I can bang out a thousand words on just about anything (and some of the shit you wouldn't believe) well in time for any deadline going – so she uses me a lot. Pays well. Lately, she's been . . . not *nice*, no: less vile. And I know why: she has detected how unhappy I am (I have watched her probe and plumb the depths of my misery) – one pointer to this state of mine very possibly being the fact that I am forever bursting into tears whenever I hear a voice that does not spring from Lulu, for it brings in closer, if not into focus, the truth that the world is simply jam-packed and chock-a-block with people whose voices can never be Lulu's, and here is something one must either live with or else settle down to nuzzling round the scary and grimy edges of the other thing. (That, you know, is one of the bravest things I have thought for months – and I didn't even cry out once while it was occurring to me.)

And of course, women just love deeply unhappy men – just love that. Women? Or women in power? No – just women, pretty sure. Because then they can cajole – begin to fish around the business of winkling them out from this carapace of despair (I don't think I'd actually go ahead and use that image in any final copy – the subs'd rip it out anyway) – but always there dangles the threat to plunge you back in, and deeper.

All that said, she's a good-looker, Tara. All you need. Not a good-looker like *Lulu* (let's get that straight – Lulu, my Lulu, is in a class apart from the rest of the planet and God I love her, God I do). And she lives alone, which has got to be favourite. What must she be, Tara now? Late thirties? Probably late thirties, I'd say (but not to her). And lately, very recently, she's been making pretty encouraging noises – if, God help me, I am still capable of discerning even the shadow of any such things. She says she's got a little place in Bath: studio flatlet. Nice for her.

I'm going to open just one more of these, and then that's it . . . this Screwpull's marvellous, you know – used always to put my back out with the other bugger. The novel I am working on now (untitled – and, of course, largely unwritten) is not, in fact, my first. The first took years and it was rejected by every publisher you know about, as well as all the little crap ones; some bloke I met who called himself a novelist (never bloody heard of him), he said to me: don't be discouraged – get down and write another. And I didn't say Yeah? Oh yeah? And what if *that's* bloody rejected too? I didn't, because I just knew I couldn't bear the answer. But here I am – sort of doing it. And Jesus! *Some* of the muck you see published nowadays . . .

Right now. Now this minute. God – I'd *love* to have a woman, right this very second: one who would take care of me, find my dissolution no more than endearing. Someone who would just put me to bed and not keep threatening to put me to death. It's a mistress I need. Not just someone to have, but somewhere to *go*. Christ knows I'm going to need it – because believe it, that lawyer of Lulu's, he's going to strip me of everything because I am apparently guilty of – how can she *do* this to me? – mental cruelty. I expect I shall be paying his fees.

Think I'll go to bed, now. Or maybe just have a couple of brandies and spend the night right here, where I seem to be. Like I did last fucking night. Oh God. But the thing is, you see, I get scared of standing up, for fear of falling down. And the joke is (huh!) that it is *Lulu* who is the sullied betrayer! It is Lulu who has surely taken leave of her senses, and yet now it is I just left here, alone and awash, well down the road to annihilating mine.

PART TWO

Cats and Dogs

It had been yet another of those breathlessly rushed and delicious phone calls to Carol that always made Colin swell and flush with a tingly blood-heat, and yet left him cold and void all the way down to his melting centre the second the receiver went down after the dozenth foolish but heartfelt reluctance to end it. But he felt so charged and swooning while still they both chattered into the mouthpieces so damn far apart, his voice giving way only to the no less urgent sweetness of Carol's – the thrill of that for Colin only just tempered by his awareness of the clicking phone card's pacy erosion.

'So tomorrow, yes?' checked Carol.

'Oh God yes – tomorrow, tomorrow,' moaned back Colin. 'Wish it could be now. Wish I could see you now. Oh God I wish you were here with me now, Carol. I love you. Love you so much.'

'I love you too. Silly.'

'But I mean I'm *always* loving you,' gushed Colin. 'Always. Can't wait. Soon is never soon enough. I want you now now now and for ever! Oh God – I think the pips are going to go. Love you, Carol.'

'I know. I know. Look – I'll see you where we said, OK? Only I've got to go cos I've been on the phone for ages and I think my Dad wants to use it.'

'Don't go!' gasped Colin. Childish, he knew that, but he felt it – yes he did, he did: it just came right up and out of him.

'*Got* to, Colin. Tomorrow at ten. You do *know* Camden Market, do you? Yes?'

'Hm? Oh yes, yes,' Colin assured her distractedly. No, actually – heard of it, vaguely, but all that Camden stuff was way across the other side of London and this had been most of the trouble all through the summer and the autumn and now the sodding winter; that and bloody *school*. At least now there was the time – so tragically little money and so few opportunities: just *time* to fill, *time* to fill, *time* to fill until he could be back with her and remember again how *breathing* goes. But I'll find the place, wherever it is; I'll crawl to a war zone, if that's where Carol is because listen, look – just where Carol is is all I want to be.

But here was time that would surely never pass: ten tomorrow! Ten o' clock (did you hear her?) tomorrow morning! It was hours and hours till ten this evening, never mind tomorrow. And then the night! The night, the night – another of those year-long nights in his caravan coffin to kill his groaning and churn up thoughts and bedclothes while becoming chillingly lucid and alone, racked by turmoil, before practically exploding under pressure of wide-eyed dreams of softly and then not so softly taking hold of Carol and feeling stunned again by the almost electrically shocking tenderness of all of her skin before heat and gasping dispatched all that – and then when he tugged quite gently at the roots of her hair – dragged it back more firmly – that's when her eyes would widen and melt and a slight catch in that throat at the back of her open mouth would do it for both of them and from there on in all there could ever be was a hot, brief, savage melding. And I want it now, I want it now.

Which was all Colin was still feeling that following morning – jostled by crowds at the black gate of what he prayed to God was the main entrance to Camden Market (how many entrances could there possibly be?), his nostrils just about coping with incense and onions while his eyes

92

were intent on scanning, scanning – the brain behind them busily shuffling and dealing out all sorts of dread possibilities for now, oh God, she was *late* – and yes, she was always late (Sorry I'm late, she said – sorry to be so late: those were the first words she would ever utter), but still, you never know, do you? *Anything* might have happened.

But Colin wasn't late, oh no. He had been turning to ice for nearly two hours, now, due to over-zealous planning. He had slaughtered a part of the awful evening before by sitting in Howard and Elizabeth's garden (wrapped up in a sleeping bag, yes, but still bloody freezing to death) trying to make some sort of sense of a tiny little Tube map and an ancient *A–Z* with the not-much-help of a grudging and flickered light from the Jesus-we-never-ever-have-any-bloody-batteries-in-this-pit Durabeam. He had calculated that if he got neither lost nor attacked, the journey would take about an hour so he allowed an hour and twenty minutes – say an hour and a half (safe side) and then rounded it up to two hours because look, I've never actually been to Camden before, right; and then he became so fed up waiting for eight a.m. to crawl round he had set out not much after seven. Journey took no time. And here he now still stood – his feet no longer anything to do with him and just another impacted part of the frozen London clay beneath – praying to God that this was indeed the black gate of the main entrance to Camden Market and those bloody fried onions were frankly turning him queasy and the joss-sticks stung his eyes and someone bloody *else* had cracked into the back of him, now, and it was just as well Colin was in love, that's all, because otherwise he just might not be quite so forgiving; that, and the fact that everyone he *did* scowl at looked so damn big and severe.

Colin was wearing sort of turquoisy-green and suedette trainers because apart from those awful school lace-ups, that's all he had that just about fitted him. And a black puffy zip-up jacket kind of coat thing – no *not* an anorak, actually

93

Carol, he had been quick to make clear, the first time she had laughed at it. It makes you look like you're expecting, was her follow-up remark, to which Colin had said absolutely nothing at all while knowing that it was one of those comments that he would never ever in his life come close to forgetting even if he lived to be as old as his bleeding father. Talking of whom – Colin was wearing Brian's gloves which were, it almost goes without saying, perfectly shitty, but Colin had been left with no choice at all, here, because one of his ski-type mitts had gone missing (You have to look *after* your things, Dotty had remonstrated – before threatening to, oh yuck – *knit* some, can you oh Jesus believe it?) and so Brian's great horrible and creaking things had become the only alternative to just standing there and watching his fingers go black and drop off. (Where's my gloves? Dotty? Seen my gloves anywhere, Brian had wanted to know. You have to look *after* your things, Dotty had remonstrated – before threatening to, oh yuck – *maim* him, can you oh Jesus believe it?) And rammed down into the coat-jacket-thing was the scarf from his old school – the actually pretty decent school, where every day you went to learn things with your mates, and not skulk bent double in an effort at invisibility and fearful of your life: black with yellow stripes – pretty cool. But he didn't wear a hat because a baseball cap was just too, well – just wouldn't want people to think he was the sort of person who would wear one of those, frankly; and he turned down Dotty's offer of a scratchy little woolly pull-on number with a bobble on top on the grounds that he did not want, please, to afford to Carol the slightest chance of suggesting that he now resembled nothing so much as an oh-so-cosy pregnant teapot.

I am losing all feeling. I stamped my feet a while back so that my blood would remember to shoot all around me, but the really odd feeling of not feeling at all very quickly gave way to this awful, jarring and fizzy pain, so I'm not too eager to do it again. Why could Carol never be on time? I know women are famous for it, of course – I know that. It would help if she could, is all I mean. I mean – I'm not *criticizing*, or anything, because I love her, as you know, with all my, um – thing and thing. Heart and soul. It's just when it's so bleeding bloody cold it would be nice, for once, if ten meant ten and not – Jesus, God, coming up to nearly half-past, now. What if this isn't the right place? Oh Lord – what if Carol is turning into a glacier at some other bloody damn gate and cursing me and sick to death of incense and onions and (Jesus) maybe even approached by *boys*. I'd never forgive myself. Particularly if she talked to them. What if right now, right this second – somewhere over on the other side of this massive market (why Camden Market anyway, actually? What's it for?) she is not only quite happily chatting to some guy, some – I don't know, slightly older sort of guy who's maybe left school and maybe has a car, or something, and *certainly* is wearing decent and designer gear and – and what if she thinks he's actually pretty cool and he says, he says – *well*, Carol (because Jesus – she's already told him her name!) – all alone, are we? And she says yes! And off they go! And I'm just left here to solidify into the night and then maybe it'll snow and settle and I'll just become a rooted mound of whiteness and then some kid could jam a carrot nose into my face and *then* some creep would stick on me a scratchy little woolly pull-on number with a bobble on top and then when I die I'll be in all the papers and Carol will scream out Oh God Look How Hysterically Funny – he looks just like an oh-so-cosy pregnant teapot!

'Hi, Colin – sorry I'm late. Sorry to be so late. You OK?'

'Carol – thank God.' Yes indeed – in danger of losing it, there.

'Have you been waiting long? Sorry. Tube.'

Colin shook his head in a throwaway, God-no-just-this-moment-got-here sort of a way and aimed his mouth at her mouth just as she was maybe thinking of other things and glanced away, so there was a fresh and Polo-minty softish clunk of pink and fleshy wintry noses, and then the moment sort of passed.

'So what shall we do?' asked Carol, brightly. 'There's actually some candles I want to look at, somewhere round here.'

'I don't really mind where we go,' responded Colin with wide-eyed honesty (did she say *candles*?). 'Is there – are there any indoor bits to this place, do you know? Only I'm slightly on the freezing side.'

Carol grinned and linked arms with Colin. 'Come on,' she said.

'Why are you so warm?' said Colin. 'God you're so warm – I wish we could – '

'Well we can't,' cut in Carol, at her horribly most practical. 'Can we?'

Colin shook his head at the big, deep sorrowful truth of this (God, you know – the way people just barge into you – Carol's got a pretty tight grip on my arm at the elbow and if I'm not a bit more assertive, here, the rest of me won't still be on the other bloody end of it). 'I love you, Carol. It's so good to – '

But Carol was setting up one of her shrieks; she did that, Carol – Colin had been quite scared the first couple of times he'd heard it but all it was, he'd decided, was her wonderful way of expressing this girlish enthusiasm.

'*There* they are,' she whooped, breaking away from Colin now and rushing over to a stall quite literally weighed down with all manner of, to Colin's eye, deeply unpleasant and somehow rather filthy-looking stumps of sulkily livid can't-be-beeswax, some as thick as your leg and loads of them writhing in purple and orange and often dusted over with sparkles, too.

Colin stood slightly apart from Carol, happily watching her scanning these lurid totems from Middle-Earth – could never tire of the endless flicker of thousands of minutely calibrated hints of expression dancing all over her really quite painfully lovely face, until the mind behind settled on one or other of them – sheer pleasure, this time: so large and simple as to suddenly render her no more than a five-year-old at her very own birthday party (tall for her age, and wobbling on top of her mother's platforms).

'This! This one – don't you just adore this one, Colin?'

Carol held before him an extremely tapered conical candle that looked as if it had been maybe not lovingly moulded from a down-to-earth blend of Bird's Custard Powder and superannuated blood clot, with an under-pinning of possibly mulch by way of a bracing afterthought.

'What do you want it for?' asked Colin – and here was not so much diplomacy as out-and-out amazement.

'Oh I just *adore* having lots of candles. Particularly the scented ones – this is sandalwood, pretty sure.'

Colin nodded; the collective stench from the stall was bringing him close to throwing up or passing out.

'What I do,' resumed Carol – eyes bright and warming to the memory – 'is I dot them all around the bath, no lights on, and then I have these essential oils and hot, hot water and God I could just drift there for days and days.'

The sharing of this intimacy had lit her up, and Colin was held and then felled by his vision of it all. He thought he could very happily forgo the remainder of his life if just once he could be a big part of this throbbingly hot and scented experience . . . and then when she rose like Venus from the water, soft and streaming and exuding – oh Christ, whatever it is that girls *did* exude after doing all this stuff – then Colin could wade into all the warm and sticky peace she was feeling and make them both remember just where it was that vigour came in. Could burn the bloody house down in the process, of course, but hey – all the two of them would know of that was just a bit more heat.

So she bought the long and swirly number ('It's like

Merlin's hat – don't you think so, Colin? It's just like Merlin's hat!') and then she chose a midnight-blue pyramid as well, and a round dull pink and cream one, about the size of a cricket ball.

'Let me get these,' said Colin. 'Let me get them for you.' And he hauled off one of Brian's big and loathsome gloves and stuck his hand into the pocket of his jeans and sort of left it stuffed in there, but God – if Carol didn't begin to protest at the generosity of this must-end-today offer fairly damn soon, then Colin could see little alternative to dragging out some cash and actually paying for the things . . . but yes, it was OK, it was all right: Carol was cooing no no no no no and she'd got them now, she'd done the deal, and the fourteenth-century Bulgarian gypsy who hazily ran the stall and dipped the wicks had already wrapped up her waxy treasures in the sort of thin and floral tissue that you only ever see on garage forecourts when they sling it around your fume-choked pinks – and now he rammed the lot into a too big and just still whitish Sainsbury's carrier, as frail and thoroughly lined as a human being of indeterminate gender captured in a grainy snapshot in the local paper when confronted by its similarly ancient offspring, a hundred candles of a very different order, and no puff left at all.

Colin had not enjoyed the charade; there was nothing remotely mean about Colin – he yearned to give, was longing to give Carol whatever he had. It was just that what he had was so, oh God, *pitiable* that he had already worked out in advance that if the two of them were going to have a coffee, or something (burger, maybe) then that and possibly just one more coffee (Coke, say) along with his Tube fare back to Nirvana was utterly and completely the whole sum total. How wonderful it would be – wouldn't it be wonderful? – to say to Carol – here, let's get a taxi: I've already booked a room, no – a suite (yeah!) in the Ritz, Savoy . . . Selfridges, is it? No – Claridge's, fairly sure: one of those. Or take her out of London altogether. Which – believe it or not – he was one day quite determined to do. They had discussed it, once (loosely) – it was even Carol who had brought up the shadow of even the possibility of such a thing (her auntie's flat – where did she say?). And Colin's got to come back to it and find out soon, because his need to be with Carol somewhere secret, allied closely to his even stronger compulsion to put as many miles as possible between himself and whatever perfectly bloody little ordeal his father had cooked up for this terrible and nearly raw impending winter break, had made Colin absolutely resolved on the matter: this, OK, just *must* come off.

The trouble is – had Carol actually been *serious*? Were they? Girls? *Serious*? They seemed so – you always thought so, right up until the moment when they laughed in your face and spluttered out Oh God – you didn't really think I was *serious*, did you? (Well yes, since you mench – did.) I mean OK – I'll see Carol at Christmas (Elizabeth's invited over just everyone) but there'll be *people* all over the place and her *father* might come and bloody Terry, that absolutely shitty shit-shit of a *brother* of hers – and these days, Jesus, I don't even have a room to go to, just my own personal shelf where I wedge in and don't sleep (just due north of my father's wet and open mouth, and the vapours it conveys). So you see what I mean, don't you? Yes? You do see? If there's the slightest chance I've got to grab it.

And as now we seem to be settled into the corner of some sort of clattery café – all stripped pine down to the waitress's face, clammy bits of vinyl gingham (least it's warm) – and I've already turned down a brown and porous slab of bready sort of cake (on grounds of not just poverty but revulsion, too) this maybe seems as good a time as any to launch into the thing. My time today with Carol is slipping away, and what I think I am thinking is that – how can I say? – already I cannot bear to know that soon I will be unable to bear being back in hell and without her again.

99

'Carol . . .?' Colin began – voice cranked up a little bit high, all the better to convey a casual, smirkish and altogether fairly grown-up approach (although in truth Colin always found himself bound up in a barely suppressed and whippy-white lather whenever Carol was within range of his senses – close to a cousin of panic, sometimes, but nearly loving it).

'You've got tons of milk in your coffee,' said Carol, idly. 'Do you never have these dark and strong ones? My Dad always has these – he introduced me to them. Espresso. Gorge.'

'No – don't really go for those,' said Colin quite frankly. Don't actually go for coffee in any form at all, in truth, but if you stick all this milk in and then a load of sugar it's more or less OK; it's just that tea is so uncool, and I needed to get my hands round something warming. 'No – expressos aren't for me.'

'Espresso.'

'Swat I said. Look, Carol . . . about this week. Have you actually got anything, you know, fixed up? Planned, or anything? Because I thought we could –'

'What do you mean, Colin? It's *Christmas* next week, isn't it?'

Colin nodded as vigorously as if he'd been paid to. 'Oh yeah – absolutely – *next* week, yeh – I was just wondering about in between. You know you mentioned your auntie's flat . . .?'

'Oh yeh – that,' was Carol's crushingly flat response. And now she just stirred her coffee (not without difficulty, Colin was surprised to even care, because the spoon only just fitted in to that piddly little cup).

'Well,' went on Colin, feeling quite brave and frightened (the two often went together, he had found). 'I mean – is it still, you know, empty and everything? Is she still away? Your auntie?'

Carol nodded. 'Yeah – she's gone to the Bahamas till after

New Year, for some crazy reason. Dad says it's a bloke. She's always been a bit like that, Auntie Jane, which is sick, actually, cos she's got to be fifty.'

'Yeah,' agreed Colin without reserve, 'that *is* sick. But I mean' – touch of urgency, now – 'you are still up for the idea, aren't you? I mean – you do still *want* to . . .?'

Carol looked directly at Colin and hunkered down to pondering this. Well *see*, Colin, it's not quite as simple as that, is it? I mean – yeah, in *one* sense I want to, but I can't just shove off, can I? What's my Dad going to say? He'd go absolutely nuts. And also there's Tony. I haven't mentioned Tony to you, Colin (obvious reasons), but he goes to school with Terry and you know how much Terry absolutely loathes you, Colin – I think that's why, actually, he introduced us. Tony's nice – pretty cool. But I do find you sexy, still, Colin, if that's what you mean . . . anyway, the only reason I go to the flat is to generally sort of check up and snoop about a bit, so I suppose you could maybe come round for an hour or so, if that's what you mean? Is that what you mean, Colin?

'What do you *mean*, Colin? What are you actually saying?'

Colin breathed in deep and slowly, and then got rid of all that pent-up air in a rush. '*Right* – what I mean is, what I think would be really great is if we could spend a few, er, nights at your auntie's place and – '

'*Nights*? Are you kidding? *Nights*! How can I – ?'

'But you said that – '

'Just wait, just shut up and listen, Colin – OK? You've got to be – I'm *fifteen*, Colin – I live with my Dad! How the hell do you think I can – '

And Colin just had to charge in here because the whiff of desolation was assailing him now and it made him choke and he had to ward it away because *look*, OK – this just must come off!

'But when we talked about it the first time, you said you

101

could maybe say you were staying at your friend Charlotte's – '

'Emma.'

'Emma – right. So couldn't you? Say that? Oh *please*, Carol, please – we might never get another chance!'

Carol looked at the light in Colin's eyes, and all at once she maybe saw the point. When again would there be an empty flat? (But I'd have to let Dad know where I really was.) And also look at this: in the light of Tony (seventeen, now – learning to drive: says he's going to get a Mini Cooper, which I think are just totally fab), maybe after Christmas is the time to move on. I lost my virginity to Colin, right? So it would be nice to know if what we do together is actually any good. Don't get me wrong – I *like* Colin, really do, but it's just that lately he's always so . . . I don't know what the word is . . . intense? Sort of *desperate*, you know? Kinda clingy is what I mean.

And Carol said: 'Before I go back today I want to get the second volume of The Stones' greatest hits – I'm really into that Sixties stuff, lately.'

Colin knew he must now look like a stricken deer; he hoped not a wounded faun – and let's pray for no undertone at all of Bambi, here.

'Carol . . .?!' just had to be the word that oozed out of him now, and it sounded quite as racked and longing as the pain inside that went with it – this whole fetid slurry of deep-down bad feeling that had washed right through him: it mingled now among the lights that Carol had kindled, and put them all out.

'What's wrong?' she came back – eyes far too wide, this time: just had to be playing with him, didn't she? 'Don't you like The Stones?'

And Colin looked at her, his face just daring to hope. And yes – she is smiling! Her look is telling me that she's back in again – I can feel her filling me up.

'So you *will*?' he gasped.

Carol nodded and laughed. 'Let's go for it,' she gurgled. 'I wouldn't mind another coffee, actually, Colin . . .'

And Colin piped up immediately to the waitress who quite amazingly just happened to be idling there (and how often does that happen, hey?):

'Two expressos, please.'

'Espresso,' said Carol, still smiling.

And Colin smiled too, you bet he did. 'Swat I said.'

'I thought you didn't like it?'

Colin was now mumming for Britain – looked as if he was doing his damnedest to break his own jaw. 'I love it,' he said, while thinking God I'd pay money to just fuck her right here on the table. I can't even reach her thigh from this angle, which is frankly driving me crazy, so I'll just have to make do with a few more hammy and accidental breast gropes like I did just before we walked into this place; Jesus, by the time we get to Auntie Jane's, I'll be like a bloody volcano.

Carol had paid for the coffees – which was just great because then later when she did one of her loony yelps at the sight of some ghastly and lime-green sort of bug-eyed puppet thing, Colin was able to grandly treat her (No honestly, Carol – please: I insist: my pleasure). He walked her down to Camden Town Tube, and there he kissed her, gently. Then he came at her again and his hands and arms were going at it like a blood-hot and rabid windmill and she had to practically beat him off with the Sainsbury's carrier, in the end, and then she hoped aloud it hadn't cracked her candles.

Colin turned away from the Tube – did not follow her down into its warm and breathy guts, because all bar thirteen pence of his current disposable income had of course very recently been invested in a ghastly and lime-green sort of bug-eyed puppet thing – but the thought of the coming million-mile trek did not faze him in the least. And so what if now it was raining down glinting particles of Wilkinson

Sword that seemed to slice him? The reflection of strung-up coloured lights bobbed in the smooth and oily blackness of Regent's Canal, and a flashing and tinselly sign over Dingwalls wharf was twinkling out the message 'Merry Christmas'. Colin hugged around him his rapidly whitening black not-anorak and grinned fairly manically into this now quite serious blizzard. It will be, he thought – oh God yes: now it *will* be.

❄

These underpants are a puzzle. But never mind that, for now. Dotty had no idea where Colin had gone that morning, but she hoped at least he was all right for cash. That's just about all I can do for my big little grown-up, these days – give him a couple of pounds, let him buy a couple of things and hope against what really can't, can it be, hope any more that there are at least for him a few times when he does not feel so deeply just what hell our lives have now become. And the source of the money? Dotty's part-time little job, yes? Well yes – that was the means, certainly, or else how could she have access to all those receipts? *Receipts*, did you say? Did you say receipts? Confusing. Yes look – all very confusing, maybe, but to me it has become quite everyday and utterly normal and I don't actually want to dwell on the ins and outs of it because I'm *not* a dishonest person, not – all I am is a mother: a mother to little Maria, whose last breath seeped through those tiny white lips before we had ever even spoken – she was still so tender and sweetly young, my little angel Maria, that time she left me. And a mother, yes, to another angel, Dawn – if only so briefly; but Melody is weakening, I can tell that. My bursting love for Dawn just grows and grows as her natural mother's feeling continues to diminish into near invisibility – a thing I truly, truly will never understand. It is one of my hurts: the biggest.

You can keep things from babies – it is easy to disguise

the real surroundings. All you do is recreate the time before they were forced to emerge, bloody and crying – make their lives a pinkly warm and soft and, mmm – a loving place, beyond which nothing at all can ever exist. But with Colin, what chance could there ever be of that? He sees his father dead-on, stark and floodlit: he knows just what Brian is – he knows too (how could he not?) that he was taken from a good school, taken from a good house, and imprisoned elsewhere. So all I can do is what I do – give him a few pounds, let him buy a few things – and just how I do it is no more than the way it now has to be.

But what about these underpants, though? Should she, what – confront someone about them? Brian? Colin? I mean – what I mean to say is, how did these things come to be in the drawer? One pair of ash-grey Calvin Klein Y-fronts with contrasting white waistband – far too small for Brian (not that there was a preponderance of Calvins at whatever skip or boot sale he currently favoured) and although, yes, they would just about fit young Colin, it was Dotty who bought all his stuff, you see, and what she bought was pale blue boxers from M & S (Colin's choice) so you can see her puzzlement, here. Can't have been a mistake on the part of the laundry because laundries – along with all other services, amenities, facilities and treats (together with a good deal of less than basic human necessity) – no longer applied, here.

And there was Brian now – in the east wing of the caravan, roughly a yard from where Dotty was seething at the sight of him. Mention it, should she? Worry flickered into her, now: she hoped there was nothing sinister, here. If Dotty's life lurched into one more turn – if again, screaming, she was obliged to somersault into darkness – then she would leave this ride for good and all. And what – Christ – what bloody gadget was the man tinkering with this time?! Why, instead of finding a job . . . how can he just – how can he just *sit* there like a smashed-in buddha and spread out in front of him another load of junk and just be content to *fool* with it, a look of – do you know I think it is a sort of quiet *satisfaction*, if you can believe any such thing – actually tugging at those sallow and stubbled cheeks of his.

'Brian, don't you think there's enough clutter in here without every day of your life adding to it? Hm? Why have you got an old *Hoover*, Brian? Going back into the carpet business?'

That one connected: life had been so good when Brian's carpet business was booming. Before the recession. Before everyone decided that it was wood they wanted on their floors – all that wood that Brian had spent half a lifetime obliterating with carpet, and now they all ripped it up (along with Brian and Dotty and Colin, as it happened).

'Not a Hoover, Dotty,' was his mild response. 'Think I've put it together all right – I'll try it out this afternoon.'

'Oh God, Brian – you've left all the – the sink is full of washing . . .'

'Just one or two things I left to soak: they'll want drying flat – I'll put them under the mattress, later.'

Dotty had done everything in her power to stop Brian taking over the domestic chores – but no no no, he had insisted, it's only fair, it's only right: you are going out to work, after all, and until I, um – until I can get . . . until things are more *sorted*, it's only proper I do my bit. And he did, he did, as Dotty would despairingly admit – there were *bits* all over the place: that was the trouble. He would be halfway through the ironing, while in the process of swabbing down most of the surfaces; some potatoes would be well on their way to being peeled, others not. And while a good deal of the washing would be done, the rest was left to soak. (It was maybe in the field of hand washing that Brian took the most pride: he had been amazed when he had seen in big red letters on the side of the massive carton of detergent – part of a multi-pack, cheaper that way – that due to a formidable cocktail of not just new but secret ingredients, this powder actually prevented bobbling. Brian had had no idea what this bobbling could be – and nor, indeed, why its suppression was so clear and absolute an imperative – while taking quiet pleasure, however, in wielding the power to stop it in its tracks.)

'Oh God why is it always so *freezing* in here?' Dotty now demanded to know. 'Christ – I'd get one of those terrible paraffin heaters but I just know we'd all end up in the morning *fried*.'

'Think I'll try this out, now,' said Brian softly, lifting down to the floor what could indeed be taken for some spare and primitive form of vacuum cleaner. 'Really?' he went on. 'You think the weather's all right? Oh yes, I think so – doesn't look like rain again today.'

Dotty gazed at Brian chatting to himself: this was quite recent, all this – all this was a new one. And nor were these conversations always so equable. Just yesterday, Dotty had heard Brian say Think I fancy a walk, to which he responded No, not me mate – I'm quite happy here. But, Brian came back with, It'd be nice to get a bit of fresh air, don't you think? Brian was resolute, though: No, he concluded – I'm really quite settled. Dotty had run from the place before he came to blows.

'What is it, anyway?' she asked now – grudging, yes, but Jesus: had to *know*, didn't she?

'What – this?' checked Brian, indicating his latest gizmo – and then rushing on in order to stem the force of the certainly impending *Yes*-Brian-you-prat-*that*-of-course-*that*-what-in-Christ's-name-did-you-*think*-I-was-talking-about-the-secret-of-oh-Jesus-eternal-bloody-*life*?! 'It could, Dotty, be the answer to all our problems.'

'Uh-huh,' chucked back Dotty, with huge and indolent indulgence. 'Gas chamber, is it? Or maybe it's made of gold.'

Brian nodded slowly, as a sage might do; it was one of about seven expressions he could muster at will that had

Dotty reaching out for just anything at all, but maybe best a carving knife. 'Could well be, in a sense, Dotty – could well be. What it is is a metal-detector.'

Dotty's eyes were as dulled and stagnant as a placidly fermenting cesspit, and her voice was well in tune with all of that. 'A metal-detector,' she echoed.

'Correct. It, um –'

'Don't tell me – detects metal? Did well, then, didn't it? Found this heap of scrap-iron in no time flat.'

'Funny, Dotty. No – seriously. Considerable fortunes have been amassed with the help of one of these. I was only reading the other day –'

'How much was it? Brian? How much money have you spent on this load of junk?'

'An investment, Dotty – that's how you have to see it. You put out a little – you get back a lot. Anyway, a good deal of the outlay was offset by the sale of my little schooners. Could be canoes.'

Not remotely true, this, it must now be said. Even Brian had been forced to admit that the eventual miniature fleet fell some good way short of being collectors' models; in fact, far from being authentic in every detail they were seriously deficient in the whole damn lot – and that Humbrol sticky paint got everywhere, you know, and those little brushes were so sodding fiddly and not just that but Brian had cut up four perfectly good handkerchiefs to make up the sails but in the end they just looked like bits of bandage, if he was honest, and it was maybe psychosomatic or could have been the acetone thinner – Brian will never know – but he was sneezing thirteen to the dozen for hours after that and had to resort to a John Lewis bag which was hopeless, being plastic, and after that a fistful of handy Andrex. So he had said to the woman in Help The Aged I wonder if you would like these little boats at all? Free? As a gift – so you can sell them in your shop and direct all due proceeds to noble causes and she had said No and so he dumped them in a bin in someone's front garden and the owner had barked out Oi! What's your game, then? And all Brian could do was shake his head in sorrow and hurry on – because it's not as if he *played* one, or anything, is it? And so how was he expected to answer?

Brian now stood at the open door of the caravan, peering into the veil of drizzle just hanging there, not at all invitingly.

'Oh Christ shut the fucking *door*, Brian! Just get out and shut the fucking *door*, can't you? It's so bloody bloody *cold*!'

'So,' pondered Brian. 'Shall we go or shall we not?'

'Go! Go!' screamed Dotty.

'I think,' concluded Brian, 'we will. You agree? Yes – on balance I rather think I do. Don't think the rain'll last.' And then – soon after Dotty punched him in the back and slammed shut the door – as his wellingtons ground down into the sparkling gravel in Howard and Elizabeth's driveway: 'You know the trouble with Dotty, don't you? I do, I do – indeed I do. But which one trouble in particular? Always judging, that's my opinion – always so quick to judge, put you down, laugh in your face. At least I am *trying*.' At this point Brian broke off from his dialogue to briefly wonder why that woman, there – the one with the dog and the little girl – had been staring at him so very oddly; people, concluded Brian, could be awfully strange. 'Now where was I? Oh yes – *trying*, mm. I mean, OK – the little boats didn't really work out. You can say that again. OK – no need to rub it in. But with this metal-detector, I'm telling you – just anything is possible. How do you get to the Thames from here, actually? Should've looked it up. Do they have tides and things, rivers? Or is that only seas? And just you take those underpants. There could be money in them. Well – not in them per se, maybe – but in the principle. Apparently there are people who will pay all sorts for any old junk if only it belonged to a famous person. Was reading an article about it. Well, thanks to the local paper, I happen to know that some kid from one of these dreadful rock groups lives just round the corner. (Bloody hell, look at this – Tube fares are like taxi prices, these days; I remember when you could go anywhere for a couple of bob.) So it's *initiative*, isn't it? You get yourself round there and have a rummage in his bins. Admittedly, a pair of underpants isn't quite what I had in mind – but better, I thought, than the lager cans and microwave food trays. What I suppose I was hoping for is some signed photos or maybe a pair of gold leather boots, or something. An empty packet of heroin, or whatever it is they eat. I'm not so wet behind the ears as to have expected *guitars*, or anything. Still. Try again next week. And there's a novelist too, quite near. Maybe get a manuscript.'

The rain had now hardened into glassy splinters (on a whim, God had put his foot down and finally rid Paradise of all its vandalized windscreens). 'So. Think we'll unearth any treasure on our very first trip? You never know. It would be handy if we found some bit of jewellery, or something, because I've got absolutely nothing for Dotty's Christmas present yet. And I don't have to tell *you* what she's like. Well – you can only try. And that's exactly my point, isn't it? You've got to *try* – and that's all I am: really *trying*.

'Tell you what: find anything good – we'll go halves.'

❋

God, Dotty thought – the second she had hurled shut the door and come close to practically embracing the curious arrangement of vertical slats and grilles which made up what she despaired of ever being able to call her 'heating system' without hanging the plonk-plonk irony of inverted commas around each of these dumb and lying words. But God, though – even that peculiar Peter person that works for Howard or Elizabeth or whichever of them it is (I can never work it out) – even *he* looks at Brian as if he has just crashed down from the sky. Dotty had seen that funny look in his eye just now as he was letting himself in to Elizabeth's – he just turned and gazed at Brian as if he simply couldn't believe it. Why on earth does Elizabeth have him in the house? What exactly is it that Peter is *for*, I wonder?

Dotty slung into a bucket whatever crap of Brian's he had left to soak and would want drying flat later on. She filled the kettle and looked forward to tea. The repairman had said any time between lunchtime and four; it was the – oh God, please don't ask Dotty to even think about this, let alone put any of it into words. It was the – *glah!* – the thing that passed for a *lavatory* and Dotty had purposely not mentioned anything to Brian because he would have had the whole thing asunder in no time and although in one sense it would have pleased Dotty quite profoundly to see him hard on his knees and deep in the shit, she was aware too that in rank and unspeakable pieces the whole awful thing would have remained until Dotty could have stood it no longer and one of them would have died or exploded or worse, much worse – oh so much worse than any of that: Dotty would have had to not just compound but yet again extend the boundaries of seemingly infinite humiliation and knock on Elizabeth's door and ask her quietly if it would be all right if Brian and Dotty and Colin could possibly use her loo.

And hence the repairman. How awful that there are people who spend their days just going round and doing such things. But maybe in some ways it's all any of us amount to. I shall have my tea, swallow with guilt one and then two of Colin's own Jaffa Cakes, and not think of Christmas. Or our, oh God, 'holiday'. Which I pointedly haven't asked Brian about because there's always the risk that he'll *tell* me and I don't just now feel strong enough for that.

But why on earth does Elizabeth have him in the house? What exactly is it that Peter is *for*, I wonder?

✳

'Why does Dotty go on bothering with Brian, do you think?' asked Peter, with his usual loose and only mildly exasperated air, which to Elizabeth always seemed to convey an utter carelessness as to the nature of a reply, or even whether any was delivered.

'You get used to things,' was Elizabeth's gently smiling reply, though she could almost hear herself thinking Poor, poor Dotty – what the hell else can she do? Stuck with him, isn't she? 'How did the lesson go? You know, Peter – Zoo-Zoo, you naughty thing – for one so young you really are an insufferable snob.'

So odd, she reflected, in so very many ways. It was only quite recently (Elizabeth had been amazed, at first – and then quite delighted) that Peter had asked her to call him Zoo-Zoo. Zoo-Zoo? she had laughed – why Zoo-Zoo? And those heavy-lashed eyes had nearly closed and then opened wider than ever. Because, he said, it suits me; don't you think it suits me, Elizabeth? Don't you? And now his mouth was miming the sort of kiss that would linger just long enough to warm her so that she would miss it, when it was gone – and Yes, she said – yes, said Elizabeth: it suits you, Peter – it suits you. Zoo-Zoo. Zoo-Zoo. It really suits you well.

'I don't think it's a question of snobbery,' said Zoo-Zoo. He was sort of semi-sitting and half sprawled in the chaise in the morning room, one long leg thrown wide. Those slim-cut trousers really become him, reflected Elizabeth – that slight touch of dusty pink in the creamy beige looked so wonderful when he laid on it his soft and brown and bony fingers: expensive, yes – but like all good things, worth it, Elizabeth had thought. 'It's more *aesthetics*, wouldn't you say? I mean, there are some things, some people, that should just be destroyed, no? Why not be rid of ugliness? Who will miss it?'

'A fascist as *well* as a snob,' said Elizabeth, in her mock-admonishing voice; God, you know – I could forgive this boy just anything on earth: why him and no one else? 'Oh *Jesus* – what was that? That sounded like something's broken, didn't it? Oh God, Peter – Zoo-Zoo – I sometimes wonder if Nelligan remembers that he's supposed to be a *builder* – it's a *builder*, he's supposed to be. Why do builders always *destroy* things? Anyway – can't bear to look. Do you want more pineapple juice? No? Sure? Well tell me, then – how did the lesson go? Do you think you'll pass? And don't forget you promised to help me with the packing. Will you miss me? I will you.' (Oh God look: the *Colin* thing was wrong, and *this* is wrong, but I just can't help it – and yes: people, I know, have said this before.)

Zoo-Zoo looked down, and then he sat up. 'I don't want to think about you gone.'

This so much pleased the girl in Elizabeth that the grown-up voice she now dredged up just simply didn't make it:

'Oh don't be so *silly*, Peter. My little Zoo-Zoo. It's only a few *days* – and then there's Christmas, isn't there? It'll be the most wonderful Christmas – and I've bought you something quite divine – I promise, you'll love it. And I'll bring you something beautiful from Paris: beautiful.' And then Elizabeth caught her breath as she did whenever this thing crept up and assailed her. 'Kiss me, Zoo-Zoo – oh *kiss* me, my darling. Let me feel your hands and *kiss* me!'

With no change of expression, Zoo-Zoo rose and as slowly as ever approached her. He seemed not quite sombre, but still filled with a melancholy only partly masking this shared awareness of a sweet joy to come; it was as if the moment was finally here and a seriously big and heartfelt rite was at last to be enacted. So you can well imagine how utterly pissed off Elizabeth felt (at first she started, and now she was howling) when the shrill trilling of the telephone first cracked into and then shattered all that.

'Leave it,' breathed Zoo-Zoo.

Elizabeth – anxious – nodded briefly: hadn't heard him – the clamour was still wall-to-wall all over the place – understood his intention, yes of course, but knew that she couldn't leave it, couldn't – never ever had been able to do that, leave it. So Hello was the next thing she said, just as far away from the intrusive mouthpiece as she needed to be, and a wash of cold and regret now touched her shoulders as Zoo-Zoo lowered his eyes and turned away.

'Oh Mummy,' she said, feeling near to bereaved. 'It's you.'

'Well of *course* it's me, Elizabeth. I know that. Have some sense.'

'How are you?'

Elizabeth swivelled up large and helpless eyes to Zoo-Zoo as she stretched towards him an imploring arm, stiff fingers out straight and tingling, now toying with scales on an invisible upright; still Zoo-Zoo stood entrenched and unyielding, and was Not Even Looking.

'Not good,' said Elizabeth's mother, quite tersely. 'Worse – much worse – but I don't want to burden you with any of that. Everything's yours when I've gone.'

'Oh Mummy . . . .' sighed Elizabeth. It was to be this phone call, then: there were only about five, and this was to be this one. 'Don't be so silly – you're not going anywhere. You'll outlive us all.'

Please, Zoo-Zoo, look at me: don't turn away. I simply can't bear it when you do this to me.

'Except,' went on Elizabeth's mother, 'that amethyst ring your father gave me. I thought Katie might like that. What do you think, Elizabeth? Do you think Katie might like that? It would suit a young hand – not a horrible old horn like mine.'

'We've talked about this, Mummy – we've said all this. You've shown Katie the ring and she doesn't like the colour, remember?'

'What say? Can't hear.'

'I said – '

'Do you know, there are more of those horrible brown livery spots on my hands than normal white skin? I look like a Dalmatian. What size are you, Elizabeth?'

'You know what size I am, Mummy . . .'

Oh but look! Zoo-Zoo, with just one indolent and easy eye, is nearly glancing over: Elizabeth's arm now batted up and down at him as if she was drowning or else being saved.

'No I mean your dress size. And your shoe size. I want to get you something nice for Christmas. God knows it's a trial just getting out to the shops these days, but I'm not quite decrepit yet. I've got the gasman this afternoon, so I have to listen out.'

'You're not *remotely* . . . look, Mummy – please don't bother about presents and things, honestly. You just come and relax and enjoy yourself – you don't have to – '

'What say? Can't hear.'

I cannot hear that you cannot hear me, Mummy, because the beautiful boy, my Zoo-Zoo, is looking at me fully, and soon he will idle towards me; he has done that now and I can feel his presence, just behind. It is as if he is all around and inside of me.

'What do *you* want for Christmas, Mummy? That's more to the point. Hm? Any ideas?'

Touch me. Touch me. Touch me!

'If this weather keeps up, though,' rattled on Elizabeth's mother, 'you'll all just have to have tokens. What's your size, Elizabeth? How's, um . . .? What's that noise?'

'Sorry, Mummy – I thought I was going to sneeze.'

No no – I thought I might expire. Zoo-Zoo's hands are at my shoulders, their warmth and pressure at once making me boneless and turning me rigid.

'What say? Can't hear.'

'Size twelve,' gasped Elizabeth. 'Take fives in shoes. Same

115

as last year. But really, Mummy – I don't want anything. Nothing. Really.'

But it was only want that flooded her, now – for Zoo-Zoo had reached down and laid both his hands so lightly on just one breast – and then, as it swelled, the other.

'Howard's fine,' Elizabeth now heard herself say – not surprised, this time, when Zoo-Zoo's touch just momentarily froze (she did not know why, but mention of Howard always seemed to affect him) – but now his fingers were easing up and ambled onwards and Elizabeth just knew that she had to get away from Mummy and be with her boy.

'Elizabeth – I think that was the doorbell so I'll have to run. Probably the gasman. Or if not, someone else.'

'Bye. Mummy. Take care, yes?'

Elizabeth just dropped the phone and turned to face Zoo-Zoo, now aware that her shirt was wide open and maybe knowing also that her mouth was too. Right here and right now was Elizabeth's feeling, but an appalling uproar from Nelligan in the kitchen (it was as if Goliath, in a fit of pique, had sent flying his teetering and titanic house of mahogany cards) at once made her realize that here was no good and so she signalled to Zoo-Zoo the hall and then the staircase and Zoo-Zoo was already there, and urging her on.

He was halfway up to the landing, now – his eyes their most huge and liquid and bright – reaching down to Elizabeth and hauling her up, she giggling unstoppably, the contagion of his youth now invading her bloodstream – for here was the keen thrill she had first known with Colin – a boy's breathless urgency – and now as she fell down on to the floor (the big cool bed is far too far away and we'll never ever get there) Elizabeth lay buried under the weight of Zoo-Zoo's insistence, and gave up and gave in to it all over again – flinching not from the first stab of his inquisitive tongue but yes from the hot shiver of certainty that soon it was coming.

For Zoo-Zoo could not or would not warm himself inside

her, and nor could she ever arouse him (Elizabeth had been amazed, at first, and then quite delighted) – but he gave himself utterly to inflicting pleasures that came close to stinging her, as with eyes shut down tight she flickered away from and then ploughed hard into wherever it was their blood-heat was fusing, and wherever else now his fingers and tongue would flutter and delve. Elizabeth adored the girl's limbs on the boy – quite as slim and clean and soft as maybe Lulu's – and now as she lay again, spent and panting – her mouth tugged askew by ludicrous glee, her mind (once more) marvelling at what it was her body had (once again) put her through – her exhalation was one of repletion and it underscored too the needlessness for talk of any kind.

And it was silly, you know, asking Zoo-Zoo how his lesson had gone – whether or not he thought he'd pass. His fingers on the wheel of a car, his sensitivity to the pressures of motion, would be quite as sure as this: driving to my Zoo-Zoo must just be a part of him, for daily he drives me wild, and then to heaven.

❋

It's odd, isn't it, Howard was thinking, just how easy it is to delude not just others but oneself. Case in point: those months and months when I had Zoo-Zoo hanging around the office all day long, I just refused, didn't I, to see how – what? Ridiculous? Questionable? Downright bloody *odd*, anyway, it must have appeared to simply everyone concerned. I mean, take Katie: the looks she gave me, sometimes – looks of real bafflement, if not outright suspicion. Certainly Sam and whatsername, thing, what's-she-bloody-called thought it all pretty damn funny (Jesus, she's been with me now how long? Three years? Could easily be getting on for four and I can't bloody remember her name; it'll come to me, I hope). Even fucking Norman was forever and pointedly Not Saying Anything . . . but my point here is that it was all as plain as day to just everybody that there I was employing a slim and beautiful sixteen-year-old boy to do absolutely nothing at all – and yet I blinded myself daily as to how it must have *looked*. Greed, lust – even self-importance: all those and other things can do this to you, you know. Nowadays, of course, I can see clearly that Katie thinks it equally bloody weird that Elizabeth has him hanging around at home all day – and it puzzles the hell out of me too, if I'm being perfectly honest. I mean Christ – it's not as if he's capable of *doing* anything, or anything; and his conversation, if such it may be called, oscillates between the vapid and the out-and-out creepy. So why on earth does she have him in the house? What exactly is it that Zoo-Zoo is for, I wonder?

And I wonder too if he ever thinks of me, now. It all seems so long ago, all that, and yet it was only last summer. I took the loss of him badly, I suppose – yes I did, I did: no two ways about it. If it hadn't been for Laa-Laa – if she hadn't just been sitting at the bar, that time – I don't know what I would have done, how I would have put myself together. And it is Laa-Laa now who I am on my way to see. Is there a discernible spring in my step? Is there? Are my eyes a-twinkle? What fools we are, what fools – and yet who in their right mind would wish away turbulence when it is tinged with heat and danger? I hope she's remembered the Scotch, because a very large belter is now what I need.

Phyllis. That's her name. Not Laa-Laa's name, no – the girl I employ in the office. Phyllis: I knew I'd get it. No, Laa-Laa's actual name is something very dull indeed – couldn't even tell you. That name I very deliberately put out of my head (not saying it wouldn't anyway have left of its own accord) because that's not at all, you see, what I wanted her to be. I call her Laa-Laa because her pale blue eyes are so happy and bright that you look at one and it pings alight and goes *Laa!* You gaze into the other and *Laa!* it goes, maybe just a semitone higher. She seems to like it: it suits her well and it suits me too.

'Morning, Mr Street,' called out the porter, as Howard was stamping his feet on the thick coir mat in the foyer. It was a rather nice little block, this – Howard's agency had been managing it on behalf of these probably pretty dodgy offshore clients for many years, now: precious little effort, and the percentage was astonishing.

'Morning, um,' returned Howard. And yes yes yes I *know*, I *know* – after all this time I should bloody know *his* name too – Christ, he practically runs the place single-handed, and he's only got the one arm, poor sod.

'Lovely day for it,' continued the porter, cheerily, as Howard wedged himself into the tiny lift.

Yes, Howard yearned to say out loud, as the mirrored cubicle croaked and groaned its way upwards, it is *always* a lovely day for it, Roger – with my Laa-Laa, it always is. Yes – that was the bugger's name: Roger. You know, it's a laugh, this lift – it sounds like it's in terrible physical pain – as if each time you press the button, some wizened old fool has to sighingly rise from his rocking chair, knock out his corncob pipe and then haul the bloody thing up on a rope. And there's this little enamel plaque just over the door that cautions Maximum 4 Persons: that would presumably be a brace of midgets perched on the shoulders of another couple, then. That, anyway, had been Howard's wisecrack to Laa-Laa, one time.

He slipped the key into the lock (it was always so amazingly quiet in this block, you found yourself whispering in the corridors; you'd swear it was completely deserted, and yet all ten flats were let, oh yes – Howard made bloody sure of that). He opened the door only very slightly, and with eyes tight closed, inserted just his face into the warmth of the crack – and now he was inhaling, long and luxuriously, breathing deep down into him the wonderfully heady scent that danced all over and then suffused him. Good old

119

Chanel No 5, unless he was very much mistaken; Laa-Laa had dozens and dozens of beautiful scents, and it amused Howard to be right in guessing which of them it was this time. Some men were rather sniffy about such matters as scent, but Howard saw no reason why: if one of his senses was inflamed and then appeased, what the hell could be the downside there?

'Chanel No 5,' said Howard, with pride and confidence, stepping into the small hall and opening his eyes – and God, what a sight was now before them: today it was the basque (the French one – cost a fortune: pink bows rather than red, Howard had adjudged – altogether prettier, don't you agree?).

'Brilliant!' enthused Laa-Laa – her eyes just exactly like Howard has said they are, a dazzle of springy and butter-blonde hair framing that little baby's sweet and quite white face: some pink alive on the cheekbones, though – and a wetly red and absolute mouth exactly where it should be, that hit of polar teeth just about winking within (Thomas Hardy had once likened so wondrous a thing to 'roses filled with snow', but Howard one night when plastered had called it piously an engorged and fab horizontal cunt, otherwise known to man as heaven on bloody earth).

Laa-Laa kissed his nose, and then Howard brought down his lips to that warm and secret part of her neck where it melted one way into the slope of the shoulder, the other towards the swell of her breast; he breathed it in and he breathed it out.

'You know *all* my perfumes, now,' laughed Laa-Laa. 'Have to get some more.'

Her voice was light and ravishingly friendly, just the slightest tinge of cockney lifting it at the edges; but this was not the sort of voice that had merely become mildly lazy – more that it had been worked and worked on, starting from the handicap of Christ only can imagine quite what, and here was as close to Laa-Laa's apparent ideal as it was ever going to get; to Howard it was music, sweet music.

Laa-Laa took him by the hand and the two of them toddled through the double glass doors and into the sitting room. She indicated the glistening bottle of Bollinger in the sturdy silver bucket, this atop the sort of serpentine and really pretty ritzy stand that you only now see in restaurants that haven't yet got around to changing them.

'Scotch,' said Howard. 'I'll have Scotch, Laa-Laa. You did get some in? I always have Scotch, darling – you should know that, now.'

Laa-Laa affected that dumb little pout that had the power to move every single man she had ever met in her life in quite the most extraordinary way: the blood drained away from the whole of their bodies, and then just one second later twice as bloody much pumped right back in – and it's red and bursting, we're talking now. And Howard, as we surely have seen, was no exception at all:

'Christ Laa-Laa, oh Christ,' he hissed. 'Want you. I want you. Want you now.'

And Laa-Laa teased out the moment (of course she did).

'Champagne is piles more *romantic*, Howard,' she playfully sulked.

'*You* be romantic, Laa-Laa – you drink it. I'll have the Scotch. And then I'll have you. Or maybe I'll just have you and *fuck* the bloody Scotch. If you see what I mean.'

'First you have to come and talk to me,' admonished Laa-Laa – she had teetered over to the sofa (how does she walk at all on those pin-thin jacked-up spike-heeled shoes? Who cares, so long as she goes on wearing them) and now patted the cushion next to her quite authoritatively and put on her no-nonsense face – in Howard's view no less than simply fantastic. So Howard padded over there and was perfectly content to feel like a spaniel as Laa-Laa gently pawed him.

'Haven't seen you for three whole *days*,' she said.

Howard gulped down a fair deal of whisky (she'd got in

121

a litre of The Macallan – good little girl) and then he nodded with vigour.

'I know, I know . . .' – it came out as a sigh. 'I've been *aching*, Laa-Laa – aching for you. Simply aching, darling, just to *be* here.'

He held the back of her neck as she squatted on the rug beside him; the view of her spectacular cleavage from this vantage point was tremor-inducing, true – but Howard loved too the wrinkle of her nose as she pretended to be encountering her bubbly grown-up champagne for the very first time ever.

'And now you're going away and *leaving* me – going to Paris with your beastly horrid wife and *leaving* me. I've never even *been* to Paris.'

Laa-Laa wasn't really upset, though – Howard knew that. It was all just part of the beautiful game. That was the really great thing about her – there was no malice, no grudge; no moods and no fights. Howard truly did ache to be here, just like he said – because here was quite simply nothing bloody short of perfect.

'I'll take you, darling – promise. After Christmas, I'll take you.' But Howard had to rush on quickly now – yes, he saw that – because even with women as mild and forgiving as Laa-Laa, you don't really want to go mentioning Christmas – not in these sorts of circumstances, you didn't. 'And she's not actually beastly – or horrid, my wife,' he tacked on, gently – but sensing that here was no great improvement on the Christmas line of thought, Howard now threw in a sure-fire winner:

'Tell me what you want for a *present*.'

And he didn't actually care if the girlish squeal of pleasure and delight was cooked up or not, to be perfectly frank with you, for the simple truth is it rippled right through him anyway, and now he was glowing.

Laa-Laa turned and held him and then withdrew so she could look right at him and he could now lose his mind as he latched on to first one bright sparkling eye (*Laa*!) and then the other (*Laa*! again) – and now the great big startling pair of them – live and liquid lights among the downy beauty of the rest of that *Christ* will you Jesus just look at that *face*?! (If I die, when I die – can I maybe just die with this in mind?)

'Let's choose it together,' she gasped. 'I love being out with you, Howard – looking at lovely things. And London's really lovely at the moment – with all the lovely lights. Tomorrow? Yes? Yes, Howard? Please say yes. Yes? Yes, Howard?'

Howard just gazed at her. 'Yes,' he said.

And then Laa-Laa's mouth seemed to double in size as she lopsidedly wrapped it around the most lascivious expression of all, and this made Howard's heart stop, stutter, and go on thudding. The sight of her was shut out to him then as she ducked low and huddled within the welcome of his legs; now she was peeling back his clothing with a long-fingered delicacy, as one might the four corners of a napkin concealing ripe fruit. All Howard had to do was just be there – and now, while sensation was still at its freshest, and some good way before the deep-down volcanic demon could brew and then twingeingly stir before doing his stuff – Howard simply lay there amazed and slung into the midst of contentment, glancingly regarding with a sort of stricken awe the dipping up and down dazzle of Laa-Laa's golden hair. And now he set to wondering just how it came to be that again his loins were set a-quiver by the molten tongue of a worldly angel.

She must really love him. But yes, Howard was ready to concede that possibly the rent-free flat and a thousand a month must surely have some little thing to do with it all: just another part of life's rich, er – what's the word? What's that thing? Travesty, is it? Think so, yeah. Might as well be.

CHAPTER SIX

Edna Davies really was (truly) trying very hard indeed to not at all be troubled – to blank out all these rather harsh and frankly worrying sounds coming at her from the kitchen. They were not the sounds made by madcap dailies, no – it was not at all as if this girl she'd hired was enacting on a shoestring some gimcrack cut-price parody of a cleaning lady's crudely slapstick and enervating incompetence, no not that. But some sounds whispered to you, didn't they, that things were being carried out with both method and care – the comfortingly slight, almost wearily inevitable and intimate noises of a good job being well done by a willing and able pair of hands busily demonstrating their skill (wreaking their magic) just south of the elbow-grease department, and not much below a strong set of shoulders – beyond which again you felt sure was confidently bobbing an unfluffy head you could believe in. And these were not the sounds.

I am not easy, thought Edna now – sitting on the window ledge of what one day would become the breakfast room, and stirring tea she might not drink (here was normal – Edna would habitually make tea as a way of punctuating an otherwise interminable tract of day: enjoyed too the business of cream jug and sugar lump – simply loved the tinkle of silver on crockery. From then on in, the ritual lost its flavour and grew increasingly tepid and then cool to the point where it just had to be over with – flushed away until the next time).

Yes, you know – it's a terribly odd thing about woodchip,

Edna was reflecting now, while running the tips of her fingers up and down the coarse and random grain of the horrible stuff. Because that's what everyone *thinks*, isn't it? You mention woodchip wallpaper to just anyone at all you care to name and that's just what they're going to come back with, isn't it? *Horrible* stuff, they'll say – and they're right, they're right, because it is. Bane of everyone's life, when you buy a new house. And I think very possibly deep down it annoys people more than all the other and more obvious horrors put together: *right*, you say – central heating system's utterly obsolete, so that's number one for starters. Touch of a suspect and lurking odour in the far corner of the cellar, so that'll have to be looked at and seen to. God Almighty – did people really go into a carpet shop, do you think, and actually *choose* those dreadful patterns? This one looks like dead giraffes, and here is a spoiled risotto. The bay windows want replacing, no two ways about it – arctic gale blowing in the front room; and if you want patio doors (light in summer, snug in winter) well then you just have to bite the bullet and put the whole thing in train, don't you now? It has to be faced. And your eye skips over things like bathroom fitments seemingly cobbled together from old palettes and driftwood (held together by masking tape and nails) – you actually quite enjoy the ritual demolition of blockboard units apparently purpose-built (it surely did seem in our case, anyway) to house a collection of those dreadful dull and round sort of metal things, what are they? You see them in the street and set into the *pavement*.

What I'm really getting at is that you expect all this – it's all part and parcel of moving, isn't it? And if you're not up to all the upheaval and trauma, then best stay put is my way of thinking. And according to Cyril – who, I rather believe, knows a very great deal more about trauma and stress than many amateurs who profess to, thank you – moving house truly can be more upsetting to one's personal equilibrium than absolutely anything in the world except, um – something and something else; forget – doesn't really matter. I *should* remember, of course – should – because Cyril spent what seemed like weeks and weeks explaining it all to me in quite some detail, but I certainly shan't be requesting a brief recap because first he'd lose his temper and then, oh God, launch into a recap that would, I'm afraid, be far from anything that you or I might recognize as being in any way *brief*. But there – the way he is: it's his job – does things to him.

But this woodchip is just the limit, isn't it? You feel so terribly cheated when you airily instruct your builder Oh God yes of course all *that* stuff is coming off right away, ecch, can't stand it – and then half the *wall* comes down with it and there you are faced with the awful and not at all *fair* dilemma (and don't think I'm the only one): a massive and additional bill for a total replastering job, or else spend your life with the one thing on earth that truly everybody without exception utterly and totally *loathes*. So who – and yes I know I have been rather roundabout, but it really *exercises* me, all of this – who is it, please, who actually buys it and puts it up? Hm? And who are the villains who *make* the stuff – that's what I should truly love to know: there ought to be a law – for everyone's sake, I think.

But bitter thoughts of woodchip fled from Edna now as an awful grating and then quite booming bark of metal on metal became the first of today's intrusive sounds that she could truly not ignore; this one she actually identified as the main deep drawer of the dishwasher being cranked in at an angle (and it's smooth, so smooth, if you just go careful), this slapdash action maybe not just harming the mechanism but possibly also quite needlessly putting at risk all of Edna's lovely tableware: the Riedel glasses, I hope not the Baccarat bowl (I've *told* her about that) – and I don't even want to *think* about my Doulton.

'Melody – for heaven's sake,' was Edna's opening – but she got no further than 'What on earth do you think you're – ?' because at that point Melody spun round on her haunches where she squatted in front of the dishwasher, and the glare in her eyes Edna could barely believe. I'm not sure, not at all sure about you, young Miss Melody, Edna was thinking – despite all the recommendations, no matter what Elizabeth has said to me, I remain deeply unsure whether Melody is remotely *right* for all this. Even now as she rises, Melody is still just *looking* at me – no word of apology: why on earth is it that she goes on *staring*?

The gist of what was busy weaving around in Melody's mind throughout this latest brief and potentially explosive encounter was Jesus Aitch Christ, what in fuck is the old bat staring at me *now* for? It's not a home help this one wants, it's a bloody sacristan – Christ Almighty, the look on her face you'd think I'd just smashed in a crucifix with a hammer: it's only bloody *stuff*, for fuck's sake – how can all these women *care* so much? Can I really be the only one who just doesn't *mind* about all this shit? I mean – OK, Elizabeth, we all know about her: as soon as her stately home achieves its stateliest, thing – status, you know what I mean – she embarks upon a programme of improvement. Well – that's Elizabeth's temperament and Howard's money (a true bloody marriage of convenience) and there's not much more you can say.

Of course, that's the whole thing with Elizabeth, isn't it? When she told me that Edna next door was 'having trouble finding someone' I said Me, I'm someone – I'll do it, yeah: tell Edna Me. Took me how long to convince her that no in fact I'm *not* joking, Elizabeth, not – deadly serious, OK? *Broke*, you see – broke. And Elizabeth had just sort of looked at me (people, women, do that – men too, but it's different then). She couldn't, could she, ever even remotely understand the concept of broke: Got No Money, Elizabeth, I had practically bawled – and she had become so piteous and perplexed as she wrung her helpless hands that for some bloody reason I began to feel sorry for *her*. But, she had stuttered – you don't want to do *that*, Melody: cleaning and polishing for Edna Davies (and her face, Elizabeth's face – getting sicker and sicker at every syllable) – and *No*, I screamed back, *no* Elizabeth – of course I don't bloody *want* to do that but it's a case of just *having* to – right? Got it? I tried the supermarket, didn't I, but I just couldn't get into the swing of swiping those barcodes and then they said I'd stolen a bottle of vodka and I shouted back well if *that's* what you think you lying bastards, you can bloody well *stick* your sodding job and then I went home in tears and drank the whole fucking thing in an evening.

And even Dotty! The one upside of skivvying for Edna – apart from the food and Cyril's drinks – is that I can dump Dawn on Dotty next door: all the other crap jobs I've had, most of anything I got went straight out on some dumb childminder. But Dotty – she'd pay *me*, I think (which is something I think about more and more). But even Dotty! Reduced to a bloody caravan and still every time I go there she's cleaning, cleaning – tidying, tidying (I have to, she says, because Brian is in charge of all that). But we can't just be put on this earth to bloody *clean* things, surely to Christ? And what – single-handedly raise our daughters so that they can grow up fit and strong and clean things too? That just can't be right. If God is as good as they say, why does he go letting his sodding Universe get so bloody dirty all the time – and then just sit back and watch all of Creation kill themselves *cleaning* the fucking thing? That's why, maybe, it's only heaven that ever stays white (He's no fool).

And now here's Dame Edna – deep breath now, having cranked herself up to the summit of indignation's very own and most awesome Water Chute: soon would come the heart-stopping descent and then the whoosh of castigation as she dealt with the serf.

'I think,' said Edna – icy at the brink – 'that you and I had better have a little talk – yes?'

It occurred to Melody right now, right this second as the

anger rose within her – just caught the impending howl of Fuck You, Cuntface, as it was damn near up her throat and all the way out of her mouth – that she was in prime danger of forgetting the very principle that she had been at pains to get across to Elizabeth: I *need* this job, right? Need it. Bloody Edna pays well over the odds, I've got Dawn and Dotty next door modelling for a remake of the Pietà and there's, yeah – not exactly a jostling queue of juicy alternatives. So it looks like time to spurn cold cuts and turn to gorge again on cold and mouldy humble pie – platter of the month (dish of my lifetime).

❊

Oh God it's just absolutely *typical*, this, thought Cyril, vaguely willing his vexation in the direction of what he supposed really ought to be – professionally speaking – out-and-out fury at the interruption. But if he was honest, here was no more than an inner, automatic and token display of irritation; if he was being *really* honest, the arrival of Melody slap-bang in the middle of this session with a particularly tedious neurotic was actually rather a welcome, not to say lovesome thing (hm – éclairs on the trolley, it very much seems – I am rather something of an éclair man, as Edna well knows, and even your workaday toasted teacake is not to be sneezed at – not when there's a good strong pot of Earl Grey alongside, it's not. I have even in my time been known to be partial to slices of both Madeira and Battenberg, and at a cursory glance – rattle-jiggle, rattle-jiggle: here comes the trolley now, oh goody good-good – all seemed to be present and correct).

Cyril had sat up in his claret-coloured leather and deep-buttoned captain's chair, his eyebrows' best effort to convey dark and not-to-be-forgotten disapproval to this rather sullen young woman called Melody more or less wholly undermined by not only the rubbing together of hands, but also just that hint of a pinkly wet and slavering tongue. The patient, however – stretched out fully on the couch (a very Freudian couch, Cyril would have told you – a veritable twin to the one in dear old Sigmund's Hampstead museum, replete with Persian throw) – did not appear to have noticed so much as a shift of dust in the stifling air, let alone the tinkling clatter of approaching tea.

'So the thing is, Doctor Davies,' he mournfully intoned – and it sure seemed to Melody like Jacob Marley had visited early this year (Christ, you know – people actually pay money to come here and do this) – 'I *do* want to see her again, I deep *down* do, yes . . . but she's so, I don't know . . . I sometimes feel like I'm back in a classroom, with her – and that I ought to, I don't know – put up my hand . . .'

'Put it *down*,' instructed Cyril, sternly.

'I didn't put it up!' panicked the patient.

'No not *you*, Mr Driscoll – you, Melody: put down the tray – put it there – no here, look. Yes. Now go, please. I'm sorry, Mr Driscoll, for this, ah – unfortunate, um . . .'

Yeh yeh, thought Melody, stomping away – well don't bloody blame me, that's all: I *said* to Edna you don't like to be interrupted in the middle of one of these bloody crap appointments and *she* said it's all right, it's the end of a session – and I said Not according to his diary, it's not – and *she* said Oh do stop *arguing* about everything with me, Melody, and just take in the *tea*, will you, Godsake – and now *you're* bloody glaring at me, Cyril, like I'm one of your itinerant nutcases and all I think, all I know is that if I ever win the Lottery I'll buy a bloody great machine-gun and – OK, Edna comes first, but then I'll blast away at, oh – pretty much everyone I've ever met in my entire and shitty life on earth.

As soon as the door had shut behind Melody (none too quietly – I think I'll have to keep a weather eye on that young girl) Mr Driscoll took up the muted but still plangent howl of his heartfelt lament, continuing quite seamlessly in much the same spirit; Cyril, meanwhile, tucked in a napkin, sipped at tea and with no more than one or two of his very studied yet detachedly noncommittal grunts of deep comprehension, very real encouragement and a truly big and sincere confederacy, lost no time in getting down to some serious cake.

' . . . but then I think there's something in me that craves a certain strictness,' Mr Driscoll was moaning. 'Do you think that's true of me, Doctor? From what I've told you?'

This actual Madeira before me now is the one with those crunchy glacé cherries dotted inside – utterly moreish and also, I might say, very easy on the eye.

'Is it something you feel to be true about yourself?' came back Cyril, with practised ease.

'Well this is it, this is it,' enjoined Mr Driscoll – eyes bright and picking up a bit of pace, now. 'All the time I feel I am holding back, holding back with her – you know?'

'Go on.' (Well, face facts: he will anyway.)

'And yet while I find that very frustrating, it sort of – I don't know – excites me too. And it's this, basically, I don't understand about myself. Am I blinding myself? Am I? And if so, to what?'

I've got a bit of that cherry stuck in my teeth, now, but it's nothing a jolly good big gulp of Earl Grey can't deal with: it's just got to be a chocolate éclair, next time round – simply can't bear them staring at me for one minute longer.

'Do you *feel* blinded? That you can't shee?' Cyril chucked in, while chomping.

'Sometimes . . . sometimes, yes – I think sometimes I do, really do feel that, yes.'

'Blinded to what?' They're really awfully gooey, but maybe licking your fingers is actually the best bit of all this.

Mr Driscoll's brow was furrowed. 'To . . . to *myself*, I suppose.'

And Cyril did not speak but nodded gravely and slowly, the better to indicate the import of Mr Driscoll's own words, still hanging in the air (also: mouth now crammed to bursting).

'You're very wise . . .' said Mr Driscoll, really sounding quite relieved. 'You really do know me so very, very well.'

I am rather wise, thought Cyril – also a bit full, now. As to knowing you well – well: you've been coming to me long enough for me to venture without fear of any contradiction whatever that you certainly must have a good deal more money than sense, if that's anything at all to do with whatever you're meaning.

And here is the point where Cyril would dearly have loved to sigh conclusively, rise with finality – dust off the crumbs from lap and fingers and generally wind up the session with a *Well*, Mr Driscoll . . . and sometimes he could get away with that – shave off five or so minutes with ease – but the bloody man would know he'd only been here for three-quarters of an hour at most (seemed like days) so better let him witter on a little longer. And while he does so, I shall gaze out upon my one-hundred-foot garden – all I have now are some rather fine and mighty oaks, not-good leylandii and a quasi serviceable lawn – but you just wait until this cursed winter is over: just you see the magic then. I am the most brilliant gardener – just ask Edna. And talking of the garden – do you know that among the many skips-worth of junk that my builders unearthed there was a wartime cistern tank packed with old wellingtons? Plus four, or was it five lawnmowers – none of which could ever have come close to actually *working* – and behind a high and barbed wall of bramble not just a lean-to shed but also a lean-to greenhouse, both of which – once the mass of vicious tangles had been hacked and slashed away – had lurched violently and leaned-fro, shuddered further and then with seeming weary gratitude collapsed into shards of splintered glass and a heap of rotten debris. I reckon that if I had the previous owner of this bloody house on my couch – Brian Morgan (lives in a Huntley & Palmers tin, just next door) – before I even got close to assessing even the most prominent of his very evident psychoses, one of us would surely die of old age.

'I think,' Cyril thought he vaguely half-caught from Mr Driscoll, 'that what I must do now is confront her. This might, what is the word? *Empower* me . . . and yet if I *do* confront her, what if she . . . ?'

'What if she what?' Cyril slotted in.

And Mr Driscoll replied brokenly, his eyes imploring: ' . . . *leaves* me?'

Cyril nodded. What a shame, he was thinking, that that absolutely wonderful woman Lulu Powers does not consider herself as in any way in need of psychiatric treatment; she and her husband, though, are apparently utterly convinced of each other's insanity, which is fairly piquant – and I did recently hear a rumour (with Elizabeth being the probable source – she's forever slipping Edna's way some deep confidence or other that must on no account whatever go any further) that the two of them are finally and formally breaking up for good. Maybe then, possibly (God, how we can delude ourselves when the whiff of desperation is all around), Lulu might feel in some need of a little gentle counselling, hm? Christ, though – if I could only get that Lulu on my bloody couch for just one session, well then gentle, mate, could go out the fucking window.

'Do you *want* her to leave you?' sighed Cyril.

'No!' barked out Mr Driscoll. 'No. Well. When I say no, maybe what I feel is . . . do you think that secretly, deep down I *do* want her to leave me, Doctor? Is that what you think?'

Cyril's smile was miles away from humour, or anything.

'What do *you* think?'

'I think, I think . . . I think maybe ultimately I *do*. Oh God. Doctor – you really are quite wonderful. I feel almost . . . *happy*.'

133

Well, modified Cyril, I don't know about wonderful, but not so bloody dumb as you, anyhow.

'*Well*, Mr Driscoll,' he now said – a well-reined-in and just avuncular jolliness tinged with inevitable regret, 'it seems as if our time is once again up for today, so . . .'

Mr Driscoll rose and turned with such shy pride, his large and trusting eyes so packed full of don't-think-me-foolish-but-love-me looks that it took everything Cyril possessed to restrain himself from reaching down to the bowl on the trolley for a couple of lumps of bright white sugar and cramming them in between those wet and slackened lips before subjecting the lankness of his forelock to a damn good tousle.

Mr Driscoll strode to the door, shoulders braced by eighty-five quidsworth of new if spurious grand self-assurance – grasped the handle and twisted it one way, wrenched it round clockwise and then started tugging hard at the thing, just prior to applying his shoulder to the panels. Cyril gently shook his head, an amused tch-tch playing at his lips as he redirected Mr Driscoll to an alternative door alongside. But Mr Driscoll still was glancing with panic at the first one and saw now that yes, oh Christ – it wasn't a real door at all: the *knob* was real, no worries on that score, but the rest was just painted grain and rubbed-in shadows. His open-mouthed gawp towards Cyril was now one of utter anguish – was this a *symbol*, was it? Was this, what could it be – some kind of *test*? Cyril could only smile as the whole eighty-five quidsworth of whatever visibly plummeted to the very soles of Mr Driscoll's shoes, where it oozed out meanly, through the Goodyear welting. And no, dear Mr Driscoll, no I'm afraid not – even if you were to ask or pay me I couldn't for a moment hazard as to why my wife has seen fit to have painted an imitation door slap-bang next to a real one: believe me, there simply aren't the hours in the day to start on working out Edna, not on top of you lot. So all I can say to you is goodbye, Mr Driscoll, and try not to go too mad until the next time we meet.

I am now lying comfortably on my Freudian couch, and I see by my diary I am soon due to listen to the next of my loonies: a strange young woman – spends most of her session trying to wheedle out of me any insights going as to why she remains convinced that her formative years had been spent in fighting off the determined and voracious sexual advances of a three-legged, spayed and tortoiseshell pussycat to whose permanently stale and fishy breath she still attributes her phobic revolt and intestinal convulsions at even so much as the mention of haddock in batter. I shouldn't really have that smallish wedge of fruitcake, but it seems to be calling out to me, and I do so hate to disappoint.

❋

John Powers hauled towards him again the big red notebook, just as usual, and then (quite normal, this) it more or less fell open at page seventeen and that damn bloody sentence that not at all triumphantly concluded 'and Gregory went down to the car'. That's as far as John could get with this bleeding novel – and every time he gazed at this horribly familiar, endlessly rejigged and ultimately no damn good sentence he felt the cold slice of fear invading his entrails (just as was happening again to him now) and once more it seemed sure that he had simply used up his very last words on earth.

But look, look – OK OK, John was urging himself now – so Gregory's gone down to the car, right? (Gone down to *get* the car? Gone down and *sat* in the car? Gone down and kicked in the fucking headlights of the car?) – so apparently he's going somewhere, yes? So where? Where is it that Gregory's off to? Search me – ask sodding Gregory (and why did I choose such a prat name in the first place?). Look: I just don't *know* where he's going, do I? Well – is he going to see Isobel? Or maybe just popping round the corner for a packet of cigarettes. Does he smoke, then, Gregory? Can't remember. Maybe he does. And who the fuck's Isobel? You see this is the whole bloody trouble – only seventeen pages in, but I can't seem to keep it in my head: all I do is read and reread these seventeen pages until I'm close to screaming and then fall headlong into a shocking standstill and there I am again confronted with this freeze-frame image of Gregory going down to this bitch of a car of his – what can I tell you? How did I get the other one finished? All of fifty thousand words, that was – not that anyone cared. Total waste of bloody time. I think maybe I finished, though, because it was the first; I think it was the bliss of that. It was new and it was clean (alight with hope). But this thing now is already brackish – I back away from the staleness that rises up from page seventeen. Christ my head hurts. Maybe Gregory can go down to his car and fit a hosepipe to the exhaust and briskly gas himself and then we can all just stop this caper and get some peace.

Was that Lulu in the hall? That noise? Was she leaving this place? John passed a hand over his heated forehead (which fleetingly felt to him no more than damply cold). I actually, today, feel no worse than usual – which is to say, pretty bloody bad. But I haven't had a drink yet, which I'm reasonably pleased about. Well – *not* pleased in that I know well that a couple of large ones would sort me out and pull me in – stop my long pale fingers seeming like new and just translucent fleshy shoots, caught in a breeze and faintly a-quiver.

'Oh sod sod *sod*!' came Lulu's quite unmistakably tetchy and shriller than usual voice from the hall. 'Oh damn and bugger – don't come out, John – God's sake don't come *out*.'

So John was through that door in a jiffy and his so brief glimpse of the wonder of Lulu was knocked clean away from him as his foot skidded so suddenly in the golden puddle of whatever thick liquid lay there that the amazement on his face told Lulu that yes I too am quite as surprised as you are that I have at this moment elected to perform a middle-aged man's version of the splits while busy too miming the antics of one who is a slave to the rhythm of the castanets, but this very much seems to be the way things are surely going – and now, in addition to the general and clunking barks of pain and strain that tend to be part and parcel of troubles such as these, John was now aware of a quite overpowering and very heady scent, just before the no-holds-barred agony of so fierce and quite eye-popping heat and now *burns* – heat and now *burns* – tore searingly into his stockinged foot, sending north-wards a quiverful of flaming arrows.

Lulu for her part was screeching with frustration: was it not bad enough that she had dropped her brand-new bottle of Guerlain's Mitsouko (nearly saved it – just had it and then it went) – and of *course* it had to break, oh yes of *course* – and now all the scent and glass were just everywhere, all this gritty slime well streaked too with what had to be the lifeblood that until so recently had been happily coursing up and down a few of Johnny's toes and now was smearing the maple floor and John was clearly even more directly aware of the general thrust of this because the howls he was setting up were close to yelps of disbelief and would have moved anyone but Lulu well down the road to pity – made urgent in them a need to hunker down and help.

And Lulu registered within her the lack of even a trace of any such compulsion; how little time it takes, she thought with alarm, for two people to come to this: how I have changed.

'Cold water,' she said, quite crisply. 'Cold water would be best, John. I'm late. I'm sorry. I have to – '

And before she said go, was gone. John was crying, now – physical pain and the other sort too – and tugging at his saturated sock while dragging himself away and out of range of this toxic mess (the stench alone was making him retch). Cold water, yes – Christ oh Christ it *stings*, I tell you

– and possibly some, what is it? TCP – Savlon, that stuff. Maybe I've got that thing, contracted that thing, and they have to give you a thing, injection. The phone rang, then – and simply because it was handy and the bathroom was very far from being that, John picked up the handset and murmured into it some indeterminate noise.

There came at him another big voice, at the same time strident and dismissive: 'John – you sound even more drunk and useless than usual!'

And there really *are* such things, you know, as straws and camels' backs, and John had quite frankly had it up to his gullet with these bloody women and if he was going to be betrayed and scarred by his wife (my wife!) and now lambasted by his bloody fucking editor then by Christ he wasn't going to go down without making some sort of a stand and so he blazed right back with:

'Now *look*, Tara – just you look: for reasons I do not even remotely feel like bloody going into I am in considerable pain and in a ludicrous position on the floor of my hall – I feel sick, I am bleeding and I need *help* – not this. So just fuck off.'

There was a pause, and a new voice came back:

'Are you serious, John? All that? Are you *really*?'

John sighed deeply. 'Yes,' he said.

'Do you want me to come over? Help?'

John sighed deeply. 'Yes,' he said.

❄

'Every day it gets colder and colder.' And then Lulu half-widened her eyes at Elizabeth as if to make up for the leavening smile she felt she maybe ought to have worn when she said it.

'The weather?' checked Elizabeth. 'Or is it John we're talking about now?'

Lulu let out one laugh of ironic if mock despair. 'Both! Oh God, Lizzie – let's forget it. It's just too depressing. I adore your new cases, by the way. Are you really taking *all* of these clothes, Lizzie? I thought you were only going for – '

'Oh I *know*,' deplored Elizabeth. 'I'm *always* like this. It's just that when I'm away I like to have a *choice* and you never quite know, do you, what everything's going to be *like* and I always end up dragging along absolute mountains that I never so much as unfold – '

'And then go and buy a whole load more,' interjected Lulu: a quiet and mutual joke, packed with affection – Elizabeth entering into the spirit, now, by wagging her head this way and that as her big eyes asked hopelessly what on earth could be done with her.

Not just Elizabeth's dressing area but the whole of her bedroom and a fair deal of the bathroom too were swathed in plain and coloured layers of Elizabeth's brand-new or pristine winter things and gorgeous sundries. Lulu was busy exploring the taste of many emotions: of course the usual liquor of relief at having got out of her house and away from Johnny – made effervescent by the sparkling addition of Elizabeth. Sad, yes, that she was going to Paris not with her but with Howard: Lulu had just minutes before only playfully intimated a tiny degree of this feeling (the smell of smoulder, but shielding the flames) and Elizabeth had hooted at the bare bones alone of any notion that anybody, let alone Lulu, could hint at so much as a smidgen of even quasi jealousy over something so silly as *Howard*. And then further saddened by that: Lizzie knows that I love her, yes, but not of the way and nor how deeply. But I am happy, though, simply to be here with her – watching her move and inhaling her things. The sight of the bed, quite sumptuously strewn with silks and velvets – this and the lingering aroma of Lulu's shattered Mitsouko had truly nearly driven her to touching more boldly – this time not breaking the kiss and finally allowing her hot hands to wander. She maybe would have, but that strange child Peter was around – he would come in silently, while making

139

palpable the waft of his presence, maybe with a newly laundered froth of chiffon: place it just so, and quietly, and then exchange that glancing contact with Elizabeth that Lulu could never fathom (was not meant to) and that left her coping with the stirrings of unease and even the just-there odour of potential anxiety.

'So,' said Elizabeth. 'Mrs Bramley's done now, is she? I just hate to be leaving you with all the work *and* the house. I think if I take this pink, I won't actually really *need* the fuchsia as well.'

'Is that fuchsia, would you say?' asked Lulu, considering it. 'I suppose it could be – I suppose so, yes. I prefer it to the pink, I think. She's *nearly* done, yes – I've got the tree up and the wreath anyway, but now she's decided she wants table decorations as well: it's not as if she's having anyone *over*, or anything. She's very odd. I really like her, actually – she's so awfully funny. She comes out with the weirdest things.'

Elizabeth peered at both these dresses, one suspended from each of her outstretched arms: it was as if she were threatening to break their alibis – gain real insight into which of them had perpetrated the lie.

'Oh blow – I'll take them both. What things? What sort of things?'

'Oh God – I wish I'd had a tape recorder. Oh I don't know – we were talking about food, we somehow got on to food, and I suddenly thought I wonder if she's a vegetarian – don't know what made me think that: maybe because she's called after an apple. Oh and *God* yes, Lizzie – you will not believe what her first name is! I nearly *died* when she told me. It's not Naomi at all!'

Elizabeth smiled broadly at the sight of Lulu's pleasure.

'Charlotte?'

'Better! It's Pippa! Believe it?' And then Lulu tacked on – amid the hiccuping jerkiness of her and Lizzie's laughter – 'Philippa, actually – but everyone, she says, calls her *Pippa*. Pippa Bramley – I just love it. Anyway, I asked her that –

being a veggie or not, and . . . I simply *adore* those shoes, Lizzie, the cream ones – I had some just like that but they got ruined in the rain. So I said so do you eat meat, then, Pippa?'

'And *she* said?' supplied Elizabeth.

And now Lulu cranked up her voice a few notches and approximated her mouth into haughty-but-nice absent-minded dowager mode:

'Oh of *course* I do, dear Lulu – what *else* can you do with it?' Lulu then cackled in actually quite an un-Lulu-like way and erupted now in her own voice: 'Isn't that *wonderful*? And then she started on about recipes and things, which surprised me because it was apparently her late and very *un*lamented husband who did all that stuff – but she started telling me about this meatball thing she'd once invented: You need *really really* lean beef, she said . . . *yes*, I said . . . and the yolks of six eggs – six eggs, I went: uh-huh. And then you add – and this is true, I swear – half a large bar of melted Bournville chocolate – !'

The cook in Elizabeth was profoundly shocked, but amusement won over.

'*Kidding* . . .'

Lulu shook her head for all it was worth. 'And there I was trying to keep a straight face and saying *Gosh* – that's, um, pretty unusual – and Pippa starts nodding away and then she says It is It is: it's also completely uneatable – quite ghastly. I don't at all recommend you try it.'

Arched eyebrows and incredulous hooting held sway for not too long a time, and then Elizabeth was Pulling Herself Together and saying You know if I don't seriously get down to deciding just exactly what it is I am and am not taking, the holiday'll be over before I even get my bags packed. And then, much to Lulu's this time extremely intense irritation, that Peter person was idling back in. And that voice! That eerily light and wheedling tone – to Lulu's ear just stranded amid uncertainty, between a whisper and a sneer.

'Melody's just arrived, and she took a drink. Is that all right? And Mr Nelligan wants to talk to you about something to do with pipes, I think he said.'

'Oh Christ *I* don't know anything about *pipes* – I tell you, Lulu, I've just about had enough of Mr Nelligan – promised me faithfully he'd be out by the weekend and just look at the place. Don't want to even *think* about doing Christmas in the middle of *Nelligan's* mess – never use him again, tell you that.'

Lulu smiled sympathy: I wish we could swap problems, she was thinking: give me Nelligan, and you take John. And also – I'd love to kiss you. 'I'll go and talk to Melody, Lizzie – you go and stop the man flooding the place.'

'Oh God *don't*,' chastised Elizabeth, not remotely joking.

'And it's all right, then, is it?' pursued Elizabeth's Zoo-Zoo.

She was halfway to the door, but Elizabeth paused now in puzzlement.

'Is what all right, Zpeter?' she asked.

'Melody. Taking a drink, like that.'

Elizabeth hesitated – good humour vying with bafflement on her face. 'Well of course it's all *right*, isn't it? Hm? Melody's a *friend* – of course she can have a drink. What on earth can you mean?'

Zoo-Zoo was expressionless. 'Just so long as I know,' he murmured (sounded to Lulu like no more than a smug and officious trumped-up jobsworth).

The three of them came down the stairs more or less together, Zoo-Zoo peeling away on the first floor landing (maybe gone to polish his nails, thought Lulu drily: have you *seen* his nails? Well *have* you?). Lulu now swung into the drawing room, having just caught the roll of Elizabeth's eyes as she trudged like someone doomed into the kitchen sighing loudly and with resignation *Well*, Mr Nelligan, what does the problem appear to be this time?

'Hi, Melody,' said Lulu, brightly. Don't in truth actually

know Melody all that well – she had gone on holiday with Lizzie last summer but Lulu barely saw anything of her in The Excelsior: forever with that absolutely ghastly salesman person – the one John was so damn stupid as to actually think was with *me* (Christ alone knows what she saw in him). Even now Lulu found it so totally, well – she would say laughable, but as a result of all that and other things too, laughter for Lulu and John was so long dead as to render impossible even recalling the nature of its trigger – to begin to remember just how it had gone.

Melody nodded in a way that said so far, anyway, she was still so bloody knackered – utterly done in by whatever – as to manage no more than this heavy-lidded demonstration from amid the depths of her slouch. She indicated a bottle of Sancerre, well on its way to being pretty bloody knackered itself.

'I won't, thanks,' said Lulu, flopping down on a damn big sofa some way away. 'So what have you been up to, Melody? Christmas shopping? *You're* not going away, are you?'

'Ho ho ho,' came back Melody – and if any of the red-cheeked ebullience of Santa had been meant here, then she'd let the whole side down badly. The deadness of heavy irony, devoid of all trace of a lighter side: that seemed to be much more the message of the moment. 'What I have been *doing*, Lulu, is cleaning Edna fucking Davies' fucking kitchen, washing Edna fucking Davies' fucking dishes – '

'Yeh yeh – OK,' smiled Lulu, one hand batting the air in a not too hopeful attempt to stem the tide.

' – and serving Cyril fucking Davies his fucking *tea*,' concluded Melody, defiantly.

'I'd forgotten you were doing all that,' said Lulu. And she had – forgotten completely: couldn't care – couldn't care less.

'Yeh well,' sulked Melody. 'I'm reminded of it every bloody day. And no – to answer your other question, *no*

143

Lulu – haven't been Christmas bloody *shopping* because as per fucking usual I've got no Christmas bloody *money*, have I? I hope you lot aren't expecting anything, or anything, because you'll be bloody disappointed. I can tell you.'

'I don't want anything,' said Lulu, softly.

And Melody looked at her. Yeh well – I didn't even mean *you*, did I? Hardly know you. Meant Elizabeth and Howard, didn't I? Actually I will get something for Elizabeth – have to, really: she's so bloody good to me. And Howard. Still miss Howard. Why am I thinking about *Howard*, now? Because I can't, just can't, go on thinking about that bastard *Miles*, can I? No I can't – just can't: it simply kills me. Christ, though – if it wasn't for Howard and Elizabeth, I'd barely bloody *eat*.

'How's John?' said Melody, suddenly, while not giving a damn. 'Same?'

Lulu looked away and nodded briefly. God – does everyone know about John and me, then? Well, to be fair, Melody was hardly likely to forget the summer party, was she? When crazy John attacked shitty Miles and blood and tattered shirts became the order of the day.

'Same,' she said. 'And you? Do you still see . . . that person?'

'Miles. His name was Miles. Is. Was. Whatever.'

'So – no, then?'

Melody nodded, looked up and drank wine. 'No,' she whispered – and then more forcibly: 'Men really *are*, aren't they?'

'Bastards?' queried Lulu. 'Oh yes. All of them. Complete bastards.'

Melody poured more wine. 'Never *used* to think so . . . well, they're not *all* bad, I suppose. Howard, say. He's not like that.'

Wish he was, thought Lulu: wish to God he was.

'Yeh,' went on Melody, quite carelessly now. 'Howard's

144

all right. Howard's the only one I've ever . . . I mean, I really liked it, liked it a lot, when we were . . .'

And Lulu now looked at Melody. Well, she thought. Well well well. Well, now.

'I didn't know,' said Lulu, quietly – thinking what is it, exactly, that I feel about this?

'No,' sighed Melody. 'People don't. Nobody does. I think even *he's* forgotten, sometimes. Sorry, Lulu – I don't know why I . . . I maybe shouldn't have . . .'

'It's OK,' said Lulu.

'It's just that I'm so – !'

'OK,' hushed Lulu. 'It's OK – really.' And then she smiled. 'I'm going to see how Lizzie's managing with the dreaded Nelligan, and then I'm off. You know I'm housesitting, yes? So I'll probably see you, if you're going to be around next door.'

'Yeh,' agreed Melody morosely. 'Hoovering Edna fucking Davies' fucking carpet – sorry, *Dysoning* Edna fucking Davies' –'

Lulu laughed. 'Oh God's *sake*, Melody – don't start all that lot up again. Look – it's a means to an end, right? Life is – it's all it is. Means to an end.'

Melody smiled wanly as she watched her go – Lulu herself unspeakably depressed by all she had just uttered. And Melody, some while later (Christ – I've finished that whole bloody bottle, you know: didn't even notice it going) when she herself was seeking out Elizabeth so that she could say hello and goodbye and then tender her customary gratitude, together with a vague and all-encompassing apology (safe side) – had been surprised to find Lulu still in the house. Much more surprising, though, was glimpsing her through the barely ajar door of the morning room, her arms softly hard around Elizabeth's waist – just audible faint gasps of could be anything from sweet bliss to amazement (warm fallout from both of their big hot mouths, locked together as they were, open and probing). Melody

145

glanced too at that very odd young man Peter, just some little way off – so pale and rigid as to appear made of stone: his eyes glinted liquid and his face was stricken.

CHAPTER SEVEN

John could not have told you, not right away, just what it could be that was different about Lulu. There was a sort of, what – muted elation, conceivably? Was she the privileged custodian of fat and secret knowledge? Maybe nothing so intricate – might even be nothing at all. Yet there was something, something ... And then he had it: happiness. Happiness was all – pure and simple. Lulu looked as she used to look when she and John had been *happy* together – and he fell into a well of sadness, now – sad, so sad, that this huge and dead-eyed melancholy had driven out happy. But here was the big change coming: John was not drowning, floundering or even panicked in this black and familiar cold, dark well, no: he briefly wallowed and then climbed right out, practically refreshed – was now all but subjecting himself to a brisk and vigorous towelling down. He could take it – accept the fact now, he thought, that any pleasure or even contentment for Lulu just had to be sourced from way beyond their dank and wretched, soon to be split asunder mutuality; could take it, yes, because as from this very afternoon, John maybe had for the first time since summer somewhere to go and somewhere to be.

And Lulu too was aware of a shift – almost as if all the old air in the house had been siphoned away and replaced by great gusts of the fresher sort. She didn't feel blanketed by the oppression of John, skulking – and nor did he seem so sullen. Hell – he appeared only partially pissed, which in his case passed for sober. The mess in the hall – through which Lulu had been wholly resigned to scrunching – was all cleared up, every trace, and nor were there any signs of John having spilled, cracked or overturned anything else at all while she was away. (Sometimes in the past, a really heavy and you would have felt safe in thinking immutable piece of furniture – bureau, say – once, that massive chest-on-chest in the corner – was suddenly brutally askew and jutting, as if the local poltergeists had nipped in for a malevolent quickie; no more than the result of a staggering and legless, blind drunk John colliding heavily into the thing and wondering only why now his shoulder should be killing him, before he slithered on down to the floor.)

John and Lulu both tried smiling, and it really didn't go at all badly – not quite mawkish, not too painful. And when Lulu made her usual move towards the staircase, John did not lurch forward in his customary attempt to head her off at the pass – and consequently Lulu had felt under no compulsion to make an anguished dash for it. John was content, it seemed, to let her escape with whatever warm thing she carried inside her, for now he was strolling back into the room where he poured a really very small drink for himself – no more than the merest couple of nips – and settled into an armchair just as a regular person could easily do: he relished all of the normality – this new elevation within the ranks of the human condition.

A new light – that thing you see things in. Or was it just perspective? People talked of these, didn't they? How the advent of some new and undreamt-of element could penetrate murk and even illuminate the shadows that were left, while blocking out a good deal of the glaring. How vertiginous and seemingly unbreachable barriers could suddenly be negotiated with all the ease of a five-bar gate; and there, lurking amid walls that had blacked out all hint of day, was a door, small door (searched and prayed for how many times? And now quite plain and teasingly ajar, the light beyond it winking welcome). In short, it very much seemed as if John had got another girl.

When he had put the phone down after that briefest and unbelievably non-aggressive little chat with Tara – she had hurled no abuse, even seemed to care a bit (can't do, can she?); hadn't even hit him with whatever ghastly commission of a thousand words on exactly which particular variety of crap this time, I wonder – John had been perfectly content to continue slumping in the hall, hurt and broken amidst the breakage. If she was truly coming (and she said she was on her way – people don't generally, do they, say that if they're not?) then she might as well be party to the full extent of the carnage. The tremendous and acrid pungency of the scent had all but invaded him, now – he felt as if it no longer mattered what in life he ever stuck his nose into, for it would always come up smelling of not roses but this. And when the doorbell rang, at least he was well within hobbling distance.

'Christ Jesus,' was her opening shot. 'What a fucking stench. Like a bloody brothel. God, sweetie – you really *are* bleeding. Have you put anything on it?'

'I should think this stuff could cauterize anything – but no, not in the sense you mean, I . . . no.'

This was so weird. Tara had never been to the house before – well why would she? She could be foul and cantankerous in the office, as well as by phone, fax and e-mail: no sense in going in for overkill. And yet she seemed, well – John would have said softer, but that was plain ridiculous: I mean OK – Tara was surely softer than unhewn granite, but there the comparative ended. Though she was coming over as not maybe quite so dominant as usual. Don't know, though: still no slouch when it came to dishing out orders:

'Right, sweetie – you go and lie down on the sofa, can you manage? And tell me where the kitchen is and the bathroom is and I'll get all this cleared up and then I suppose I'd better do something or other with that foot of yours and then we'll go off for a drink, how's that?'

'Perfect,' said John. Well – it came damn close. Tara was a

capable woman, he'd have you know; despite everything else she might or might not be, she sure as hell could get things done (and you better count on it, sweetie).

John lay down on the sofa; his inclination would have been for the armchair just east of it, but one did not question one's commanding officer. Lulu would not at all care for this woman (any woman) rootling around in the kitchen and certainly not in the bathroom; and John rather surprised himself then by thinking Who actually gives a toss? Hey? She's the one who went out and left me like this, isn't she? Yes she is. And Tara's the one who's come over to help me, right? Right. Too damn right. So as far as John was concerned, Tara could fool around with Lulu's special and secret little bottles, phials and packages for as long as she bloody well pleased (which, of course, she would do – there was yet to be born the woman who could enter an alien bathroom in noble quest of analgesia, plaster or antiseptic, locate same and swiftly emerge: some things, it must be faced, are simply contrary to nature).

There was the rush-rush noise of brushing from the hall, bit of tinkling, and then the muted groan of severe wet-wiping, probably by way of what Lulu would be bound to put down as The Wrong Mop. And in no time at all, Tara was kneeling in front of John and telling him that there's just the teeniest bit of glass here, in the ball of your footsy, sweetie, and it's just as well that I have these famous red fingernails of mine because I couldn't find tweezers anywhere. She then gently dabbed on some sort of sticky and creamy stuff (it did sting, yes – but not like the bloody *scent* had stung, let John leave you in no doubt on that score) and soon one of those clean-smelling and big Elastoplasts was firmly in place – the old-style clothy ones that always put John in mind of not just Aertex vests and Shreddies, but Southern American waffles too.

'Florence Nightingale,' he said.

Tara smiled shortly and not too frighteningly as she rose

from her crouch and faced him. 'I never thought I'd hear you saying *that*,' she said.

No, John reflected – never thought I'd be bloody saying it, did I? He offered her a drink, of course he did – needed one himself, but maybe not quite so badly as usual, in that he hadn't yet cried out for several. But Tara seemed eager to be away: let's go to my club, she said – I'll carry you on my back. And John was aware too of a frisson, now – not just due to the fact that here they both were, the two of them, for all the world getting *acquainted*, for God's sake (in fact, if John is being honest, he couldn't really believe that he was actually dealing with himself, here, let alone Tara: this just had to be two entirely different people altogether). No – this feeling in the air was maybe too because each of them was conscious of the truth that Lulu could arrive back home at just any second at all and although this shouldn't in the circumstances (and on the face of it) matter a single jot, it somehow most certainly and very much did.

So they drove into Soho and Tara parked her rather super car wherever she bloody well liked and then led the way down into the mauvish gloom of her damn famous club, such designer-misery soon giving way to a dazzle of orange and vermilion at the bar where they perched high on stools (Can you manage, sweetie, yes? Yeh yeh – fine, I'm fine) that seemed to be fashioned from the lithe and sinewy hind-quarters of half a herd of aluminium springboks. To the left and right of John there buzzed not only the odd bristle-headed, sharp-suited and moneyed hooligan, but also tight gaggles of successful women all arrayed in neat and leggy armour – not just black but colours encompassing every shade from charcoal to blood-clot – each one of them so very much younger than John, their collective light of confidence blinding.

'So, sweetie,' said Tara, energetically horsing around with the plastic stirrer in her long tall sally of a drink (looked like a lava lamp), stomping down all the fruit and leaves good and hard. 'Counting the days to hanging up your stocking? Have you written a list to Santa?'

'Waiting for the commission: one thousand words on What I Want For Xmas.'

'I'm not that bad, am I? And what *do* you want, sweetie, hm? What do you want for Christmas?'

'Peace. Crates of booze and peace.'

'Sounds heaven. Sounds terribly like *my* Christmases, actually. Always shoot up to my place in Bath – Tuesday, I'm going. Told you about it, yes? It's good to get out of London.'

'I'm sure. Envy you. Except, well – I couldn't.'

'Couldn't? Why? Why ever not? You just *go* – that's all there is to it.'

'In your life, maybe. You live alone.'

'So? Soon you will be too. Practice.'

'I know. I know that's true – but though we've, you know – Lulu and I are, er, oh God – breaking *up*, I still feel I always have to keep an *eye*, you know? It's crazy, I know, but I still get so terribly jealous if she's ever away from me. Can't bear it. Can't.'

'But sweetie – she *will* be away from you, won't she? Hm? Permanent. Face it. What're you going to do when she's gone? *Stalk* her? When it gets to this, it's just over. You have to move on.'

'Cowboy talk.'

'So be a cowboy. How about riding out to my spread?'

'What – Bath, you mean? What – a visit?'

'A visit, a lunch – a weekend. Christmas. Your choice.'

'It sounds . . . that does sound good. But – '

'It *is* good, of course it's good. If *I'm* there it's got to be good – right? But what?'

'But, well – I'm a bit . . . I mean, I didn't even think you *liked* me. You never *seemed* to like me.'

'Of course I *like* you, sweetie – why else would I go on commissioning all your stuff? It's not that good.'

'You never said it wasn't good. Anyway, I'm writing a novel. And that *will* be good, I promise. It's got to be.'

'Oh it's not *bad*, the stuff you write – I'm not saying that. And the reason I never said anything is because I'm so *nice*. Don't you think I'm nice?'

'Not particularly, no. Not really.'

'Well I'm being nice now. Tell me about your novel.'

'It's seventeen pages long. Christ.'

'Uh-huh. Needs work, right?'

'Right. Yeh. Right.'

'So come and work at my place. You can have your very own room at the top. Peace. Peace and crates of booze. Well?'

'Well . . . what, you really *mean* it, Tara, do you?'

'Don't I always, sweetie? Mean it? Don't I just *always*?'

Tara held up her glass in salutation, and John clinked his against it. She had a striking face, it had to be said. And the body too was pretty bloody good: she went in, she went out – just like in the magazines.

'You do,' he agreed. 'You do indeed.'

In short, it very much seemed as if John had got another girl.

❋

Which was more than could be said for young Norman Furnish – and don't think it wasn't on his mind. The trouble with this mind of his, Norman felt, was that although it always seemed to be chock-full to bursting with all manner of worry, doubt and pain (and hesitation and panic – and longing, mainly: mainly it was that) there never seemed to be anything there he could actually get to grips with – certainly nothing he could (big sigh) act on. His mind, then – or could it be just the skull – was possibly packed only in the way that dusty cavities between walls of flimsy plasterboard are charged with hardening foam: just soft then rigid stuff, to keep out the worst of the chilling, but leaving

153

Norman nowhere near even the threat of warmth, sometimes in anguish, and fearing he could well die of mildness.

Without Katie, nothing was any good at all any more. The reason being that although Katie had been frequently dreadful (and still Norman cringed away from all those hot humiliations, shivered at the memory of the *danger* she put him into), when Katie had been both there and lustful, it had blotted out not just all that but also the sheer weight of dismal nothingness that made up the sum total of the rest of Norman's bare existence on earth – the part that, post-Katie, lingered on like some grey disease with a decidedly dry but nonetheless warped sense of humour (malignant only in that it was forever within and wished him no good. There were no sudden and dramatic deteriorations, it is true, but nor was the patient giving any hopeful signs of rallying round). So not benign either, in that sense – and a little benignity, to Norman's way of thinking, could only be a good thing, now.

Maybe it would help him to feel better, bit better, if where he had to be was not so unremittingly vile. Norman had actually spent time this very evening (well why not? Evenings were just full of nothing but time) in trying to decide whether in fact this fetid little bedsit in which he crouched and paced and – due to the huge trombonist in the next room – suppressed his howling, was (a) just about as disgustingly similar to the last one as you could feasibly get, or (b) not just worse by far, but quite possibly the very nastiest little room in not only London, no, but in the whole of the universe and cosmos beyond it (for Norman well knew you can bypass global and think astronomically when all you are is approaching atomic). And if there were life on Mars, as some people possibly as lonely and distracted as Norman would tell you, then it surely had more intelligence than to live like this; Christ – even *organisms* had standards.

You see how it is when you are alone too much? All the critical faculties shut down and you end up nodding like a sedated llama at some inane conclusion to a non-con-undrum. So let's liven things up – what's on TV, then? Doesn't really matter, does it? Soon find out because now it was on and fizzing, fizzing in that way it did (normal, the people at the rentals company had said) and now here was the noise of a nation plugging in their deep-fat fryers while delivering huge expectoration (you get this, the people at the rentals company had said) and next there swam up a quasi picture that after a brief bout of nerves settled down into just what have we here, now? Ah yes – an early evening serial, how very pleasant indeed. Now let me see, let me see – a young and tousled man in a sofa with no socks on (*yes*, the young man – keep a grip for God's sake, Norman) blindly riffling through his newspaper at the rate of one page every half-second, and here was a girl at the door now, yes – so what she'll do, if Norman's any judge, is finger the edge of this door for a bit (and now she was pawing, now she was clawing) while putting a whole lot into getting that canine to slide over her lower lip as her eyelids batted with enough uncertainty as to make you wonder whether she'd forgotten the line. But no – here comes the line right now. And what she's going to say is . . . yes, here it is: 'Mick? Mick? Look – about last night . . .' But Mick doesn't want to talk about it, does he? No he doesn't – and Norman can't stand any more, can he? No he can't. Hear him? So he hurls the remote control at the buttons on the set and it bounces right off so he retrieves it straight away and bloody throws it back again and this time it connects with the Off switch and all is silent save the high-pitched whining (it will do this, the people at the rentals company had said) – because the remote control, Norman would have you know, doesn't remotely *work*, or anything: but all it is is the *batteries*, those smug and lying bastards at the rentals company had said, but batteries cost *money* – *don't* they *don't* they *don't* they? Yes they bloody do so go and get stuffed and leave me alone.

But you see how it is when you are alone too much? Norman knew, Norman knew – don't ever think he was unaware of the shadowy risk of losing it altogether. But the only way to get out and in with someone was to wade into that other world of serious spending – because however he broke it down (whenever he did his sums) all he surely ended up with was a bill for services rarely rendered: just you take tonight. The first blind date from this agency he'd signed up with. Oh God oh God – to say that Norman had spent a fair part of the day in a state of barely suppressed anxiety would not at all come close to hitting the mark. His moods had not so much swung as suffered convulsions: would this be the worst evening of his life bar none (not bloody easy) in the company of a woman who looks like a horse and she shouts and spits and swears and drinks too much and then rounds off the evening by cleaving me in twain? Or could this just be the break I have been waiting for? Could the sweet Lord have maybe remembered me? I mean – it happens, it happens: sometimes, *tell* me it happens (and not just in films?). The sort of girl who wouldn't dream of answering a lonelyhearts ad but had to take the time and trouble to use an agency so that the clearly unsuitable could be filtered out – and all she was was too demure, too shy: too damned *nice* (and maybe too busy, what with her off-shore trust fund and fab and hugely paid career) to form meaningful relationships in the normal way. Christ. Where has she been all my life?

But by the time it got to the stage when Norman was as close to being dressed as could ever really happen (he had bought a shirt and tie and hank set at the iffiest end of Brick Lane market – sort of diagonal stripes and morse code dots in not just taupe but also an olivey kind of . . . no – better, on balance, you don't know) the scale of likelihood had tipped way in favour of the axe-wielding and foul-mouthed mare of the night, but what could he do about it? He was caught now, wasn't he? Ensnared. Yes he was, yes he was – just as usual, yes he was. (Her name is Jennifer. Mm. I take a sort of solace if not outright courage from the fact that her name is Jennifer: you couldn't, could you, be an out-and-out lout with a name like that? Which is not to say I couldn't have coped with maybe a Fifi or Dolores. But it's all so bloody silly anyway, isn't it? Yes it is. Because all I want is Katie.)

Norman was now whimpering quite manfully as he patted into his newly-razored cheeks and jowls whatever heavy-duty drain-scourer was shamelessly masquerading as Givenchy for Gentlemen – Brick Lane market also (well, have you seen the prices they charge in the shops?). He then forlornly and under a cloud of doom set off for the mutually agreed-upon boozer, which could easily be a good and handy little local for anyone who lived about fourteen tube stops and three changes away from Norman's own dungeon (third floor, ring twice and then fuck off because no one here answers doors because no one ever visits – and anyway, the bell got stove in years back).

❉

And sometimes Norman wondered – whenever in fact he thought of Katie, so a good deal of wondering was often going on – whether ever she might be maybe thinking of him. And although he suspected that the answer was no, not really, no (save on the occasions, possibly, when she needed to illustrate to a gleeful assembly the epitome of one or other colossal ineptitude by way of the ultimate living example) – it would have done Norman no good at all to be quite certain that in truth he had joined the ever-swelling ranks of those whom she simply did not know any more, and who therefore had ceased to exist. To Katie, it was all quite straightforward: if you knew her, then you must adore her – yes? And if yes, then you should surely need to devote your life to doing what it is she currently wants and taking her wherever at the moment she desires to linger, however briefly, and supplying her too with all the luscious trinkets that daily she decides are required. Otherwise, what in Christ's name is the point of you? None: there is none.

Miles McInerney was well down the road to knowing all about both the inside and the out of this – and was it bothering him? Well was it? Trouble him at all, did it? Well at the beginning – *nah*, forget it: name of the game, isn't it? Course it bloody is. Some kid wants Dom bloody Wossname, Perrier, Pérignon, whatever the fuck – then in steps the smooth bastard to supply it, right? Hey – been tuning this fiddle for how long? But all games come to an end, OK? I mean – business conference, two days tops. Yeah – that Melody thing, whole week: mistake, as we now know all too bloody well. Too much, see, and they won't leave it. I get a lot of that. Clingy. Understandable, yeh sure – but a fucking pain in the arse whatever which way, right?

But this one, Catherine – I mean OK, yeah, knockout bird, I'm not saying otherwise (not bleeding eighteen yet, believe it? Last girl I had that young was, well – didn't know *how* bloody young did I cos she *lied* to me, didn't she – scheming little bitch: bloody jailbait – I was out of there well quick, I can tell you). But Catherine, she doesn't seem to quite get the ins and outs of what an affair actually entails on *both* sides, see? Now I admit, I admit this – at the beginning I thought Oh Jesus, Miles old lad: jackpot time. She knows you're married, knows you've got kids – couldn't give a shit; and is she hot? Is she *hot*? Come on – I've been around hot, son: I know hot when hot's around and this cat, I am not joking, could bloody *burn* you. So yeh – what can I say? Sex on a plate and no strings and none of this bloody loony talk about phoning the wife and falling in love and all the rest of these women's bloody caper: just what you want, just what you're after, sweet as a nut.

Fact is, I had a couple of them going on and off at the time: one at work I'd oblige with a good seeing-to whenever her Malcolm was off on some bloody load of bollocks in the Midlands (he wants to hang around, doesn't he? You don't wanna go fucking off up the Midlands when the action's down here right on your bleeding doorstep). Jenny or Joanie or something's her name: she's not going to win prizes – she ain't any sort of traffic stopper, is what I'm saying here, but always OK if you've got a minute and nothing better on (and she's no fool – she knows all right what side of the toast the jam's on: they don't meet too many like me, these birds – not like me, they don't). So there was her, like I say – and then there was that one I bumped into down Crawley way, one time. Had to get a bit strong with that one (which don't come up too much) but not long after she was gagging, wasn't she? Anyway, what I'm saying, right, is that soon after Catherine and me was really into it – I chuck 'em both. Well – when you've got a lady at home, you don't want to go pushing it too far: can't be working late *every* bleeding night, can you? Mind you, I always make a point of taking care of the wife – you have to. And Sheil's not a bad kid: always bring her flowers of a Friday (favourite for keeping them sweet) – and none of your garage forecourt muck neither, if you don't mind, no: proper florist's job, done up like a bloody Easter egg, yeh nice. Wives are funny bleeding things, I know, but they appreciate a bit of thought – and hey, what does it cost you? Lose it on some expense sheet or other and who's crying, hey?

But the main reason I chucked these two was Catherine. She was enough, you know? Also – less of a risk. Also – another league, body-wise, yeah. There's only one real trouble – just one thing that gets to me about Catherine (well two, maybe two – but never mind two for now, let's just get this one thing out of my system): she seems to think that an affair is any time of the night or day she bleeding takes a fancy to – doesn't seem to get that it's got to slip into non-existent weekend sales trips and the odd sly lunch which hangs about. Apart from anything else – they're the only times you can offload the bloody bills. I mean – take right now: we're in a bleeding Park Lane hotel (Catherine's

159

in the bath right now – singing away like a bleeding thing, birdie in the trees – else I wouldn't have a moment to think) but there's no way I can swing this one, no way on God's earth: nothing in my diary, is there? And we're doing this, what – twice a week? Three times? First time in my life I'm beginning to feel it. Dragged me to Tiffany's, just before – said she wanted that blue and silver pen. But look, darling, I said, I've got you *how* many bleeding pens and Christ knows what else from Tiffany's (and all the rest of these bloody places, oh yeah – you don't wanna know, believe me) but she just ups and says Yeah but I don't have the blue and silver one, do I? And then she gives you that look that makes you want to fuck her on the spot – which would certainly liven up the joint: bleeding quiet in Tiffany's, I don't know if you know – and what you do is you buy the bloody blue and silver pen, right? Yeah right. And between Bond Street and here, she saw some sort of velvet scarf thing in orange and black – and come on: guess which tart of my acquaintance is now the proud owner of just this bloody thing? So you get my drift. And even now – we're two bottles of Bollinger down already and that ain't nothing to her, you gotta believe me. Telling you – the money I've spent on this girl we're talking a pair of world-class hookers delivered to your door on a bloody velvet cushion twice a week for life. So why don't I chuck it in? Hey? Call it a day. Get some bird that isn't bent on breaking me. Well why? Yeah well – that's it: that's the other trouble, like I said.

'Miles!'

She's calling me.

'Miles! Come in and make me dry. And bring me some champagne.'

She's calling me. She's telling me to rub her down and fill her up and that's just what I'll do. And that's the bloody funny thing I was on about, see: I don't *do* what birds tell me to do – no way, never have: not my style. I mean – I'm *nice* to them, yeah sure: smile when they say something

160

fucking stupid, laugh at some crap non-joke they just come up with – and pay for bloody everything going (don't I know it). But all this Miles Come Here bit – well, you gotta be joking, right? You know me by now – I don't go nowhere: they come to me, OK? So like I say: bloody funny.

But Christ: take one look at this. She's only standing up in the bath with her arms stretched high above her head – she knows that gets me going – all the warm foamy water pouring right off her and glistening, like that. Oh Christ I've got to have her – bleeding got to. And even now that I've lifted her out and I've soaked my bloody suit (and it's Italian, a one-off) I'm not even minding, am I? Her tits fit my hands like two halves of the same thing and Jesus when those fingers of hers slip down and sod around and then get a hard bloody hold on me that'd make you cry out if you hadn't got her down on the ground by then and whacked the palm of your hand right over that wide and squealing mouth so only those fucking sexy eyes of hers are flashing bloody up at you – and now I'm bleeding in her, now I'm bleeding up her – it feels like she's sucking my blood out and I'm really like doing a locomotive on her now, mate – thundering in like you wouldn't believe and Christ I'm crashing, Jesus this is – uh – *it* I'm bloody telling you: *God* when I come in her like that I'm looking to see everything I've shot come jetting right out of her mouth and her ears and her eyes and it's now when I'm collapsed, now when I've really bloody had it and she sighs like that as I fall on her – it's then I start to feel like I'm falling inside too, falling – yeah far deeper than I ever wanna go and this is, yeah – oh yeah: this is the other bloody thing about Catherine, cos I don't *fall*, you get it? She can be a real shit, this little kid, but she knows more than any other bird I've ever been with just exactly what the fuck it is she wants and Jesus she gets it, she gets it – whatever it is she gets it; and now as I look at her and I see the whole lot of the thing, then I just know that

161

she reminds me of me – and do you know what? I say do you know what? I'll tell you, son: I think I bleeding love her.

❉

Norman Furnish had allowed himself hours and hours for the journey to this really rather classy and darkish boozer, in the far corner of which he now stood, wavering. He was ten, twelve minutes early; Jennifer would be ten, twelve minutes late (this is how it went: it is known). The point is, the barman was eyeing him, wasn't he, because Norman hadn't yet got around to ordering a drink because he was not quite sure of the form, here: would being well around the larger part of a pint when she arrived (and please God – she *would* arrive, wouldn't she?) in any way constitute having started without her? Also, if he had one he'd have two and then he'd start slurring and she would surely have heard tell and maybe had first-hand experience of men like that and be off like a shot. Can't, on the other hand, ask for some nancy little mineral water or Britvic of a drink because then the barman and these ho-hoing weightlifters to the left of him would immediately think whatever people like this habitually did think of people like him and then on top of that if she *didn't* arrive (and please God – she *would* arrive, wouldn't she?) it might even seem as if he had merely been loitering or touting – or even, Christ help us, *procuring* and then the police could be hastily summoned and before they arrived amid a frenzied blur of klaxons and burnished steel Norman might have to smash his dinky little Babycham glass and drag the jagged bambi across his bulbously blue-veined and cheesy wrists in a last-ditch effort to evade the strong clutch of arrest and the further shame of living any bloody longer. So yes – even the business of ordering a drink in a pub assumed strange proportions and askew perspectives in Norman's world (for now I think you well see just how it is when you are alone too much).

He ordered a large Bell's, on the rocks, and stared at it in frank disbelief when it was plonked before him: Norman never drank whisky (too dear – also too nasty) and nor was he a great one for ice. This aberration, he thought, need not be unconnected with the general confusion he had felt about himself ever since he had, from within a miasma of escalating bafflement, filled in as well as he could the extraordinarily lengthy questionnaire demanded by the dating agency. Initially, no probs: surname, first name, address – very few crossings-out there. Then it got tricksy: 'I am seriously interested in meeting someone', the form said – well yes, absolutely no argument there – but then you were meant to tick boxes that went Single, Divorced, Widowed and Separated; so Norman ticked those, regretting only that there was no Married option as well for quite frankly there wasn't one sector of the community save Dead And Buried that he wished to exclude. He did add on in red felt pen, however, *Female* – because they hadn't at all, to his mind, made this clear and he didn't want any elementary slip-ups at the very outset. Then he did indeed see a box marked Sex, so he ticked that too and underlined it in red.

Now the next part he found quite appallingly difficult: you were meant to write in the tiniest spaces imaginable Age, Height, Occupation, Religion, Build (Slight, Medium, Large) and then, heavens, *Attractiveness* (Very Attractive, Attractive and Average were the options here – bloody hideous is apparently a figment of our collective imagination). Norman had been halfway through his second supplementary sheet, itemizing with quite abandoned gusto all the occupations, builds and ages that would be entirely acceptable to him (he drew the line at nonagenarian embalmers in excess of six foot four) whereas only Very Attractive would do for him – and only then did he realize with a sinking of not just heart but other organs too that all this stuff was intended to pertain to *himself* – at which realization he was utterly floored. He made tea, and resumed some time later, putting in his age at twenty-six (did that sound too young? Too old? Too average? What?), but as he didn't really have any height, build, occupation or religion to speak of, he left those blank. As to Attractiveness, he plumped for Average, with the judicious insertion of a couple of minuses.

Education: oh dear. Norman pounced on GCSEs (Eng Lit, Eng Lang, Elementary Maths and Ancient History) but as to Technical Qualification, forget it: that's why he was an estate agent (sort of). But from here on in it became at first faintly and then progressively more out-and-out hilarious because it seemed that now Norman was being asked to assess his *personality*: was he ('tick which traits closely describe you') Affectionate, Serious, Considerate, Shy, Romantic, Fashionable, Practical, Conventional, Reliable, Adventurous? The word No agilely sprang to Norman's mind, but he simmered down and eventually and with huge reluctance settled for Shy and Conventional (which is just certain to make all those nymphomaniac supermodels rabid and gagging for me, isn't it? Christ oh Christ).

Now he was faced with the 'Your Attitudes' section and already, he thought, this doesn't smell good. 'Do you involve yourself with community activities?' Um, let me see – No, I think just about sums it up. 'Are you looking for one special relationship?' Well yes – that's why I'm fooling around with all of this, isn't it? So yes – one will do, ten would be nice. 'Does your work make it difficult to meet new people?' Very droll: my 'work', such as it is, makes it difficult to meet any people at all: sometimes – on the days I'm late and skive off early – I practically miss *myself*. 'Do you want to extend your social life as well as finding a special relationship?' Let's do this thing one step at a time, shall we? Why don't we try and latch on to someone who doesn't actually laugh in my face or isn't physically sick at the sight of me and then just take it from there. 'Do you devote a lot of time to your social life?' Ha! You mean apart from filling in this fucking form?

Norman did his best to persevere with the thing, but if he was honest was now losing interest. So the next section, 'Your Interests', signally failed to rouse him. He crossed out 'Wining/Dining' and substituted 'Eating a Bit'; but as to Sports, Keep Fit, Politics, Reading, Travelling, Science, Technology, Pets, Theatre, Arts, Astrology, Children, Gardening, Countryside, Music in any shape or form whatever and (oh please) *Homemaking*, Norman was forced to draw a negative conclusion. He couldn't even bring himself to tick off 'Watching TV' because OK he *did* it, sure – of course he *did* it, but it wasn't so much an interest as an alternative to suicide.

And as to details of his 'Ideal Partner', Norman thought Katie, and simply marked 'Don't Mind' throughout; he'd gone off the Very Attractive idea as maybe unrealistic because look – all Norman amounted to (and here it was before him, in his very own hand and alive with leaky blue biro and red felt pen) was a twenty-six-year-old we presume male, with four GCSEs and bugger-all else who's interested in absolutely zilch and is willing to pay this agency just about all he has in the world to forge for him a Special Relationship with a preferably blind and insensate half-witted woman of indeterminate age, creed, colour and bulk who will let him bore her at length and then screw her briefly, while he gives himself up to thoughts of Katie.

So when this Jennifer finally did arrive (ten, twelve minutes late – but never mind all that: she's *here*, isn't she? At least she's *here*) Norman was somewhat surprised that she did not in any way come over as a ringer for the Medusa. Plain sort of a girl, was his first impression – quite plainly dressed and not, he thought, in any way a raver (that much was plain). Well look – what was he, then? *Fancy*?

And how had he known it was her? Easy. She had come

right up to him and said You must be Norman (plain sort of voice). And *yes*, thought Norman, just must, mustn't I? Of all people in the world, it just has to be me. What she probably means, he was thinking now – while busy battening down the wilder elements of his face into some sort of smile that might maybe not come across as maniacal – is that everyone else at the bar looks older and younger and not only occupied, interested and solvent but also Very Attractive, Attractive or even bloody Average and so all that is left is *me* – who just must, mustn't I, be *Norman*: yes oh yes – *I* have to do it.

He was undecided as to whether to take a manly pull at the Scotch and then start up the talk, or maybe say something now, should he, and drink as she was responding? As it was he both put the glass to his lips and started prattling straight into the tinkling depths of it, this having the twin results of two faint rivulets of golden Bell's coursing away from the corners of his mouth, and Jennifer's name emerging like a bad ventriloquists's guttural gurgle; it was possibly time to proffer the icebreaker (maybe a gottle of geer?).

'Well, um, Jennifer – drink. A drink of some sort, yes?'

'Mm. Lovely. That would be nice. I think I'll have a kir.'

'Absolutely. No problem. God – they're always up the other end, aren't they? Barpeople. When you need them.'

'It's a nice pub. Do you like pubs?'

'I – they're, yes – fine, pubs are. Pubs are good. I mean – not, you know, *great* or anything, but good when you want a drink, or something. Then they're good. You know, I sometimes think they avoid your eye on purpose . . .'

'So anyway, Norman – you're in real estate, is that right?'

'Yes, I – yes, I sort of am. Very boring, I'm afraid. But never mind all that – tell me about you, Jennifer. Awfully good of you to turn up, by the way.'

'Oh don't be silly – looking forward to it.'

'Christ – they do *serve* drinks in this place, do they? Sorry about this, Jennifer, I just can't seem to get him to notice me – ah! Here he is now. Yes, right – I'd like, um . . . sorry, Jennifer, I've completely forgotten what you, um . . .?'

'Kir, please. If that's all right.'

'Yes, oh yes – absolutely. That's what I *thought* you said – I just didn't – oh Jesus would you believe it? He's pushed off again now. God that's just typical – ah no, OK, he's coming back, I think – yeh, here he is. Yes. Right. I'd like a queer for the lady, please, and um – large Ball's. Bell's. Sorry.'

'Here, Norman – let me get this one. So that's one kir, please – and a double Bell's, is that right? Thanks.'

'Oh no, God no Jennifer – here, I've got it here – look: five-pound note – got it, been waving it about.'

'It's OK – I've done it now. You can get the next one.'

'Oh. Right. OK. Thanks, then. Cheers.'

'Cheers.'

'Cheers indeed. Yes indeed. Cheers. Very much so. Oh yes. Nothing like it, is there? Quiet drink – friendly pub . . .'

'Nice.'

'"*Tis* nice. Very nice. Very nice indeed. So anyway – cheers, then.'

'Cheers.'

'Mm. Nice whisky. Good whisky. I don't actually like whisky, if I'm honest – but this one is very good indeed, I must say. And is your, um . . . are you enjoying your drink, Jennifer? It's a lovely colour.'

'It is pretty, isn't it? I love the bubbles.'

'Oh it's got bubbles, has it? You like sparkling queers, then – yes, must be very nice, I can see that. Maybe try one later. Look, um, Jennifer – I was looking at their menu just before you arrived – they've got a sort of a place at the back, apparently, and, uh – I was wondering whether you might, uh . . .?'

'Pretty hungry, actually, yeh. How about you?'

'Hm? Oh yeh – hungry, hungry. *Starving*, in point of fact. Eat a horse.'

'Ha ha!'

'Two horses.'

'Ha.'

'A whole *herd* of horses!'

'Mm.'

'Yes. So anyway – what looks good? Fish, yes – they seem quite heavy on fish. Scampi, they've got.'

'Like scampi. And cod. Cod, I like.'

'They've got cod. And steak. And pies. They've got most things, actually.'

'Can I have another drink?'

'Already? I mean oh yeh – course. Gosh – miracle, he's actually *here*, this time. Yes, um – same again, I think. Yes, Jennifer? Same again? Yes. Right: same again then, please. Thanks. So, Jennifer – do you, um, do this sort of thing a lot?'

'What do you mean? What sort of thing?'

'Well I mean, you know – all this sort of dating business. This is my first time, I have to say. Learning the ropes. You're the guinea pig. Ha! What's wrong, Jennifer? You've gone very quiet.'

'I've been with the agency for quite a while, if that's what you mean.'

'Have you? Have you really? Ah – drinks, here we are. So – one of the house's very best sparkling queers for you, coming right up, and more of this bloody stuff for me – I don't know why I'm ordering it, really. Start as you mean to go on, I suppose. So, what – you must've been with a lot of men, then, yes?'

'What do you *mean*?'

'Well what I mean is, um – all I mean to say is that if, you know, you've been with the agency a fair old while, then you must presumably have been out on quite a few sort of *dates*, is all I mean. I mean – I can see you're the choosy type.

168

And why not? You don't want to spend the night with just *anyone*, do you?'

'Look, Norman – I think I'm not actually that hungry, now I come to think about it, so maybe we just ought to –'

'What, just make a booze-up of it, ay? Oh yeh – I'm all for that, absolutely. Last one to fall over turns out the lights, right?'

'Actually, Norman – I've just remembered I'm meeting my sister later on. We're going to see my mother – not been well.'

'Oh. Really? I'm sorry to hear that. So – no scampi, then?'

'I don't really think so. I'll just drink this and be off.'

'Uh-huh. And cod? Can't tempt you with a nice piece of cod, at all?'

'No – really. Honestly. Look, Norman – oh God, I didn't realize it was actually this late. Anyway – really nice meeting you.'

'Oh – and *you*, and *you*, but . . . do you really have to go, Jennifer? It's early, and – I mean we've hardly even got to know each other and look! You haven't finished your queer.'

'Bye, Norman. Take care. Happy Christmas.'

'Maybe another time, then, yes?'

'Bye.'

'Bye, then. Jennifer. OK. Bye. I hope your mother's, um . . . not too bad. Happy Christmas. Yes. Um – just a large Bell's, then, please. On the rocks.'

And on his way home soon after (nineteen stops and four changes, this time, because he messed up badly somewhere on the Circle Line) Norman had spent all his cod and scampi money on a full bottle of this very same liquor and now he sat in the centre of his dimly lit room amid a medley of odours, but mainly that of laundry yet to be laundered, trying to blot out the throb of terrible lowing that the big trombonist just next door emitted nightly for hours and hours, no one ever twice suggesting he might maybe desist or even tone it down a bit because he wasn't just big but mad to boot and once had threatened to hang Norman by the neck in the stairwell and had actually upturned a tea-chest in his room and set to with avidity beating its booming sides while he rummaged for rope.

Maybe I'm having all these problems because what I am doing is deep down *wrong*. Could there be some sort of higher and moral judging going on here? Maybe, all that time ago when I was living with Melody, I should just simply have stayed there. Because she's all right, Melody, you know – not too bad at all. Bloody sexy, that's for sure. Bit crazy, yeah – but what woman isn't? Bloody sexy, that's for sure. Christ – will I ever have a woman again? The last was Katie (oh God, Katie my Katie), and that was on a par with having twins set about you. Can't think about that, now. Can't actually *stop* thinking about that, now, but leave it, leave it – I've just got to leave it. But the thing about Melody is that I wanted and wanted her for ever and ever right up until the very moment that she wanted me too. Which was when Dawn was born. And that of *course* meant I should have stayed because Christ – what sort of man and father is it that walks out on a jobless woman with a new-born baby? This sort, I'm afraid: my sort, yeah. But Katie never for a moment agreed to be with me always – every time I brought it up she'd either scream or hit me, but more often than that she'd simply laugh, which just about says it all, I suppose.

Norman wanted to go to the lavatory, now – one more ordeal he always tried to defer for as long as possible because it involved resignedly picking up the roll of Izal (always handy, by the door), creeping past the big trombonist's room, then climbing two sets of stairs and groping his way down a corridor now permanently in gloom because tenants persistently nicked the twenty-five-watt light bulb to the point where whoever it was who replaced this thing simply ceased to do so; then he must try the door of the bathroom which seemed at any normal hour to be thoroughly engaged and then trudge back down again, his bowels in torment – taking solace only in that at least he had been spared the insidious pain of hard and unforgiving Izal in and around the pinkly tender crevices of his put-upon bottom. Within and between such disciplines, Norman's life was measured out.

Maybe tarts are the answer; not tarts like that awful, oh God, *so* awful thing he had gone with down King's Cross, that time – and still Norman cannot relive it (he will one day, yes he must, if only because he's running severely short of things to look back on, but in the light of the timbre of today, absolutely not now, I think). No, what Norman is maybe getting at is these fabulous women you read about that get summoned via a madam to the Plaza suite by a Hollywood star. The ones that look like centrefolds – the ones who at least take your breath away as well as the money. I think I'll save up: bound to be cheaper in the long run. I wonder how you find them? Not those cards in phone boxes, presumably; hotel porters, maybe. Meanwhile, I've got one more date lined up with this sodding agency, before bowing down to the inevitability of the stark and lonely Christmas that is surely looming. Well maybe the next one will at least hang around a little longer than our fleeting little Jennifer friend. I don't believe for a minute that her mother isn't well; and if she *isn't* well I hope she bloody dies.

Norman kicked on the television, while swigging Bell's from the bottle. What is it this time? Ah yes – one of those moody and unshaven Italian westerns, probably seen it. The barman's got a huge moustache and he's wiping a glass and there's a tinkling of spurs and the gringo comes in through those creaking swing-back half-doors and every-one does their turned-to-stone-for-just-a-split-second routine and then the joanna jangles back in and from the extraordinary contortions the barman's lips are going through you'd swear he was mouthing from memory three of the four gospels, but all we hear is *Dreeeenk*, señor? And his mouth is still juddering like a headless chicken at the end of it. Yeah, thought Norman – fiddling now with a video cassette – seen this one a thousand times.

It was Norman's one and only video – the fantastically erotic (not to say downright rude) minidrama that he and Katie had made in Chicago, just last summer: their joint production. But could he play it? No he couldn't, just couldn't – *couldn't*, you hear him? Nothing to do with the plangency of heart-strings, nor the dread of aching for all he had lost. No, entirely down to the lack of the relevant machine, I'm afraid – and even if he did spring for the extra, wouldn't it in all probability melt the tape just prior to bursting into flames (you have to expect this, the people at the rentals company would tell him). Pity, though: quite in the mood for a bit of auto-stimulation – and the Izal's just within reach. But this tape is far too precious to risk – this tape just had to be Norman's passport back to Katie. She had responded to none of his cards, none of his letters (don't suppose she got the last one), and so now although it pained him to do it, the time had come to bring threats to bear: *know* me, Katie – *know* me again. Let me love you and have you back! Otherwise we will both have to brave the agony and wrath of your father, Howard, when he settles down in his favourite armchair and tunes in to the truth of what not just Norman but Katie did. Sorry, so sorry my love – but finally and at last, that's just how it has to be.

Norman *really* wanted to go to the lavatory, now. He picked up the roll of Izal (always handy, by the door), crept past the big trombonist's room – the loony has stopped: he must have had his injection – climbed two sets of stairs and groped his way down a corridor now permanently in gloom and tried the door of the bathroom – which gave! Yes it was dark within – the atmosphere redolent of not just shaving foam but sewage, true – but in the light of just about everything today, this simply had to be the best news yet.

CHAPTER EIGHT

'I know, Mummy – I know it's terribly good quality and all the rest of it – of course I do, I remember it well,' Elizabeth conceded dutifully into the telephone, 'but I still don't think it's for Katie – young people just don't *wear* mink coats, Mummy, they're just not into it. Hardly anyone is, now . . . yes . . . yes I know, Mummy, but Marlene Dietrich's *dead*, isn't she? I say she's *dead*, yes. Oh hang on, Mummy – I think I hear Howard. Howard? Howard? Is that you?'

Howard had dropped his heavy briefcase noisily to the floor, yawned like a Disney dozy ogre, thrown his keys (bloody keys – bane of my life) into the brass sort of bowl thing on the table just west of the drawing room. He now wandered over to where Elizabeth was clutching hard her cordless and mouthing *Mumm-Meee* at him with rigid lips, and hugely.

'It's me,' he exhaled. And then he sighed in the very same tone.

'That was Howard, Mummy, so I'll really have to go. Howard. My husband. Yes – yes, everything's packed and ready – far too much as per usual, but still. Well of *course* we'll be careful – it's only *Paris* . . . yes, the tunnel. No, you don't drive through it – you sit on a train. It's just the same as going on a train anywhere else . . .'

And now Elizabeth made a great show to Howard of forcing her eyebrows to all but hit her hairline while bulging out the eyes and giving the chin a good, long, slow wag – the ultimate demonstration of stoic endurance (though she was aware too, as always, that she herself remained guilty of plaguing Katie daily with all this sort of nonsense: it was, she supposed, just what mothers did – unstoppable, however ghastly for all concerned).

'Well bring it if you really *must*, Mummy, but I'm telling you she'll never wear it . . . me? *Me*? God – I've got so many furs I don't know what to do with them. The best ones are in storage – can't even remember what they *look* like . . .'

Howard strolled into the drawing room; Elizabeth had told her mother that she Really Had To Go just the once, so far, so there were at least a couple more of those to come, along with an awful lot of repetition and assurances, and so here was the time – as it so often was – to pour for himself a nice big drink and try to forget all about work, Paris, Christmas and the looming loss of Laa-Laa. (Still he was pained by the look of love as he left her; they had shopped – Laa-Laa had skittered by his side and linked arms in the way that made him feel so very manly. Too many beautiful things he had bought her, and he loved it even more than she did. Then the moment came when they had to, just had to get back to the flat and Howard had been astounded, this time, by the nearly frightening pleasure she gave him and the way she soothed him out of it, and now he was pained – only by the look of love as he left her.) And if Howard had to put into just one word what it was he felt on entering the room and finding Zoo-Zoo lounging there, it would, he thought, probably have to be awkwardness, plain and simple – which was strange, wasn't it, in his own house and with the beautiful boy so recently his lover? But there it was and there was no point denying it: when things like this changed, they *really* changed, didn't they? But here was no ordinary End of the Affair-type scenario, no, for the very obvious and rather weird reason that Zoo-Zoo was still very much *around*. Certainly at this particular moment, he looked a lot more at home than Howard seemed to be.

A sort of smile flickered briefly at the edge of Howard's quite dry lips – parted now, in order to say Christ in heaven knows what – really hadn't the slightest idea. So maybe say nothing, hm? Just move over to the drinks table and quickly get myself a good, large Scotch.

'I'll do it,' offered Zoo-Zoo, easily – and already he was ambling with his usual cool laziness in the direction. 'I know how you like it.'

Well Howard had absolutely no arguments there, so he settled into the corner of a damn big sofa, grunting his contented assent to that particular scheme. And Zoo-Zoo handed him the chunky glass from behind his shoulder, as he always used to, but now it was not accompanied by the lightest of touches, just to the right of his neck. So often, Zoo-Zoo had eased out all the tension there, the gentle and then quite hard probing of those long brown fingers rendering Howard both dreamy and boneless. He was aware of the shift, but could not in truth say he honestly minded. In the light of Laa-Laa, he saw Zoo-Zoo now in a way that had never before struck him – and this Howard found quite frankly incredible. It was just that – for all his grace and languor – Zoo-Zoo seemed merely boyish and little more; feminine in one sense – plain to see – but never female in the way Laa-Laa always was to him (but then, of course – be fair: she was a woman, after all, and therefore had the edge).

'So . . . what?' opened up Howard (three great gulps of whisky inside him, now – good and warming it was). 'You'll still be popping in, will you, time to time? While we're away? Talked to Lulu about it, have you?'

Zoo-Zoo appeared to be addressing this question with considered gravity – as if world peace or the other thing could well depend upon the nature of his reply.

'I shall,' he eventually responded, 'be around. But it won't be the same, you know, with the two of you gone. Houses, I always think, very much assume the odours of their owners – not odour in the literal sense, I think, but more in the way they mean it when they talk about an odour of sanctity.

In this case, of course, it's much more that of possession. Wouldn't you say?'

Well look, Howard never had been terribly good at dealing with Zoo-Zoo when he started on all this *talking* business: conversation, as far as Howard was concerned, had never been a part of the deal. And now that the whole deal was dead anyway, all this stuff was more cumbrous than ever.

'I sort of see . . .' chucked in Howard, by way of a make-weight. He thought (was that him? Think so) – thought he had caught a glimpse of Brian, just then, flitting momentarily by the flank of the bay window with some sort of bucket in his hand, looked like, and his usual bag of tools. Poor Brian – forever trying to mend the irredeemable, it always seemed to Howard; why could no one take him aside and quietly tell him that some things in life just get so smashed up, you really have to leave them: they're just no good any more. Hm. Might maybe pop out and have a quick word – freshen up the drink and get away; the merest suggestion of Zoo-Zoo goes a very long way, these days, I am increasingly finding. How odd that all I ever used to do was yearn for any stolen moment; time and circumstance have seen to all that – that, of course, and Laa-Laa.

I am walking towards the drinks table, now, and I notice that this time Zoo-Zoo has made no offer; was I expected to have done something in return, then, for his pouring me a Scotch? Some plausible sign of a white man's truce? If so, can't think what. All this business about *behaviour* and second-guessing – it's all so terribly *wearing*, to my way of thinking. For me, whenever I'm with someone, I'm just ad-libbing my life away – not a clue if it's the right thing I'm saying, or whatever the hell might or might not be coming to me next: I just wing it. And you get all this in novels, don't you? Characters who just deep down *know* at any particular moment not just the feelings and thoughts of others but their entire bloody destiny from this day forth.

Well that's not me. Everything I do and everything I say is no more than just a shot in the, er – shot in the, oh Christ bugger it – shot in the what the hell is it you have a bloody shot into? God oh God – my mind.

Howard took a scarf from the rack in the hall: even the few steps to Brian's caravan could turn you to ice, you know.

'Anyway,' he concluded a bit jovially by way of Zoo-Zoo, who had casually followed behind him. 'At least you won't have the slave-driver that is Elizabeth breathing down your neck for a few days, anyway. Maybe put your feet up.'

'Oh please don't worry,' came back Zoo-Zoo with generosity. 'My feet, I assure you, are very often up. Anyway – I have to say I don't in any way regard Elizabeth like that at all. No no. I actually think she is quite delicious. As does Lulu.'

Is that what he said? *Is* it? Howard couldn't quite be sure, and he certainly wasn't asking for any repeats. It had very much sounded like that to his ears, however – and if so, what a perfectly astounding way of describing Elizabeth. What on earth could the boy be meaning by it? Or was it just one more lazy example of how young people spoke, these days? Could be, could be – but as is usual, I couldn't come close to actually telling you.

Howard inhaled sharply as he heaved open the front door and the cold wind gripped him. So depressing, isn't it, this time of year – not much after teatime, and yet just look at it: black as night. *Dark* – that's it, yes indeed: that's what you shoot into – the dark.

❋

'Christ, Brian,' stuttered Howard, stamping his feet on the floor of the caravan, this causing Dotty's collection of miniature teapots, china piggies and God alone knew what else to jiggle and judder on shelves that very much had the air of being Brian's handiwork, the way they were slightly leaning, like that. 'It's colder in here than it is outside, man.'

Brian nodded like one condemned. 'I know, I know – I've been trying to fix it – been on it most of the afternoon. Dotty'll go mad if she comes back and it's still like this. She'll go absolutely crazy. And I can't even find my gloves.'

'Well – can't you get someone in, or something? I mean, well – you don't know about heating systems, do you?'

'Not much. But then this isn't much of a heating system, frankly. There's so little that actually *can* go wrong with these things – that's what's baffling me. I've checked every little part – every single stage of the thing. All I can say is – it *should* work.'

'But,' said Howard, quite gently (and you had to go very easy with Brian, oh yes – if there was any heart in you at all, you just had to, believe me), 'it, um – clearly *doesn't*. Does it? Hm? So why not get someone in?'

Brian shook his head as if under the weight of a massive sorrow, forced into denying a sentenced and desperate man all hope of an eleventh-hour reprieve. 'Too expensive. Can't be done. And even then, there's no guarantee they'd fix it.'

'But Brian – how expensive can it *be*? If Dotty's coming back with Dawn – isn't that what Elizabeth told me? Christ, Brian, they'll freeze to death if it's like this tonight. Look, let me –'

'Forty pounds call-out fee alone, I've checked – and that only covers the first half-hour and they always spend that just drinking tea and shaming you.'

'Brian. Listen to me. *Call* someone – use my phone. Call them. I'll see to the bill – early Christmas present, yes?'

Howard held out his mobile while wishing to God Brian wouldn't look at him like that – it went right through you, when he got this mournful.

'Thanks, Howard – you're a true friend. I wouldn't, you understand, if it weren't for Dotty and Colin. Dawn, of course. I mean, if it were just myself. I'd quite happily solidify and die here – you do know that?'

Howard had a vision, then, of that sheaf of Brian's aborted suicide notes he had come across in the old house, one time. This, and the knowledge that just last summer Brian had elected to leap off a cliff made Howard think that maybe we fast change the subject, yes?

'And of course you know,' rushed on Howard, 'that you all would have been perfectly welcome to stay in the house while we're away? That would've temporarily solved the problem, anyway. I was going to offer, and then Elizabeth told me you're going off somewhere too. Good. Excellent. I'm pleased. Do you all a lot of good – getting out of this bloody caravan, for a while. Set you up for Elizabeth's famous festivities.'

Brian looked frankly terrified, now, which Howard didn't understand at all, so he carried on anyway. 'I mean don't think I'm, you know, in any way – uh – *criticizing*, or anything – but just *anywhere* you go for this break's just got to be better than *here*, hasn't it?'

What little colour Brian ever had now hurried away from him.

'That's what Dotty said,' he uttered, drily – and then without one more word set to tapping out the heating engineer's number on Howard's very tiny mobile.

'So where are you off to?' pursued Howard chattily – aware now, quite painfully, that the tips of his fingers were actually turning blue.

'Oh – I'll tell you when Dotty gets back. Haven't told her yet. I'd like you to be here when I do. Oh – hello? Hello? Yes – I've got a bit of a heating problem, and I wonder if you . . .? Well, rather difficult to describe the set-up, really – if you could just send someone? Yes. Yes. Oh good. Well I'll just give you the address.'

And Brian did just that, adding on: 'But not the house, no – we're in the caravan alongside. Yes. Perfectly serious.

179

Oh . . . oh . . . tomorrow afternoon's not really any help, I'm afraid . . . you see, we're going away in the morning and –'

Howard was mugging and miming It's OK Lulu Can Let Them In Just Leave Her The Keys and was mildly amazed when Brian merely shut tight his eyes and shook his head in a frenzy of denial and went on to practically plead with the engineer and finally and after a hell of a lot of talk about a freezing baby got him to agree to come round himself and in person in, well, let's see: what time is it now? Say, what – hour-and-a-half suit you?

Brian handed back to Howard his really very dinky phone.

'He says hour-and-a-half. Thanks so much, Howard.'

Howard nodded and waved away any of that.

'Let's wait in the house,' he said. 'Have a drink.' Oh yes please, he was thinking, or else one of my thumbs will turn indigo and fall to the floor (clunk!) while the other plumps for maybe imperial purple and shortly follows suit (clonk!). 'What's that thing, Brian?' he tacked on at the door, pointing to an extremely Brian-like contraption.

'Ah yes,' said Brian, pride of ownership just tinged with let-down, maybe. 'It is my latest acquisition. Metal-detector. Fortunes have been made, or so I am told.'

Once more Howard felt clouded by sadness.

'Uh-huh,' he said. 'Made one yet?'

Brian had the goodness to smirk self-deprecatingly.

'Alas,' he sighed. 'I've taken it out just the once, and I must say I was a little disappointed. I was making for the Thames – asked Colin along – thought he might be quite keen. Well, didn't really; anyway – he wasn't, not a bit – just gave me that look, can't really describe it. Poor Colin. Not his fault. Anyway – read somewhere or other that it's best on the banks of the Thames at low tide – well, *obviously* at low tide because otherwise you'd, well, you know – drown, or something – but I couldn't actually *find* the Thames, if I'm honest – it is quite twisting, and I think I was just at the bits of land where at that point it wasn't, if you get my drift. But I did find a sort of a sandbank thing that looked fairly promising, so I put on the headphones and everything and started sweeping. Hours I was there.'

Howard could barely bring himself to ask. 'And?' he prodded.

'Nothing,' Brian was forced to concede. And then he trained his poached-egg eyes quite fully on Howard. 'And that was the terribly odd thing – I mean *literally* nothing: no old bicycle wheels, biscuit tins – no prams or any of the usual junk. Not even a baked bean can. So I thought it might not be working . . .'

Oh dear oh dear oh dear, thought Howard. 'And?' he prodded.

'Well – got the whole shooting match back here and tried it out on my manhole covers – you know, the ones outside. Christ – the blast I got through those bloody earphones: nearly blew my bloody head off.'

Howard pulled on a sort of smile and laid his hand on Brian's shoulder.

'Let's wait in the house,' he said. 'Have a drink.'

❄

'Carol. Oh thank God. Thought I'd never get you.'

'Was it you who phoned earlier, Colin? I just couldn't get there quickly enough and Terry answered. Is that why you hung up?'

'Look – never mind *Terry*, for God's sake – is it all done? Have you, you know – oh *God*, Carol – I'm so looking forward to this, I just can't tell you.'

'I've got to be quick, Colin, cos Terry's still around so *listen*: have you got a pen?'

'Yes. Got loads. Always do with another, I suppose. Why are you talking about pens?'

'I mean can you write something *down* – times, and things.'

181

'Oh got you, right. OK – hang on, right. Pen. Pen pen pen pen. Christ I've got just loads of pens and I can't seem to –'

'Oh come *on*, Colin, for God's sake.'

'Pen – got it. OK – fire away. God I can't *wait*, Carol. Hang on – paper . . .'

'OK – the train's at 10.20, Victoria. We go to Hove, and there's a bus, apparently. Now I *think* it's Platform 3, but –'

'Hang on, hang on – bloody pen's not writing, shit. Platform what, did you say?'

'I only said it *might* be Platform 3, but you never really know until you get there. But you got the rest of it, did you?'

'Yup – absolutely. Ten-thirty –'

'*Twenty*. Christ, Colin.'

'Ten-twenty, check – God I just *love* trains. Did you ever see *From Russia With Love*? When they stopped off at Zagreb and –'

'I've got to go, Colin. See you in the morning. Be there by ten at the latest – kay? We'll meet at the ticket bit.'

'God I love you, Carol. I just love you. Can't wait. Ten tomorrow at the ticket bit. Was it Paddington?'

'Vic-*tor*-ia – oh *Jesus*, Colin.'

'Victoria Victoria – I meant Victoria. It was Victoria I had in my head, honestly Carol – it just came out as Paddington. I'll be there – don't worry. Can't wait. Love you.'

'Love you too. Got to go.'

'Love you love you *love* you.'

'Got to *go*, Colin. See you soon.'

'Can't wait. Love you. Love you, Carol. Carol? Hallo? Hallo? Oh. Right.'

Colin replaced the receiver in the phone box, and emerged into the biting cold quite literally dizzy with delight. He had sort of felt like this just once as a child, when he had closed his eyes and extended his arms and turned and turned, round and round until the red of the sun beyond his eyelids tilted up and shadowed and he fell to his knees in the grass, his fists clutching at dampish daisies while his head and eyes marvelled at such groggy distortions; a similar giddiness had swum into him when he was entwined around Elizabeth at the hotel last summer, his temples coping badly with the fallout of the latest two, three, four cold bottles of champagne – but what he felt now was so utterly different: what he felt now was *clean*.

❋

'What a simply ghastly time of year to have heating problems,' deplored Edna – not particularly for Cyril's benefit: they just happened to have coincided in the hall, and Edna felt she might as well put a name to exactly why her nose should be stuck deep into the folds of her rather splendid brocade and interlined curtains – this vantage point generally proving reliable if next door's comings and goings were the fascination of the moment.

Cyril was enjoying that thrill of release he always experienced whenever he closed the door on the last patient of the day (some woman who harboured a near-psychotic hatred of her mother it was, this time – but as the mother in question, so far as Cyril could understand it, lived quite blamelessly and two hundred miles away, he couldn't really see the problem; but twice weekly he went through the motions of listening, of course – well of course he did: got to earn a crust).

'Heating problems?' he murmured. 'Something wrong with the heating? Seems quite warm.'

'No, not *us*,' Edna was quick to reassure him. 'Next door – Elizabeth's. There's a van outside – and they're going away tomorrow.'

'Ah,' said Cyril. I really do think Edna should try to get out more, you know: not at all healthy, this sort of thing. 'What's that noise? Sounds like a pig being stuck.'

'I've sent her up to the very top floor with all the ironing, and *still* you can hear it,' came back Edna, with frank disgust. 'I tell you, Cyril – friend of Elizabeth or no, I've just

183

about had enough of Melody. I mean, the fact that she's no damn good is one thing, but when she brings that *baby* of hers – !'

'Oh – it's the baby, is it? Well what's wrong with it? Why is it crying all the time?'

'Well that's what *I* said,' rejoined Edna. 'I mean, God knows I don't know anything about babies, never having been *blessed* – '

'Yes all right,' Cyril interjected tersely. 'Don't go into all that again, for God's sake.'

'I wasn't going to. I'm simply saying that whether you're a mother or not, it just can't be right to have a baby that just never stops bawling, can it? I mean – it's not natural, is it?'

'Well what does Melody say?'

'Oh she just starts up with some ranting of her own. I mean I sort of see her point, yes I do – what I mean to say is if she *could* stop her, she would, I suppose. But I mean just *listen* to it – been like this all through the afternoon. No, my mind's made up – Melody has to go, and the baby with her. I'll phone the agency – get someone reliable.'

'It's nearly Christmas,' said Cyril, mildly.

Edna looked at him quite blankly. 'Yes?' she said.

'Can't go firing someone at Christmas, like that.'

Edna hardened her gaze. 'Wrong, Cyril: quite wrong. I can and I will.'

And then she swept away. I should behave like this more often, I think – show the world that I'm not just the little woman everyone I am damn sure believes me to be: no no no – inside and deep down I am a very big woman indeed, as maybe even Cyril will one day discover. Thank God Melody's time is practically up for the day; I'll let her go, yes I will – couldn't anyway make myself heard over that shrieking baby – and tomorrow I'll tell her, quite kindly, that her services are no longer required. Pay her for the week, of course – maybe even put in a bit extra (it is, as Cyril said, nearly Christmas – and yes it *does* affect me, of course

184

it does: I am *human*, you know). She can whistle for a reference, though.

Cyril passed through the breakfast room and into the kitchen, telling himself it was tea he wanted, though in truth it was the vision of an éclair that was luring him – and so he felt immediately crushed by the most prominent of the latest batch of bulletins littering Edna's board: 'Cyril – there are no éclairs'. Well bloody why *not*, was his first bitter thought – but he was partly and almost immediately mollified by another little note just tucked into the side: 'Cyril – there are doughnuts'. Oh well, they would serve the purpose – I am, I admit, quite partial to a doughnut, particularly if Edna has taken heed of what I said the last time and given the traditional sugary ones with the hole a very wide berth, and plumped instead for those globular and thoroughly sinful numbers, engorged with fluid crimson that always made a playful beeline straight for the chin.

He had barely extracted the sticky big thing from its paper bag when Cyril became aware of the distant and near subliminal mewling swelling now at first quite gently, but soon rising sharply in both pitch and volume until the terrifyingly inevitable moment when Melody barged right in to the kitchen and the full awful force of little Dawn's lungs and tonsils were unleashed upon a startled, deafened and now butter-fingered Cyril (oh fuck – that's the bloody doughnut on the floor, now – shit shit shit), and while Edna's tasteful wall arrangement of lobster and salmon-shaped copper moulds continued to shudder and tinkle, Melody launched into a barrage of farewell in the fully big-hearted and booming manner that was second nature to her now – and Cyril's attempt at a grin turned out as a grimace that was close to gurning as he batted the air and tried not to hold on to his head as if in a desperate effort to save it from shooting into orbit and didn't even remotely manage that at all and so now he was clutching it hard and with both hands and Melody was bawling out maybe apology and all Cyril could do was hold his stricken pose amid the uproar, sending various features of his face scurrying wherever they would in some faint hope that they might eventually pull themselves together and gang up to express just any form at all of Goodbye so that this roaring girl and her infant from Hades would actually please God leave the bloody house in peace and give the very mortar at least some chance of reasserting its tenure on the shimmering bricks, and maybe then the roof would cease its hover of arrested flight and finally when convinced that the coast was clear and the danger passed, settle back down if gingerly to hugging fast its gables.

It's all right for *them*, was Melody's morose and grudging way of thinking, as she trudged next door with the dead-weight of Dawn at least now firmly in her buggy (which had come ready fitted with a full and heartening array of buckles and straps, but alas no gag) – they don't have to live with it all of the time like I do. I just hope Dotty's back, that's all, because otherwise Elizabeth and Howard and everyone else there will start hating me too: it's just not fair – it's *Dawn* who makes the noise, so why is it me who has to take all the blame?

❋

Dotty had been really quite cool about it all, oh yes – just the way she always was, but she deep down knew it was reckless to use the very same shop as she had the last time, not much more than days ago. It was just that she had to be back in good time for Dawn – Melody was bringing her round and (oh – joy of joys) leaving her with Dotty for whole days and nights, and this to Dotty meant that whatever grim and grimy place on earth Brian was set on taking her, it really hardly mattered for she would be out of that caravan and with a blissful angel at her side. Maybe why she had put up no more than token resistance when Colin had quite casually though with singular purpose, it surely seemed to Dotty, announced just this morning that no matter how (ho ho) wonderful his father's holiday plans might or might not turn out to be, they most certainly could not, oh dear, be including him, you see, because he, Colin the Brave, was actually, um – well, if you want the whole truth of it I'm actually staying with a schoolfriend for a few days, yes, just fixed it up, as a sort of run-up to Christmas, I suppose you could call it – and actually I should think we'll get a whole pile of prep done because he's got this really cool new computer, OK, with all the latest software.

Well look, Dotty had reasoned, Colin was growing up, wasn't he? Plain to see. Had to start doing his *own* sort of thing, now – yes? And God knows he didn't want to be cooped up with his *father*, somewhere. Also, of course, although he's nearly sixteen now, he still requires, oh – *you* know, all the things males of whatever age always seem to: clean shirts, hot baths, endless food and someone to moan at – and if Dawn were there, all of this could only be a distraction (as to Brian – he could look after himself: and if not, not). So all Dotty had said was Well Colin, tell me a little bit about this boy – why have you never mentioned him before? (Didn't, of course, ask Why have you never brought him home, because you just wouldn't, would you? School was maybe tough enough for Colin already without word getting out that his home life was on a par with that of a suspect and dowdy outcast Romany.) His name, responded Colin, is, um, Cary – you know, like in Grant. And, he tacked on – quite as expected – he's very nice, promise.

So yes anyway, as she says – if Dotty hadn't been so hopelessly desperate to get back as soon as she could for baby Dawn, she most certainly would have followed the quite rigorously drawn up timetable and taken a bus to Kensington and done the necessary business in that rather comfortingly large and anonymous branch of the store, and not so stupidly broken all her own rules and used another shop again the very same week. Because there had been an atmosphere, this time – Dotty truly thought for the beat of one heart-clutching second that took just years to tick by and pass away that this time the game was up, chum – though all she could think was Oh no, oh no – please not this time: please don't pick me up and put me down and send me away because it's all for Dawn, you see, it's all for her, and she's waiting for me now and I can't let her down because she is only an innocent and nor must you deny me the pleasure of her, although I know that for me, sweet innocence is a thing I have sullied so often it is dark enough now to be taken for guilt.

My part-time job is of course – as everyone must have gathered but none, in a spirit of mercy, has ever once suggested (at least to me) – is not, let's be frank, at all much. I used to, long ago, be a personal secretary, you know, to a man quite high up in the publishing world – PA, I understand, they call them now. It had been Brian who persuaded me to give up the job (almost impossible, now, to remember a time when I actually listened to anything at all that fool had to say). Look, Dotty love, he had urged her – and still she can hear the evangelism, still can she see in his big and pale moon-face the spurious confidence there, as if he had just changed into his brand-new Fully-Fledged He-Man dressing up kit and had maybe invested too in some optional extras – accessory packs of not just Pint-Sized Arrogance but could be too A Beginner's Guide to Halfway Capable (all this, of course, years and years before the very business of breathing in and breathing out came so near to closing him down). Look, Dotty love, he had pressed her – why don't you pack in all this secretarying lark, hey? I mean – it's not as if we need the money, is it? I'm telling you, the business is just coining it in: Christ, sometimes I think I've carpeted the whole globe twelve times over and still they keep coming back for more. And Colin needs to see more of

188

you, course he does – and me, me too love: want you at home for me, don't I? So Brian got his drudge, and year by year so very much of Dotty's resolve and maybe even some healthy self-loving were steadily rinsed away – but in truth she did not mind it all that much because look – they did have a beautiful house with Elizabeth as a neighbour and Colin, of course – and then the ultimate joy of baby Maria (heaven, heaven – an angel from heaven) and never mind that Dotty's remaining spirit was just oozing now because the money, anyway – just as Brian had said it would – went on pouring in, and it lapped around her, warmly.

Maria went back to heaven. The money and house went to hell and Colin grew up and now away and all that was left to Dotty (save dreaming of Dawn) was this: she tidied up – made things nice – on the fifth storey of the flagship store of one of the best-known chains of all; she wasn't on the shop floor, no – more on the office side. And no – *not* a cleaner, oh no, this must be understood from the outset, please: no, all I do is put people's desks in order, give the phones a rub down, maybe, and tend to those big sad plants they all have. There's no Mrs Mopp about it at all – no buckets, God no – maybe a very little light Hoovering and that's all. And no of *course* I'm not happy doing it, and no it's *not* the job I applied for – would never even have dreamt of such a thing. It just became, oh – quite embarrassingly plain in the personnel department that awful afternoon that what with the very long time-lag since Dotty's last employment (during which, it was borne in upon her, the world had gone high-tech, supersonic and just about Martian) as well as your, um, how can we put this Mrs Morgan – *age*, this was just about all she was fit for (and, it was made clear, lucky to get it).

And it had been one evening last autumn – not too late, but later than usual due to some or other extraordinary meeting that six or seven of them had without notice and quickly convened, leaving behind them to Dotty's mind a similarly extraordinary mess of a room, given the brevity of the whole palaver – as well as just one or two wholly disingenuous and mumbled apologies vaguely in Dotty's direction. The men, wouldn't you know it, were far and away the worst: women, in meetings, Dotty had observed, seemed to sip at half their Perrier (you could see the lipstick) and then just leave. Men, on the other hand – oh, Dotty can barely describe it: it looked as if they had all been living rough there for the better part of a week – several cold and milky coffees apiece slopped into saucers, cigarette stubs just all over the place and some in ashtrays, pages of mindless and sometimes quite rude screwed-up doodles and blotter pads and chair cushions so deliberately and even violently askew as to suggest that given just a bit more time and a plentiful armoury, then the favourite option by far would have been drawing and quartering the things, prior to maybe plugging them full o' lead.

So Dotty had cleared away all that (at least it's overtime – eight more quid, oh God, oh Jesus) but the last of the rubbish collections was long gone, now, and she couldn't just leave it all in the corridor so that everyone would collide with it in the morning, as maybe some people might well have done – Dotty could not have told you – so she took the service lift down to the sub-basement (bit spooky – not too many lights: Hellooo? she went – Hellooo? But it seemed like no one was around) and there amongst great bales of crumpled paper and boxes and all manner of debris awaiting maybe incineration Dotty came across not one but look – here's another one: two receipts from that day's trading – and then, not really understanding why, and with plenty of furtive glances towards the lifts – she actively sought out more. She quickly amassed close on a dozen, and not quite knowing what it was she had here (but feeling it just must be *something*) she crammed them into her handbag and let herself out of the building in quite the usual way – Bert on Security saying Night Love, as he did, and Dotty coming back with Night Bert – this trust-and-love-me aria sent up from a bursting ribcage and then expelled with a big and wide-eyed gusto from a mouth chock-full of unmeltable butter.

And here, Dotty saw later, was a vivid example of all this new technology you kept on hearing about. To her mind, a receipt was a receipt was a receipt – never really studied one before. But not only did this clutch before her all bear today's date – yes, OK, you expect that – and the amount so recently rendered (the whole point of the thing, as Dotty well recognized) but also itemized were not just whatever department we were talking about but a potted description of the actual article itself, right down to the colour or fabric, in some cases. Just as some people keep or even file such things for years and years, Dotty could only suppose that other more impetuous and what-the-hell types just left them to flutter wherever they would – this time, unwittingly, right into Dotty's increasingly nerve-racking life – and, more specifically, hard and tight between her hot and guilty thumbs and fingers. And the scheme was hatched even before she had time to feel appalled at being capable of hosting so brief and covert an incubation. Maybe, then, she thought, this is the way – and yes yes I know, I know – of course I know it *can't* be the way but maybe, just maybe, in my case it is?

❈

'Dotty! It's Dotty!' screamed out Elizabeth, as maybe would a trusted courtier finally unleashing his King Is Dead Long Live The King routine – but possibly with more outright and heartfelt gratitude than any mere form of ceremony. 'Melody – Godsake: give her to Dotty! Do it! Oh you are – oh you have, oh thank God, thank God: I thought I'd lose my mind! What on earth have you been *doing*, Dotty? We were waiting and waiting – !'

This last passionate enquiry came out far too raucously

191

and grated on everyone – though maybe none more than Elizabeth herself – because suddenly, quite suddenly (it was simply eerie, uncanny, how immediate it was) – just as Dotty took Dawn so gently in her arms, this wet-faced purple child's unnerving and pitiless ranting utterly ceased, as surely as if a switch had been pulled – and already: Ahhhh! Just look at her! Pink and gurgling again, little teddy bear black button eyes glistening like stars up and right into Dotty who was now quite somewhere else – entranced and in love, miles and worlds away from whatever it was on earth she'd been doing – which in fact, Elizabeth, is this: what I have been doing – and what would you think, what could you say if only you knew – is . . . oh Dawn, sweet Dawn, you are so precious to me, my darling Maria . . . what it is I have been doing, Elizabeth, is stealing, stealing. Again, yes again. With Dawn now, you see, it is the only way forward. But it shreds me – oh yes it shreds me, the fear of it – and never more than this time, today: it is only when I look down at Dawn, though, that I feel so sure that all the risk is worth the taking.

Just under two hours ago, I went to the women's fashion department in the very nearest store (and no, Elizabeth – I don't suppose you ever use it for clothes: lighting, maybe – or possibly that set of twelve, was it, Le Creuset saucepans you showed me, all gleaming volcanically and ready for the custom-built unit in your brand-new kitchen, which will be unveiled to us all, I suppose, just any day now). And I took from a carousel a dark green cashmere and lambswool sort of sweater dress, I think you might call it, in a size sixteen, and then a dusty pink angora dressing gown in a twelve and a very smart Jaeger two-piece, black and white houndstooth (my size too – might have been tempted to have it for myself, but there's so much I need to do, now, for Dawn). The difficult part in all this is to as surreptitiously as possible – and as I say, it's not at all easy – slide them into the large and brand-new plastic carrier that I have to make sure is always with me. I then browsed. I resented the time it took – I knew I had to be back soon for Dawn, you didn't have to *remind* me, Elizabeth – but this part is truly essential: you have to make sure, as sure as you ever can do – they can be terribly sneaky, these floorwalkers, you know – that no one is eyeing you oddly. And I'm quite good at acting, now – I've really surprised myself: I angle some dress up and away from the rack, while leaving it hanging, and I then put on all of the expressions – is this my colour, I wonder? Would it do for the party? It's not too . . . is it? Let's have a look at the price – ooh no, don't really think so: what about *this* one . . .? After a suitable interval, I then empty my haul before one of the bored and tetchy salesgirls (and you can almost see them mouthing their displeasure: oh no, *returns* – that means bloody forms to fill) and then from my bag I produce the precisely corresponding receipts and I smile and I explain that they were presents for friends, you see, and not *one* of them is right, isn't it awful? – and it's so hard, isn't it, choosing for other people – *so* hard to please – so I think I'll just settle for a refund, if that's at all possible: just give them the money and let them choose for themselves. Yes. I paid cash, yes (which is something, by the way, you have to watch quite closely: I go down to the sub-basement most evenings, now, but all of the Switch and Visa and Mastercard dockets are a total write-off, terribly wasteful – only payments by cash and cheques are any good at all, so I really do have my work cut out for me, as well you are beginning to understand).

And then I saw my big mistake: it was the very same salesgirl as last time – and was there a flicker? Across her face? Was there? Or was it just this uncut fear, rising within me? Was she thinking Here, hang on – isn't this the woman who came in Tuesday and changed a, what was it – kingfisher ball-gown, think it was (and it was, it was – alive with sequins)? There was a frisson, now, as the girl went through the motions of checking over the stuff for damage. And then she looked full at Dotty and said with maybe challenge in her voice *Cash*, you said, and Dotty said Yes I did say cash, yes, and then truly thought for the beat of one heart-clutching second that took just years to tick by and pass away that this time the game was up, chum – and while she was thinking Oh no, oh no – please not this time (should have taken the bus to Kensington) the girl started in on the first of the returns slips and then the others and summoned someone quite stern with a ballpoint on a chain to authorize all that (if she could, would she?) and then the money and Dawn's holiday were both safe with Dotty and she left the salesgirl maybe thinking Oh fuck these returns – got to hang the bleeding things up again, now.

Anyway, it will all have to be gone through just once more this year (Christmas shopping – absolutely vital: can't have Elizabeth thinking of me, oh – even more terrible things than she must already; I just have to, somehow, keep my end up). Dawn, Dawn – oh my sweet Dawn – you will never know how good it is for me to be calm and back here, safe and warm and holding you.

'I've brought all her, you know – gear,' said Melody, feeling, oh God – just *tell* her how much better she's already feeling: whole days and nights without Dawn! Still too, of course, without that shit Miles, God damn him, but look – it's just no bloody good me thinking and thinking of him, is it? The bastard. Love him. Miss him.

Dotty nodded as she eyed the little heap of not quite clean Babygros, the plastic bib with Peter Rabbit's ears practically rubbed away and an assortment of half-used jars and packets thrown just anyhow amid a muddle of scuffed and not-nice toys. You really needn't have bothered, Melody, she was enjoying thinking: I have bought just everything for Dawn – all in shades of delicate rose and of the very highest quality, because that's what she is, and that's what she deserves. And then Dotty for the first time looked up and registered the presence of not just Howard –

well, no great surprise: his house, after all – but Brian, too: her husband. Yes indeed – my husband, my husband, oh God, oh God.

'I thought you'd be packing,' she said to him, flatly. And then to Elizabeth: 'I was all set to pack first thing this morning, but Brian for some reason just wouldn't let me. I rather *assumed*,' she went on, building into it a hefty dose of sardonic, 'that that meant that he would do it instead, but apparently not. Or have you already, Brian?'

Did Brian look startled? Or were his eyes just always like that now?

'I, er . . . haven't actually done *all* of it, no Dotty.'

'Have you contracted alopecia, Brian, since this morning?' came back Dotty, the tenderness in her arms as she cradled baby Dawn very much at war with the rigour of her face as her mouth moved only as much as was strictly necessary in order to enunciate these tight and spiky words of hers. 'Or has a sheep been grazing on your skull?'

Melody let out a fairly fat guffaw that well matched her smirking – she had noticed Brian's head (well how could you not?) and it wasn't that she didn't like to *say* anything so much as she hadn't yet got around to letting rip with it.

'Gave it a bit of a trim,' said Brian, quietly.

Howard thought he might just as well step in. 'Have a drink, Dotty? Yes? G & T?'

But Dotty was talking to Elizabeth: 'He cuts his own hair. As you can see. He clearly sees this as a wise thing to do. I will just have a very quick drink actually, thank you, Howard, and after that I've got to see what sort of a mess Brian has left for me, and then I'll settle down Dawn for the night. Because I think she's a very sleepy ickle baby girly – aren't oo, Dawn? Hm? Yes I think so – I think you are, I think you are, I think you *are* – intoo, lickle Dawn?'

'Someone in there seeing to the heating at the moment, Dotty,' said Howard, quite casually, pressing into her hand

195

a generous highball of gin and tinkling ice, the tonic still hissing. 'Like a fridge – but he says he can sort it out.'

'What – the heating's packed up?'

To which Brian could only nod.

'*Again*? Well at least you've had the sense to get in a professional, this time – amazing in itself. Last time Brian – don't laugh – *fixed* it, I spent the next morning thawing out the taps with a bloody candle.'

'So tell us,' said Elizabeth brightly. 'Why don't you tell us all, Brian, about this mysterious holiday of yours? Where are you going? Will it be fabulous? I mean – fair's fair: you know where *we're* going, so why won't you tell us?' And then, to Brian's considerable relief, she tacked on to Dotty: 'Is Colin terribly looking forward? Bet he is.'

'Oh didn't I tell you?' rushed in Dotty. 'Not coming. Quite the little man – off to stay with a schoolfriend, apparently. I must say I'm quite pleased, really – I was beginning to wonder if he would *ever* make a friend at this beastly new school – no it *is*, Elizabeth, it *is*, it's just got to be said. When I think of that lovely St Alfred's we took him away from – he was so happy there, loved it. That's before his father decided he ought to suffer something else.'

Howard glanced at Brian – caught the flinch in his face, as if all the bones there sought to cower within more deeply. I suppose she never ever gives him any sort of a break, these days; no, the time for breaks, I imagine, has surely and long ago passed.

'Well they *do* that,' said Elizabeth, choosing to ignore that last and rather nasty bit. 'I mean look at Katie – Chicago last summer: didn't want to be anywhere near her boring old mother. We *did* ask her to Paris, didn't we, Howard? Not for a minute thinking she'd actually *come*, of course, and naturally she said no. They can be quite devious, you know, young people today. I said to her Oh I see, Katie – a lovely hotel in Paris not good enough for you, is that it? And she comes back with Oh Mum, it's not that – it's just there's

Christmas *shopping* to be done – and then she said (I nearly died): there's the *house* to see to! Can you believe it? *Katie* – seeing to the house? And so I told her *Katie* – you have never in your life –'

'Howard,' put in Melody, 'any chance of another, um . . .?'

'Surely, surely,' agreed Howard. 'Give me your glass and I'll just . . .'

'So *Katie*, I said,' went on Elizabeth. 'Never, not once, have you so much as lifted one finger in this house as well you know and anyway as you *also* know I've got Lulu staying for just that very reason. Maybe it's just that you cannot bear the thought of your mother and father's company?'

'Thanks, Howard,' said Melody, who then drank half of it.

Elizabeth expressed her displeasure at this second interruption only by smiling tightly. 'Oh it's not that *either*, Mum, says Her Royal Highness Princess Katie. You'll both have a better *time* without me. Of course it turns out after just about *forever* that this man, this American person she met in the summer is coming over early, apparently, and so of *course* he comes first, oh naturally – a complete stranger would just *have* to, wouldn't he? And she's not yet eigh*teen*.'

The doorbell rang, then, and Elizabeth – still filled with a righteous indignation – strode away in the direction, sighing out to no one that she didn't know who on earth this could be, unless it was Lulu, but I'm sure she said it was first thing in the morning she was coming.

'Yes?' she said to the rather red-faced and somehow slightly absurd young fellow who stood there. 'Oh you must be . . . oh come in, it's freezing with the door open.'

'Mister Walmeley,' said the man. 'Heating.'

'Ah *yes*,' Elizabeth comprehended (she had been right when she concluded that he must be . . .). 'I'll just get, um, Brian. Is it all right? Mended?' And then she left the man standing there and crossed the hall calling Brian? Brian? while thinking that it was really too too perfectly enchanting that this heating person should actually be called Warmly, of all things – aren't they just bliss, things like that?

Both Brian and Howard came out to meet him.

'Thanks so much for coming out at short notice,' said Howard, expansively, while Brian hung slightly behind, thinking to himself You know, it's hard to believe I know, but I used to be a man like that, one time – one like Howard who could say quite big grown-up things and accompany them with the sweep of an arm. He clutched more tightly the hard twenty-pound notes that Howard had very subtly and without a single word slipped into his hand – so at least I can, you know – *pay* the man, even if it's really Howard.

'I tell you,' said Mr Walmeley, wagging his head like there could indeed be no tomorrow. 'I'm not making no guarantees. It's out of the Ark, that set-up, I'm telling you. Whole thing wants getting rid of and replacing. Anyway – what it's worth, got it going – chugging quite nicely – but like I say, God knows how long.'

Brian nodded and stared at the bill: sixty-five pounds, God Almighty: he'd been there, what? Hour? Not even, I shouldn't say. Why can't *I* earn sixty-five quid in an hour? Christ Jesus – I can't seem to raise close to that much over a whole bloody week. But he's right about the heating system – it's shot, Brian knows that. And so's the toilet. Don't too much like the look of the underseal, either; the suspension seems soft and loose and there's as much rust round the doorsills as you like – although that little tin of Hammerite went a fair way in making good, I'm not denying. The whole bloody caravan's a nightmare, let's face it – but what it is is home.

Back in the room, Elizabeth was right in the middle of saying: 'So *anyway* – I implored Mister Nelligan to stay on as late as possible tonight so that at least the garden end of the kitchen will be anyway sort of more or less finished – I must say despite all the mess and the noise and everything it is beginning to look terribly *nice*, I'm really quite excited –

but I'm determined that neither of you sees it till it's utterly, utterly perfect for Christmas, yes?'

Both Dotty and Melody nodded: independently and together, they could live with that stricture.

'And oh God it had *better* be,' rattled on Elizabeth, 'or else I just don't know *what* I'll do – feel dreadfully guilty about leaving it all to Lulu because she's got three more women to sort out this week as well – but she promises me faithfully she'll keep old Nelligan at it and God, I do so *need* the break – you know? I bet you do too, Dotty. But poor Melody's not going *anywhere* . . .'

'Oh God don't worry about *me*,' laughed Melody – and here was no face-saving bravado – she meant it, she really did. 'I can *sleep* – you just don't know what it means – I can actually *sleep* at night and watch TV and *read* and oh Christ all the things I can never do with Dawn around.'

And instinctively, all three of them looked at the baby, so contented and adorable – it seemed quite incredible that all you had to do was be so rash as to simply remove old Dotty from the scene, and the next second Dawn would be giving Damien of *Omen* fame a bloody good run for his money.

'Ah Howard,' said Elizabeth now, as he meandered back in to the room (making a beeline for the Bell's) trailing behind him an ever more disconsolate Brian. 'Are *you* looking forward to your little holiday, darling? I was just saying, I simply can't wait – I really do *need* the break. Is the heating OK now, Brian? Yes? Oh did I tell you? The funniest thing – that little man's name was *Warmly* – isn't that fun?'

And Howard was thinking A break from *what*, Elizabeth? What exactly is it that you do? I've often wondered.

'Yes,' said Brian. 'Everything's simply tip-top now.' These words were delivered in the ponderous tone of a resounding oration over a deep and open grave.

'Good,' approved Dotty. 'Then we'll be off. God, Brian – it's *late* now, and there's still the packing and you *know*

I've got Dawn. What time are we actually leaving in the morning? Not *too* early, I hope.'

'Are you flying, Brian?' asked Elizabeth. 'Oh Brian stop being so secretive and *tell* us, God's sake. I'm sure *Dotty* wants to know – I know *I* do. Only if you're going to Heathrow or somewhere we've got this really good car firm we use – truly reliable.'

'Oh I don't think we're going *abroad*,' doubted Dotty. Of course we're not bloody going *abroad* – and I almost wish Elizabeth would just stop asking and asking because yes of course in one very real sense I want to know where in Christ's name this bloody thing is to be, but in so many others, I really just don't.

'No no,' said Brian, softly. 'Not abroad.'

'Well *where*, Brian?' pursued Elizabeth.

'Tell me what time it is we're leaving, Brian,' insisted Dotty – partly, maybe, to sidetrack Elizabeth.

'Well,' said Brian slowly, thinking Well this is it: had to come eventually, didn't it? Yes it did and here it is and this is it. 'Any time you like, really.'

And after just one moment of silence, as most people began simultaneously to voice their thoughts on this one, Dotty was straight away all bustle and very anxious to be away. She threw all of Melody's awfulness into a carrier bag and made for the hall, her precious cargo now sucking at a finger and practically asleep.

'Come on, Brian,' she called – and who heard the urgency, now, in her tone? 'We're going. Things to do.'

'All sounds bloody odd to me,' grunted Melody – not, in truth, at all caring either way: just so long as nothing was *cancelled*.

'Well if you *really* won't tell us, Brian,' laughed Elizabeth, 'all I can say to you both is have a really *lovely* time and we'll see you very soon when we all get back. Oh and Dotty – don't be worried about the caravan, or anything, because

Peter and Lulu have sworn to me they'll keep an eye on it – but best leave your keys to be on the safe side, yes?'

And just before Dotty in the hall could be out of that door and into the night, Brian set up his mournful intonation, just as suddenly she had feared and then known he would do:

'No – see, the thing is, you won't have to actually keep an eye on it, because it won't, in fact, be here. The truth is we're, um, taking it with us. Why I had to get the heating working, you see. Yes. Anyway – saves packing, doesn't it?'

Dotty stared at the panels on the door.

'I'm hiring a car in the morning,' went on Brian, 'and then we'll just – you know, hitch up and be off.' And he added on in a hardboard voice steep-dipped in the varnish of misery: 'Quite an adventure, really.'

❉

And later, much later that night, as Brian lay stiff and still in his bunk, unable to sleep (Christ knows what that heating bloke has done with the thermostat – like a bloody oven in here), he was muttering softly: Well, on balance, I don't think I really handled all that too well. But be fair on yourself – how else could you have done it, man? Well – maybe I should've told Dotty about it first? Think so? I don't know about that – you know what she's like. Mm. Anyway – done now. Try to get some sleep, ay? Big day tomorrow. I can't sleep: *you* sleep. Well I'm certainly going to give it a try. Well OK – you sleep, and I'll just lie here thinking for the two of us, all right? If that's the way you want it, old son – but I'm telling you, you're going to feel like hell in the morning – don't say I didn't warn you. No – honestly, I'll be fine: really. Sure? Yeah yeah – truly, thanks. It's good that you care. *Course* I care, course I do – we're in this together, aren't we? You're right, you're right – it's true that we are; and do you know? I really wouldn't have it any other way. That's a kind thought – kind of you. Anyway look – it's really late: I'm turning in. OK, then. We'll talk again in the morning: goodnight.

Goodnight.

Oh – and, um: happy holiday!

Thanks. You too. Night.

Night.

202

PART THREE

Bitter Out

CHAPTER NINE

'I think I must have got it wrong about Hove,' said Carol – Colin just about bursting with pleasure on the concourse at Victoria, drinking down the sweet sight of her, eyeing up the flickering Departures board. 'Best go to Brighton and get a bus from there, think. We've got about twenty minutes – what shall we do?'

You mean short of tearing off our clothes and lying down and entwining in front of Smiths and banging like pistons and then sluicing a litre and a half of Evian down and between our sweating bodies clammily impacted and beating as thing, one – and then doing the whole dreamy all of it over again, and maybe not just one more time? Short of that I'm pretty stumped for an answer, Carol, quite honestly, because as per usual I got here simply hours and hours early and I have at least twice investigated and appraised every single point of not just interest but spectacular tedium too that Victoria has to offer – and that even includes the Brent Cross type effort they've built upstairs, not just the Tie Rack and the chocolate doughnut stand and also that funny little shop in the corner, there, which seems to sell nothing but Kleenex tissues and stunted umbrellas, for some strange reason or another.

'We'll have a coffee,' Carol decided. 'Want a coffee?'

'Not really. Had five already – and expressos too.'

'So you like them now, do you? And it's *espresso*, Colin.'

'Swat I said. Look – tell you what, let's just buy a sandwich or something for the train, and maybe get a paper. What paper do you like? Gosh – there's so much I don't

205

know about you, Carol – but I will, won't I? Know everything.'

'Don't be embarrassing, Colin. We're in a *railway* station. I don't actually read any newspapers – there's always the box, if you want to know what's going on. Do you read papers?'

Colin shook his head. 'No,' he said. And we don't so much have a box as live in one, see, so that avenue too is well closed down; but I think ignorance of everything save Carol is increasingly suiting me. 'I don't actually read much of anything any more. Used to. But now I don't. The trouble with these huge baguettes – Christ, look at the size of that one – is that you break your jaw getting your face around the thing and they never actually come apart when you bite them and you end up having a tug of war with yourself and all the tomato bits go sliding out everywhere.'

Carol laughed as she paid for the two baguettes. 'Why do you see everything as a *problem*, Colin?'

Colin was panicked. 'Oh God – I don't, do I?'

Carol was nodding vigorously, although her eyes, anyway, were still busy enjoying the laugh. 'You do – you do. You should be more like my Dad – he sees everything as a challenge, or else as a joke. He's actually pretty cool, my Dad.'

Yes, thought Colin, he is; I remember thinking just that very thing on his boat, that time, a few moments before I threw up over your brother and fell down amid slime and prepared for death.

'So long as I'm not like *my* Dad . . .' he grumbled. 'I'm not, am I? Oh God *please* say I'm not like him! Is this the train? Are you sure? What a piddly little train to be going to Brighton in. Looks more like a Tube.'

'I haven't *met* your Dad, have I Colin? All I did was watch him drop off that cliff – 'member? He does seem pretty odd.'

They were picking their way through the aisles of truly

dazzling and migraine-inducing blue and stiffly fuzzy seats, Colin carrying both their cases and feeling fully twice the man as he did so.

'This'll do,' pronounced Carol, settling herself into one of a pair of seats with two upturned styrofoam beakers, a caved-in McEwan's can and just the one crumpled-up crisp packet forming a tableau on the grudging ledge between them – the sort of installation that would get you a grant: less junk than elsewhere, though. 'Can you clear away all this stuff, Colin? It's so yuck – I just can't stand yuck and mess. Hate it.'

Colin lobbed the holdalls up into the rack and scooped away all the yuck and mess (vile and sticky from other people) and vaguely and in vain glanced around for some sort of bin or something and soon settled for shoving it all under the seats across the way.

'Trains weren't always like this, apparently,' said Carol now – as Colin flopped opposite her, his guts in lusty torment or pent-up bliss at being on this train, any train, with Carol – off to a secret place for days and nights! 'When I said to Dad I was making this trip – '

'How did he . . .?' put in Colin. 'What did you tell him?'

'Hm? Oh – I said that Auntie Jane had said she'd give me a hundred pounds if I'd clean the flat from top to bottom and redecorate the bedroom and listen Daddy *darling* I'm really keen to do it cos I need the money for Christmas.'

'And he said?'

Carol sighed. 'He said he was proud of me – showing such enterprise and that Terry at my age would never have dreamed of such a thing. Felt a bit of a shit about it, actually. Still. Anyway – the point is he was telling me that there used to be what everyone thought was a really fabulous train to Brighton called the Brighton Belle and it left every morning at eleven and there was this dining car, right, but there was never any dining in it cos the journey's so short, OK? But there were proper tablecloths and silver and china and things and what you did, right, was wait a million years for the dressed-up waiter to take your order for coffee, and when it eventually came it was always so scalding hot that no one could actually drink it, and my Dad said that it was always pretty worrying at this point because you thought Oh Jesus – we get there in five minutes and it'll never be cool enough in five minutes but just then the train always started swaying back and forth at really high speed for those days, and all the coffee slopped into the saucers and over these brilliant tablecloths and so no one ever got to drink them anyway – but it was this point of absolute honour and sort of tradition that each and every single time, this is what you *did*! And it cost a fortune, too. My Dad's just hilarious about things like that.'

There was the boom of buffers, then, and the train – suddenly damn near packed out – lurched once and began to draw away from the platform. Colin and Carol exchanged their unstoppable grins.

'Love you, Carol.'

'Love you too.'

'Love you so much.'

'Don't go on.'

Carol set about the clingfilm on her baguette, while Colin settled back and gave in to this big and fleshy grin of his that now tugged so hard as to threaten the splitting of cheeks and bone. I have got away from Mum and Dad and the caravan: I have left them all behind me. I am on a train. I am on a train with Carol, as it scythes its way through the icy grey beyond these filthy windows. God oh God – I *am*, you know: off to a secret place for days and nights!

❄

Brighton, to Colin, surely felt a helluva lot colder than London (don't you think so, Carol?) – more exposed, he maybe thought it must be. Certainly *he* felt exposed as the two of them trudged down the hill from the station and towards a blank and distant wall of looming slate, which now turned out to be the vast and dispiriting sludge of sea. He hoped that Auntie Jane's flat was nice and cosy, because quite apart from not being able to face a gelid rerun of the lowlights of caravan living, it was for Colin not at all a question of merely wrapping up warm or *layering*, or anything, because he was already wearing practically everything he had – the non-anorak, but of course, zipped tight over various horrible woollen and scratchy things, no cuff or hem coming close to doing the decent thing and covering up his bony wrists and ankles, all of which felt utterly whipped.

There are buses right here, Carol, he had said at the station. I know that, yeah, Carol had acknowledged, but last time I did this Auntie Jane told me that if you got on one of those you had to change, or it didn't stop – or went only halfway, or something, and it's best to get one of the cream and green ones down at the depot. And God, the waiting under glass in a corridor of bitter gusts had practically done it for Colin – whichever way he turned or hunched, he felt nearly knifed by it. It's only *fresh*, Carol had said: this isn't *fresh*, Carol, Colin had retorted – this, believe me, is bloody *raw*. You see, she came back – you're doing it again: anything at all you see as a *problem*. Not a *problem*, Colin had said more quietly – I'm not saying it's a *problem*: it's just cold – that's all. All I'm saying. It's cold – OK? Carol had looked at him and then she said Here's the bus now – come on if you're coming.

A mile or so on, Carol told the conductor that they wanted that little place – do you know it? – just a short way beyond Hove, yes? And he had really full-bloodedly enjoyed coming back with Ho no you don't, miss – not on this bus you don't, leastwise, cos I'm going to Rottingdean, aren't I, and that's what we in the trade call the opposite bloody direction, innit? So they had got off a bit shy of Rottingdean and hung about for longer than either of them cared to and then had got on another bus that was only going as far as Brighton (sorry, love) but they couldn't, simply couldn't, just stand there any longer and so all in all it cannot have been much short of an hour when they found themselves back at the depot surrounded by a further sea of cream and green buses, all of which now Colin deeply distrusted.

'Look, Carol – I know what'll cheer us up: why don't we buy a bottle of champagne? Yes? Celebrate at the flat with a nice bottle of champagne. Our secret holiday.'

'Hm,' approved Carol. 'I do actually rather like champagne, as it happens, Colin. My Dad lets me have some, sometimes.'

'There was a shop – we passed it on the way down the hill. Then we come back for the bus.'

But it wasn't just that now Colin came to *see* this as a problem, as Carol might well have suggested – because to Colin's mind there could be no doubt about it: this was a problem, plain as day – in fact, oh shit, it was two. One – he would never, he knew, have the faintest hope of passing himself off as old enough to do this deed (no way in hell – which pissed him off, quite frankly, because among the many things that Colin yearned for, being older was among those jostling for pole position). And Two: have you ever actually seen how much they *charge* for this stuff? Colin was goggling now at the prices in the window – he had had no idea. His taste for champagne had been sown, fostered, nurtured and then brought to full and heady bloom by Elizabeth – and with Elizabeth you just never even thought of the business of *paying* (and nor, to be fair, did she: this was, after all, what Howard was for). But Carol – God she's great, this girl – said Oh don't worry about any of that stuff, Colin: you don't have to get *real* champagne – there's some really good Cavas you can get now for about a fiver, and Colin had been terribly relieved to hear it and said Oh great well let's get some carvers, then, and Carol nodded briefly and went into the shop and came out with not one but two cold bottles of bubbles and said Yeah, I never have a problem – buy stuff for my Dad all the time; which reminds me – I haven't yet got him anything for Christmas – and Colin said Well let me give you the money for those, Carol, and Carol said It doesn't matter and Colin said Well it matters to *me* and Carol said Look, Colin, I've got them now, OK, so just leave it. And Colin said Well at least let's go halves, shall we, and Carol said Oh Christ sake shut *up*, will you Colin and let's just try and find this bloody bus.

When they got back to the depot, there was only the one bus there – empty save for the driver (and, thank God, this time it was the type where you pay your fare as you board the thing, so at least you know well in advance whether or not you are once again on the verge of making a right bloody fool of yourself) – and it even bore all the appearances of being the very one that was needed: all rather suspicious, don't you think? But this did indeed prove to be the case ('Just the ticket', Colin had quipped – and Carol, who was busy buying a couple of these at the time, threw over her shoulder Sorry Colin – Say again? And Colin had mumbled Nothing, I just said – doesn't matter). By the time the bus sputtered into life and swung away from the shelter, there was only one other passenger, sitting bolt upright in the very front seat – a pale and even faintly luminous thin, tall man who could have been, God, any age at all, really (couldn't even get close), who looked so adrift in pain as to be gripped by fear and he sighed out as drizzle made pinpoints on the windows. 'I'm coming home,' he said out loud – 'soon, soon, I shall be there.' And then, just a short while later, 'But will *you*? Will *you*? Will *you*?'

Colin lost no time in mugging gleefully to Carol and jabbing his thumb in the direction. 'Christ, what a nutter – hope he's not a neighbour.'

'I think it's very sad,' said Carol, quite seriously. 'When

211

people get like that. They must feel so terribly alone. It's *sad*, Colin – I don't see anything to laugh at.'

'My Dad talks to himself,' came back Colin – just a touch moodily and thinking You know, I just kind of wish she'd stop getting at me all the time: why is it that everything I say is wrong? 'All the time. *Argues* with himself, sometimes. And simply *everyone* laughs at him.'

'You really don't like your Dad, do you? God – look at all that sea! It looks so *cold* – amazing that just a few months ago people were on the beach and swimming and laughing and things. And look at that shop! Do you see, Colin? The rock shop – all lit up like that, and the others just boarded up. Fairy lights are pretty, though – I love Christmas lights. Who buys rock in the rain?'

'Same people who buy ice-cream when it's snowing, I suppose,' considered Colin. And then, in precisely the same tone, 'No. I don't. There's nothing in him to like. Mum doesn't either.'

The distance, thought Colin, can't be very much, but this old bus seemed to be taking for ever; on the inclines it barely felt like it was moving at all – almost as if it was being sucked all the way back to the depot by some unalterable gravitational pull, or maybe just a yearning to be back with its mates. But eventually, Brighton became a thing of the past, and then there was a stretch of nothing much at all, to Colin's mind (but the view, qualified Carol, must be great in summer – and Colin had responded Yeah, you're right: let's come back here next summer, shall we? Yeh? Carol? Why don't we? . . . and then he left it). Hove soon passed by too, but it was only the indecipherable and quite guttural call and then gesticulation from the driver that alerted either of them to this, and suddenly all was grabbing action and balance-keeping while a rapid roll-call of holdalls and clinking bottles was conducted (if we don't get off quickly we'll end up right back in that bloody depot, I'm telling you) and Colin was off the bus now and standing on wet and puffed-up quite squeaky grass and one arm was outstretched towards Carol who took it and gave a brief and sympathetic smile to the man in the front seat whose eyes became even more imploring as he said to her gravely You know, I don't now think she'll be there when I come – and that means that I'll be not just alone, but astray.

They took the right fork (Carol telling Colin that Auntie Jane had said to her that if you take the *left* fork, right, you end up falling off a cliff – bit like your Dad) and although the rain was maybe not quite lashing, it was surely more than spits and spots, Colin's smarmy hair alone bearing drippy testimony to that. And now they were at the outskirts of what could easily be a, yes, quite pretty village – except that it was grey and vilely wet and therefore hateful – and Carol said Here, here, this is it and Colin had said Really? Really? This is it? and they went into the narrow and dark floor-boarded hall of what you somehow just knew to be really rather a large house and Carol said We're right on the top floor and Colin mock groaned and sagged at the knees the better to suggest to her that now their luggage comprised solely the lead flashing and gargoyles from atop at least the transept and nave of one of our better-known cathedrals. In truth, the idea of the flat being at the very top of the house just utterly thrilled him – and at once and once again he was flooded by the awesomeness of simply being here with his Carol in this secret place for days and nights and he husked out Oh Carol I Need You and he made a rush at the stairs and called back after him Come On Come On Come On Let's Get There and Carol laughed he hoped quite delightedly, and certainly put a good deal more into it when Colin in his lusty haste slipped badly at the landing and cracked his shin quite forcibly on the coming riser and now he was calling out Oh Shit Oh Bugger Oh Christ I'm Hurting and Carol had passed him now and looked down at him pretty suggestively from this sexy eminence of hers and actually now raised an eyebrow which was a thing Colin always yearned to do and had tried to often but it just came out as a loony's squint and now as she said Well? Well? You coming or not? all thoughts of pain ran right away from him as his thoughts clankingly switched gear (and to hell with the clutch) into gorging on the other thing and the only regret now in life was that Carol was wearing jeans and Doc Martens and not that tiny little black skirt she had on just once last summer – and maybe too a pair of anything strappy and heely because then he could have gazed up her legs to the point where heaven was closed down to him by the horizontal and abruptly no-no hem but still and for all that his blood was boiling and Yes, he called out, Yes You Bet – Coming, Coming: I Am Coming For You.

Don't ask Colin what the décor was like; once the door of the flat was shut behind him, he surrendered to his senses – and they all were telling him that there, over there, that door there I just know it is the bedroom, my blood can smell it – and he dropped the bags and made for Carol and hauled her by the hand and was not having her drawing back, and nor was he hearing her protests while tinglingly aware of the effect of them and so he tugged at her harder and hurled open the door and charged on in with her and now what she was yelping at him began to make more sense so he charged back out of the fucking kitchen and across the hall to that other door, another door, and here was a bedroom all right with the bed there to prove it and the two of them spun before falling into it headlong and Carol was whispering with urgency Love Me Like A Lover, Colin – I Don't Want Another Sixty-Second Thing, and that was absolutely fine by Colin because this time there was no way on earth he could drag any of this out that long – Christ it was touch-and-go if he'd have time to deal with these bloody trousers – but the good news now was that they were hanging off one leg at least, and playfully coiling tight around the other and he gasped out *Carol* as he found her and entered her and came quite deliriously and Carol made a tutting sound and sighed out *Jesus*, Colin, and Colin sighed too in bliss and panted I know, I know, And I Thank You. Fantastic.

As she lay there, gazing at the ceiling (Colin now busy retrieving his pants and faculties), Carol opined: 'You know what, this room really *could* do with a bit of decoration – d'you know about all that, Colin? Painting and wallpaper and things?'

And Colin – free now from the ferocity of that brace of Bengal tigers that had been straining on chains from deep within him – came back quite airily with What – you're not actually seriously thinking of going through with any of that stuff, are you? And Carol said M'yes – think so. Case my Dad checks up. And anyway – it's something to do.

❊

'I *just*,' intoned Dotty with an emphasis fully bolstered by the tang of something well on the way to approaching uncut hatred, 'thank *God*, Brian, that Colin, at least, did not have to be a part of this awfulness – and that little Dawn is too mercifully young to ever remember what you have *done* to us all.'

Brian nodded sadly as he edged past Dotty to get to the sink at the farther end of the caravan; not yet even one day in, but Dotty had already delivered quite a few not really very varied variations on this ominous and sombre theme – and Brian took the point, of course he did. Maybe, once more, the time has come, then – no, not maybe, no: there's no maybe about it, is there? This is the way his thinking was going as he dropped a couple of teabags into a couple of mugs – was hunching, now, ready for his recoil when the gas popped and hissed at him at the approach of a match. *I* think – you wanna know what *I* think? I think that if it weren't for Dawn, Dotty would've killed me, by now. Which could indeed be an end to all our problems, except that no, don't want it like that. Why not? Hey? I said why not? Well – that way, Dotty's going to be in line for *blame*, isn't she? See? And what will become of Colin and Dawn? Yeh – get your point. Well I knew you would – because you're a decent bloke, same as I am. Well – I try: do my best, for what it's worth (precious little). But yeah – we can't have Dotty shouldering the blame because blame is all *mine*, as well you know. This is my territory. I blunder through uselessness, crushed by guilt, and blame is what I've got coming to me, as well as the final sentence. Which will be soon, oh yes – very soon now, in coming. Get my drift? I want out, son – no two ways about it – and when that old feeling creeps up on me and sort of seeps right in, rather in the way of the back corner of the basement, I don't know if you recall – that time the damp course wanted seeing to: just a bit of discoloration, at first, and then maybe a touch of musty whiff; it doesn't take long for the paper to peel away and reveal to us all the fungus and the rot beneath. The big difference here, of course, is that the basement got fixed (best part of a weekend, I spent on that); but me, well – I just let it go, didn't I? Let it drift for years. And now I'm riddled and dilapidated – a bloody dodgy structure, decidedly unsound, and soon – oh yes – soon to be condemned.

'Oh and Brian,' tacked on Dotty – breezily might have been the intention, but that tone was fooling no one, believe me – and least of all Brian. He well knew that this casual afterthought style of approach was no more or less than that old velvet glove we've all heard so much about, and so already Brian was braced and resigned to spitting out teeth like so many bloody peanuts following his receipt of a faceful of iron. 'Is this actually the holiday destination you had planned for us, is it? Hm? Or is here just some sort of impromptu stopover? An impetuous and romantic gesture on your part this, is it, Brian? Well? Were you struck by the natural beauty of your surroundings? You can *hear* me, can you, Brian? Over the roar of the bloody motorway? I'm telling you, Brian – ' and here was Dotty getting to the point:

lips compressed by so much venom, the words squirmed out only because they craved an airing and couldn't remain within for fear of festering: 'If we get shunted by a juggernaut – if Dawn gets harmed – I'll kill you, Brian, kill you – I'll kill you twice, and I'll do it slowly.'

Dotty now glanced at Dawn (while Brian studied nothing at all just anywhere else) and wished her to be awake. When Dawn was awake, nothing else in the world could matter, but without her to care for – well then, then there was just nothing, full stop: a void, spiked by Brian.

'Tea, Dotty?' he enquired. Best try to keep it light.

'To hell with you and your *tea*, Brian – I hope it chokes you. When are they *coming*? We've been sitting here for just *hours.*'

'They said they'd be as quick as they could. Women on their own get priority, apparently. I told you. And members, of course. But they shouldn't be long, now.'

'Women on their *own*,' retorted Dotty, 'are the luckiest people in the *world*: hear me, Brian? Why don't you phone them again? I just feel so vulnerable, here – the noise is simply deafening and what if we're hit? What if we're hit? What will we do if we're *hit*?'

Brian shook his head. Die, I suppose; if we're hit we'll die.

'We're pretty visible,' said Brian. 'And it's not yet dark.'

But it wasn't a good situation, as he very much acknowledged. All had gone as well as anyone not completely detached from all the realities, here, could reasonably have expected for, oh – sixty or seventy miles, Brian would suppose. Dotty had been in the caravan, clucking at Dawn, and Brian thought he was finally getting the hang of the hire car (never actually driven a Ford before, oddly enough – had had enough Vauxhalls, the old Austin – and the Volvo, of course, before I had to sell it – but never, oddly enough as I say, ever a Ford) but when he had with care filtered on to the motorway – pleased as you like about not having buggered up at the roundabout and so having to do the

217

whole damn thing again – he had felt a, don't know, lightness towards the rear, sort of thing – a kind of increase in the tow and sway that you expect with a caravan (or so, anyway, Brian imagined – he had never actually pulled one before). So OK, he had thought, better safe than sorry – pull on to the hard shoulder and check it out, why don't I: think that's best. And dear oh dear oh dear – by golly was he pleased he did: as he squatted down to the coupling between the car and the caravan (from within which already Dotty was calling out Brian? Brian? What's wrong? Why have we stopped? Brian?) he was quite appalled and then almost physically sick when he saw that despite all his best and textbook-assisted efforts back at base, the two were just this side of complete separation. Can you imagine . . .? No. No. And nor did Brian want to. So he had played the whole thing down to Dotty and had laughed like a fool as he assured her It's nothing at all, love, just needs a bit of a tighten and Dotty had said AA, Brian – call the AA – and Brian had said Well I don't really like to trouble them, Dotty, not for just a little thing like this, and Dotty had said Phone the AA, Brian – do it now – and Brian had said Well the only thing is I actually, uh, cancelled my subscription to the AA, as it happens (seemed sensible – commensurate with no longer having any money, not to say a car), and the other thing is, now I think of it, we haven't got a phone – so why don't I just get out my tools and . . .? But any shred of that was obliterated by A fucking *A*, Brian! Do it! Do it! Get out and find a bloody phone and *do* it, Christsake.

So he did that – had never felt so castaway and alone as he had during every single step of that long, long journey, stumbling over wet grass verges with his icy breath hanging before him as cars screamed by, their white eyes flashing shock at him. And now he was back – been back ages – and despite what he had said to Dotty, there could be no doubt that although it was barely teatime, something quite as good as night was clustering about them – and *yes* he had the hazard lights going like the devil: he had even quite properly stationed one of those red and reflective triangle things way to the rear, but a BMW had clipped that just seconds after Brian was clear, and now it was lying and very possibly broken on the fast lane quite close to the crash barrier and despite Dotty's frenzied commands for him to *get* it – don't just stand there – *get* it, he didn't really care to (despite the fact that here indeed and on a plate could be the much to be desired and quick way out, but almost certainly others would be put at risk, and with that sort of thing there was no way at all that Brian could cope).

And still Dawn slept; she slept through all the thunder and wailing of determinedly relentless traffic, unterrified by the black beyond the windows and the buffeting of the caravan each time something particularly monstrous roared and shuddered by. She did not stir when Brian yelped with real pain as well as huge surprise when Dotty stabbed his hand with the nib of her fountain-pen (she had been quelling anxiety and doodling, keen for just any sort of relief: Brian's white and stupid hand was outstretched there, so she had gone for it without even raising her eyes).

Brian sucked the wound, but said no more. He had been for nearly an hour now (and Dotty had a point: was this bloody AA man *ever* going to come?) trying to make any sort of headway at all in something in the evening paper laughably entitled the Quick Crossword, and with his customary grasp of mood and situation, thought it might help pass the time and ease the atmosphere if he could maybe make Dotty a part of it too.

'What do you think this is, Dotty? Wild cat. I've tried Lion, but there's not enough letters. And Leopard's too many and so's Jaguar. And Cheetah.'

'Prat,' muttered Dotty.

'Don't think there *is* a wild cat called that, Dotty!' pitched in Brian, giving his all to this hopeless attempt at levity or even the vestiges of friendship (doomed to failure, he knew) before rushing on with: 'Well how about this one, then? Hercules, For Example – that's what it says here. Funny sort of a clue.'

'Prat!' spat out Dotty.

'Well,' allowed Brian, 'it's four letters, anyway. Would you like some soup? Spot of soup?'

'Is that a clue?' shot back Dotty.

'No – it's me asking if you'd maybe like some soup.'

'The answer to the first one's Tiger – and the other is Hero. Go and make your soup, Brian – make your soup before I throttle you.' And then just so much pent-up tension whistled out of her as she panted Oh Thank *God* – because at last, now, there was a tapping at the door, and it was maybe just that or the whoosh of freezing air as Brian opened it that finally stirred Dawn into shrieking, and Dotty had her quiet and comforted in next to no time, true, but not before the AA man had convulsed with fear (what banshee has lured me to this dark and dangerous place?).

'Christ,' said the AA man, now, looking down at the spotlit towbar. 'Christ. How far you come like this?'

'Sixty miles, maybe,' considered Brian. 'Seventy, could be. Christ it's bloody cold out here – would you like some soup?'

'You're lucky you made it sixty *yards*, mate, state of this. Christ. Caravans are a right bloody nuisance at the best of times, but this . . . Christ. What sort of soup is it?'

'I've got Mulligatawny. And there's a thick vegetable sort of broth thing – diced carrots. Will it take long to fix? The thing, I mean – not the, you know, soup: that'll take no time.'

'No, won't take long – it's just a question of doing it *properly*, isn't it? Christ. You're bloody lucky – you know that?'

'Am I?' doubted Brian. 'God it's just *freezing* out here – I expect you're used to it.'

'This could've broke loose at any second, son, telling you.

220

Right. Get my gear. A drop of thick vegetable might just hit the spot. *Is* cold. I'd be nothing without my thermals – used to be a martyr to winter, one time, me.'

Brian was almost offensively upbeat as he scampered back into the caravan (God – don't envy *his* job: like the Arctic, out there) and was full of big, broad assurances for Dotty: On Our Way In No Time Now (true he had estimated their time of arrival today at maybe with a bit of luck just before dark, while it now seemed that shortly before sunrise was nearer the mark – but at least very soon they would be on their *way* again, yes?). And then he busied himself at the Belling stove, muttering contentedly as he groped around in his box of cans – let me see, let me see now, here's the Mulligatawny – tomato, yes, oh – didn't know I had any chicken noodle left. Ah, here we are – thick veg, very nice – sure you won't have any, Dotty? No? Please yourself, then.

'Just make sure he does it properly,' was all Dotty had to grudgingly say. 'All right baby Dawn? Izzoo all right my ickle angel? Yes oo izz because ooze chuckling, izzuntoo? My ickle happy baby girl. When we're back on the road again, I'll sing you your very favourite song – would you like that? Woodoo?' And then – from treacle to battery acid in the blink of an eyelid – 'In fact, Brian, *I* shall see that he does it properly – not ever again going to leave anything to *you*.'

The caravan stirred slightly and seemed to tauten; then, with a clank that had all the air of being final, it just wheezily settled back down again. Brian now poured the piping hot soup into two large mugs (plop plip plap – that'll be the carrots) and made for the door.

'Of course he'll do it *properly*, Dotty – he's an AA man, isn't he?' It's not that I'm worried about – how much is he going to *charge*? 'And anyway, you'll freeze to death out there, I'm telling you.'

'I don't care,' said Dotty stubbornly. 'I just have to be *sure*. I'm just sure of nothing any more and I just have to be

221

sure of *this*. Now come on, little Dawn, let me wrap you up nice and warm in this and we'll go and see what the funny man outside is up to.'

'You don't have to bring *Dawn*, for God's sake,' protested Brian.

'Oh yes, Brian,' said Dotty, quietly. 'Oh yes I do.'

Brian shrugged and led the way down the two short steps – almost collided with the AA man, who was wiping his hands with a rag.

'Right,' he said with conclusion and a weighty assurance. 'That'll do you – tight as a drum, now. She won't budge. Ah – thick vegetable, lovely.'

'You're really sure it's safe?' urged Dotty.

The AA man nodded, eyeing Dawn with caution: she's a right worry, that little bundle, and no mistake about it. 'Telling you,' he said, 'sound as a bell.'

And as he and Brian more or less as simultaneously as it goes both now lowered their heads towards their steaming mugs of comfort, they sensed independently just as Dotty did too a sudden shift in the air and the noise that filled it; the constant swish and thunder was for some small part of a second arrested as a dazzle of lights caused them to flinch and then scatter and Dotty heard only the awesome droning of a klaxon amid the pitched scream of lesser horns and then it was as if a train had torn roaringly from its under-world tunnel and as Dotty screamed and scrambled up a sheer and cold and slimy bank and Brian shouted and clawed himself up behind her, so the AA man – white and panicked – darted towards his van and then he stopped, turned and sprinted away altogether as the night erupted and the caravan rose up into the air and fell away, cracked up, and lay there broken-backed, as the lorry slewed on through it and ripped the thing asunder, a brutal splitting overlaid by breakage and the tearing shriek of brakes as the sky and bare trees were lit by white beams, suddenly doused. The terrible noises ceased, and just humming, hiss and tinkle boomed in the darkness as Dotty, face-down and trembling, clutched Dawn to her, her hands dashing out to each small part of her and joining to hug her into safety. The AA man was moaning at the sight before him, as more and more cars drunkenly collected and startle-eyed men came forward stiffly, not at all ready to do whatever one did when faced with whatever this was.

'Dotty! Dotty!' rasped out Brian. 'Oh my *God*, Dotty – are you all right?! Are you! Are you both OK?!'

Dotty could not see him. Was that him? Yes, she could see him now, sprawled quite near (there is a smell of scorching). 'I'm fine. My leg hurts. Dawn is OK – she's safe, she's safe!'

Brian closed his eyes. (Yes – I think I'm all right too: which is good because although I want to be dead, I can't face hurt.) When he opened them, anxious faces were peering down at him, and beyond them – strewn over an amazingly large area of cold-lit road – were the crumpled and seemingly cardboard flanks and shattered panels of the caravan and the stove-in rump of the hire car, all amid the smashed-up bits of anything at all that was left to any one of them.

He could hear his Dotty sobbing, but he felt airily distanced from any of this – hovering somewhere above the hurt of it. All he could think, as he wiped away at the wet and lumpy mass that coated his chin and chest, was Oh my God what a waste, what a waste: what a shocking waste – all that soup's gone everywhere, now, and I didn't even get to so much as taste it.

CHAPTER TEN

Melody hadn't been to Waterloo for simply . . . oh, couldn't
even remember when – and God, it certainly didn't look
like this, not way back then, it didn't. She felt childlike
and awed by the scale and sleekness – and to the growing
irritation of Howard, if not quite yet Elizabeth, she would
keep on trying to convey all this.

'Yes,' agreed Howard. 'Very swish.'

'It's more like an *airport*,' enthused Melody.

'The trouble is,' said Elizabeth, 'it gets so awfully *full*.
People have no manners at all. You see that man in the
perfectly vile yellowy sort of jacket affair? See him,
Howard? *Twice* he's barged into me now, and you don't get
so much as a single word.'

'It's more like,' Melody went on – her eyes sweeping up
and over the huge glass and arching curve of the roof –
'we're going to be getting on Concorde or something,
instead of just a train.'

'Yes,' agreed Howard shortly, 'very swish.' Jesus – it's a
station, right? How will Melody react in the unlikely event
of her dying and going to Heaven? Twenty minutes I've just
spent, getting her a ticket – still, at least I suppose she's
grateful.

'Oh – thanks so much, Howard,' she had said, as he
handed her the thing. 'I'm really looking forward.' And
again she felt that cheesy buzz – as if a kindly uncle had just
awarded her a bumper pack of Jelly Tots at her best friend's
birthday party for having come *nearly* top in the face-
painting competition. Was this real, this dopey feeling? Or

am I putting it on for just my benefit and my benefit alone? I think a bit of each, is maybe the truth: that cow Edna bloody Davies was so fucking beastly to me this morning so Christ – I deserve *some* sort of a treat, don't I? And then I think it's partly Dawn, if I'm honest – when Dawn's gone, I quite like to be a little girl again.

But it was Edna's beastliness she supposed she had to thank for this one-off day trip out of the blue (silver lining time again): Elizabeth had in so many ways felt just so *awful*, just so *responsible* – and of course, yes, it was nothing to do with her, but she never could bear things going *wrong* in life, do you see? Her own most particularly, true, but in that of selected others, too.

'But I simply can't *believe* it,' Elizabeth had hooted, wide-eyed that morning, while she and Howard had been standing in their hall in the midst of just so much luggage (to Howard's way of thinking, wholly beyond credence, had it not been so utterly predictable). 'What – she just said *Go*, just like that?'

'More or less,' sulked Melody. 'She said I broke things and spilt things and didn't clean things properly and that Dawn was driving her mental.'

Four bloody good reasons for getting shot of her, was Howard's take on that: didn't, naturally enough, *say* anything. Even Elizabeth was having a teensy bit of difficulty in sweeping away that lot, but still she made a fair old stab at keeping up the outrage.

'*And*,' tacked on Melody, 'she accused me of nicking all of Cyril's sherry.'

And that gave Elizabeth free rein to crank up the God-I-simply-can't-believe-it stakes, but it was Howard who grunted And Did You?

Melody was smiling slily. 'Yeah,' she agreed, cat-like. 'I hated the stuff, but it was all they ever seemed to have around.'

She's an odd one, Melody, Elizabeth was thinking. And

then – just as the black cab swung into the drive and Howard started saying Right a good deal – she on impulse came up with another of her corkers:

'Melody – come with us to Paris for the day! Mustn't she, Howard? It'll do you the world of – '

'Oh *no*, Elizabeth – honestly. I'm always muscling in on your holidays! I'll be fine, I'm fine – honestly.'

'Howard,' commanded Elizabeth, 'do make sure the soft bag, the black Gucci, this one – make sure it doesn't go on the bottom, yes? Nonsense, Melody – you're most welcome. Howard can arrange the ticket when we get there, yes Howard? It'll be great fun. Now no more words – we *insist*, don't we Howard?'

Oh Christ, thought Howard – helping the driver with the rampart of baggage – who really *cares* any more, actually, hm? I mean look – I'm perfectly happy pottering about at home, as you know, but if I *am* going to Paris, if that really is the deal, then I would opt for preference for the Ritz with Laa-Laa, so accepting that this is a no-no, how can it in any way really matter what other little extras are bolted on to this pointless little package? Let's ask the cabbie along too, why ever not – seems a niceish sort of a bloke. God, you know – I truly thought I'd squared myself up to all this, but suddenly now as the cab doors are slamming, I feel like no one so much as the condemned man – you know the one, confronting a firing squad and being proffered his very last, um – his very last, oh Christ, *thing*: tobacco, white tube, Player's – *cigarette*, yes. Cigarette, blast it.

And now among the swarming masses in the concourse of Waterloo International, Melody found herself gently edging over to the borders of a café, pulled by the near-palpable hit of dark-roasting coffee, tempted by all those crusty baguettes: well Jesus – she hadn't even had time for breakfast at Edna's, before she was given the shove.

'Oh you don't want to be bothering with any of *that*,' deplored Elizabeth. 'We eat on the train – they do a wonderful lunch in First Class, don't they Howard? Champagne and everything.'

Howard nodded. First Class, yes – the fares hadn't really been too ruinous, this time around, because I suppose it's winter and they were tied in to the hotel and booked well in advance. *Melody's* spur-of-the-moment and what-the-hell ticket, however, had been altogether something else entirely – but hey, as usual, what could he do? Stick her in the baggage car while he and Elizabeth swanned along up to the posh bit? Don't quite think so.

Howard had squintingly ascertained their access gate, and now as the announcement came, set to trundling behind the hordes. Elizabeth carried an Hermès Kelly bag in a mustardy colour, and fashioned from the bobbly skin of some strange thing, and Melody sported a sort of shiny tartan knapsack arrangement while Howard manhandled a trolley so piled high with assorted cases that it rather looked as if he might be selling samples. But Christ – First *Class*: it's a total joke, really, isn't it? You fetch your own trolley, you work out where to go, you wait around, you queue, you budge a bit and stop; you wait around, you queue, you budge a bit and stop; you find the carriage yourself and then all on your own you buckle down to stowing the bags. The First Class bit is when a grinning ninny in her bloody red waistcoat just stands there and says to you Hello And Fucking *Welcome* (all part of the service, sir). And Elizabeth can't have been the only one on board who firmly believed that seven pieces of luggage was more or less right for a three-day stay: most of the bays and bins were already choked by the time Howard had heaved his lot aboard, and so having rammed in a couple of the smaller items, he was forced to traipse to the other end of the carriage to try his luck there: two journeys, that took, and he was frankly sweating and murmuring fiercely by the time he'd kicked in the last case just anywhere (the soft one, pretty sure, the black Gucci, think) and all the while some other toothy

227

woman in a bloody red waistcoat beamed at him encouragement. And when finally he collapsed into his seat and Elizabeth said Oh Howard I've just remembered (how silly of me) – I've left my magazines in the pocket of the tan case Howard very uncharacteristically shot back *Tough*. And very soon after the train drew silkily away, yet one more girl with a colossal smile came round with a trolley and offered in a voice that promised blue skies forever – Champagne? Orange juice? Mineral water? And Melody grabbed her plastic flute of champagne and downed it pretty much in one and sweetly asked for another (and got it) while Elizabeth was still in the process of reaching out as Howard said Whisky, please, and the girl came back with Red wine? White wine? Lager? And Howard now groaned out loud and said No, whisky – *whisky*: you must have heard of it, and the girl smiled even more broadly and said she'd check.

And soon they would be in Paris. And Laa-Laa is in London. So would some kind person please explain to Howard just what precisely is the point of *that*?

❋

Lulu could see by her hand as she put down the phone exactly how much she was trembling – and this was utterly in tune with the flutterings of her heart and she swallowed now hard as if to make quite clear she would brook no revolt from within.

'Is there something wrong?' asked Zoo-Zoo from nowhere – and the suddenness of that made her jump.

'Hm? Oh Peter – I didn't hear you. No. Nothing, thank God – but it could have been . . . oh God. And to think they had the *baby* with them . . .' Lulu became abstracted, then, and wondered out loud Should I call Lizzie? No – they maybe won't even have got there yet, and anyway there's nothing to be done. But she was tweaked abruptly away from all that when Zoo-Zoo said quietly:

'You very much like Elizabeth, don't you?'

Lulu looked down now at this very strange boy.

'Yes,' she said – on the way to falteringly, but well bolstered by a sturdy undertone of what's-it-got-to-do-with-you, whoever you are.

'I do too,' said Zoo-Zoo – and when he added on, 'I think you must actually love her,' Lulu simply said Yes again and continued to observe him, while thinking what, exactly?

'I do too,' said Zoo-Zoo – and then he turned away.

Oh God, thought Lulu, what a bloody odd day. And yet she'd more than vaguely known it was going to be one of those from the moment she'd opened her eyes, far too early, in the big white bed that once, quite incredibly, she used to look forward with eagerness to sharing with Johnny. Who was, it surely seemed from the general and distant clatter of things, already up and about – and it wasn't even . . . what? Christ – it was only just after six: as black as night outside, and not only was John conscious (rare, before noon) but the telltale clicks and taps of his movements, the urgent economies of journeys to and fro, were all suggesting to Lulu not just unaccustomed bustle, but a definite purpose, too. And then she remembered: he had said, really quite casually and just last evening, that in view of Lulu's decision to go ahead and house-sit for Elizabeth, he had, um, thought he might as well take off somewhere for maybe just a few days; could be longer – who knew? P'raps even for Christmas . . . well, let's be honest here, Lulu – it's not as if I'd be *missed*, or anything, is it? And he had been sober, you know – quite lucid – which was startling in itself. This, of course, was very good news for Lulu, but at least she had the goodness to wear a don't-be-silly smile, while nevertheless not so much taking care to censor all enquiry as to just where it was he thought he might be going, but rather more forgetting to let it occur to her to so much as pretend to care about asking. He's off – great: I'm going to Lizzie's. And now I'm awake, I might as well get myself going (can't wait); I wonder if John's left any hot water.

John stepped out of the shower (it had suddenly turned tepid, and he was well versed in judging the moment to call it a day before the wash and caress of any remaining warmth turned like a traitor into glancing rain). I'm not at all sure about this Tara thing, he was thinking, wrapping about him a towel and padding wetly into what used to be termed the spare room, once, but now was just the space he crookedly fell into, sometimes even overcoming the long crawl to the divan – on those rare evenings, that is, when the prospect of the stairs hadn't utterly floored him. But the odd thing was, since that afternoon when he had agreed to go up to Bath and stay a while with Tara – the duration honestly unspecified (maybe shied away from? He had been far too wary to commit, she just shrugging and saying Whatever, genuinely seeming to be cool about going with the flow) – since he had actually gone and said Yeah, OK, Why not, I'd like to, he hadn't seemed to need the nightly and headlong plummet into a vat of booze that he was lately used to, hoping maybe to drown there. I mean sure – he still *drank*, of course, but only maybe two, three . . . well, rarely more than four bottles of red over the better part of an evening: helluvan improvement, think you'll agree (feel quite proud of me, point of fact). I think what it must be, John thought now – feeling tugged by something he felt sure came pretty close to his memory of what if not outright *happy* was like, then at least something approaching carefree – is that for the first time in such a long time, there's somewhere I can *go*. Somewhere I can go where I am not vilified, sneered at, dreaded or despised: she *asked* me to go, for Christ's sake. But how very odd that this was *Tara*, of all people in the world – for years I have dreaded her sneering and despicable vilification of me. Can people really simply alter their attitudes like that? Is it just a bit possible, do you suppose? Well no they don't – it isn't, is it, let's face it – so what's going on, then – ay? Oh God, oh God – I really mustn't dwell. What I must do now is pack up not just dwelling but both my bags and put right out of my mind any lurking possibility that Lulu, when I am away, will encounter some *man* (while knowing she will, while knowing she must!) and cling on fast to this not really consolatory and, I have to admit it, rapidly dwindling sensation of release that just for one brief minute back there came close to at least something approaching carefree.

He was ready to leave long before Lulu, and now as she watched his controlled franticness at the hall table – checking he *had* everything – Lulu found herself not really within striking distance of stirring the memory of just how it had once gone to actually *feel* for him, but certainly less far away from the shadow of it, anyway: pass a brown cardboard box strung on rough twine over his woolly hat and then his ruddy cheeks and let it dangle around his dark blue gabardine shoulders, and what you had was an admittedly pretty raddled soon-to-be evacuee, the light of adventure in his eye, the bat-squeak of optimism just suppressed by the compression of lips – both doing their damnedest to wipe out the prickle of fear that made him tremble.

And now it crossed her mind to ask him where he was going, and so she touched his hand and said:

'Take care, John, yes?'

'Yes,' agreed John, quite readily. 'And you too, Lulu – and you too. Um – Lulu, when I'm gone – you won't, um . . .?'

'Have fun, won't you, John? And you know where I'll be.'

John nodded – stopped that, then did a bit more of it. 'Mm. Yes – it's just that, er – oh *God*, Lulu, you know what I'm like – it's just that I can't bear the thought of you –!'

'John – two things: I will be with no man. OK? No man. There never *was* a man, Johnny, but never mind any of that now. And after Christmas, John – '

'This is the second thing, right?'

231

'Right. After Christmas – in the new year, there will be no you. You've just got to get that – it's an absolute, John – OK? An absolute.'

John's eyes were blank as he picked up his cases. He was nodding now as if he had been at it for months – had long ago broken all Guinness records going, and no one had got around to telling him to stop.

'Bye then, Lulu.'

'Bye, John.'

Not till he reached the door did he whirl round, wild-eyed (all of this was so much worse and so much harder, when there was no drink inside to dull you).

'Don't you want to know where I'm going, Lulu? Who I'll be with?'

Lulu held John's eye, smiled into him not unkindly, and nudged him through and out of the door.

'Bye, John,' was all she had to say then, aware now of something like a kick as she ground out the fag-end of their years together.

❋

It was Mrs Bramley who had delayed her, as usual – dear Mrs Bramley. Lulu had been quite determined to get to Elizabeth's in good time to see her off – but Lizzie did know that there were three of their ladies to see to that morning. Mrs Stein had been easy: she'd bought four pairs of shoes in the Manolo Blahnik sale (divine – *non?*) and she needed Lulu to match each of them with any of her hundreds of outfits, and this would see her through the bulk, anyway, of the coming festive season. But you must come *today*, Mrs Stein had insisted, because if you think there's nothing here quite *right*, then I'll just have time to buy more – and you will, won't you, tell me exactly what (I don't know how I ever existed without you). Mrs Henderson had taken a wee bit longer – Lulu had to finish off a giant Christmas cracker she had started yesterday – over three feet long, terribly realistic, and fashioned from stiffened gauze and the very finest pastel silk, guaranteed to shred into luxurious tatters when she and her (don't breathe a word – but I know I can tell *you*) brand-new lover tugged at its opposite ends; as to the bang, she giggled, that would come later. She intended to tell him she had made it herself over days and out of sheer adoration, and Mrs Henderson was just yearning, now, for Christmas Eve to come – their own very *special* day, when Mister Henderson, she told Lulu huskily, always – every year – played golf. Did Lulu think her man would simply adore the cuff links, the silk shirts, the Cohiba Robustos and then the Beluga? Yes, said Lulu – oh yes (thinking God how on earth can she begin to be *bothered*? Christ Almighty – it's only a bloke).

And so, eventually, to Pippa Bramley's – who more or less admitted that she couldn't, in truth, think of anything more for Lulu to do (the house was just dripping with Christmas – everything rustled, and some things chimed) but she had got so used now to just *seeing* her and so tell me – did Lulu have time, did she think, for just one cup of tea? And Lulu, my dearest, will you take cake? Lulu stayed – and no Pippa, no: no charge at all for the visit – 'tis nearly Christmas, isn't it, hey? And Mrs Bramley had gazed about her – took in the stars and the cherubs, the massed holly and semi-bells, caught mid-peal: soothed a death-still robin by stroking down the downy crimson at its throat and with wide eyes that mirrored coloured baubles she said quite dreamily Do you know, dear Lulu, I think it must be.

'When Gilbert and I were married,' confided Mrs Bramley, now – she and Lulu were clustered round the fire – 'we used often to go to this charming little restaurant in old Bloomsbury – I don't doubt for a minute that it's not there now – and always, every time, we would both of us eat the very same thing.'

Lulu nodded happily, knowing well there would be more to come.

'I can't,' went on Pippa, more slowly, 'for the life of me remember what it *was*, or anything – but I do recall well one warm summer evening when the waiter – head waiter, I suppose he must have been – came over to our table and informed us rather gravely that tonight, alas, the dish was off the menu.'

'And?' prompted Lulu (look – I know I must leave, but I can't leave yet: could just go on listening to this woman for ever).

Mrs Bramley sniffed dismissively. 'Well – we ate something else, I expect. Of course, all this I'm telling you – all this was before Gilbert died, do you see. I used to *love* dining out, you know – because there was none of that at all, you see, not when I was a girl. I was very *ill* as a child, you know, Lulu: very ill indeed.'

'Oh?' said Lulu.

'Yes,' Mrs Bramley verified. 'But I'm much better now, thank you for enquiring. Are you quite sure, Lulu, you won't even take so much as just a single langue de chat?'

And so by the time Lulu finally did get round to Elizabeth's, she and Howard had long gone, of course – but not to worry (ring her soon). The first thing to deal with was Nelligan (he seemed to be making a fair deal less clatter this morning, which might or might not be a good thing: at least it didn't sound as if he was ripping out something instead of if not building, then easing it in). Lulu well knew that if Lizzie came back to find even so much as a speck of sawdust in this grand, so grand, kitchen of hers, she would be felled at the outset and quite despair of Christmas, and such a scenario was totally unacceptable from all sorts of points of view: despair, or anything like it, Lulu was quite determined, must never ever visit upon her Lizzie's shoulders because what, please, would that do to the rest of us? How, then, could we face it? Also – I *need* this Christmas, need it (and maybe others do too, yes maybe, but not like me, no not like me – it's more important for me, because . . .

because, very soon after it I am walking away, and although until recently that seemed enough, I now simply must have somewhere to go to).

But Lulu was calmed when she walked into the kitchen – apart from the dust and still quite a few details, here indeed was something truly covetable. The deep fielded panels on the simply dozens of units bore the strong graining of aged oak, and yet were glowing with all the dark and reddish richness of could be mahogany. The ranks of halogen spots already were warming the wood, and once all the granite was given its final swabbing, the room could well pass muster as a handsomely endowed and latter-day chapel. Chunky and simple, circular and heavy bright brass drop handles awaited their billet and Nelligan, you could see, was pleased, very pleased, with how all this had gone. Lulu chivvied him on for form's sake (You are on schedule? It will meet the deadline?) but had time only for four or five of his beatifically pacific Shore Twills before the phone set up its warble in the hall, and Lulu scooted off to field this next thing (maybe could be Lizzie? No – too early, too early by far).

'Elizabeth, darling,' gushed a full-throated woman's voice – so damned loud that Lulu started – 'please do refresh my memory – is it pink or blue that you love? I know it's one of them, and there's something divine I've seen for you and – '

'No – no,' stuttered Lulu, 'it's not Elizabeth, actually. You must be her mother, yes?'

There was a pause. 'Yes,' agreed Elizabeth's mother, 'I suppose I must. And you are?'

'Lulu. I'm Lulu. Friend of Lizzie, Elizabeth. Looking after the house while she's away. Did she not, um . . .?'

'Away? Is she away? She tells me nothing. Is she gone for Christmas, or what? She never tells me anything, you know – and I'm her mother.'

'No – no – Christmas is *here* – *you're* coming for Christmas,

235

aren't you? She and Howard have just gone to Paris for a few days and then they're –'

'Can't hear. What say?'

'Paris! They've gone to –'

'Ah yes, Paris. That's where Elizabeth is. She told me. Well now do tell me, dear – I'm so awfully sorry but I've forgotten your –'

'Lulu. It's Lulu.'

'Lulu, quite. Now Lulu, dear, do you at all happen to know whether it's blue or pink that Elizabeth loves? Only they've got this thing in both and I want to be sure.'

'Well . . . she likes blue *and* pink, pretty sure . . . of course it depends on, um, the actual shade and, I suppose, what exactly the thing is . . .'

'I'm sure you're right,' said Elizabeth's mother, with energy. 'When you speak with Elizabeth, do please tell her that I would have phoned yesterday but it's my leg.'

Lulu was quite pleased when the doorbell rang, because now she could pipe up with justifiable truth:

'Oh look – I'm so sorry but someone's at the door.'

'Can't hear. What say?'

'The door, the door – someone's at the –'

'Ah yes – this happens to me. Well if someone's at the door I think you must answer it, um – I'm so awfully sorry but I've forgotten your –'

'Lulu. It's Lulu. Sorry. Bye.'

Lulu skittered across the hall because the ringing was becoming shrill, now, and she didn't have time to wonder who on earth it might be. (Even as she swung open the door she thought gulpingly and too late of that warning John had always tried dinning into her, quite without success: What is the point – tell me Lulu – of our having all these bloody expensive Banham locks and grids and alarms and cameras if in the middle of the bloody day the doorbell goes and off you toddle and just bloody *open* it, hey? People don't go crawling up drainpipes in the dead of night facing death or detection, do they? No they don't: what they do is they ring the front doorbell in the middle of the morning and stupid bloody women let them *in*.)

It only took a bit of a split second for that lot to whizz through her brain, but too long to allow time for safety chains and spyholes, and so Lulu was wholly relieved to be not now confronted by a couple of grim-faced heavies bent on shouldering their way in, wrapping her up in parcel tape and subjecting Lizzie's things to a ransack and pillage – prior to barking coarsely into her terrified eyes while playing with knives: OK Darling – where's the keys to the fackin sife?! No – all we had here was Cyril and Edna (better by far, oh yeah sure, but still this side of a delightful surprise).

'Come in, come in,' she said (well – what else could she?). 'God it's so c-c-c-*cold*. Come in. You know Howard and Elizabeth aren't here?'

Yes indeed, Edna was thinking – the thought tucked well behind that smile of hers – how else could I have managed to get to snoop around this bloody wonderful kitchen I've heard so damned much about? I'd never get past Elizabeth, would I? Cyril too, of course, was well aware of the situation (why, in fact, he had agreed to Yes – why don't we pop round, put on a friendly face, the second Edna had suggested it; and this had pleasantly surprised her) – but kitchens, you may be sure, didn't feature in his way of thinking, oh dear me no. Already, as he unwound his scarf and grinned like a halfwit while agreeing out loud that Yes indeed – 'tis cold, 'tis, and much more of it to come, they tell us – snow on the horizon, is what they're saying – already Cyril felt stifled by the closeness of Lulu's uncompromising and seemingly effortless beauty, wall to wall, all over the hall. Imagine, just imagine the twist on the whole of one's future life on earth – how there could be no more room for dread, or even a dull contentment, if only daily one could open one's eyes and fill them brimful with the loveliness of Lulu.

'No – we *did* know,' admitted Edna. 'Of course Elizabeth told me about Paris – envy her terribly, but what with the builders and everything, we didn't really feel we could honestly get away this winter, did we Cyril? For a break. Talking of builders . . . how's the, um – how's the kitchen coming along?'

'Oh very well,' said Lulu brightly. 'Would you like a coffee, or anything? Cyril? But I have to tell you, Edna, that I promised Lizzie faithfully that no one must see it until it's absolutely finished. She wants it to be a Christmas surprise.'

Yeah you old bat, thought Lulu – I know your type, what you're up to. And why's Cyril keep on leering at me like that? Working his stupid eyebrows. I think he thinks that because he's a psychiatrist, or whatever he is, that this somehow makes him something special; well it doesn't – all he is is just yet another (yawn yawn) *bloke*, and therefore bloody zero. Funny they never seemed to see it like that, all these men.

'Oh but *surely*,' teased Edna, 'just the *littlest* peek . . .?'

Lulu smiled, or did her best to. 'Sorry. I promised.'

'Well,' acquiesced Edna, sourly, 'a promise is a promise, of course. Anyway,' she rallied round, 'we just really popped over to say, you know – if you ever *need* anything over the next few days, you know where we are. And of course in the evening, maybe, if you feel like dropping round . . .?'

'Thanks, Edna – thanks. I've actually got a whole load to do before Lizzie gets back but yeh – thanks a lot. I might just do that. Did you say you did want coffee, Cyril?'

Cyril opened his mouth, but not before Edna had cut in with I don't really think we will, actually Lulu, if it's all the same to you – I've got quite a lot to be getting on with myself: haven't we, Cyril? I think so.

'I must say,' she went on – lowering her voice into a look-

I-know-it's-terribly-awful-and-I-probably-shouldn't-say-this-but-I'm-jolly-well-going-to-anyway tone – 'it's *bliss* not having that eyesore caravan cluttering up the view. Only *temporary*, I suppose . . .?'

'Fraid so.' grinned Lulu.

Edna nodded, accepting this with stoicism. 'Thought as much,' she said.

They left soon after, which Lulu was pretty pleased about – but before she could quite close the latch on the freezing outside, Cyril popped back in to the crack and whispered conspiratorially while standing horribly near: Look, Lulu – I know we don't know each other or anything (more's the pity) but I am by way of being a professional in, ah, certain matters as well I think you are aware – so if ever, you know, you feel like just – *talking*, you know? Talking? Just maybe if you ever need a *chat*, yes? Then possibly I could help. And Lulu tried hard to subdue the jerking around of all her features, wildly desperate to be an unmissable billboard spelling out in three-foot neon letters You Have Got To Be Bloody *Joking*, Mate – and instead put at least a sort of effort into conveying no more than Message Received But I Really Don't Think So, and then just shut the door.

A bam-bam thumping on the staircase made Lulu glance round, then: it was only Katie – in search of some breakfast at long past teatime, yawning hugely and ruffling her hair as if to dislodge an infestation. From Lulu's vantage point quite close to the foot of the stairs, she could see whether she liked it or not that Katie was wearing just a brief T-shirt, and nothing else at all; and how odd that so slight a creature could make such a bone-jarring noise on carpeted steps in just her bare and scarlet-toed feet: she must, thought Lulu, want to.

'Hi,' said Katie – casual, this was, to the point of dismissive. 'Mum gone?'

Lulu nodded. 'Hours ago. I'll be fixing a bit of supper in a minute – salad, maybe. Want some?'

'Nah – I'm not great on salad. I'll just get something from the fridge. Can I go in there now? Only last night that old Nelligan creep was banging on about grouting the floor, or something – whatever bloody grouting the floor is.'

'I think it's all dry now,' returned Lulu, with caution. 'But, um – do you think you should go in there – dressed like that, Katie?'

Katie laughed. 'God – you sound just like Mum!' And then she gazed down at the jut of her breasts through the pink cotton of the T-shirt (from nipple to nipple was printed in bright red the word Easy) and then on to her bare brown thighs beyond. 'What's wrong?' she queried, guilty as hell of wide-eyed innocence. 'Anyway,' she tacked on, idling across in the direction, 'give the silly old sod a thrill, won't it – specially if what I want's on the bottom shelf. Hee hee.'

Lulu briskly washed her hands of all that: I don't care, do I? She's Lizzie's daughter, not mine – she can charge at Nelligan and rape him for all it means to me.

'I'll be phoning your mother later on, Katie,' she called. 'Do you want to speak to her? Any messages?'

'No,' said Katie, simply. 'Just tell her I'm out. Actually – I will be out, as it happens. Rick's in town – can't wait.'

'Who's Rick?' threw in Lulu, not much caring.

'Mm? Oh – you don't know, do you? He's this absolute hunk I met in Chicago. Just can't wait to fuck him again.' And then just a smidgen of hesitance: 'You won't say to Mum I said that, will you?'

'No,' said Lulu. No, she thought, I won't: I'm not in the business of hurting Lizzie. Maybe I'll ring her *now*, yes? Just can't wait to hear that voice again; still a bit early, though. 'Oh by the way, Katie – Mister Nelligan said that someone called Norman rang you this morning; said can you ring him, or else he'll keep trying.'

'Norman?' queried Katie, quite blankly. 'Who's Norman? Oh Christ *Norman* – oh well: fuck that. He's nobody.'

Amazing, thought Lulu, that she's Lizzie's daughter:

simply amazing. And that reflection (not the first time it had struck her) was cut short by the trill of the phone again, summoning her as ever with so much urgency – and wasn't it often simply the most trivial thing?

'Oh hi, Dotty,' said Lulu, with wide coo-fancy eyes and huge surprise (here is one call I surely wasn't expecting). 'Lizzie's not here, you know – she went off ages ago.'

'Lulu, listen: I'm in a police station. Something rather ghastly has happened, and – '

'Oh my *God*, Dotty – what is it? Are you both OK?'

'Thank the Lord, yes. Dawn is fine – she's with me now. And I'm all right – bit shaky, but OK. Now listen – the caravan was in a smash. It's all too complicated, but by the grace of God we weren't in it at the time. Brian's just giving a statement to the police – it wasn't our fault, or anything – and then – '

'Oh yes – Brian. He OK?'

Dotty turned from the ash-grey cubicle in which she and Dawn were tightly wedged and glanced across the ugly room to a dull steel desk where a shirt-sleeved copper was animatedly cross-checking with Brian some other damn question, and Brian – just slumped there – was slowly nodding, while appearing confused: seemingly beaten and utterly drained.

'I suppose so,' said Dotty, shortly. 'The thing is, Lulu, we've – ' and the voice cracked now, as Dotty sucked in her lips and revolved wet eyes up and around her, taking strength finally from the bright light in the blue of Dawn's. 'We've – lost absolutely everything, and – '

'Oh Dotty! Oh poor poor Dotty! You must come home immediately. Stay here – Lizzie would really really want that. Come now, Dotty – I'll set everything up.'

And Dotty softly replied (I never thought Lulu could be so tender): 'Thank you, thank you. That is what I wanted to ask.' And then, more distantly: 'What a day, what a day . . . oh dear me – what a day it's been.'

241

'Come soon,' Lulu urged once more; and then she slowly replaced the receiver.

'Is there something wrong?' asked Zoo-Zoo from nowhere – and the suddenness of that made her jump.

'Hm? Oh Peter – I didn't hear you. No. Nothing, thank God – but it could have been . . . oh God. And to think they had the *baby* with them.'

Soon after, Lulu was lying (nearly sprawling) on Elizabeth's big wide bed, idly stroking a peach silk La Perla nightdress, selected for the purpose. Now, she thought, I must ring her – I shall try to break all this as gently as I can, but maybe she and Howard will anyway feel that now they ought to come home? Perhaps a shame for Lizzie – but lovely for me, to see her again. But then, oh God, I won't be *needed*, will I? My God, my God: with Brian and Dotty there won't even be *room* for me, will there? Either way, now, I'm not too happy.

Lulu tapped an impatient fingernail on the side of the handset, as it went on placidly purring in her ear; no matter how bloody posh, these foreign hotels, they still took an age to answer. But no, Madame, was all she eventually got – I am getting no reply from the suite, I regret. God, Lizzie – you're not out shopping already? You can only just have got there! I'll try and get you on your mobile.

❄

And she was, you know – out shopping already! Elizabeth knew it was childish, yes she supposed she did – but there was just something, just this buzzy *thing* about Paris (and so much more so at this time of year – everything so stylishly lit with clusters of little white diamonds, so much less garish than London) that just made her practically desperate to get out there and *buy* things. But it's not as if it's just for *me*, is it? There's Zoo-Zoo's present, isn't there? Already got him something divine from Peal in the Burlington Arcade (don't tell him) – he's unspeakably irresistible in cashmere – but I'd like to get him something else as well. And Lulu – sweet Lulu. Howard, of course. Melody, Dotty, Katie – everyone. Anyway – I've made a list of possibles, so it's silly hanging about.

'You two will find something to do with yourselves, yes?' checked Elizabeth. 'It seems mean to be going off on my own, I know – but I want everything to be a *surprise*. Just can't wait till Christmas, now.'

'Well I've only got a few hours,' smiled Melody, 'so I think I'll be a bit of a tourist – Eiffel Tower, all that. Ages since I was in Paris. Years and years. God, Elizabeth,' she added on, gazing around the mushroom-coloured plush-ness of their Louis Quatorze suite, 'you're wonderfully lucky – it's the most gorgeous hotel.'

'Well you two potter off, then,' allowed Howard expan-sively. 'I'll just make a couple of work calls, and then maybe stroll round to the Crillon – book us into an earlyish dinner, yes? And then Melody'll be fine for the nine o'clock train.'

'Great,' grinned Melody. 'Double dinners.'

'Pig!' laughed Elizabeth. 'OK, you two – I'm off.'

Still giggling, they parted in the Place de la Concorde – Elizabeth unerringly weaving her way to the Rue St Honoré, Melody ambling vaguely towards the mist-hung Eiffel Tower. The bare and frosty branches on all the trees in the Tuileries gardens seemed to her impossibly romantic (maybe quite sad) – and as the cold stung her cheeks, she tried not to think about the bastard Miles, and the great times in this city that in some other lifetime they maybe might have had.

Howard, still in the suite, sighed with huge contentment: it was great to be alone – I'm just so used, I suppose, to being my own boss and doing my thing. He poured two miniatures of Teacher's into a chunky tumbler and thought how terribly small and forlorn they appeared and added a third for company. And now, he thought, as he pulled on that – now I'll phone my Laa-Laa.

No reply. Pity. Try her later. I've never actually wondered what she does with her time, all the hours I'm not around: something, I suppose. Maybe shopping, like Elizabeth – always seems to have new things. Anyway – I'll just amble round to the, uh – Christ, the um . . . oh God I've forgotten the name of *that*, now, Jesus; anyway – *there*, and have a quick drink and book us a table. Expensive place, yes (whatever it's called, but they actually do a rather surprisingly very reasonable set lunch and dinner, you know; I often book places working on such a principle, but Elizabeth always seems to go à la carte anyway, so it never actually gets to work, any of that. Laa-Laa too, come to think of it).

And now Howard was back from the Crillon (it was called the Crillon – it said it outside) and was quite in the mood for a bit of a kip, and maybe try Laa-Laa again – and so to be frank, he wasn't at all overjoyed to find Melody there.

'That was a quick tour,' he grunted. Sod you, he might well have added.

'Oh,' sighed Melody, 'I got a bit lonely. Do you want a drink, Howard? You don't mind me being here, do you? I can go, if you like.'

'I've just had one, actually . . . yes all right, why not. Course I don't *mind* you being here, Melody – what a daft thing to say.'

Melody crouched to the minibar and poured the last three whisky miniatures into a fresh glass (she knew her Howard) and added just a touch of Evian. While she was down there, she broke the neck of another little Smirnoff, and topped up her not-that-Bloody Mary. Howard received the drink with a smile of thanks – and yes of course he noticed that she was yet to withdraw her hand from his.

'Melody . . .' he said slowly, undercut by maybe a friendly note of caution. Because she did this, Melody, from time to time: she knows that what we had – good at the time, I'm not denying – was well and truly over years back, and yet whenever I try to be no more than kind to her, she starts up all this Howard-I-still-need-you caper. Mind you – it had worked on him that evening last summer, had it not? That evening I drove her home when Christ alone knows I could barely even walk: a very swift and dirty and really quite frightening fuck in the back of the Jag (a tomcat had shrieked as I jetted right into her – practically finished me off). But as I made it clear afterwards – that was a one-off. Joke is – at the time, all I could think of was Zoo-Zoo as I did it; now I just want to speak to Laa-Laa, and here comes bloody Melody again.

'Melody . . .' he tried again, as her other hand snaked up to and then around his neck – she teased the fine short hairs there, which she remembered he used to quite like, and Howard now registered electrically that he still quite did.

'Come on, Howard . . . oh come *on*,' teased Melody, brushing his lips with hers, as he felt her fingers on his thigh, and rising. 'Make it as fast as you like – I don't mind. I *need* it, Howard, I *need* it – do it to me hard. And now. And now.'

Well Jesus he was only human and filled with hot blood – and so, by Christ (the feel of those breasts, still damn firm) was she.

'Melody for Christ's *sake* . . .' Howard was practically pleading. '*Elizabeth* . . .'

And now she knew he'd cracked, Melody became both breathless and insistent:

'She'll be gone for *hours*, Howard – you know that. She only leaves shops when they throw her out. Take me. Take me.'

And when he opened his mouth to say Christ knows what she went to devour it and he brought up his hands to her hair and tugged it gently and then not gently and Melody grunted, loving it, and now Howard crushed himself against her, hugging hard, and the kick his heart

245

gave him as he leapt back and away as the door flew open came too close to stopping him for ever.

Elizabeth's whole face was bursting with news, but now she cut dead her headlong rush and a ripple of perplexity flicked across both eyes as her mouth fell slack and she cocked her head by way of asking someone to quell this for her.

'Ah Elizabeth!' blustered Howard, in a tone that suggested she was long overdue. 'Poor Melody – came over a bit tearful, didn't you, Melody? What with Paris and Christmas coming – all got a bit much for you, didn't it love?'

Melody had turned away, but she swivelled back now – and Howard was mightily relieved to see her big wet eyes that she now was busy dabbing at, while sniffing rather well for back-up.

'Silly of me,' she whispered. 'Sorry, Howard. To burden you.'

And they both faced Elizabeth, to see how it had gone.

There was still uncertainty there, just a glimmer – an almost childlike confusion, or maybe the doubting of all her senses. But the issue of the moment just had to win through – must first quickly get this out of the way: *Silly*, Melody, Elizabeth affectionately chided, stroking her arm in a sisterly way – you'll have *us* for Christmas, won't you, hm? *We* won't leave you alone. And then she could hold back no longer from hitting them both with the startling and really quite shudder-making events back home which she had only just this minute been learning from Lulu – and the line on her mobile had been terrible, just terrible, and she had had to keep asking for repeats.

Howard was shaking with shock. Never before had Elizabeth come anywhere close to catching him out at simply anything at all – a hint of any of that would be bound to destroy her. And just think – just five minutes later and . . . what was he bloody talking about! Thirty seconds on, just thirty seconds (she had got him so hot) and he and Melody would have been on the floor, mad-eyed and dishevelled, with dragged up and dragged down clothing – sticky with sweat and for his part, spent. And as to the news about Brian and Dotty and Dawn (dear Christ, *Dawn*) it made Howard feel quite physically sick. As for Melody – only the kid's *mother*, God's sake (Jesus, what a woman) – all she said was But you are sure, are you Elizabeth, that she wasn't actually *hurt*? And having been assured on that score, she seemed to just put the whole thing out of her mind: Dawn was, after all, still with Dotty, she said quite glibly, and what actually could be better than that? Howard could not say what now made him tremble. I will, he said on impulse, go straight back: give me your ticket, Melody – I'll get the nine o'clock (Brian, poor bugger, won't know where to turn).

Elizabeth was nodding, fairly abstractedly. 'I suppose,' she said, 'you must.'

Howard nodded too, and started beating energetically at all of his pockets – he tended to do this when any hint of On The Move was on the menu. 'Think it's best. Ring you, of course.'

'Maybe *I* should . . .?' put in Elizabeth, still bewildered.

'No point, is there?' returned Howard. 'No love – don't worry: I'll see to everything. No one's *hurt*, are they? Thank Christ. It's just a question of sorting them out. You enjoy the holiday – and Melody, Melody – you can take *my* place, yes? All paid for, after all.'

Melody went through the motions of bluster, and after a short while Elizabeth cut through that with no more than a tremor of doubt: Yes, yes – yes Melody, of course – that is the obvious answer. And then Elizabeth was thinking You know, it's quite funny – or do I mean odd? Normally (and is this somehow not normal, then?) it would have been me, insisting on that.

❋

247

Some time into the earlyish dinner at the Crillon, Elizabeth seemed to come to (from what?) and started in on Howard as to all the now essential domestic rearrangements: when poor Colin gets back from wherever he is, he'll have to, obviously, have a room of his own, so clear all your junk out of the boxroom, Howard (should've anyway done that years ago). Lulu is fine where she is – but Katie, Katie will have to move to the spare room – are you listening, Howard? Because Brian and Dotty will need the larger room and their own bath, poor things; and if Katie kicks up a fuss, as she probably will, just tell her *tough* – we all just have to knuckle down and make the best of it.

But right at that moment it seemed that Katie wouldn't, in fact, mind too much at all, because all she would want to do when finally she got home that night is sleep sleep sleep, oh God just sleep, crash out – because this guy Rick, let her tell you herself: Jesus, this guy – he wears you to a frazzle. But hey, that's cool – it's pretty much all I've been dying for, yeah? Rick is for real; the other boys I've been out with lately – well, that's all they really were: no more than little boys. But Rick's a man, all right. Masterful? Didn't know what it meant – didn't think I'd ever like it, but it's sort of OK – at the moment, it is; just for now I'm like, cool about it. And he chucks money around like confetti, and that's OK – that's cool too.

Take dinner. They had gone to this really spare and stylish sort of *designer* Indian place, Katie supposed you'd call it (he was staying at the Ritz – it's where he stayed – and she had thought OK, they'd be eating there, but no: that's one example of the masterful bit – just upped and said we're going, period. No nonsense about Fancy an Indian? Nothing like that: we're going, period). He had glanced at the menu in that very offhand and rather superior way people sometimes had when they already knew damn well what to order. And then he had cocked an eyebrow in Katie's direction and drawled out of the side of his mouth something that to her mind was just about the most inane and inexplicable thing in the world: You Feelin' Lucky – *Punk*? And Katie, being an English girl, had fluttered the smile of mild consternation and then tacked on I'm *sorry*? It was only later she twigged (hadn't noticed it before) that Rick was given to letting fly with bits of script from films, in what he maybe imagined to be the authentic voice of the actor concerned (his Connery-Bond in particular was shame-makingly and squirmingly quite horribly embarrassing, but look – all Katie was saying was that Rick was OK, yeah? Cool for now, a good big guy – not *perfect*, or anything).

And how many times had he insisted to the waiter with almost a fanatic's fervour that his curry, right, should be but *really* hot, got it? Like I mean not just what usually *passes* for hot, but the hottest of hots – kay? Make it the hottest of hots, mister, and then make it hotter again: think you can handle that? When it came, Katie watched him down a disdainful forkful and waited a bit and then said Hot enough for you? *Nah*, he sneered – nah, never is, baby – never is. Only one place I know in the world that makes it like fire, and that's a diner on the main drag in Reno – anyplace else it's just like a pussycat. Katie had tried just the littlest bit and felt her tongue cook as all her internal organs threatened an eruption. Look – just what more can she tell you about this guy? Huh?

And all afternoon in the long broad bed he'd come at and into her like a runaway train. We were not, Katie would like to make plain, talking Sensitive New Man, here, attentively caring for a woman's needs and tenderly exploring all the Cosmo secret places like armpits, napes, backs of knees and soles of feet (all those bits that just don't grab the headlines like all the sinking in and jutting out stuff does). By the end she was feeling not so much knocked up as down – maybe by a Cadillac; she just dragged herself to somewhere cooler, the aching victim of a big collision.

And after dinner, the menu on the bed had varied not at all – except that now his curried tongue was probing and scalding her deeply. Some time later (he was swigging Cristal, to cool him down) Rick got the front desk to order her a cab. He didn't actually ask her to stay over, and this was fine by Katie: all she wanted to do was just get back home and sleep sleep sleep – oh God, just sleep, crash out – because now you know just how it is that Jesus, this guy – he wears you to a frazzle.

Rick sat up amid the screwed-around debris of bed-clothes, one white sheet half cradling the thick dark fur that covered his chest. He clipped and lit an Upmann corona, and as the steel-blue smoke hissed away from him, he croaked out Of all the gin joints in all the towns in all the world – you hadta come inta *mine*. And Katie – attending to the last of her make-up – could only smile tentatively as one might well do to a declaiming loony in a night-time doorway, because she had not a clue in hell as to what he was on about.

Then he said: 'In the restaurant.'

'Yeh?'

'There was a guy. Guy looking at you.'

'Yeh? Didn't notice. So what?'

'And in the lobby downstairs – two other guys. Looking.'

Anyone else and Katie would have screamed at him to please just fuck *off*, OK? But this was Rick – right? And there was something about him – you just didn't mess with things like that, this much she knew; not with Rick, you didn't.

'There are always guys, Rick. Half the world is guys, right? And they look – guys look at girls. It's what they do.'

And now his voice hardened. 'Not no more. Not now they don't, baby – cos now you're mine. And no one – but no one gets to look at my girl. Capeesh?'

Katie gave him her Silly Boy smile, which was just about all she dared. And then, for something to do while she kicked this around, she started to pick up Rick's clothes which he had hurled just anywhere, so mad had he been to get at her (and when will they tell her the taxi's arrived? Oh God oh God – I'm so bloody tired I'm dropping). The tie and the shirt and the thong and the socks – those she dumped on a chair. She picked up the jacket, heavy and soft (can't seem to see the trousers) and his wallet and pen slipped out from an inside pocket and she slipped them back there and tried not to falter when she felt and then saw the snub-nosed automatic. Look – just what more can she tell you about this guy? Huh?

❊

And only Katie that night was big in the mind of Norman Furnish, even though he was just that minute about to pop out and quickly see a prostitute. Well look – when it came down to it (and that was the point – in Norman's life, it rarely did) then truly and honestly, it just had to be the only way, now. It was the last agency date that had finally done it for Norman – he just couldn't, could he, go on shelling out money and hiking miles across London (and why did it always have to be *their* side of the river? Good bloody question) solely in order to be summarily humiliated, roundly jeered and then just left there? Even for Norman, there was a limit, he would have you know – and last evening that had surely been reached and then breached in just another unknown pub, with yet another nutter. This one had been called Davina, and she was already propping up the bar by the time Norman arrived ten or twelve minutes early, and once they each had established with roughly equal measures of near-tangible distaste, if not out-and-out revulsion, the awful truth of the identity of the other, the first thing she said to him was Where in hell have *you* been, Norman? Getcherself a drink, then: call me Dive – everyone does.

'Dive?' checked Norman (why does everyone?)

'Not *Dive*,' she practically roared at him (and she was a

sizeable woman, please believe Norman – this woman came only as a bumper pack). *'Dive,'* she clarified, 'as in Dye-vid fuckin' *Bowie.'*

'Ah,' breathed Norman, 'right.' And then to the bargirl, who much to her own disgust had failed to time the back-turning and then make good her escape: 'Large Bell's, please – with ice.' Still wasn't quite sure about the taste, in truth – but this stuff *worked*, right? And tonight it would have to work bloody fast, let him tell you.

'What star are you, Norman? You wanna get me another vog-ka?'

'Pisces,' said Norman, 'if that's all right. Yeh sure – if the girl ever comes back. Anything with it?'

'Are we eating? Only I'm famished. No – just as it comes: large one. And how old are you? Pisces isn't *great* for me actually – it's not a *disaster*, know what I'm saying? But when I hear Pisces I'm not like, *wow* – you know? Me I'm Gemini, yeh? I go most for the fire signs. How old did you say you were? You look quite young and quite old, I reckon.'

'That's pretty much how I feel, a lot of the time. I'm twenty-six.' And so nervy was he that he very nearly added on If That's All Right, again: he felt rather as if he had strayed into the high ground of a no-man's-land somewhere between the Yes and No interlude and a nerve-breaking initiation into West Point Academy.

'Yeh? You look older than that, I think. Maybe just a bit beat up. I'm in my thirties, if you wanna know. But every-one says I look really amazingly young.'

'Yes?' checked Norman (why does everyone?). And then the bargirl made the huge mistake of having her eye caught again (Christ, she maybe thought, I must be losing the talent for this game) and so Norman was able to get in the vog-ka and another large Bell's for himself because the first one (big surprise) was now just vapour.

It's bloody crowded and noisy in here; I don't, thought

Norman now – a wash of misery suddenly all over him – actually *like* pubs, if I'm totally honest . . . but then where else were poor people cooped up in freezing little rooms expected to go? How else could they partake of and savour the finest cask ales and wines and spirits – all part and parcel of the bogus gilded mirrors and the lying fucking brewers – while exploring the spirituality and sheer animal magnetism of wonders such as Dive?

Who now said: 'Cheers, then, Norman – Christ I'm bleedy nungry.'

Norman nodded, sipped and then gulped. I don't like this woman, he thought – she scares me to bloody death. OK – breasts are good – yeah huge – but that red mouth has teeth in it, you've only got to look. And her thighs could break me in half; and I bet she's got misshapen feet – boats are bloody massive. Plus, there's not a single thing I want to know about her: I don't want to know what her job is – *nor* for how long she's been doing it, and certainly not if she's happy there. I don't want to know where she lives, whether she shares, or if it's handy for the Tube. I could not care if she has brothers, sisters or living parents, what sort of movies she goes for and nor if she has a favourite book. Her birthday is anathema. I know she is a Gemini, and that is surplus to requirements. And neither am I concerned as to whether she currently fancies a Chinese, Indian, Big Mac, spag bol or something posh and Frenchy – and here now we come to the nub of the thing: despite my desperation and all my pent-up craving, I do not wish to spend even one more second in the company of this thing (and yet she's no worse than many) – and nor do I wish to pay for food and watch her eat it. My icebound room seems better than here, and if I drink more whisky it'll warm me. Think I've got to go. Katie, oh Katie – why did you leave me? Just look at the things I'm reduced to now.

'You know what, Norman?' said the diva that was Dive, nudging him.

Norman did not, and he admitted as much.

'I really go for you – you know? And I don't normally – I'm pretty, like, picky. But I'm getting vibes – yeh? You getting them, Norman? You feeling karma?'

No, thought Norman – feeling more nervy; I'm stifled, now, and jangled.

'I think,' he stuttered, 'I have to go.'

'Go? What chew talkin' about – go! You've only just bleedin' arrived. What about grub – ay? And I wannanother drink.'

Norman shook his head and tried a smile. 'No. Sorry. Go. Got to.'

And then she became raucous and oh dear God – people were *looking*.

'Yeh? *Yeh*?! Well just you let me tell you this, fuckin' Norman whoever-you-are – you *can't* go. Know why? Ay? I say Know why? Ay? I'll bleedin' tell you – cos *I'm* going, that's why. See? *I'm* going – *me*. No one walks out on me, mate – and specially not a spineless little weasel-faced bloody cretin like *you*. When I said back there I *liked* you – huh! That was shit – I just felt *sorry* for you, cos you, fuckin' Norman, are just *pathetic*. You're dirt – you're lowlife – you're just fuckin' *nothin'*, son.'

And laughing now (her big face flushed with delirious scorn) the woman walked clean away – while men hid sniggers with pints, eyes beneath raised brows sneaking sideways to contact others (Christ Almighty – poor bloody sod: bit of a laugh, though).

So he couldn't, could he, go on shelling out money and hiking miles across London solely in order to be summarily humiliated, roundly jeered and then just left there? Which is why now the next day he had come to his senses and bought a *Men Only* and got on the phone. And the first thing he asked of all the women was where the hell *are* you, hey? Because if you're not local, forget it. And Jesus – what, could every bloody female in London live across the river?

254

It surely bloody seemed so – until eventually, at last, about time, he got one – sounded gorgeous – who was not just nearby, he even knew the actual street. Mind you, when they touched on the money side, Norman wavered (maybe *Men Only* was enough?) but then he came down on the side of Oh sod it – I'm going to do it, have to, if only to remember how it *goes*.

And she'd banged on about how warm and lovely her pad was and everything, which was damn good news to Norman, believe him, not just because he longed to get out of his, but also because he had yet to even begin to obliterate the memory of that awful encounter in King's Cross, that time, in a room that makes even this one appear palatial. And maybe yes, one day, he would haul back into his mind all of the detail – mull it over and then be done with it for ever – but not now, he wouldn't, oh dear me no, oh no. And anyway – look: I'll be late if I don't go now (you only get an hour – Christ, the money these birds must make; she said she had a special rate to stay there overnight – and God I'm sorely tempted).

But despite or even because of what he was about to do, as he slipped out and into the whippingly bitter night, it was only Katie who was big in the mind of Norman Furnish.

❄

And he wasn't the only one: Miles McInerney was scarcely able to believe not one bit of what he was bloody *hearing*. Christ Al-bleeding-Mighty – there's no woman ever, not ever, what's tried to pull this one on me. I mean – Jesus: I call up some tart – she's all over me, right? And so she bloody should be. But this! This just ain't the way it bloody goes. I mean oi – what the fuck is going on here? Miles had physically recoiled from the earpiece on his handset – pulled the car in just wherever he happened to be and parked it bloody badly: Up Yours! Up Yours! he furiously mugged at whatever death-wish fuckface he'd cut right up – him with his blaring bloody hooter: you come back here and I'll do you, mate!

'What do you mean "*no*"?' he repeated, genuinely amazed. 'I've booked the bloody thing – you said when we were there the last time for me to bloody book it again and I've booked it – champagne laid on, the works.'

'Yeh . . .' sighed Katie. 'But something came up – you know?'

'Something . . .! What's your game? Ay? Some *bloke*, more like.'

'*Yeh*,' came back Katie, with defiance. '*Is* some bloke – what's it to you? I'm not your bloody wife, am I? You've *got* a bloody wife – remember?'

'You said you didn't care I got a wife.'

'I don't. Don't care. Don't care about you, either. I'm hanging up, Miles – so sod off.'

Miles caught his breath and panic flooded him: this was all wrong – this was upside-down: it's me what says all that.

'Catherine! Don't . . . don't *say* that. We're all right, you and me.'

'*Were* all right,' amended Katie, with big emphasis. 'We were fine. And now we're not. I don't know what you're getting all so bloody het up about, Miles – I mean, we both of us knew it wasn't *going* anywhere, or anything, didn't we? Just a bit of fun, that's all.'

'No!' protested Miles, barely able to believe that it was he who was doing all this. 'I never thought that, never. I thought – you and me – we could've made a real go of it.'

'You're *married*, Miles! Why does this fact keep slipping your little mind? You've got two kids. Face it – you're *stuck*.'

And that one sent him reeling.

'Never! Me? I'm not . . . *stuck*? Me? Get out of it – I do what I like, when I like – got it? So I'm married – yeh, big deal, so what? People get un-married all the time. It's nothing, these days. Come on, Catherine – be sweet. Let's meet and we talk about it, yeh?'

'What – you're going to leave your wife, then, are you Miles?'

'Yeh,' agreed Miles like a shot. And yes, he'd said it before (face it, he'd said everything before). But with all the other birds, that was just to shut them up; this is to stop her going. So yeh – I could leave Sheil, why not? She won't bloody care. And the boys? Well – boys are tough: they get over things, don't they? Bleeding got to – what's the choice?

'I don't believe you, Miles. And even if you mean it, I'm not interested. Got it? Not. We are over, Miles – it's not that tricky to understand. You go back to Sheila – or whatever other little new bit of skirt you've got in tow –'

'Catherine!' Miles barked out, eyes quite wide with shock. 'Please –'

'And I'll go back to Rick, and we'll all live happily ever –'

'Rick? *Rick*?! Who in fuck's name's *Rick*?!'

'Oh Miles . . . just leave it. Christ's sake. Look – *Bye*, OK?'

'*Can't* leave it – *can't*. Catherine? *Catherine*? Jesus.'

Miles stabbed at Redial and an android told him the cellphone he was dialling was currently switched off, and to please try later. He stared ahead of him. Christ. Later just ain't no bloody use to me, is it? When it gets to later – I've bloody well lost.

CHAPTER ELEVEN

'That was my Mum,' Colin had said simply, replacing the receiver on the old-fashioned phone – still a bit surprised that Dotty had called him (I mean yeah – gave her a contact number, had to really, but I didn't for a minute expect her to ring it) – and shaking too with a silly relief that it just happened to be he who had answered. Carol, for her part, was furious (her face was white and taut and hard – never seen her like that before) because *what*, she had demanded, what on earth would've happened if it'd been my *Dad* – hm? I mean Jesus, Colin – I'm supposed to be here alone and slaving away to pick up a bit of Christmas money from bloody Auntie Jane: what would he have thought if some *boy* had answered the phone? I am not, Colin had returned (quite hurt – was this childish?), just some *boy*, am I? Carol had snapped back oh Christ God*sake*, Colin: you know what I *mean*. Anyway, Colin had tacked on sullenly, it wasn't your Dad, was it? It was my Mum. Yes yes yes I *know* that, Colin – I'm just saying – what are you? *Thick*? I'm just saying what if it *had* been. But Jesus, Carol – it *wasn't*, was it? What more can I tell you? And a sort of impasse descended, each of them glaring at the other's very evident incapacity to get hold of the *point*, here.

'She sounded a bit funny,' Colin now said (God I can't stand it when Carol's just silent, like this – she never used to be: not last summer, she wasn't). And then, when she made a fairly large show of Not Responding, Colin went on a bit, more or less for himself – because he knew, now (this much he had learned), that if Carol ever opened her mouth again to speak, it would only to be airily dismissive: something on the lines of Sorry, Colin? Wasn't Really Listening. 'Said something about she and Dad not going away after all – going back to Elizabeth's. Apparently we're staying with Elizabeth. Don't know why.'

The look that Carol now gave him – you could tell she couldn't care. And no, she thought now – I don't care, actually; why in fact should I? I don't know that it was a great idea, coming here like this: the worst bit's having to lie to my Dad. Every time I've rung him today, I've had to feed him a load of nonsense, and it's just not in me to do that. On the last call he'd said Oh my poor little angel Carol – you sound so down: why don't I drive over and give you lunch? And the thought had so pleased and thrilled her that she very nearly came back with Oh *Great*, Dad – that would be fab, super – until she remembered (well OK – she hadn't forgotten) that this was very much a no-no.

But you see, Dad's great *fun*, that's the point – and this, all this . . . I don't know: not sure. Colin's pretty sexy – don't get me wrong (he really does have quite lovely hands) but it's just that whenever he *says* anything lately . . . oh – I don't know: it just kind of drives me nuts, you know? I don't *think* it's me – but he always seems to be taking the negative view, watering down my ideas so that they almost don't exist any more. Become invisible. I mean look – we've just come back from shopping, and never mind all the rain and heaving it up the stairs and all the rest of the crap – just the business of Colin having *reservations* all the time about practically *everything* – and Jesus, some of the things he seems to like to eat! I mean – frozen chicken *nuggets*? Puhleese. And he said No, don't get French sticks because by tomorrow they'll all be hard and horrible – and I said what do you mean *tomorrow*? These are for eating today – tomorrow we'll get more. Not difficult, is it? And he doesn't like olives (what he in fact said was I've never actually eaten olives, Carol, but I'm sure I wouldn't like them: too oily).

259

And when I said let's get some chockies for the evening he said oh yeah great – and he wandered off down the aisles and came back with a titchy little box of Milk *Tray*. Christ. I suppose it's upbringing, isn't it? The parents. I forget what it's like to have a Mum (let's just say the divorce wasn't the friendliest thing in the world – doesn't matter now) but my Dad's really taught me about stuff that *matters*, you know? As to *Colin's* Dad, well . . . what can one say? Colin hates him, clearly – and yeh, I suppose it's easy to see why – but even he, you know . . . even Colin maybe doesn't yet see the extent of the damage. Poor Colin. Anyway – let's get all this stuff put away, and then I can sit down and have a drink. Or maybe make a start on that bedroom? We've got all the paint and everything – God, even that was a bloody battle: let's get *this* one, I said. Ooooh I don't *know*, Carol, he says – it's practically *red*. It *is* red, Colin – it is, yeh: Auntie Jane'll like that. And then he goes, Why don't you get something a bit less . . . I mean, something like this, say? Because, I shot back, that looks like the colour of *porridge*, Colin – it's *boring*: dull dull *dull*, right? So we got the red stuff (it's brilliant – like a pillar box) and Colin just muttered Well, it's *your* aunt's flat – and I said yeh, yeh you're right: it is, Colin. It is.

Weird thing was, when we got to all the other bits you need he was going Hm, we'd better have this sugar soap, I'm pretty sure he said (sugar *what*?), and Polyfilla and *two grades* of sandpaper and some sort of knife thing and then instead of a socking great brush to whack it on with he went for a roller and some piddly little brush called a, what did he say? Hitch, pitch, bitch – something. Mitch, witch – whatever. And I said Jesus, Colin – how come you know about all this stuff? And he went kind of pale and kind of white and he just said I don't know, Carol – I simply cannot tell you. Weird huh? He never used to be: not last summer, he wasn't.

'It says here,' Carol now called out over her shoulder (Colin was in the kitchen, quite enjoying stowing away all their groceries in cupboards, fitting things neatly into the fridge – it was really good to be living in rooms again, like people did) – 'that you don't have to stir it.' She gazed into the bloody murk of two-and-a-half litres of alarming emulsion and sniffed at it a bit. 'But there's a funny sort of filmy bit on the top and it looks more maroon than red at the moment. What do you think? It's got a hell of a niff.'

'Well,' came back Colin, 'if that's what it *says* . . . maybe you're just meant to move it around with the brush for a bit. Are you really going to start on that now, Carol? Wouldn't it be best to wait till the morning? Ah – that's where it is: I've just found the cutlery. And the glasses.' It was pretty good, all this – like preparing for a siege: stocking up the bunker and then hunkering down and ducking from fallout with the woman you love.

'Yeh but we haven't *got* a brush, have we? Only that witch thing.'

'Fitch,' corrected Colin. 'Yeh well – when we pour it into the roller tray, it'll all even out, I expect.'

'What roller tray? We didn't get a roller tray.'

'Ah,' breathed Colin. Oh Christ how dumb – I didn't get a roller tray: oh Jesus how stupid.

'Well it's going to take just years with this little titch.'

'Fitch,' grunted Colin.

'It's still a *titch*, though, isn't it? God, Colin – I thought you were supposed to know about all this sort of stuff.'

'I never said that. Maybe we could use something else.'

'Well you were banging on about all that sugar crap for long enough,' snapped Carol, actually getting a bit pissed off, now, if you really want to know.

'Soap,' said Colin quietly, now standing beside her. 'It's not crap – it's soap.' These are simple words, is what he was thinking, so why can't she bloody remember them? 'What about maybe a baking tray? Oven tin, thing.'

'Oh yeh great!' exploded Carol now. 'And then possibly we can clean the bloody roller and the bloody little ditch on

261

Auntie Jane's *bedspread*, why not – and if you say "fitch", if you just dare say *"fitch"*, Colin, I'll dump this paint all over you, I'm telling you now.'

'Like you did the ice-cream,' tried Colin (can we maybe make a joke of this? Hope so, hope so – cos I'm getting upset). 'But I wouldn't recommend it – think of Auntie Jane's carpet.'

Carol at least had the goodness to snort: even an aborted laugh was better than none. 'What *ice*-cream – what are you talking about *now*, Colin?'

'Don't you remember? You *must* remember.' Can she really not? God – I do: it's the only moment in my entire life that changed things (well – apart from getting drunk and losing my virginity to my mother's best friend: something I now think I'm maybe not yet old enough to even *think* about, let alone to have actually done). 'When we met. On the sands last summer. The van – yes?'

Carol's hand darted up to cover the snuffling laughter and her eyes creased up in delight, thank God.

'Oh God *that* ice-cream – oh God, Colin, God – you must have thought I was such a prat, spilling it all over you like that.'

'No,' smiled Colin. 'I thought you were lovely.'

'And then I bought us both another,' laughed Carol, 'and we sat down on that dune thing – and that's why we know each other now! Yeh, life's funny. You never know about anything, really.'

Colin sat next to her on the rug in front of the (shall we soon light it?) fire. 'Actually it was *me* who bought more ice-creams, but doesn't matter. Yes – I loved that day.'

Carol froze, and looked at him. 'Christ, Colin,' was all she said.

Colin now pulled away too – shocked by this new coldness, and just about utterly confused.

'*What* . . .?' he attempted.

'*I* bought the ice-cream – *I* did: distinctly remember. Not that it actually matters.'

'It doesn't matter!' hooted Colin. 'Of course it doesn't – I'm just saying that in fact it was me, that's all. That's it. Nothing more. It's just that I remember the whole scene so well and –'

'Oh and I *don't*, I suppose. I wasn't *there*, right?'

'Look, Carol –'

'No *you* look, Colin – oh Christ you drive me crazy! How can you go on and on about a bloody *ice*-cream? I mean – how mean can you actually *get*! Oh look – I'm going to have a bath, it's the only thing I need, right now. All this is doing my head in. Just get me a drink, yeh? Open a bottle of that fizz – you can *manage* that, I suppose? And bring it in to me.'

Shock – maybe shock took up the lion's share of all that Colin was feeling: how could Carol *be* like this? Shock, yes – but also hurt: that cruel and dismissive jibe about opening the fizz. Did she have to? Say that? Apparently – or else she would have kept it down. Shock and hurt, yes – but the skin-crawling kick of lust: this too was leerily going about its business (the momentary prick of the moment when he would be sucked into the clammy warmth of the bathroom, and see her sprawled there).

And on a point of order: no – no he couldn't actually manage this palaver with the fizz, since we're bloody asking. Never actually done it before, had he? But thank God that at least Carol is elsewhere and not just *looking* at him (he didn't even attempt the neck wire until the air was filled by the hot gurgle of taps and the sweet whiff of maybe mimosa). The cork – having been up till now intransigent to the point of immutability – suddenly assumed a life of its own and shot off like a mechanical hare into Auntie Jane's saucepans, which maybe Carol hadn't heard – and the realization that his arched eyes and enquiring nostrils had been so whisker-close to the thing still made Colin shudder (he had felt the draught as it whistled by) but he forced himself

263

into finding a sort of cloth thing quickly to mop up the floor and wipe away the sticky coursing from his fingers – and now he must wash out the very prettiest glass that Auntie Jane had to offer. Maybe then (always assuming he didn't skid on the bath mat and crash the whole caboodle into the centre of her face) Carol might soften and smile and care for him again?

And the very thing of prettiness – wholly subjective, isn't it? Very much famous for being so (beauty is in the eye of the whatever – right?). But this little glass here – this surely struck Colin as maybe lovely: it was smaller than an average wine glass, he supposed, and the bowl was more like a delicate and inverted cone, than anything. The stem took in a bulbous ball about halfway up, and then the glass turned pinkish – little coloured garlands around the rim, and this was trimmed in gold. *Nah* – what am I thinking of, Colin suddenly chastised himself: this is like one of a set that my Mum would have collected by mail order over a succession of months and months and months: she had been a sucker for so long for just anything like that, poor old Mum – could never seem to get that Send No Money Now just came down to Authorize Us To Siphon Off A Bucketload Later.

So no – dump the little dolly glass; how about this one, then? Seems nice enough – slim, plain, straight-sided – but how is one actually expected to *know*, hm? I mean – I couldn't tell you the first thing about this or just anything else in the world, it keeps on seeming, but I so terribly don't want to make another *mistake*. Well – all I can do is plump for this one: it's either that or a *mug*. Take it in now, shall I? (Just can't wait to see her, awash and warm.) Or is now still a bit too early? I mean to say, it would be just awful if she was attending to, oh – I don't know, some *part* of her that women, girls, maybe like to keep to themselves. Or if she's only halfway into the bath – or maybe not got to the bath bit at all yet, and still just sitting on the loo. There was a lot to think about here, and quite a bit at stake – so possibly leave it a tad yet, yes? But the bubbles in the fizz were looking none too frisky – though what finally had the effect of spurring him into action was Carol's still quite tetchy voice coming loud and clear from behind the door: Colin? Colin? Where's That Bloody *Drink*?

He had not known quite or even remotely what to expect – but the picture on kicking open the bathroom door (I know, I know – but with two full glasses, how else can you?) came quite close to making him gasp. He might well *even* have gasped, he now acknowledged – though here could be something too to do with the throat-gripping rasp of a thousand scents, as well as the winking and shadowy vision of Carol's sweet face and long and perfect limbs spread out in warm and oily water as if on offer, as all the flickering candles in opaque and frosty potlets smoothed her into honey planes that curved off into darkness. He wanted his voice to mellow in harmony and come up meltingly only with the enraptured exhalation: *Darling*! What he said was Holy *Shit* – which yeh, he knew, was even worse than the Gosh he'd abandoned.

Colin crouched down to her, low. The look on her face, now, was one of perfect pleasure – and while Colin would not at all have minded being the sort of older, wiser and generally more cool sort of guy who could have dwelt on this, locking into the light of her eyes, he had to admit to coping badly with this whole carnival of distraction some way to the south of all that because God, I'm telling you – I just don't think I'll ever get over the way these girls are put together (hope not, anyway); but it's simply astonishing, isn't it, how they just come out in a jutty sort of a way and then swoop back in again and then before you know it, out again looms some other rounded part, soon hiding one more secret: all they have to do is lie there, quite frankly, and it seems like they're thrashing about.

'Do I get this drink, then?' she said. But softly: all the essential oils marbling the bathwater allied with the musky

flowers around her were clearly having their lulling effect
(they certainly were on Colin – he felt half strangled and
blind). And even as he handed Carol her glass and managed
to nudge one of the squatter and peachier tea-lights over the
rim and (plop) into the bath, there was no more than a
flicker of maybe not even irritation across her creamy brow.

'You know, Colin,' she smiled – shifting all the warm
gorgeousness of her just so slightly (enough to cause an
easy swell in the water, before it slopped back lazily, and
over her). 'You're the only person who hasn't thought I'm
silly when I've told them about all my candles and oils.'

'Really?' breathed Colin. 'God you look so lovely, Carol.'
God, I want her badly.

Carol nodded – smiling now in affectionate memory. 'My
Dad's ribbing me about it all the time – says I make the
bathroom smell like a perfume house on fire. He always
buys me more, though – always gets the good ones. And as
for that beastly brother of mine – Terry just laughs at me out
loud, the pig. He still absolutely *loathes* you, you know,
Colin. He'll kill you, I think, if he ever sees you again.'

Colin maintained his expression, or so he very much
hoped.

'Even my best friend Emma – thinks I'm crazy: lots of
girls at school do, some reason. Tony too – he thinks it's all
pretty funny.'

And then Carol gave out a yelp that had Colin leaping to
his feet in alarm – was she burned? Can she be choking like
me?

'Oh *look*, Colin, *look* – look at the window! Oh God how
perfect, how beautiful, how utterly romantic!'

Colin glanced up at the black of the window, where early
night had taken its hold. Fat and fluffy, big flakes of snow
were softly hitting the glass and subsiding, already banking
up into a cloud upon the sill – and soon the whole pane was
patterned with dancing white polka dots, as Carol sighed
her deep contentment. Oh *God*, she was thinking, just think

266

if it's like this at Christmas! What bliss, what bliss, what absolute and utter heaven that would be.

While all Colin could think was Sod the snow: who's this *Tony*?

❋

'Oh *Dotty* . . .' exhaled Lulu – a hopeless sigh, dripping with sympathy, but chock-full too of what-can-mere-words-*say*? And 'Oh Dotty . . .' was all she could think of following it with; and then she shook her head a bit.

But Dotty was well on the way to having a jolly good stab at bravery (well *someone* had to, didn't they? *Someone* had to be brave for Dawn – and who else, then, but Dotty? Melody, you think? No you *don't*, do you: Melody's in Paris, having a holiday. Brian? Well take one look at him, and then please tell me your verdict).

He was over there in the corner of what (until just that morning) had been Katie's room; he was slumped deep into a chair, gazing out of the window at the thickish sleet falling and now wetly settling on the patch of Howard and Elizabeth's driveway where used to loom (until just that morning) all that was left on earth of Brian and Dotty's life together. Brian's head shook sadly too – while his fingers idly plucked at the silly fringe of something or other that must be Katie's. All that lingers is my nicely spaced out collection of (white-flecked) manhole covers: what will become of them now?

'Well look,' attempted Dotty, 'this really was one of those times, you know, when it truly could have been an awful lot worse. I mean – we're *here*, aren't we? In one piece?' You know, she thought suddenly now, in a way this might even be better: having just nothing, instead of so little.

'Yes of course that's true,' Lulu readily agreed. 'Of course you're right – that *has* to be the way to look at it.' But *I* couldn't – Jesus no. I think by now, had Johnny brought me down this far, and not merely to the brink of leaving him,

267

then I would maybe want to see him gaudily die – before I ran away just anywhere, in tears and in pieces. 'Now look – I've sorted out some of Lizzie's clothes – oh and Brian: Howard too says to take from his wardrobe anything you need, right – but he'll be back a bit later so you can talk to him, OK? OK? Brian?'

Dotty said quietly: 'Just leave him.' I feel, she thought, almost sorry: even for him, even for him – and that I haven't come close to doing for practically ever. When I phoned Colin, he had sounded so . . . *free*: I simply didn't have it in me to tie him down again; so all I said was that I and his father and baby Dawn were doing fine, but that we were coming home to Elizabeth's – and that met with no more than an ironic if not utterly baffled or maybe couldn't-t-care silence (Yeh? Great). Thank heavens for his schoolmate, that's all: at least he was somewhere else and having fun. And otherwise, despite all his protestations, he might well have been with us, no? And would Colin have stepped out into that freezing evening, just to see the AA man? No no no – I can't think like that, or else I shall start to tremble again. Poor Colin; he will of course not be sorry to have seen the last of the caravan, but what when he learns (when he takes it in, as I have yet to do) that here was the end of the line: the time when there is no *instead*? Because face it – do you think that for Brian the word contingency has remotely or for an instant entered? Well take one look at him, and then please tell me your verdict.

When the phone rang, Dotty merely glanced at it dully (who would be ringing me?) while Brian seemed not to have registered at all. Lulu could have picked up on Katie's handset, but here was maybe a good chance to leave them now, yes? She could not again say where there were towels, and nor any more could she demonstrate sadness.

This, thought Lulu – making for the phone in the drawing room, comfortingly two floors below – just has to be my

Lizzie (but please God at this hour let it not be her mother: really not up to a bout of that).

'Lulu?' came the breathless enquiry. 'I'm so glad it's you who answered. It's, um – me.'

'*Yes*, John,' hissed Lulu. 'I know it is.' She had toyed with feigning an aloof surprise, although with John there could never be anything approaching that: even when he was gone, he was somehow still there. Instead, Lulu gave in to quite real weariness.

'I just wondered . . . well, no reason – not calling for any reason at all, really. Just to know you're safe. Settled in, sort of thing.'

'You mean,' amended Lulu, quite sternly, 'that you're checking up I'm here.'

'No!' came back the huge protestation, full of shock at the very idea. 'No, I just . . . well I *said* . . . just saying hello, really. You notice I am quite sober? I mean – I've had, you know – *couple*, yeh – but I'm really quite OK.'

'Good,' said Lulu, with forced patience. 'In some drying-out clinic, are you?' Damn, thought Lulu – damn damn: I was quite determined to show no curiosity at all as to where in hell he is (and in truth, I feel none).

'No not, as a matter of fact. Do you want to know where I am, then, Lulu? Tell you, will I?'

'John – it's late . . .'

He was crestfallen, now. John had not been certain whether he would have told her, had she asked (dangerously boat-burning: if the front door is bolted, and the back one too, should we not all leave open at least a cat-flap?) – but it would have been mighty good to know that she minded either way.

'So,' he said slowly – with some sorrow, yes, but not nearly so much as he was ladling on, here – 'you don't, um – want to know?'

Lulu sighed heavily. 'Right, John – right: I just don't want to *know*.'

She turned off the phone, in defence of any milksop call-back. The silence in this darkened house was new to her: Mr Nelligan's familiar and grumbling movements in the kitchen had ceased till morning (the very last of the work, he had told her tonight); Katie presumably with whoever this Rick was – and Peter gone to wherever he goes; Lizzie in Paris, of course – and Howard not back yet. The only people here are refugees, and they so seldom make noises, for fear of maybe further shame – or else just losing a toehold, so hard fought for.

❋

John felt like hell when he woke the next morning: took him a devil of a while to work out just why what he was feeling was so far from the usual dull heaviness, presaging the true and would-be storming hangover which might not come till evening (when he would redouble the day's puny alcoholic efforts to hammer it back into the dungeon where it belonged, and not surge through him, killing his parts as it went).

The reason I feel just terrible in quite another way, I now just about recall, is that I had far too little to drink because of Tara's insistence that some ochre and truly nasty-looking joint would be far better for me (far better for me!) before we went on to, Christ – must have been at least a couple of chopped-out lines of coke and *Look*, I said, look: I've never actually been into any of this, can I tell you, Tara – and couldn't we just open a case of something maybe red or golden, huh? And she said *Sweetie*. So I dragged down the joint, honked up the horse. *What* did you call it, then she hooted. *Huh*? I had said: huh? Just then – the coke: you called it 'horse'. I did? Yeh I did – isn't that what they call it? *Horse*, sweetie darling, is *heroin*: heroin, my angel, is horse. Oh right, I said: right. And then she came back with *Want some*? And here I put my foot down (hell – I was floating just above the floor anyway: it didn't have far to go) and so

270

she went off alone to get even higher in the bath and I – don't ask me why – I just phoned up Lulu. (Well ask me why, then: I just had to check she was *there*.) And I felt so lucid: it only hit me later.

So at least now I have worked out just why this room – these curtains, that chair, the thick air around me – why it all seems so utterly strange. I am at Tara's place in Bath, then – right? And just beyond these curtains is the soot-stained and not-at-all honey-coloured pediment of must be next door's door, a watery sun doing its pitiful best to warm its coldness.

When Tara had come to bed last night, I was jolted from I-wasn't-really-I-don't-think-asleep and headlong into wide-eyed and hard-boned, red-throated lust. Felt I would *die* if I didn't have all of her now now *now* – and booze alone, believe me, just doesn't work like that. She had stumbled over something as she gigglingly approached and I had called out to myself Oh My Poor Sweet Darling Are You Hurt? Come To Me, My Woman! I do not recall just how or which way we conjoined – felt near gone again, and this time with even my limbs inside her; a deeply seeping just-pubertal near-orgasmic tremble made me then aware, rather than overtook me – and for maybe hours it seemed as if all my blood and spleen and marrow were sweetly siphoned elsewhere, leaving me only oozing with a gently insistent and genital tingle, the rest of me progressively weakened into chalk-white and brittle – caved in flat, and sucked out soft. Then she was away from me, Tara – swaying towards the door of the room – oh God, oh God: way over there – and she stumbled over something as she gigglingly left me and I had called out to myself Christ You Fucking Clumsy Bitch and I think I think I must have died for at least a very short while, before I spent just one more year suspended, falling out of and then into the trick of sleep.

It's later in the morning – close on lunchtime – and now it's sort of snowing; all the streaked and darkened stone on

271

those strait-laced façades beyond the twelve-bar window –
it seems it's almost weeping. Tara's eating something eggy:
I just couldn't face it.

'So, sweetie – have you decided? Staying, are you? It's
just that I'm going off out to get some things in a minute,
and I'd sort of like to know.'

'I think I am. Well – I'm not going *now*, anyway. If that's
what you mean. How can you sit there and eat that stuff?'

'Protein. But I mean Christmas, sweetie – Christmas. I can
still fry you a couple, if you've changed your mind? No?'

'Christmas . . . yeh, I – yeh, spose so. Sorry, Tara – I don't
mean to sound ungrateful, or anything – I'm just a bit . . .'

'Enough! Let's just say you *are*, yes? I'll just get in all the
stuff and anything we don't use I can freeze. Last call for
eggs?'

'Oh God – no really, not. A drink, maybe . . .'

'Bit early after last night, don't you think so, sweetie?'

'Tara – you are smoking a *joint*! And I distinctly saw you
sprinkling something that was decidedly not salt over that
awful omelette thing.'

'Different, sweetie – totally different. This stuff doesn't
dull the brain.'

'Oh yeh? Oh yeh? It practically annihilated mine.'

'That's just because you're not used to it. Anyway – it was
probably the snow that did that. Not *horse* – remember?'

'Yeh. I remember.'

'And you had wine. And whisky.'

'Wouldn't mind a whisky.'

'Can't.'

'Can't? Why can't? I thought you said if I came here
there'd be peace and crates of booze?'

'You'll get your peace when I go out. And the booze,
sweetie – you can have all you like *after*.'

'After? Oh Christ – what's this, now? After what?'

'After you *write*, of course sweetie! That's what you
wanted, isn't it?'

272

'Oh God don't tell me – One Thousand Ways to Use Illegal Substances in Scrambled Eggs! What do you mean *write*, Tara? It's practically bloody Christmas.'

'Your *book*, sweetie – you can't have forgotten? The *novel* – yes?'

'Oh . . . Jesus. You know what, Tara – it doesn't seem possible, I know, but I had pretty bloody well forgotten, you know. My mind these days is just a . . . Christ.'

'You have *brought* it?'

'Hm? Oh yeh – *brought* it, sure: what there is of it.'

'How much did you say you'd done? Do you want a drag on this before I put it out?'

'No – told you, not into it. And you won't even give me a drink.'

'You'll love me for it one day. Now answer – how much?'

'Mm? How much? Oh – the book, you mean . . .'

'Don't stall.'

'OK, OK . . . seventeen pages. Christ.'

'Well here is your perfect opportunity: you've got the whole of the afternoon, and the promise of not just my gorgeous self but an ocean of drink to come. Well?'

'It's not as *easy* as that, Tara . . . you can't just switch it on and off, you know. It's not like that.'

'Mm. What's it called?'

'Don't even know that. I wanted to call it *Catch-22*.'

'*Catch-22*? Why on earth *that*? Pretty famous book.'

'I know, I know – it's just such a good title. Or *Nineteen Eighty-Four*.'

'I think, you know sweetie, you're going to just have to start thinking on slightly more original lines. That, frankly, is what's wrong with a lot of your pieces, you know: derivative, very.'

'Maybe you're right – but only derivative from the last bloody one I wrote. All this stuff – it's all the bloody *same*, isn't it?'

'No more chat. When I get back, I expect results. Now tell

273

me – anything you want while I'm out? No? Sure? And another thing, sweetie – don't worry too much if the words aren't quite right the very first time. I read somewhere that each of Jeffrey Archer's books goes through seventeen drafts.'

'Seven*teen*?! Christ. But I've only got seventeen *pages* . . .'

'Better get going, then, hadn't you? Now what can I do for you before I go? Tea? Coffee? Sandwich for later? No? Shall I suck you, then?'

'What . . . you mean . . .?'

'Well yes *obviously*, sweetie. I wasn't referring to your *thumb*.'

'Well, um . . . that would be very, er – nice. If you're sure you've got the time.'

'All part and parcel of the Bath Experience, sweetie – *plenty* of time. But you will, won't you sweetie – write some more of your novel, yes? Mm? For me?'

'Oh *look*, Tara – maybe it would be better for everyone if I just *chucked* the bloody thing, hey? I mean . . . ooh, hey . . . ah . . . oh *God*, Tara . . .'

'Nice? Now will you? This afternoon. Mm? Just for me?'

'Oh *Tara* . . . ah ah ah. Christ.'

'*Yes*, sweetie? You will?'

'Oh my Jesus. Oh God. OK. Yes. Yes. I will. Uh! Uh! Uh!'

'Just think of me, sweetie, as your special muse. Yum.'

274

CHAPTER TWELVE

Howard hadn't got home till way after one (Eurostar had
been fine, but he was damned if he could get a taxi at, um,
where was it? Waterloo – which is just bloody typical, isn't
it?). And still he had crept into the hall with extravagant
care – because look, getting out of Paris had been excellent,
a windfall, but of course now as usual there were *things* to
be faced (though quite why Brian and Dotty always seem
to end up being *my* problem, I simply cannot work out) but
I surely can't be facing any of them bloody *now*, OK? They
ran out of Scotch on the train (believe it?) so I had to get
down this succession of little bottles of champagne and
they've done my stomach no good at all, I can tell you –
stabbing kind of pain in my sort of side, just to add to it:
sure it's all those bloody bubbles.

Anyway – made it up to the bedroom, thank God (quietly
did the landing lights). Thought of ringing Laa-Laa – of
course I bloody did – but then I thought Oh Christ, it's late
and she'll only be asleep. But it's true that she never ever
minded being woken; on the very few occasions he had
done this – checked on the sleeping form of Elizabeth, stolen
downstairs and dialled her – she had dreamily welcomed
the sound of his voice, husky pleasure alive in her own,
and enchantingly cut by dozy and childlike small grunts of
contentment. But if he rang her now, he'd want her – yes?
And Howard simply had to confess to himself as he yanked
off his tie and unbuttoned his shirt – his big yawning near
breaking his jaw – that although for this night alone there
was nothing at all to stop him just getting out the Jag and

going round, he couldn't – despite the wanting – actually be fagged. Which is a sign, I suppose, of becoming older. What a shame, Howard drowsily thought – as he opened his arms to sleep – that such things as Laa-Laa cannot be subtly delivered and later, quite as deftly, spirited away.

And the following morning, Howard had quite naturally and for as long as possible postponed even the thought of all the business of getting up and getting down to it: what, actually, was it he was supposed to *say* to Brian, hm? *Sorry*? Is that all he should say? Sorry to hear your, um, *news*, Brian. Not quite enough, is it? Was he expected to give him money? If he offered to rent for them another caravan, would Dotty just scream and then kill him? And I don't suppose for a second that dullard Nelligan has done all he promised to; have to ask Lulu. And Lulu – is she still staying, now that I am back? or what? I do hope Zoo-Zoo isn't creeping around and looking accusing – I almost can't stand to see him, these days, and if you had suggested any such thing to me just last summer, I would happily have pronounced you a madman. Seems to have been snowing, here; oh Christ, that reminds me – Christmas. Haven't done a damn thing about it, you know – not a damn thing. It must be wonderful, I suppose, to be like Elizabeth and look *forward* to it all; God – these days, the only bit about things *I* ever look forward to (apart, of course, from my Laa-Laa) is getting them over and bloody done with. Which must say something. Because I never *used* to be like this, you know – not once, I wasn't.

Anyway – here I am, dressed and ready for the fray, so let's be getting on with it, hey? Once more into the, uh . . . once more into the *thing*, dear friends – once more! Into the what, though – what is it? What would it be that once more you go into? A decline? Well in my case, the hall – because that is where now I surely find myself: here is Lulu coming towards me (damn fine-looking woman, this Lulu, you know – and yet I don't quite want her, don't know why;

276

think it's my Laa-Laa – she's both lovely and *easy,* which is all you really want).

'Howard,' smiled Lulu. 'Welcome back. Sorry I didn't wait up last night. Not much of a winter break for *you!*'

'Oh well – you know me, Lulu – I'm not really much of a one for any of that. Much more Elizabeth's thing.'

'Lizzie OK? Buying up Paris? Where's Melody? She not with you?'

And then Lulu all but bit her tongue: what a damn stupid thing to say – of course she wouldn't be *with* him. Just because Melody once and boozily let slip that she and Howard had one time had a 'thing', it would hardly still be going, would it? And even if it were, he wouldn't bring her home just because Lizzie was away, now, would he? No, not, of course: so there – a damn and bloody stupid thing to say. But I look at Howard with new eyes, these days: how could anyone, ever, want anyone but Lizzie? I never would; I never do.

'Melody's staying on with Elizabeth. Taking my place, as it were. Where's Brian and Dotty? How are they taking it?'

Lulu heard herself say Hm? Oh, Brian and Dotty – they're out, they've gone out – went out early; but deep inside she boiled with something real and new – this was a slash of hurt, a scarlet jealousy that maybe can't be quelled: I feel it getting hotter. Lizzie is in a suite in Paris with *Melody.* Why *Melody?* What in hell has *Melody* to do with anything? If anyone is there it should be *me* – me me *me*: not *Melody,* not anyone – not anyone else but *me.*

'Out?' checked Howard. 'Really? How very odd. What – out *together,* you mean? Even odder.'

Lulu hauled herself back to the here and now, but her face was on fire, and she knew it.

'No, not,' she said. 'Brian was up at about *dawn,* I think – went to the garage for some funny gadget or other.'

Howard nodded, and then he shook his head in a hope-lessly despairing sort of way, tinged with nearly affection.

277

'That will be his metal-detector. He stored a few bits of his junk in the garage – just about all he's got left now, poor devil.'

'Is that what it was?' responded Lulu, not caring. Why doesn't Howard go off with his bloody *Melody*, if she's so wonderful, and leave sweet Lizzie to *me*? 'And Dotty took Dawn off somewhere, an hour or so ago. Think she said she was going to that shop she works in.'

'*Breach*,' said Howard, quite suddenly.

'Sorry, Howard?'

'Mm? Oh nothing, nothing: sorry. It's just that thing you go into again, doesn't matter, not a bit. Right – so, they're out: that's a pleasure deferred, then. And what of Nelligan? Walls still standing, are they?'

'Nelligan's about done, amazingly. Do you want tea, Howard? Do you have breakfast, or anything? He's just fitting the door handles and all those brass switch-plate things, and then he says he's off.'

'Hm. With another massive cheque. Some tea would be good, actually Lulu – if you can be bothered. But no – nothing to eat, thanks.' The whisky doesn't taste as good in tea, but it looks a lot better if someone walks in.

'OK, Howard,' said Lulu – now quite brisk, in the light of the decision she found she'd just made. 'I'll do some tea, and then I'll be going. You don't need me here, now – and anyway, you've quite enough lodgers as it is!'

'Really?' checked Howard. 'Sure?' Right, he was thinking: good.

'Mm. But it's Christmas so soon, now – and I'll be back for that, of course. Can't wait.'

In fact I'll be back the very second I hear that my Lizzie has landed. And now I must ring her. And then what? Where next in this new and nomad existence of mine? Home? No – not home: John might come back at just any time at all, and that, I know, I cannot bear. So where, then? Don't know. Just must ring Lizzie.

And then the thing rang, and Lulu jumped and made for it as just that single word was sizzling behind her eyes: *Lizzie.*

'*Colin . . .?*' she queried, to whoever it was that had asked. 'No he's *not* here, I'm afraid – he's actually gone away for a couple of days. Do you want to leave a message? No? OK, then. Bye.' What a waste of time: not Lizzie at all. 'Some friend of Colin's, apparently,' she smiled at Howard, as he ambled away in quest of Nelligan.

Must ring Lizzie.

And now I've done that. But they regret, alas, they are receiving no response from that suite. A message? No. No. A message just wouldn't do it. Mobile? Switched off.

So where, then? Wherever, wherever – but I've got to go *now*, because all around me are Lizzie's things, and suddenly just none of this *works*.

❋

The kitchen seemed fine – even Elizabeth, Howard adjudged, would be more than well pleased with the finished result: it would be quite reasonably safe to assume that no more sophisticated, gadget-packed and superbly appointed kitchen could exist anywhere at all in the whole wide world, and for this reason alone, Howard felt pretty confident, Elizabeth would love it (always depending, of course, on what Cyril and Edna had pulled off next door).

He left the house and walked round to the Jaguar – quite surprised (talk of the what is it, devil) to see Cyril come crunching with purpose across the gravel drive; Cyril too seemed to be mildly taken aback by the appearance of Howard – even faltered a bit, before smiling and striding on, gamely.

'Ah Howard,' he hailed him. 'Thought you were away.'

'Change of plan,' said Howard. 'Christ it's bloody freezing, isn't it? Snow's stopped, at least. Brian and Dotty – you remember? Brian and Dotty?'

'The caravan – right?'

Howard nodded. 'Right. Well they've smashed it up. I'm afraid – they're OK, and everything, but they're staying with us, pro tem, until, um . . .'

Well, Howard asked himself: until what? Hey? Good bloody question.

'Oh. Well at least they're all right. Bit of a blow, though. Not really their year, is it? Don't seem to be able to hang on to anywhere to live. They might need counselling. People get very funny, you know, when they keep on losing their nest – has a sort of snowball effect: seen it, oh – countless times. It *is* bloody freezing, you're quite right – I didn't even put on a coat, because, well – only next door.'

'Yes . . .' agreed Howard slowly, attempting to put into it a fair deal of enquiry. He was aching to sit in the warmth of the Jag – fed up completely with jangling keys in this bloody bitter wind. 'Was there something . . .?'

'Ah well no – well *yes*, obviously – but it wasn't you I was actually coming to, uh . . . well, thought you were *away*, of course. No – I was just popping round to see if Mrs Powers, Lulu, was all right, and everything. Neighbourly.'

'Ah – right,' understood Howard, with gusto: good – excellent: nothing to do with me, so now I can go. He opened the car door, and prepared to swing in.

'Um – *actually*, Howard . . .'

Oh dear God: there's more.

'Look, Cyril – I'm actually turning to ice, standing here, if I'm honest: come and sit in the car, if you want to talk, yes?'

'Good thinking,' agreed Cyril, with real alacrity. 'My hands are going blue. It's a bugger, isn't it? This winter.'

'We had a good summer, though,' Howard found himself inanely saying, as he settled himself behind the wheel – Cyril now next to him, and staring ahead: two people in a car going nowhere.

'So, Cyril . . .' prompted Howard.

Cyril's face crinkled into a look-I'm-going-to-drop-all-pretences-here-and-talk-to-you-man-to-man sort of expression.

'Look, Howard,' he opened. 'I'm going to drop all pretences here and talk to you man to man. It's Lulu. It's Lulu.'

'*Is* it?' came back Howard, wholly confused.

Cyril nodded as frantically as a patient, or something.

'She's really, really got to me. Been on my mind since I first clapped eyes on her at your summer party – remember? She was there?'

Good heavens, Howard was thinking: how perfectly extraordinary.

'Yes,' he agreed. 'Elizabeth met her on holiday.'

'Oh *that's* the connection, is it? I see. Well the thing is – what do you know about her? I mean – I know her marriage is in pieces, but . . . well: do you think I've got a chance? Any sort of a chance? It's just that I'd almost die, just to have a chance with her.'

'Well . . .' tried Howard. Christ *I* don't know – *I* don't know, do I? What the hell are you asking *me* for? *I* don't know a damn thing about her. 'I don't see why not . . . maybe on the rebound, sort of thing, do you mean? All this is more your field than mine, I have to say. She is a very attractive woman – I can see that.'

'Oh *God* . . .' moaned Cyril now (and where had all his professional detachment wandered off to, Howard could not help but wonder). 'She's the most gorgeous thing on *earth*. I mean – I can see, Howard, that you're perfectly happily married to Elizabeth – I know all the signs – and Elizabeth is, of course, a very fine and faithful woman and you're lucky. What I mean to say is, you'd probably never dream of contemplating anything like this and you're *lucky*, Howard – hear me? You're a lucky, lucky man. But I tell you this in confidence, Howard – I'm *bored*, you know? Edna is excellent in very many ways, please don't get me wrong . . . but as a *woman* . . . you know? Well . . . you know what I'm saying? I mean – as a *woman*, well – she doesn't really make it. Not for me. Not now. Not any more. And yet I've never, you know – *done* anything about it, not once. Well – there was that Californian patient I had one time, but that doesn't really count: had her more or less hypnotized, and I thought oh what the hell – shouldn't think she'll remember. But you see – you see, no woman's ever *moved* me like Lulu does, and I just feel that if I don't do something about it I'll maybe just *explode* . . . and certainly I'll regret it for the rest of my life.'

'Well,' sighed Howard, 'all I can say is if you *are* going to do something about it, you had better be quick off the mark because she's off. She was going to be here for a few days, as you know, but now that I'm back . . .'

The white of panic was alight in Cyril's eyes.

'What? Leaving? She's going? When?'

'Just about *now*, as I understand it. I –'

But Howard found himself addressing an empty passenger seat and a door flung wide (ill-mannered sod – all the leathery warmth has gone, now) and as he hauled it shut, Howard just caught the tail-end of Cyril's sprint across the drive, his energetic jabbing of the bell and then finally – as the car cruised smoothly past and away – Lulu's face as she opened the door.

God, thought Howard, as he picked up speed while the light stayed green – can't some men be odd? But never mind Cyril and never mind Lulu: they can sort it out between themselves. But whatever happens there – not very much, I feel fairly sure – it will never ever approach the bliss of what I have with Laa-Laa. Who, at long long last, I shall so soon be seeing, kissing, holding and having: oh thank God I'm not in Paris.

❋

'Oh God oh *God*, Elizabeth – this is just such *heaven*,' enthused Melody, more or less again: Elizabeth was pleased she was pleased, of course she was, but did Melody really keep having to *say* so all the time? It could be wearing, very; Lulu, had she been here, would surely have sipped her caffè latte with appreciation, yes, but (equally surely) quite as discreetly as Elizabeth, not at all studiedly, found herself doing. Maybe, though, this could be some sort of counter-balance at work: smiling quite thinly, as one might if treating a grinning if gluttonous prep schoolboy to tea at The Grand, and trying not to wince as he practically swallows whole his fourth cream bun, and then sucks on all his fingers. Of course I didn't *plan* to be in Paris with Melody (only asked her for the day out of *kindness*) and I can't really say I'm quite *comfortable*. There are several things here that I'm not too happy with: firstly –

'Would it,' sang out Melody – and maybe this time there was just a hint of furrow on Elizabeth's brow – 'be just *too* awful to order another of these crock things, whatever they're called.'

'Croque-monsieur,' said Elizabeth quietly; she had tried for a spot of gaiety, here – more for herself than anyone – but quietly is how it had emerged. 'Of course – if you want one.' How on earth could anybody, Elizabeth wondered, eat *two* of the things?

Firstly – Melody has no money. Now obviously, this is no sort of a problem whatever in the day-to-day running of this was-to-be wonderful winter break (what I mean to say is, Melody is more than welcome to as many croque-monsieurs as she can decently handle); no, the worry arises when I consider what exactly it is that I should be doing *next* – how I quite handle it. I mean look – ask anyone (ask Howard): the whole point of *being* here is to buy all sorts of lovely *presents* and things, yes? I mean just look at the city, how lovely it is. Right now from this brasserie window, through the red and gold lettering on the glass, I can see most of the sweep of the Place Vendôme – just the most subtle Christmas lights making each of the cobbles gleam with pips of shiny light. And there is Boucheron, and there is Cartier – and Charvet is close (just imagine Zoo-Zoo in one of their scarves) – and just a street or two behind us is simply everything else and my *point* here, of course, is what precisely am I expected to do with Melody? It would be cruel to make her *watch* me (and anyway: don't want that, don't want that at all – don't *like* being watched, hate it) and yet I can't just *leave* her, can I? Well maybe I can – she is grown *up*, after all, although she so seldom seems it. She is a *mother*, for God's sake – a fact that Elizabeth so very often had as much trouble remembering or believing as Melody herself. And secondly, well . . . *secondly*, I'm not at all sure about . . . oh dear oh dear – I don't know *what* it is I feel – I've never had to cope with even the *suspicion* of feelings like this before and I *want* to cast them out (laugh them away) – I do, I do – but it's just, I suppose, you can't *un*-see something, can you? And back in the hotel, in the suite that time, what I saw in Melody's eyes was nothing to do with the tumult of the impending festive season, and nor in Howard did I catch just the caring and solicitude of a good old friend. Which leaves me where, exactly? Where? Oh it's just not fair – I can't bear shadows, just can't stand them. I am here to be a carefree shopper, not a damaged flower – and certainly not any sort of *detective*. No. No no. It's too silly – I don't know what's got into me. All I saw was *nothing*, because no more than nothing is all there was.

'Elizabeth,' Melody now piped up, 'I don't suppose you're on for a trip to EuroDisney, are you? God these sandwiches are really good. I'd quite like a brandy.'

Elizabeth stared at Melody. 'Euro*Disney*?' she repeated – unbelieving, yes, but also frankly appalled. 'You're not *serious*, are you, Melody? Oh my God you *are*, aren't you?'

'I didn't really think it was your thing,' smiled Melody – although Elizabeth was fairly sure she heard an undertone of sulking there too, if you can believe any such thing. 'So look – shall we meet back at the hotel this evening, then – yeh? I just don't know if I'll ever be in Paris again and I really don't want to miss it, you know? Heard it's really good.'

'Yes yes,' agreed Elizabeth eagerly. 'Of *course* you must go, of course. Shall we say – what, then? Eight? Later?'

'Eight should be fine. But I can ring you, yeh? Um – Elizabeth, I know this is really tacky and I feel *really* bad about it, but I haven't actually got any, er . . .'

Elizabeth was already nodding and rummaging, and now she crammed very probably far too many French francs into Melody's hovering hand. Standing now, Melody gulped back in one the tawny Armagnac that Elizabeth had not been aware of her ordering, and with a girly wave was gone. Elizabeth was left with not just the bill (she rifled now through plastic cards, not actually minding which one she used) but also the sudden thought – which teetered now with unease atop the pile of splintered other thoughts – that Melody had not even considered phoning Dotty to just maybe hear from her first-hand that Dawn was truly OK; since Howard had left, indeed, the subject hadn't arisen.

Enough, enough, thought Elizabeth finally: I really do want now to look at beautiful things. Do they include the service here? I think they do, but I'm not quite sure – ah they do, they do – 'Service Compris', it says at the bottom: better leave a bit more anyway (is a hundred francs enough, do you think? Howard would have told me, but he's not here; well *Howard*, of course, would have seen to the whole thing, which he always *does* do because he really is so perfectly sweet. So perfectly sweet. Yes).

Can you imagine *Lulu* wanting to go to EuroDisney? Elizabeth smiled at the thought. No – no I really think not. And yet the two of them *could* have gone together, Elizabeth now realized with a pang of regret and missing her; she would ring soon – talk to her, talk to Howard; talk to poor Dotty, of course – poor Dotty. And find out what Nelligan's up to. But first I must shop – and I tell you what's worrying me now: the Charvet scarf I have in mind for Zoo-Zoo is a wonderful sort of winey colour with a rich mustard-gold embellishment and plenty of black in the background – but I *always* seem to be buying him dark red and pink things (I think it's his skin, his skin, his skin that makes me tingle) – so would it just be too daring of me to get him something royal, get him something imperial? Could he seem richer to me, draped in purple? I do so wish at this moment that just that silk could be all there was between the warmth of his shoulders and my tantalized fingers. All these feelings are fighting inside – and it's awful, I know, but total peace would seem dull to me, now.

❄

'Was that Howard you were speaking to earlier?' asked Edna, quite casually – knowing it was, because she had been watching from the hall (something she seemed to be doing more and more as each day went by). 'I thought they were meant to be away. Your patient just arrived, a moment ago.'

Cyril was making a big show of having been newly out in the cold and here, thank God, was welcome warmth. 'That'll be Driscoll. He always squeezes in an extra appointment when something traumatic like Christmas is round the corner. Ha! Along with an awful lot else, he just can't seem to face it.' And what of me, though, Cyril was asking himself in a state of high alarm: what can I face now – cling on to, even – after what I have just been through and not through with Lulu Powers? 'Yes – Howard's back; Elizabeth still out there for a day or two – but Howard's back, yes. You'll be pleased to know, Edna, that the caravan's gone for good, next door – crashed on a motorway, apparently, but no injuries, rather oddly. Morgans are dossing down with Howard and Elizabeth, it seems. Strange people – Brian and Dotty, I mean.'

Cyril was surprised, then, to see a tallish and tanned,

loose-limbed and couldn't-be-much-more-than a very young girl amble into the hall from the kitchen.

'Ah Kelly,' Edna greeted her. 'Crashed on the motorway? How awful. This is Cyril, my husband, who I told you about – yes? Cyril, this is Kelly, our new help – who I'm sure will be a great deal *more* of a help than our last little disaster – yes, Kelly?'

The girl grinned – wickedly, Cyril wondered? No – probably just youth and a touch of nerves. 'Yiss,' she agreed. 'Oil troy, inny-why.'

Cyril then observed that she must be from Australia, and Kelly agreed that she was ('Hick yiss, you bit,' is what she actually said) and then he opined that he shouldn't keep the hapless Mister Driscoll waiting for very much longer – so maybe tea and cakes in about an hour, then, Kelly – yes? Edna will let you know what I'm partial to.

'Cyril has a very sweet tooth, I think you'll find – haven't you, Cyril?'

Cyril said Yes, feeling foolish doing so – but there, Edna tended to play tennis with her aimless dialogue, so what could you do but briefly conform, and lob it back down the other end? The mention of cakes now drove him towards his consulting room, yes, but by way of the kitchen. As he swiftly devoured a sort of hot cross-bun without the cross, his eyes rested dully and glumly upon the massed and overlapping messages clustered across the notice board: 'Buy both gold and silver marker pens for gift tags'; 'Bought pudding? Or ingredients?'; 'Cyril – I shouldn't be late back this morning – just gone round the corner. If you get back first, that's where I am'; 'Buy gift tags'.

I think now what I need to do is settle Mister Driscoll as comfortably as possible – set him well down the road to calling up and expanding upon all his latest worries and fears, traumas and disappointments for this will allow me ample scope to detach myself utterly from nonsense of that sort and try maybe to work out what exactly has just gone on, here, in *my* life – possibly I can make myself see other and more positive aspects of the thing? This is, after all, what I'm meant to be *for*.

'Ah – Mister Driscoll,' Cyril greeted him – brusqueish, but not without warmth. 'Sorry I'm a bit, ah . . .'

Mister Driscoll was seated bolt upright on a hard-backed chair in the anteroom, seemingly intent upon the discreetly built-in bookcase before him – precisely filled with numbered sets of unreadable tracts, gilt-blocked and Americanly bound in brown, blue and blood together with its twinned mirror image on the wall alongside, expertly worked up in acrylic and straying from exactitude only by way of the whimsy inclusion of a semi-rolled scroll and archly poised quill, together with a couple of sprauncy blue-and-white Chinese horses.

'Cold enough for you?' threw out Cyril, as the two of them marched into the consulting room and assumed their age-old positions; because whatever you may have heard to the contrary – please let Cyril assure you in his professional capacity – comments about the weather are a good and warm way in: particularly during the viciousness of winter – always an ice-breaker, depend on it.

Mister Driscoll ostentatiously squirmed into a poised but at least some way towards comfortable position on the couch, and then tried to do what Cyril always requested of him: ease down into *ease*, Mister Driscoll. Having failed, as usual (what quite did it mean?), he plumped a cushion and muttered disconsolately:

'It's just begun to snow again. Saw it as I was waiting, through the, um. Window. It doesn't much matter to me. I'm cold all of the time – from the inside out. *She* says it's because I'm bloodless, or else because I'm putting up some sort of resistance due to cowardliness, is what *she* says. But I'm not, am I Doctor Davies? Bloodless? Or a coward. Am I?'

'None of us can be mighty and brave all the time,' said

Cyril, softly. 'How is the thought of Christmas affecting you?'

And that, as Cyril had rightly calculated, surely and instantly did it: the wailing subtone cranked up a notch or two, and Mister Driscoll was off:

'Oh God well this is *it*, isn't it? She says she's damned if she's having my people over this year because they're all so ghastly – and she's right in a way, of course, I suppose – they *are* pretty ghastly, my people . . . but look, the point is they all think they *are* coming because I haven't had the nerve to tell them – I mean, they *assume* they're coming, you see, because they always do . . . but *she*, oh God, she believes I've told them all not to come because I told *her* that I'd told them not to come, thinking I'd – you know – get *round* to it, but I *didn't* get round to it and now the bloody thing is *here*, it's upon us, and the pressure, the anxiety is just so close to breaking me I just don't know what on earth I can *do* about it, Doctor – and last night, last night late, I did – I did really think of taking my life. I mean – why not? I'm worthless. Worthless.'

'You know your own sense of worth, Mister Driscoll. We've talked of it often. Just last session, you told me you were "important". Yes? Remember?'

'I didn't, did I? Did I really? Well I must have been mad . . . if I'm not mad now. Am I mad? Am I?'

'Do you think you are mad?'

'No, I . . . no, I don't, truly. I don't.'

Well, thought Cyril, you're more or less wrong, but never mind. Let's launch you out a little further, and then I can address the business of *me* (I could murder an éclair – and my bloody knee is throbbing as well, just now).

'Talk me through the worst-case scenario for Christmas, Mister Driscoll. Remember? Like we do. Then we can address ourselves to relieving the pressure – when we know exactly what it is that causes us the most anxiety.'

So Mister Driscoll set off on his journey (all aboard the

289

most terrible train of thought) – and the first few bits that Cyril bothered to listen to were, he had to admit, pretty damn dire – while his trusted mind doctor left the man to freewheel, as he settled down to a serious bout of re-enactment and analysis.

I maybe went at the thing too strong; it was Howard saying that Lulu was just about to disappear that had panicked him – I mean to say, *where*? Where would she be going? What if she were emigrating, or something? All this flew through Cyril's mind as he ran to the front door and bullied the doorbell into setting up its clamour. Unlikely, all that, of course – but if she hadn't finally come to the door when she did, Cyril was all set to imagine her strapped into the module at the business end of a US space shuttle, and bound for planets uncharted.

'Oh . . .' was all Lulu said, when she saw him. Well OK – Cyril had not travelled quite so far down the road to delusion as to even fancy that any big-hearted display of God-where-have-you-been-all-my-life was remotely on the cards, but just that single, flat and frankly chilly 'Oh . . .' had suddenly put into perspective the distinct and not to say decided shakiness of his position: he had actually managed during these few hours of morning to concentrate and point up his now just about wild lusting for Lulu to such a degree as to believe with all his heart that some if not all of it must surely be requited. And how many times had he solemnly warned his patients against just such a folly? Could there be a surer route to profound disappointment and the spear of rejection? Bearing in his fevered mind a little of this, Cyril had done his best to dampen down whatever it was – taking into account the crazy eyes and the lolling tongue – his expression might have conveyed (something unsettling, it is fair to say) and coax it into some semblance of composure – and then he said:

'Ah . . . Mrs Powers. Lulu.'

'You've just missed Howard, I'm afraid. He's gone.'

'Yes. No, I – uh . . . God, it's absolutely like the North Pole out here, isn't it? I don't want to make the house cold . . . and you just standing in the draught . . .'

And with, even Cyril could see, immense reluctance Lulu said slowly Oh, um – do you want to come in, then? For a moment? Cyril raised his eyebrows in order to convey that the plain wisdom of such an inspiration had just then dawned, before coming out with 'Oh, er – that would be, um' – and then he nipped in, sharpish.

But between Cyril and his memory of this, there now was seeping the plangent voice of Mister Driscoll:

'Of course I don't actually necessarily *believe* that she will go for my auntie's throat with a pair of secateurs, as she's very often vowed to do, I have to say – but the threat and the worry of it forever linger. Do you think I should try to ignore it?'

'Do you think it is ignorable?' chucked in Cyril, maybe a bit too quickly.

'Mm . . . yes, I see what you mean. And then there's what she's promised to do to *me* . . . you know, when we're in *bed* . . .'

Yes yes, thought Cyril, as he spiralled away – bed indeed: how he would have simply died on the spot from pleasure of the sheerest sort, if only he could have cut all chat with Lulu and boldly taken or – maybe better – dragged her there. Not that he had ever seen bed as a prerequisite: floors, walls, tables, chairs – on any of those he was easy. But just you take one look at Lulu: icier than the frost outside – and absolutely desperate now to break in to her and out of this, Cyril then set the snowball rolling:

'Lulu, um . . . call you Lulu? Yes? Excellent. I think you are a very interesting woman. Yes indeed. Very. Interesting.'

'You don't know me, Cyril,' sort-of-smiled Lulu. 'I'm really very ordinary, I assure you.'

'No no – permit me: I am a professional, you have to remember. I know how to see . . . *beyond*.'

'Yes? Well – I'm sure you're right. Look, um – Cyril, I really have to go now and Howard's not here, as I said, so . . .'

'Listen to me, Lulu – listen: when I said you were interesting, back there, it's not entirely what I meant. I mean, you *are* interesting, of course you are – this much goes without saying . . . but what I really want to say is that I think you are the most beautiful woman I have ever set eyes on – no, please, not a word: I must say this. And I *have* thought so, Lulu, dear Lulu, since last summer – in that garden there, you maybe don't remember –'

'Cyril – *look* –'

'And what else I want to say, the other thing I want to say is that not only do I find you so utterly desirable that it turns my *mind* – and no, I do not employ such a turn of phrase lightly –'

'*Cyril*! Stop. Stop now. Please leave. Oh God.'

'And furthermore – I'm in *love* with you, Lulu, and – God, what's the matter? Why are you shrieking like that?'

'I'm shrieking . . .! I'm *shrieking*, Cyril, because if I don't shriek I'll *kill* you, yes? . . . Oh – Mister Nelligan – no, it's quite all right, thank you: just chatting with the next-door neighbour, yes – I'll be in to see you soon. *Now* look what you've done, you bloody oaf! Look, Cyril – I promise not to say a single word of this to anyone if you just leave *now* – yes? *Now*, Cyril – and I mean it.'

'This could on your part, you know, be some token form of resistance . . .?'

'Believe me – it isn't. *Leave*, Cyril.'

'So . . . what you are saying, then, is that you have no, um, reciprocal feeling for me – and yet I detect otherwise. I *am* a professional and –'

'Cyril – understand this: leave this house now or I will kick your balls up into the back of your throat. *Clear*?'

'You are demonstrating great hostility, Lulu.'

'*Right*, then –'

'All right! All right! I'm leaving – I'll go. But I think when you coolly pause to consider, you might see the folly of your ways and – ow! Ow! That was my *knee* – Jesus, Lulu.'

'I missed, Cyril – I *missed*. Next time I won't. *Out!*'

Yes . . . yes. I think that's a fair résumé of just about how it had gone: not a resounding success, agreed, but the snow-ball had yet time to gather momentum: this was, after all, no more than just the first roll and tumble. And how many women have I encountered professionally who have dis-played just such physical expressions? The stance of aggression? Building walls and concealing even from them-selves the destiny of their passion. None the less – bit of a bummer, as these things go.

'So there,' sighed out Mister Driscoll – hugely mournful, though in as conclusive a tone as he would ever come close to mastering. 'I think I have told you everything – well, the *thrust* of it, no more I suppose. There can never be *every-thing*, can there? God oh God – if I told you simply everything I'd just have a breakdown in the middle, if we ever even got to the middle. All I need to do, Doctor, is get *through* – yes?'

'A step at a time,' came out of Cyril – a half-asleep reac-tion, as if by rote completing a well-known phrase or saying.

'Exactly!' Mister Driscoll shot back, really quite excitedly – quite as though this confrontation with his own paralysis and sappingly morbid dread was instead some kind of spectacular breakthrough.

'In a sense,' said Cyril – faraway and mildly – 'it's all any of us does.' Here was not textbook stuff: it was simply what he had felt, and then it was in the air. But although Mister Driscoll could not have put a finger on precisely the trigger here, this one nebulous observation had served to plunge him backwards and down, more deeply than ever, and now he was reprising his fishy stare, which he knew could presage just about anything. Difficult to say – when Cyril routinely wound up this even more ragged than usual session – which of them lay closer to despair.

In the kitchen (where was that Kelly girl, with the bloody tea and cakes?) Cyril's black mood, starkly highlighted now by tetchiness too, was maybe just partly ameliorated by the sheer fresh sight of her: Kelly was halfway through her preparation (give the child her due) and the bright-cheeked vigour, the taut-faced sheen of her – eyes that always seemed poised on surprise – made Cyril at once feel both oleaginous and old, and yet strangely heightened, for all that. And then she said:

'Are you reely a proper soy-coya-treest?'

Cyril smiled (couldn't help it – rather liked this) and said just Yes.

Kelly smiled too. 'Jeez,' she said. 'That's reely quoit sixy. Oil jiss tike up this tea to Idna.'

And this left Cyril storming within: Yeah? *Yeah*? Well I can think of someone who doesn't agree with you, Kelly; it was the *look*, more than anything – more than Lulu's words (and they had struck like bombs) it was the *look* she had trained on him constantly: as if she was recoiling within from the annihilating stench of warm and new-dumped shit, and he, most surely, was the offending source. Cyril wagged his head and glanced around for solace; he had that chocolate éclair in his mouth and down him before he even realized that had he only just concentrated on remembering to taste it, it almost might have helped.

❄

Upstairs, Edna was sitting at her dressing-table and glancing at the sleet falling slantingly, sucked in by the ground as it touched. It was pretty much the same view as from her familiar haunt in the hallway – more raked and elevated, but essentially the same. It was from here that she had been at first surprised, then puzzled – now quite galvanized – by the sight of Cyril stumbling very limpingly

294

out of Howard and Elizabeth's house, his hot and puffy face so pronounced amidst all the dark and ugly coldness; he had protested just once more as he rubbed his knee, and then that Lulu, white with fury, slammed the door on every single vestige of him – Edna not yet ready to feel anything, when Cyril dashed his knuckles across his eyes (a sight she could scarcely remember).

No thank you, Kelly, she had said softly: no tea for me at the moment – kind thought, thank you – but no, not for me, not just now. When she had gone, Edna rose quite deliberately, and – as if dissociating her mind from what she knew she had to do – began to pluck off, one by one, all of her layers of clothing – dispassionately avoiding an imagined eye, beadily lodged within the skull of someone who had sternly told her to. She approached a cheval mirror and stared at the white and sometimes spilling over expanses of matter that made up her body – idly hoiking a breast: heavy and liquid, yes, but still somehow seeming semi-filled; she let it sag back down again to where it would lie. That little bruise on her elbow still hadn't quite cleared: these days it took a lot longer than it used to, all that sort of thing.

Edna padded away to the window and stood there. Had anyone in Howard and Elizabeth's house just glanced across, they surely would have seen her – but although she stood there until she became quite chilled, no one did; or if they did, she did not see them. And had someone done so – so what? What would he or she have thought? And what, thought Edna quickly, is it in fact that I imagine I am doing? It would be easier, somehow, if I knew I belonged; it would be easier, by far, if I or someone could draw me gently aside and simply tell me what it is I'm *for*.

CHAPTER THIRTEEN

Elizabeth had had to get a taxi back to the hotel – a thing she rarely did, seldom having to stray from the first and second arrondissements – but on this occasion there were simply too many glossy and rope-handled carriers for her to manage (well look – there wasn't all that much *time*, and everything is just so beautifully lit and temptingly displayed and yes, all right – I suppose I have, yes, gone just a wee bit overboard but it's only once a year after all, and it's not for me, it's for everyone else). Well – I say that, but of course I have slipped in one or two absolutely divine little things for myself as well that I simply couldn't leave behind – they seemed to be calling out to me, and none more so than the reversible and utterly dreamy Hermès belt with the silvery buckle in the form of an H; got one or two similar, true, but this was subtly different. I am reminded now of Howard who – under instruction, but not, to be fair to him, any hint of protest at all – bought for me the first of them. He had affected the symptoms of an impending coronary at the sight of the price, and then had muttered darkly (I suppose with humour – it's sometimes hard to tell with Howard) that the whole business with an H would, on the surface of it, make a great deal more sense if her name were Helizabeth, but no matter, leave it – so long as you're happy and it pleases you. Dear Howard. Oh Howard – why are my thoughts fluttering away from you, now?

And I have thoroughly resisted the enormous temptation (which has surprised me hugely; I didn't think I was capable – and no I *won't* succumb later) to tip out and see slither across the counterpane the rich and magnificent haul: I shall wait till I'm back at home and wrapping them – that way it will be almost as much of a surprise for me rediscovering it all as it will be when everyone opens them up on Christmas morning. Instead I shall twist off the top of this little icy bottle of Perrier (God I need it – it's funny how the cold weather always makes me thirsty: with most people it's the other way round, I'm fairly sure) and then I'd better get down to phoning Mummy. Last time I spoke to Lulu (and yes, then Lulu – after that I'll phone Lulu) she said that Mummy had rung her three times already, and I've only been gone a couple of days; didn't bother asking Lulu what she had *said* or what she *wanted* or anything, because Mummy very seldom ever really gets round to either of those – it's simply, I suppose, a form of contact, is it? Maybe it's just *like* that, when you get to be older. I wonder if I'll be that way? Do so hope not. Howard once said that if we ever got that way he'd get a gun and shoot himself and I remember laughing at the absurdity of that and he had said No, don't laugh because you'd be next – but I'm sure he was making a joke.

Thank God that's over – complete waste of time, as ever: it always is, I'm afraid, with Mummy. It turned out that last evening and night, she said, she'd telephoned the house time and time again and all she got was a noise that she said was just like a prolonged and actually quite offensive note on the sort of penny whistle she dared say they didn't now make any more – and eventually she had got on to the operator who said that that number was no longer connected and Mummy had insisted (and can't you just hear her?) but of *course* it's connected, of course it must be – that is where my daughter lives with her daughter Katie and her husband, um ... and here the narration faltered, not regaining momentum until Elizabeth had come in with *Howard*, Mummy – Howard: God, we've been married now for nearly twenty years. It turned out she had been ringing the number of the old house, the first house – demolished now – a number that had not entered her head for a decade; isn't it funny – the mind? Scary, really. (It is, you know – nearly twenty years, we've been married now.) Anyway: Lulu next.

But it was Dotty who answered, and Elizabeth caught her breath for only the merest fraction of what, she was sure, was an indiscernible instant – because I just have to, don't I, face up some time to Dotty's very personal shock and loss? So better do it now, when I have no time to think too much about what I should say – it always, with me, comes out so forcedly and not at all well when I've rehearsed it to perfection; the other thing too I have to bear in mind is that although I find it hard to imagine what the loss of a caravan can actually be *like*, it must be quite different when the caravan – not really much in itself – is actually all there is.

'Elizabeth,' rushed in Dotty – before Elizabeth's tone could even just half-set into still-warm jelly – 'please before you say anything let me thank you so very much for – '

'Dotty, Dotty – you don't have to – '

' – everything, everything, is all I want to say, and – '

'Are you *sure* you're all right, and you've got all – '

' – I just don't know where we would have turned if it hadn't been for – '

'I'll be home very very soon, now, Dotty, and then we can – '

'I hope you're having a lovely time, Elizabeth – you *deserve* – '

'Anyway look – just relax . . . and Howard and Lulu, if there's anything you – '

'Howard's not here at the moment, Elizabeth – shall I ask him to – ?'

'Probably gone into the office, poor lamb. Is – ?'

'Lulu's not here either. It's just me and Dawn at the moment and – '

'Ah! Is she – ?'

'Adorable. Just adorable. As ever. Elizabeth, do you want me to – ?'

'Don't want you to do *anything*, Dotty. I'll try Lulu at – '

'Yes, at home – she could be at – '

'I'll try her there. Now listen, Dotty – you know where I am if you – '

'You just have a good time, Elizabeth. I'll see you – '

'Soon. Very soon. Looking forward to – '

'I am – can't wait. It'll be so good to be – '

'We *all* will be. It'll be great fun, you just – '

'Simply can't wait. Bye, Elizabeth – oh, and – '

'Bye, Dotty. See you soon – oh and yes, you might ask – hello? Dotty? Ah – gone.'

Oh God, thought Dotty – was Elizabeth halfway into saying something, there? The phone was just too far from my ear and I might have put it down before she'd . . . oh well, she can always ring again, if she's anything to say.

The doorbell rang, and it was Brian – Brian was back. Was his stoop of dejection just slightly more pronounced? Or could he be just ducking any brickbat that might come his way? He stole (like a thief) just one glance at Dotty who quickly looked away from that, and who can blame her? She maybe, thought Brian, yearns to know exactly what comes next, but she of all people just must understand that there's no point whatever in asking me. I have foreseen not one of these disasters, so how could I predict how much lower I can drag us (not too far, it's pretty fair to say); and as for opportunity – if it ever knocks, I'm bound to be out.

They're building an extension to the ring-road system just past the shops, so I had the metal detector down there earlier. What I should expect from so much flinty excavation I do not know (the Crown Jewels? Something more?); what I got was what very much seemed to be a rather badly dented and wholly corroded maybe child's bicycle bell – the sort they had on those Triang trikes, now I come to think of it – the ones with willow baskets slung beneath the handlebars

299

and a plumply rounded and proper big boot at the back, just like that on a Morris Minor. The chrome on the bell was severely pitted – didn't ring, or anything; I chucked it – and some bloke shouted at me *Oi*! This isn't a bleeding dump, you know – what you think this fackin is? So I stooped low, apologized, picked it up, stood again to apologize and left quite quickly and still he was hurling abuse. Later on, I chucked it somewhere else.

I don't know if you remember about the author I mentioned – oh, way back now. The one who lives in the same street as the pop person whose bin yielded up the underpants, I don't know if you recall. Yes – well I did a bit of research on our writer friend down the library; turns out he's got two novels on the shelves, not at all my cup of tea – not that I have any time for fiction; I like a good war tale, or else a biography or a bit of travel. These were all about very dysfunctional and rather selfish people, it looked like to me (I only flicked), and most of them seemed to be obsessed by sex; no doubt such things have an audience. It said on the back it was hysterically funny, but it didn't raise a smile in me. Anyway, the books aren't the point – it's the relics and their value. So I had a good old rummage in his bins – and all I can say is he must have been wholly displeased with quite a run of tins of Italian tomatoes, else why would he just open them up and tip them away? (There's a hell of a stain on my sleeve.) What I did find, though – gave it a bit of a wipe – is one of those green plastic Pentels and I thought well this just has to be a stroke of luck because what could be more relevant to a writer than a pen? Hey? But then I thought Ah no – because they don't any more, do they? Write with pens. It's all this computer business, these days, isn't it? (Did Shakespeare need a computer? Did the lack of a computer unduly cramp the style of a certain Mister Charles Dickens? I hardly think so. Progress? Dear oh dear.) And then, of course, there was this: even if he had, this bloke, written one of his grubby little novels with the pen, how could I persuade Christie's or Sotheby's (they're the big boys, aren't they?) that this indeed was *the* Pentel he used and not, in fact, just *any* Pentel? Hey? Always assuming they'd heard of him in the first place: I hadn't, I confess. So I chucked it. And then I had second thoughts and hauled it back out again (forgot about the tomatoes, didn't I? Course I bloody did) and then I took the top off it and scribbled across my hand and then I chucked it: didn't work, or anything.

This is my life. Why am I going through more of it? I don't at all think I want to – not for too much longer.

❄

Norman Furnish now stirred lazily in half-sleep, aware only – as he nuzzled his head deeper into the pillow while his palate was clucking away drily like a dozy duck – that the chief and heavy sensation was one of deadness, yes, but he felt more alive too than he could even dimly remember (and all because these unfamiliar feelings coursing in and out of him encompassed the whole and gorgeous gamut from cared-for and peaceful to comforted and mmmm – yes yes, even that big thing: happy). And now, more and more, as new wakefulness progressively edged out pleasantly drowsy, he knew just why all this should be so. The sheets were clean and sweet-smelling – despite the warm overlay of night-spent heat – on this large and deeply wonderful bed. The chill grey of morning that each day speared him through the grime of a raw windowpane was masked from him now by the thick good weight of not so much lined as near-upholstered curtains, their dusky pink just barely decipherable in this rose and easy half-light. There were table lamps, there – two, in the form of could be Tuscan columns (pleated silky shades in some sort of other pink – or is it Ionic, the one with the curly bits?). And on the soft cream of the carpet, there lay there strewn and awry not just Norman's rags but black and peachy other things – and

301

now we can work our way round to it: maybe just twelve inches away from Norman's side – it could barely be more (he felt the warmth) – lay the wondrously curved and gentle form of Sophina, deep in sleep – his goddess of the night. For yes yes yes – I am still with her (did not leave – couldn't, couldn't – not by the time I'd felt her and had her and had this and felt it, no). I was compelled to promise to Sophina not just every penny I possess in the world, but also the major part of next month's admittedly dismal income – if only, Sophina (oh listen to me, please bright angel), you will not cast me back into the night – will not sentence me to walking the length of your road in the icy and coal-black drizzle, turning left at the lights and – filled with grief – on past that Indian shop which even at this late hour will be aglow with the hope that someone close by needs something *now* (and never mind the price: we need it *now*) and then just two streets on to the accursed hole I live in, where so soon even the essence of you – let alone the scented reality – will evaporate and blend with all the taint of just everything that touches me. Let me stay, will you, Sophina? Let me just be here for one sweet night, and then wake up beside you? Give me something – oh please you will, won't you – at least I can learn to remember? Having written the card number on the back of his cheque, she then had said OK.

I think that a part of it – wanting to stay, my needing not to go – was that on the way round here (can it just be last evening?) I finally committed my terrible act of vengeance: I posted, in a Jiffy Bag, the video; I posted to Howard – Mr Street – in a Jiffy Bag, the video, yes; the video I made in Chicago of Katie being lewd (being fab and being vile) and now I wonder should I have. It was just that Katie never ever did return a single call, utterly ignored each and every one of my cards and letters – and it was not that I wanted her father to hate her (no no no – not that). It was just, I suppose, that I simply had to make him know that I wasn't lying – I *had* been on holiday with her, just like I said, and she and I, yes: we did these things. So I was not deranged or imagining I loved her – I loved her truly (I love her still – oh, I love her *now*) and she – well she, she cannot, can she, have loathed me utterly because look, view and see it: we did these things. But still and all, I wonder if I should have; only pain is what it will cause, when all I want is Katie back. Maybe, due to the chaos of very-last-minute Christmas parcel posting it won't, in fact, arrive. We hope, though, it does not get opened by some curious Mount Pleasant official if, say, the label becomes detached (which is likely, quite likely – it was a very old label and I felt so weak and I had no lick); and did I enclose my name and address? Yes oh yes, very surely – you must by now know just what sort of idiot I persist in being. On the plus side, I failed to affix any stamps – not just because I didn't have any, but also because I forgot. Anyway, it's finished with now – it's out there somewhere – because I, Norman Furnish, have done it (although maybe – and not really at all maybe, you know, now I come to think of it – I really wonder if I should have: no, I really shouldn't).

And although I could never myself actually play the damn video (I wonder what I would have felt, seeing it again? Randy then lusting – and afterwards, awful), having it just lying around had meant a great deal to me: all I ever had of her, really – and yes I know you can get tapes copied, but not this sort you can't (even full-time idiots have the odd day off). And then on my way here (not knowing what it was I would find, while having a fair idea of what I would do – God, I was feeling so sexed up and scared) I was finally and irresistibly reminded of that terrible time in King's Cross, whenever – and it was the thought of all that that nearly had me turning away (call off the whole thing, shall I? And slink off back to my horrible den).

And now as I sprawl here, I'm so glad I came; I don't want to wake her, Sophina, and so I must just ease myself

over on to the other side as gently and as quietly as I possibly can (inch at a time, inch at a time) because no I surely
do not want to wake her: I have to prolong the moment, the
illusion that each great day of my life I wake up to a clean
and ordered existence with a bloody gorgeous bird; also, if
she wakes, she might tell me I have to go now – that now is
the moment to leave. But Christ – the contrast between this
and the last time just couldn't be greater; admittedly the
first humiliation had set me back just forty quid, whereas
for this sweet but so brief night of delight I have more or
less hocked my whole being, present and future – but God,
are people generally aware of the range of *levels*, when you
start in on playing this sort of game? It's maybe good I have
found out that they are not all like that rat-faced and evil
witch who fleeced me (lucky I got away with my life) –
because it is very possible now, you know, that this is the
only way I will ever get to be with a woman again – and at
these bloody prices, it could easily just become a Christmas
and maybe a birthday thing.

But back to rat-face, and how I found her – if, indeed,
that's how it had gone. I mean – let's face it: what had
drawn me to this place that up till then I'd only sort of heard
of? King's Cross – what is King's Cross? A station, yes –
handy if you're going to Edinburgh, or somewhere – and
next to it that terribly daunting (vertiginous, to me) vast
and grimy pile of stalagmites they call St Pancras. I read
somewhere that it was an architectural jewel; I just can't see
it – to me it's a terrifying nightmare, and nothing could ever
induce me to enter. So – not catching a train, then, so why
was I there? The slab-like orange library? I very much doubt
that; on the plus side it's warm, and you can sit down for
free – but I'm none too given to the book side of things (I
heard once that they've got a copy somewhere of every
single book ever printed in Britain, but I doubt they go a
bundle on my sort of thing – which is currently someone
called Zane, um – *Grey*, I'm pretty sure – I don't know if you

know – but only because I found it on the Tube. The person who had infested my room before me left behind him a box of books – there was an algebra textbook dated 1954 and an old Red Cross manual and junk like that – also a pamphlet about taxidermy, I remember, and a couple of *Mayfair*s that I've still actually got; I am not remotely surprised that someone whose tastes encompassed these things should have lived in my room before me).

Anyway – you catch the drift: the British Library had not, believe me, been the attraction at all. So what was it? Had I seen one of those murky documentaries where a motley crew of chain-smoking deadbeats is spilling the beans, their faces blanked out by a flickering chequerboard (say what you think the man from the Beeb wants to hear and then run at the money and chase another dragon)? It could have been one of those; or maybe a Sunday redtop had been particularly explicit about the sort of vice they were deter-mined to vigorously expose and then see cleaned up (and with PR like this, who needs to advertise?). But the puzzle-ment of it is – it didn't at all seem *seductive* to me: quite the reverse. It looked sordid and dangerous – as, indeed, it turned out to be.

She had emerged from shadows I was unaware of and said to me, quite simply, You wanna gel? (hard G, as it happens, but of course it needn't have been) – and Christ oh Christ, fool that I was, I started looking around for what might be on offer. By the time I'd twigged it was her, it . . . oh, I don't know – it seemed rude, really, to turn her down so I said Er, well – you know. And still all I was aware of were two thin, so thin wrists – and hollows, big dark hollows that maybe sheltered eyes, but no light gave them away. She said then: I gotta place – twenny, OK? She didn't wait for an answer – just hustled me back into those shadows I hadn't been aware of and quite soon after we went up a metal staircase and I was wishing I hadn't left the bright lights behind and all I knew was a smell of pitch or

305

maybe bitumen, and in the small and dismal cupboard of a room, now, the air was one of dead sweat and a sadness that gripped me.

I faced her; she was pitifully slight – God knows how old. The complexion was made up of fag ash and mascara – pummelled dough and endless sleepless nights; she could have been one of those fifteen-year-olds who long ago left school to save from starvation the younger siblings – equally, she could have been the mother and cause of just such a tragedy. So, she said – hand out – Twenny, then? And what could I do but pass it over (I so much didn't want to touch a single thing in this terrible room, and I was almost sure that went for her, too – but twenty quid is twenty quid, right? So what did she mean to do?). So I asked her that, and she gave a rat-like twist of her face that may or may not have been conceived as a hellishly salacious grin and said right at me *Well*, mate – depends what you pay for, dunnit? And I said But the twenty – that was payment – wasn't it payment? Again the twist of her face – pointy teeth in evidence now (more, at this juncture, than I wanted to know). Give me another twenny, and then we're talking – the first twenny, well – that's just to *be* here, right? And you know I really think I must have said Right to that, and two more of my so few tenners had somehow already been clutched. She advanced on me, then, and put a hand down to my groin. I closed my eyes – not just because at times like this I tend to, but also, then, I didn't have to see her. Nice? That's what she said next. And I said Yes, because no matter that all my other senses were being stormed by repulsion and the urge to be somewhere cleaner – it *was* nice, I couldn't deny it, because this one sense is always the winner in the end, isn't it? With me it always is.

And then my eyes were open again, because just a second earlier I had understood that her hand was no longer on me, and this I didn't care for. My glance was maybe one of enquiry, but all she said was Come on, love – you know you want it: give us another twenny and then I'll make you feel reely reely good. And by then, by this time, even I was beginning to get a hold of the way the thing was going. (I was reminded – I don't care if you don't believe it but it's true, I tell you – this is what came into my head: I was reminded of the funfair, when I was a kid, on Hampstead Heath at Easter; you'd throw your darts or pop your gun, and the unsmiling man there, he'd give you a token – so you had another go, to build up the tokens so you could get the really *good* prize – which was always, of course, truly crap – just bigger than the others, was all; and now you were caught, weren't you? You couldn't waste the tokens tight in your clammy grasp, and so you threw and popped some more until all your funfair money was gone. And then – did you get the prize you'd been all the time ogling – while knowing that even before you got it home you'd loathe not just it but you for doing this? Nah – you never did, you never did. And this was it – what I was reminded of.)

She could, I saw, have continued like this for not so much the rest of the night as up till the moment when the last of my money was gone (at present rate of exchange, no more than about a grope-and-a-half away). Though still it is difficult – even with hindsight and the gritted teeth and heated brow of shaming – to imagine quite how I would have reacted to this latest teasing extortion had not a door in the corner, there, suddenly but quietly opened inwards to reveal a thickset man (a lot of whose muscles had admittedly gone to fat, but quite enough of them remained intact and perceptible so as to guarantee no trouble whatever in picking me up and breaking me in half). He said: Wassamaddawitchoo? Huh? Why don't you just be nice and give the lady a twenny? Huh? And at this mad and awful point I was either brave or stupid enough to say Now *Look*, before catching his eye and feeling quite alarmed by what I saw there; I turned, I ran – pleading briefly with the door to please not let me down – and practically fell headlong down the metal staircase and into an alley and into a wall and then over an upturned dustbin and out into the busyness of the garish and so welcome hamburger joints and beery kebab bars. I was not, of course, being chased – no muted shouting, no clatter or pounding of echoing feet; well naturally. I should be after *them* – what they did was *criminal*, right? But I wasn't after them, was I? No I wasn't – this was just never ever, in my life, the way things went. I took the Tube home (oh God – home) and – quite chastened – went straight away to bed with one of my predecessor's *Mayfairs*, and a lump of Izal.

But that was then and this, thank God, is here and now – and look: Sophina's shifting. What a light and lovely sigh of could-be-just-anything escaped from her now, so unlike the ugly gurgle of the waking male machine: rumbling, snorting – groping and scratching its way back into life at the end of the night; it must be so strange, thought Norman (looking at her now with real fondness cut by the reality of impending dread), to be a woman, all of the time and every day: but wasn't it good that so many were? Despite the fact that Sophina was truly a cut above (*Don't*, had been her only proscription the evening before – don't for God's sake ask me why I *do* this; and even now, it seems amazing that she does) – despite that, the truth of the matter was that the very second – and it can't be long in coming – that her dreamy stretching and flickering eyelids tipped her over the edge and back into consciousness, then would she recognize the presence, if not the identity, of another person in her bed and alongside – and what more could she do but try to piece together which particular trick this one might be (oh yeah, he's the big spender who stayed the night – funny-looking guy) and then just say thanks and bye?

She was looking at him now, and her eyes were bright. Norman was aware that his own bugged and baggy eyes could easily, in contrast, resemble the wet and nearly wounded bruises on blackened bananas; the bristles on his face itched him madly, now, and his mouth was as stale as stale – but just you look at young Sophina: her eyes were *bright*, I tell you – and all of her seemed just as new as the day. She smiled at him. There was no hint of scowling nor sign of resentment – and Norman felt almost sure that she was about to suggest some coffee, or something else equally normal: how *kind* she was, to spin out my illusions for even minutes longer. And she might – she might have come across with this coffee thing (could have easily) had she not instead become alert – eyes drawn in, now, along with nostrils (what could it be that she was sensing? Norman's mind was well on the way to cobbling up some not too damn lumpen way of asking her) – and now there was alarm all over her and just maybe the very same second that Norman possibly did hear a clunk from somewhere not very remote, her two index fingers flew up to both their sets of lips as she hissed out nearly ferociously:

'Ssshhh!'

'But what – ?'

'*Ssssshhhhh!*' came back fast, with added urgency.

She picked up and put on a featherweight gown, and lightly and quickly left the room – opening the door just inches and slithering through, and then closing it firmly and immediately behind her. Norman was aware then of the darkened murmur of some man's voice in the hall – the silences between the rumbles maybe denoting Sophina's responses, too soft to be even slightly divined. Norman was only at this stage thinking Hm – now what should I do? The situation was plainly not good – but could it yet be deemed to be bad? Maybe this was that thing they had? The pimp? Would a thickset man appear (with muscles galore, despite the gut) and say to Norman – with menace-a-plenty – Wassamaddawitchoo? Huh? It was maybe time to get, if not yet utterly worried, then certainly dressed.

Norman struggled with trousers, and was aware of rising

volume: some of the man's words were becoming distinct
– . . . *believe* it! . . . Christ oh *Christ* . . . Right, then – *right*; and
Sophina's voice rose now in what seemed at first to be a
honeyed and placatory tone but quickly veered off to one of
protestation – but Norman still hadn't located his shirt and
already she was yelping in denial and something was thumping against the bedroom door (could have been her, more
likely him) and now that flimsy door was hurled open wide
and Norman had his shirt now and found himself holding
it up close to his chin in the manner of a demure young
maiden, surprised while bathing; and as Sophina fluttered
to no effect just behind and half out of sight, the man now
strode in and glared at the floor through the hurt that was
goading him – but now his face snapped upwards and
spoke only of amazement that was surely mirrored in
Norman's own because if he or Howard had ever rehearsed
the course of their next and inevitable encounter, it surely
for neither of them had gone like this.

Howard could hold his gaze for just a second longer, and
then – his face creased now more by torment and confusion
than anything deeper (this just cruelly smouldered, black-
ening the edges) – he turned away, his wet mouth open to
speak; and though for a beat nothing came, now he burst
out:

'Christ oh Christ, Laa-Laa – how – how . . . *how*?' And
then – with reluctance facing the accursed man: 'With *him*?!'

'Look,' said Norman, quietly (not sure I get this), 'I think,
Sophina, I'd better maybe go.'

And that just did it for Howard: it looked for not so brief
an instant as if all the blood in his body had rocketed into
his face – and now he advanced on Norman.

'So-*phina*! So-bloody-*phina*! What the fuck are you talking
about? How *dare* you even so much as – ?!'

And then he lost it. He hurled himself at Norman who
stepped aside and Howard collided badly with the wall.
Norman went to help him up but Howard was batting

310

him away and then he changed his mind and hauled on Norman's outstretched arms and this had Norman keeling over in no time and they scuffled on the floor for a while – Norman trying to restore his balance and gain his feet as Howard fought on, but mainly for breath. Now they were both standing but there was somebody between them and Norman said *Don't*, Sophina – don't get involved. And that just did it for Howard:

'I'll fucking So-*phina* you – you bleeding little shit!'

And he took a swing at Norman's quite-red-and-had-enough face and Norman not so much ducked as cowered and got his feet in a terrible twist and in an attempt to ward off more blows he struck out with an arm and caught Howard in the midriff and Howard went *Oof*, and then down – and Norman cried out Oh Christ I'm *sorry*, Howard – Mister Street – and Howard lashed at Norman's shins with his heels and that soon had Norman hopping but it was only when he felt Howard's teeth at his ankle sinking seemingly to the bone that he too fell over heavily and with a howl right on top of his assailant who let out no noise this time but simply lay there as his chest pumped wildly and Norman now was being dragged to his feet and urged to go, go, go – Godsake *go*, will you, whoever you are – and Howard just registered that 'whoever you are' but had not now the heart or ability for speech or even consideration because something visceral so deep inside him was closing him down now and he gripped his side as his eyelids folded over and his teeth became bared and he just about heard his Laa-Laa yelping Oh *God*, Howard, oh *God* – you're not well, are you? Are you, Howard? Not well. I'll call a doctor – call one now. And then to Norman Oh get *out*, will you, you bastard – and Norman (putting off for now all sorts of feelings) turned to do just that, pausing only to say I'm so very *sorry*, Sophina – I really had no idea. He then turned back on impulse and knelt down to Howard and without thinking too much he said Howard? Howard? Mister

Street? Can you hear me? It's just that I want you to know that it's *Katie* I love, OK?

And that just did it for Howard: he put into it just everything it took and yanked back open both of those bloody eyes of his and through stretched-away lips and gritted teeth he was going to get this out, even if it killed him:

'I'll fucking *kill* you, Furnish.'

Norman saw that this was not the time to go into it: maybe not mention the video, or anything – although, despite everything, it did strike him as a wasted opportunity. He rose, sort of smiled for no one and simply walked out of the room and into the hall and through the front door and down in the lift and back to the street and just away from here – brimming with turmoil, and just not getting it.

Laa-Laa was kneeling down and hitting Howard's hand, in a way she felt might comfort him. (Nina Ricci's L'Air du Temps is what now wafted into and out of him.)

'I'm so sorry, Howard. I never wanted this. I thought you were *away*. You know that bloke, then, do you? Oh Christ. Look, Howard – I *meant* to tell you – was going to, honestly. It's just that, well, when you're not here – yes? I get so bored. It's what I've always *done*, Howard – I just didn't tell you before because you've been so good to me, so kind. But what you give me – it doesn't really go very far, you know – and you know how much I like lovely things . . .'

Howard gazed up at her – still his guts were burning him, but there was pain to quell here too.

'So you don't even know him?'

Laa-Laa shook her head – looking up now from a mass of business cards she had spilled over her lap and on to the floor.

'No – I've never seen him before. He's just a, oh – you know: *guy*. Look, Howard – I don't actually seem to have any doctors' numbers: plenty of taxis and takeaways and lawyers and things, but no actual doctors. Can you sit up?

Maybe you should go home. Would you like a glass of champagne?'

And Howard did then more or less struggle into a sitting position – his back up against the wall and all his insides cutting him in half.

'It's whisky I drink, Laa-Laa,' he said softly. 'Whisky.' And then, after a short pause (it's good I'm sitting up, now – because soon I shall have to stand, because that is a necessary precursor to getting the fuck out of here): 'I didn't know your name was Sophina.'

She looked down. 'It's not,' she said, quite quietly. 'Sophina is just my – it's the name I use . . . *professionally*. I'm actually called Linda. If you want to know.'

Howard had been sliding his back up the wall – clawing his way up with the help of a sidechair, digging in his heels to get a foothold. Linda was a nice, clean, normal name.

'Uh-huh,' he said (standing now – bit shaky, but up, at least). 'Well I'll tell you how we're going to play this.' I really want to cry, now: cry and be weak and unlearn all this and go back to the wonder of just coming here and inhaling my Laa-Laa and marvelling at the perfection of something that now is in pieces. 'First, you pour me a Scotch . . .'

And Laa-Laa – sensing remission – leapt at that.

'Yes, Howard, yes – of course.'

'And then you get me a taxi. Don't feel like driving. You've got, apparently, numbers – yes?'

Laa-Laa just nodded as she glugged out a large whisky.

'And then,' concluded Howard – with a heavy sigh of sad resignation that he very deeply felt, 'Laa-Laa – or Sophina or Linda or whoever in hell you are, you see about clearing out all of your stuff from this flat and depositing the keys with the porter by 6 p.m. at the latest.'

'Howard – ! You can't just – ! None of this is my *fault* – you were meant to be *away* – it's not fair – !'

'If you take anything that isn't yours, I shall contact the police. You wouldn't, I assume, welcome that.'

313

'Howard! *Howard*!' she wailed. 'You can't just *do* this – all the things you said, the plans we made –'

'Are cancelled. 6 p.m. um . . .' Oh Christ: I can't even call her by a name, now – bitch.

Howard shrugged her away as he woodenly walked for the very last time; all he heard her scream at him was How could you *do* this to me? After all this time? Hey?! Which was funny, in its way, because if he could have conquered pain just long enough to say only one more thing to her, that most surely would have been it.

CHAPTER FOURTEEN

Katie could see plainly (she was learning him, now) that Rick was working his face around to one of his voices. What he did was, he slowly lowered his knife and fork (they were dining deliciously, late at The Ivy: you'll never get a table, Katie had said – not for tonight, you won't) – and then while his eyes were beaming some maybe ironic warning notice, his lips twisted sideways, an eyebrow leapt up – and here it comes now:

'Donor *pall*agize – issa signer *weak*ness.'

Katie's uncertain smile flickered on and off – she seemed to be using it all the time, these days, so maybe the batteries were low. The trouble was – well, there were two of them, really: two troubles in all of this (quite apart from the insistence of near-fear that steadily was displacing excitement, and grew within her – the feeling recalling her last confirmed pregnancy: an unwanted child – undeniably there, though, but this was not so easy to be rid of). First – well Christ: I haven't *seen* all these bloody old films that Rick seems to think are just – I don't know, *Shakespeare*, or something (and OK, yeah – I haven't seen those either, but I did a bit at school: Romeo, Romeo – Out damn'd spot: My kingdom for a thing, right?). Plus, because Rick is an American (Jesus – sometimes, often – *usually*, Rick was like a parody of an American, the type you've seen in, oh Jesus – I suppose all these fucking *films* he keeps doing all this boring stuff from) . . . he's rich and he lives in Chicago and he visits his mother and his name is Biancardi (Ricardo): what can I tell you? (The gun we've already seen.) And to

315

me, I don't know – American sounds *American*, right? So when he does Bogart or Eastwood (and yeah, he only does tough-guy Americans) they all just sound like Rick, to me: maybe he's just no good at it. So anyway – this latest one: Donor *pall*agize, yeh OK: he's telling me not to apologize because I just did on account of on our way in here (we were checking our coats) some guy looked at me, and then he smiled. How do I know this? Because Rick told me; he told me and told me all through these fantastic fishcakes with a yellowy kind of buttery sauce, and just to stop him doing it I said I was *sorry*. Believe it? I said I was sorry because some man I didn't even see apparently *looked* at me. And smiled. What does he want? Purdah? Is that what he wants? He'd better not want that, because purdah girls are maybe born not made and I, baby, just ain't one of them – no way. And now he's telling me *not* to apologize (and I wish I hadn't, now – why in hell did I?) but he's cloaking it in some damn jokey movie voice – and now he's going to be *amusing* and tell me who in hell it was supposed to be: to me it was just another gum-chewing bloody old *Yank*.

Did he (in a big way) go for her wilful, almost defiant ignorance of all things Hollywood golden? Or was it just beginning to kinda get to him? Hard to tell from the way he was looking: amused, yes – an all-the-time-in-the-world-and-aren't-I-great sort of expression in the glint of his eyes, but always a hint of hard contempt just playing at the corners of his mouth (dry, his mouth – thin, but reddish).

'Duke,' he said easily, as if confidently flipping over the card she had been compelled to commit to memory at the outset of some tedious little set piece of trickery.

'Dook?' repeated Katie.

'Big *John* . . .' Rick expanded.

'Who's Big Jan?' chucked back Katie, looking forward not just to the end of junk talk like this, but also the blue sirloin that was coming down next – fries, Béarnaise: the whole works.

'You gotta be kidding me! *John* – John *Wayne*: the all-American guy. Numero uno.'

'How come all you all-American guys are always Italian or Irish or Jewish or black or something?' And I don't actually care if that gets up your nose, Mister Big-Shot, because frankly I'm getting fucking fed up of being spoken down to all the bloody time – and Jesus, it's not as if we're talking higher education, here: all he seems to know about is cowboy films and what things *cost*.

Rick stretched across the table (a corner banquette – and Katie just loved the way the candlelight was winking over and away from all the coloured leaded glass of the window alongside) and topped up her glass of Cristal; a thin gold Cartier tank watch pressed down on the soft black hairs thick on his wrist, and forced them flat, like fur.

'I've decided,' he said. And certainly the voice was charged with decision, though a new light in his eyes suggested too that before long some big present might well be coming Katie's way.

'Decided?' checked Katie, sipping champagne before gulping it, the way she did. 'What? What have you decided?'

'Two things.'

'*Two* things! Yeah? Two things – *two* decisions: wow.'

And she was sort of cajoling, sort of flirting, sort of batting her baby-blue eyes at the big strong man – yeh, all that: but she knew she was mocking him too, because – I don't know, somehow . . . beneath all the cash and the cool, the guy was a kind of galoot.

'Christmas,' he said. 'Christmas is *yours*.'

Katie often found herself blankly repeating whatever it was that Rick had just uttered – partly because it was always either cryptic or crazy, and also to give her a bit of time, anyway, to work out some other damn thing to say afterwards.

317

'Christmas is *mine*? What – you own Christmas too, do you Rick? And you're going to give it all to little *me*?'

Rick smiled and shook his head in a kindly, temperate, but not quite avuncular way, though this was well weighed down by a potent undertone of Cute – but don't go *too* far, baby.

'What I mean is,' he explained, slowly – and it was as if he was saying Now look, today we get to grips with the alphabet: tomorrow we'll start in on numbers. 'I'll stay. In London. Spend it with you. Kay?'

Katie knitted her brows into an approximation of how a cheerleader might complement her Ex-*cuse* me?! when – mid razzle-dazzle – asked if she was up for it.

'But Rick – I thought that's . . . I mean I *assumed* . . . that's why you're here, isn't it? I *asked* you for Christmas.'

Rick nodded. 'Bout time we had more food round here. I'll givvum a cuppla minutes. Yeh yeh – I kinda said I would, yeh – but thing is, see: there's Momma.'

He had hissed sighingly, widened his eyes and lightened his voice before and during those last two words, and Katie was left thinking Oh Jesus – what fucking film is this from, now. So all she could do was supply the inevitable:

'*Momma*?'

'That's right – my Momma. Every Christmas I spend with my Momma, right? It's what we do. But hey – I figure I'm growing up, you know? And my Momma, I guess in these circumstances, she's gonna understand.'

'Yeah?' said Katie – more intent now on the steak that was being set before her: oozing already, and she had only pressed the flat of her knife to it. 'Thanks,' she murmured to the waiter. 'Looks fab. Why are the circumstances any different this Christmas, Rick? Don't quite get.'

'It's different because *next* Christmas, Katie, will be ours.'

Here we go again: 'Ours?'

'That's right. Because here's Decision Two: you're gonna be my wife, honey – and I don't take no for an answer. And then my Momma – she's your Momma too! And then I got the best two ladies in the world.'

Joking, was her first thought. 'Uh-huh . . . and I get a say in this, do I? Or not?'

'You can say all you want, sweetheart – I'm just *telling* you, is all. Oh and honey – one little thing.'

'Yeah? What now? This steak is *sensational*.'

'I'm glad, babe – glad about that. Only you didn't have to thank the guy for bringing it, kay? He's paid to do that – *I'm* paying him. So in the future, yeh – you don't look at him, he don't look at you – and then we're all happy. Capeesh?'

✳

Look – there's no point in dicking around, Miles McInerney admonished himself: Catherine is on my bleeding mind near permanent, every day and night, and I can't bloody handle it. Not having her – not having what I want – that's bad enough: worse, much worse – face it – than I've ever known in all me bleeding life. I want a bird – I've got her, simple as that. So yeah – not having her, being told to just go and sling my hook – this, believe me, is far from good and I can't even pretend to begin to deal with it. But this bloke – *Rick*, she said – fucking Rick. She's fucking fucking Rick, isn't she? Maybe right now – maybe right this minute while I'm just sitting here, glancing at Sheil – who maybe doesn't even notice that there's something big going down here – something big is looming, Sheil, and I reckon you should bloody see what's staring you in the bloody face if only you weren't so bloody stupid to fucking *see* it. Bloody Sheil. Look at her. On her hands and knees surrounded by bloody great boxes of toys and asking me what wrapping paper Damien would like best – would he like the bloody Disney or the fucking Star Wars? Watch me, girl – read my lips: I don't care if you wrap up all this crap in old *carpets* – I don't too much mind if you torch the fucking lot and this bloody house along with it. And Christ – the number of

319

these bloody – what are they? Paper chains and bloody tissue-sort-of bells and bows and fucking lanterns, this place'd go up like a bomb, and good bleeding riddance is all I can say. Cos what you don't get, girl, is that this one's different. You did right before, Sheil – course you bleeding did, give you your due: ignoring all those other birds – the secretaries, the temps, all the shitty lot of them. Because by the time you twigged to the latest slag all she was was history, right? So yeh – you was right, basically, not to give a toss. But Catherine – I tell you, Sheil, I'm telling you – something's got to go, here, cos I'm not gonna get her unless I give her, right? And what she wants (although maybe yet she don't even know it) is me for keeps – and I can't, can I, go round making offers and promises like with all the others, can I? No I bleeding can't – cos she'll just turn round and say fuck off when she learns it's all just fucking shite. She's *already* told me to bleeding fuck off – that's what's bloody killing me. So I've got to get her back, I just got to. So what I'm basically saying here, Sheil – you in front of the gas logs with your scissors and your Sellotape and your bloody clever ribbons – is that before I lose my fucking mind, something else has got to go first – take my meaning? Give me a bit of leeway – and no hard feelings, darling, but that thing is you. Sorry, yeah – all that: it's just the way it is. Elsewise, I just don't stand a snowball's chance in bleeding hell.

✳

Colin felt funny. He also felt sure that if only he had *lived* a little bit more (as in simply been around – not suggesting fun, or anything); if only bloody youth didn't seem to last forever, with little to show for it but poverty and dread – and who said it was fleeting? Youth. Who said it? Some sad old sod who couldn't *remember*. If only, yeh, I had just anything to *compare* any of this stuff with, then at least I could know what really is a creepy and don't-much-like-it situation – probably never encounter it twice – and what too is just everyday, run-of-the-mill, yawn yawn – oh God, not *that* old thing again.

So all I can do now – and would you believe it? I'm back in bed with the girl I love and all I can feel is embarrassed and hopeless because some other damn new thing has just come up and I simply don't know what to *do*; so yeh – this is what I'm saying – all I *can* do now is play along, play for time (I'm good at this) and see where it leads me. There's only one light on, thank goodness – my face will maybe just seem warm because of a reflection-type thing, and not because it's burning.

'Oh come *on*, Colin,' Carol urged. 'It's the right thing to do. Even you must have read about the *dangers*, and everything. Put it on – go on. And then we can do it.'

Carol had ages ago torn open the little packet (where did she get them from? Why does she have them?) and Colin had eyed the wet and slug-like thing at first with only curiosity (heard about them, yeh – never actually seen one before). But as soon as she had said to him Well go on, then – put it *on* (and Christ, if she said it again he'd run from the room) all Colin had felt was embarrassed and hopeless – plus, incidentally, instantaneously neuter. And the other thing that occurred to him was this:

'But why *now*, Carol? I mean – bit late, isn't it? I mean – we didn't last summer, did we? Jesus – we didn't last *night*. Why now, all of a sudden?'

'I forgot last night. Feel a bit bad about that. Actually forgot I had them. But from now on we've just got to, OK? Oh Christ it's no big *deal*, Colin – just shove the bloody thing *on*, can't you? I bet you have with other girls.'

Oh God oh God – as if he didn't already have enough to deal with. Here was another one: what was the right thing to say? For both our sakes. How about the honest approach? Oh don't be so bloody *daft*, Carol – the only other woman I've ever had in my life is my mother's neighbour, Elizabeth, and I doubt she knows they've even been *invented*. Or should he go for lying wildly, and a touch of smarmy with it? Yeh of *course*, Carol – natch; but it's different with you – I love you and I don't want anything spoiling it – coming between us. Colin settled for attempting to subdue the rictus and tic to the side of his face, while whinnying lightly like a stagger-legged foal.

And it wasn't just this new and ticklish condom thing; in loads of other ways Colin felt but could not quite put a thing – finger on, the heady impulse of all that he loved seemed to be fading before his eyes. Last summer – after that first and mighty, wild and lusty encounter in Howard and Elizabeth's garden – their telephone calls had come in a rushed and mutual bout of panting (a combination, this, of temporary placation at just the sound of the other's noises, whipped up by a further yearning) and the laughingly hurtled and overlapping gabble of gushing avowals and a red tender eagerness that had made Colin actually acutely aware of his own rich blood racing up and down and around him, a good deal of it lurking fatly at his fingertips and groin – while his prickled brow felt akin to a brazier. And yet now here he was in the so-long-dreamed-of heaven of in *bed* with her, for another should-be fab night in a flat he could pretend was all their own. So why was this sense of, what – *loss* all over him?

Just take earlier today: Colin had tried simply everything in his power to prise Carol away from all thoughts of this crazy redecoration business. He saw now that to do an even halfway decent job they were lacking in just about everything – time, chiefly (even if they went at it day and night, they'd be due back in London long before they even got to just last knockings, let alone fine tuning; last *what*? Carol had hooted – and Colin couldn't at all explain: it was maybe just something he had heard his father say, one time, which was worrying in itself). But materials, too: they had got this ghastly red paint, yes OK – Jesus, Carol had bought

enough of that to comfortably see to the refurbishing of Hell
– and they had gloss white for the paintwork (amazing, on
the whole, she hadn't plumped for tangerine); but look –
they had no undercoat, he'd gone for the wrong sort of filler
– and anyway they had only a piddly little tube. There
wasn't a ladder in the flat, and nor had they dust sheets;
without a paint tray, the roller was useless – and Colin
didn't honestly fancy tackling the room with a half-inch
fitch. Look, Carol – the shops are shut and so much of our
precious time is, oh God, just *vanishing*: I mean, we may
never get all this time again, Carol – can't we just enjoy it
and not be *doing* with this? You make a start, Colin, was all
she airily came back with (not bossy, exactly – more like
dealing with a recurrent irritation), and I'll set about
cooking us something nice for later. But *Carol*, Colin had
tried – but only for form's sake and by way of rounding the
whole thing off: he was already levering up the lid of the tin
– and Not With *That*! screeched Carol: *Jesus*, Colin, what're
you *thinking* of – that's a carving knife. It's OK, Carol – it's
pretty blunt, I'll be OK; it's the *knife* I'm worried about,
blockhead – Auntie Jane is pretty particular. So they both
mooched around in quest of a screwdriver, or something,
but there didn't seem to be anything at all like that, so in the
end Carol said OK, Colin, use this – and she tossed him a
meat skewer, covered in could be rust or Oxo.

So what Colin had found himself doing was dipping one
end of the roller vertically into the glutinous and leery
paint, drawing it out sharpish, and then dashing wildly to
the nearest bit of wall before the carpet got the lot. He'd
spread out one or two newspapers (all he could find – hard
to fathom Auntie Jane: didn't seem to go much on anything
at all) but paint went right through newspapers, as he soon
discovered; he could maybe afterwards shift over that rug
thing to cover the worst bit – the rest was just the odd spit
or spot; and had they bought J-Cloths? Had they hell. And
nor did Auntie Jane seem to have heard of the things – and

the same was true of kitchen paper; all Colin came up with was a very off-white beach towel with Palace Hotel, Paignton, embroidered at the corner in blue, but he had already come so far with this caper to not even trouble to put it to the vote: Carol would just have thrown another of her (increasingly frequent and thoroughly unjustified – not to say bloody noisy) fits. She was never like that to her father on the phone; which seemed to be about every ten minutes, round the clock.

And she kept on playing The Rolling Stones. Me, I just thought Christ, then, this is it – here I am, squeaking the roller this way and that – can't reach the cornice (tried a chair – too wobbly, bit scary) and I'm afraid of going any nearer the skirting because I'll be bound to splodge it and I'll never have time to do the woodwork as well – and yes I did say *I* and not *we* because I just know, don't I, that I'm stuck with this (there's just no way, is there, that Carol is going to sully her lily-white pandies – Christ, she's already running herself yet another oily and pongo bath, no doubt as we speak looking out a further churchload of reeking candles) and I know too that if it's no good – and Christ how *can* it be? – then it'll be useless old Jesus-what-a-mess Colin who'll get it in the neck. Oh God – a thought: all of this seems horribly familiar.

And she kept on playing The Rolling Stones: bashing around in the kitchen, she was – in the end all we got was heated up Asda spaghetti bolognese, so God knows – don't *ask* me – what all the bashing around was about – and all the bloody time she was playing this one CD of The Rolling Stones. Now look – I do quite like all this ancient Sixties stuff (Beatles are best – but there's other good things too) and I do actually go for a lot of the Stones, but – you know how it is – the same few records again and again . . . it began to drive me dippy. I was the one trapped in a room that was very rapidly looking like all you are left with following a kamikaze attack on a ketchup plant, and all I'm getting is never mind Little Red Rooster but bleeding Paint It Black! I called out once or twice Didn't you bring any other records along, then? But all she had to say back was Aren't they great? Which wasn't an answer at all, was it? Typical Carol. She called me in to eat, thank Christ, just as Under My Thumb cranked up for the umpteenth time – and Jesus, the sauce on the spag looked just like the walls (smelt of them too, but that could've been me) and made me quite sick to look at it. So of course Carol started up with her So you're not going to eat it, is that right? I have spent time and trouble preparing this for you, Colin (yeh right – Remove Sleeve, Pierce Film Several Times and Stick in Fucking Oven), and if you're going to turn up your nose at it – I can't stand *waste* (she actually said that) – then I promise you, Colin, there'll be nothing else. And all this bawled out over *Jagger's* insistence (ha!) that despite the fact that he *tries*, and he *tries* – he can't *get* no (nor can I) – he can't *get* no (nor can bloody *I*) – satis-*fac*tion (yeah, that) – no satis-*fac*tion (too right) – no no *no* (well yeah yeah yeah – you bloody said it, mate: got it in one).

And then Carol was enshrined in her bath, and I was eating a Mars bar; do you want to come in and talk to me, Colin? No *thank* you – the stench of those candles is felling me from here; didn't actually say that – just mumbled something about having to get cleaned up – but I tell you, what with her essences and the paint, my head was really throbbing. I was so overjoyed at finding a bottle of turps under the drainer (Eureka! Auntie Jane *owns* something) that I slapped it on all over me and the paint didn't budge (I still looked like I'd come hotfoot from a sacrifice) and then the terrible stinging came – and only then did I remember that it was soap and water with vinyl emulsion but I couldn't use the bathroom because the sainted – not to say *scented* – Cleopatra was in there, wasn't she, so it was the kitchen sink that took the brunt of the fallout (cold water, Fairy Liquid – not too great) and the Paignton towel was very soon a write-off but never mind that – I'll stick it somewhere while the guv'nor continues to drift down the Nile. Oh dear. You see what I mean. When and how did all this happen? It never used to *be* like this: Carol and me together – it's all I ever wanted.

And now the day is over, oh thank God – just on midnight, and up till a minute ago I was feeling, what? Well three things, really: fairly, on the whole, knackered – because all that bending and reaching with the roller is pretty exhausting, if you've ever done it; and don't ask how it looks, the room. Carol had said she had never seen such an absolutely disastrous mess in her whole life on earth – what in God's name is *wrong* with me, she kept on wanting to know. Her *father* (oh Christ – here we go: her father and the bloody Rolling Stones – it's all I'm ever hearing) – her *father*, I might like to know, would have a piddly little room like that one over and done with in an afternoon. Oh yeh? (oh God, I wish I'd said this): So why don't you get him over here to see to the last knockings and fine tuning – you're due to ring him anyway in exactly four-point-seven-five minutes, so you might as well mention it. *My* father would still be dickering around after *years* on a room this size – agreed, granted – while *her* father no doubt would look in after tea to quickly add some bloody frescoes and maybe top the thing out with a dome: so what? It's not *fathers* we're talking about, is it? (or at least it bloody shouldn't be). It's me – *me*, Carol – Colin, the guy who loves you, if only you can remember why we're meant to be here in the first place.

Didn't say a word of that – goes without saying. So that's one thing I was feeling – tired out and pretty disillusioned; the second thing was bloody starving – I'd eaten the awful spaghetti glop (had to, really) and it was awful, yes OK, but also it was *titchy* and all there was after was a chunk of Viennetta, which is actually pretty all right but it always makes my teeth really quite hurt. But the good news was the third thing: Carol was truly soft – glowing and warm after her bath, and the one lamp in the bedroom threw all sorts of wonderful shadows over the curves of her body (aren't girls fabulous?) and so to hell with knackered and starving – here comes sex: sixty seconds worth of heaven on earth, is the way I see it – but now she's come up with this bloody *condom* thing (where did she get them from? Why does she have them?) and now even that sweet dream has turned into a job of work because look: I may not have the slightest idea how to cope with the sod, but even I can see that to make it work you've really got to be well up for it – and I *was*, of course: I *was*, before she produced the bloody thing: no way now. But I can't say that either, can I? (seems like I can't say much of anything, any more) so what I think I'll do, right, is take the squirmy thing from her (at least show I'm willing in principle – can't risk another scene) and then try to guide her hand to my chest and with a bit of luck she'll start stroking and tweaking around (I actually quite hate it when she does the nipple thing on me, if I'm honest: it kind of stings and makes me cringe and feel vulnerable and also giggle, none of which you want) and then I think just the knowledge that her fingers will be moving on down to where it really matters will probably be more than exciting enough and then I can just ram the bloody thing on before I know what's hit me.

This is very much how it went, and Colin was surprised now to find that the touch of both the latex and Carol's fingertips was actually pretty arousing and soon the thing was done and he hoisted himself over her and began to tease and probe (Colin was actually thinking Jesus, I don't know why everyone talks about these things dulling the sensation – I could shoot right now and I'm not even in her) – and then suddenly Carol tautened, her eyes wide, and now she hissed out:

'What's that?'

'Hm?' queried Colin. 'Well you *know* what it is, Carol – it's me.'

'No! No – not that! The noise. I heard a noise.'

Colin was still – not easy when you're hauling back the reins on a testy organ.

'I can't hear anything.'

'Listen!'

Colin was still: I'll maybe just do it, shall I? Will she notice, do you think?

'I'm listening. Can't hear a thing.'

Carol slightly relaxed. 'It's stopped.'

'Good.'

Colin made his lunge – quite terrifying, though (and could have been very nasty) when Carol now sat more or less upright and clamped both her open palms to each side of her head.

'There! There! I heard it again. It's someone moving around! There's someone in the next room – oh God, Colin, I'm frightened – '

'Honestly, Carol – I can't hear a single – '

And then he did: a clunk of collision, and possibly a gasp.

'Oh Christ . . .' he quavered.

'Go and see what it is!' gasped Carol. 'Oh God I'm so scared.'

'*What*?' husked Colin, out of her now, and trembling.

'Go on! Go on! What's *wrong* with you, Colin! It's a burglar, must be. Get him!'

Colin just goggled at her. '*Get* him?!' he said, frankly amazed.

'Well if *you* won't . . .' spat back Carol, making a move, 'I *will*.'

And while Colin's mind was screaming out Good Idea! (and I'll shoot out of the window and go for help) – his lips were busy with babbling All *right*, all *right* – I'll go . . . I'll go . . .

Colin could not believe he had opened the door, and

now was quaking as if electrified as his eyes coped with blackness and his ears – though pricked up – picked up nothing. He stood in the dark and silence and shivered with not just fear but cold – and now the unbearable quietness was gently broken by the plop of his condom on to the vinyl flooring (he had felt it wriggle free) and then quite terrifically by the smashing of a fist into the side of his face, and this had him stunned before his yelping even made it – though crazy with pain as he crashed back into a chair while banging his head on the wall, before he slithered on down it.

'*Bas-tard*!' was the roar now that filled the room – and Carol ran full-tilt in there (snapped on lights) and now she was screaming and tumbling over the hunched-up form of a man as he reached down for Colin's hair with one hand, while the other drew back as the fist.

'Stop! Stop!' shrieked Carol, pummelling at his head. 'Christ sake – you've *killed* him, Terry – what the hell are you *doing*?!'

'I bloody owe him,' growled back Terry. 'I just *knew* you'd be here with him, you dirty slut – very nice, isn't it? Having a *slut* for a sister . . . and as for *him* . . .!'

Carol was quivering and crying hysterically while pleading, pleading with Terry – *please*, Terry, *please* – leave him, just leave him – I swear I'll never see him again, I'll do anything, Terry, just *please* don't tell Dad, OK? *Please*, Terry, *please* don't tell Dad about this, I beg you Terry!

He stood up slowly, looking down with swinish contempt at the spreadeagled Colin – now stirring, his eyes swimming back into contact; he touched his jaw and yelled.

'Get up!' commanded Terry.

Colin did this, with huge tilting and difficulty; he felt rent asunder by hot pain and the needles of shock.

'Get dressed, you fucking *shitbag*. You *cunt*.'

Oh Jesus, thought Colin dully: on top of this I'm naked.

'And then get *out*. *Now*. I tell you, you *bastard*' – and now Terry had pressed his snarling face right up close, and he jabbed at Colin's chickenflesh chest with one hard finger – 'I *ever* see you sniffing round my sister again, and you are dead meat. Comprendo? You fucking *bastard!*'

And Carol yelled before Colin did as Terry dealt him a vicious backhander that sent him scudding into and through the bedroom door. He was conscious, just, and utterly traumatized; he found himself putting on clothes, shoving whatever was left into a bag. From the next room, Colin was dimly aware of bitten back snatches of hate-talk, fear-talk – shock-talk from the two of them: *Will* you, Terry? *Please* ...? *Knew* that bastard would be here with you ... soon as I found out he wasn't at home, knew it, just knew it ... *Promise*, yes I promise ... I never will ever – sorry, Terry, I'm sorry, but you won't, will you – *please* you won't, Terry? ... *Now* – he leaves *now*, got it? Tell him – you *tell* him ... Anything, Terry – anything: just please for God's sake don't tell Dad – swear to me you won't ...

Colin stood at the doorway, clutching to him whatever he had, looking down at the floor; the blood around his mouth was caking, and big numbness fought it out with agony. He yearned, *yearned* to launch himself at Terry – strike out anyhow – but pain and humiliation were all over him, and anyway: what would he be fighting for? The prize, he knew, was now withdrawn.

Carol hustled him into the hall, sheltering him from Terry who still stood there, poised like an animal. Now she had the door shut between them, and without looking at Colin she hushed:

'Colin. You see how it is. Oh God I feel I could *die*. I feel, oh God, I feel so ... *look*, Colin, you've got to go *now* – if Terry tells my Dad –'

'It's ...' started Colin. And then he said something else: 'It's the middle of the night.'

'There's maybe a bus. Get *out*, Colin – oh Christ get *out*.'

'I love you, Carol.'

'You don't, Colin. You don't. *Go*, Chrissake.'

Colin's jaw was ceasing to function. 'But I do,' he said.

'Maybe you *used* to,' rushed Carol, pushing him out of the door. 'Maybe we both did – but not now. And don't call me. Ever. Christ – if my Dad gets to hear of this he'll kill me – *and* you.'

Colin opened his mouth. Closed it. Then he said:

'Who's Tony?'

'Bye, Colin,' said Carol. And she hurriedly closed the door in his face.

I'll cry, soon. Soon I will, yeah. But now I plod down all these stairs and next I fiddle with this lock in the dark and now I practically keel over at the dazzle of icy cold that rushes up to me and my face! My face! My face feels slit by knives.

Colin walked into the blackness, not knowing where – oh God he was chilled and hurting, as raw as fresh-killed meat. After just a few paces he stopped and turned to look up at the top-floor flat: all the lights were on, now: look at that room – some of the wall is streaked with red.

And now the first of the tears began to roll, as Colin shook it away. So. There we are. It seems I *used* to love her . . . but it's all over, now.

331

CHAPTER FIFTEEN

The more Tara went on about it, the deeper John was driven into a morose and mute suspicion (soon to be bitter conviction) that he wasn't maybe not just quite but at all cut out for any part of this fiction-writing lark. I mean, let's face it – even struggling to the end of one of his moronic thousand-word wastes of time was becoming ever-increasingly arduous: he'd stare at the wordcount of 923 and *plead* with it, *will* it to magically enhance. I need the rounded thousand so for Jesus sake come up with another seventy-seven, can't you, because I (believe me) simply have not got a single one *left*.

He had – as promised – dug out his spiral-bound exercise book and gazed yet again at what he'd got: three characters, one of whose names he had entirely forgotten, and nor was he at all sure why he had bunged her in in the first place (just something to do, he expected). Anyway, this third character, who was called, um – there: gone again. Anyway – this woman, whoever she was, went into a shop, right, bought something (unspecified – couldn't think, couldn't think) and then bloody came out again. Tara pounced on this – because yes, she had made him read it all out to her, every word, and so now she was more or less just about as wise as he was.

'Why, in fact, does she walk into this shop, sweetie? Is it relevant to the *thrust*? How do you intend developing her?'

At which John could only stare, and consciously subdue his rising panic; it was like a nightmare – you go in to get your French Oral over and done with, and find everyone speaking in a Mexican patois.

'I dunno,' he replied flatly, feeling all of Homer Simpson.

'Well OK,' allowed Tara, 'let's see it in the wider context – in just a few words, John, what is the book *about*?'

John groaned. 'Oh God. It's about seventeen pages.'

'Funny, sweetie,' said Tara, drily. 'Seriously, though – what do you want this novel to *say*? Hm?'

John just shook his head; he then applied his lips to the large glass of whisky Tara had permitted him – pulled at it deeply, and then went back to the head-shaking thing. The truth is, he was thinking, I don't really want it to say a damn thing, do I? What I want – all I want is for the book to be *written* (come on, wordcount – put your back into it and rack me up, say, eighty thousandish words: I'll be ever so grateful) and then after that I want someone else to print it off and put it on disk and then I want another someone else – and you would do, Tara, you'd do fine – to tell me it is a sensitive and heartfelt tale of real and rare genius, the blackly comic element cut by true human emotion, the pace and plotting flawless; I then want the hot agent of the moment to hold a (fiercely contested) auction for just UK rights (tomorrow, the world); and then I want the advance that makes the news – a spectacular promotion (the cover of *The Bookseller* promising a massive campaign featuring 'stunning point of sale') followed by a glitteringly attended launch at the Groucho Club and the sort of rapturous reception in the nationals – each lead review complete with moody black-and-white study of an unsmiling and clearly fucking brilliant John D. Powers – that will be remembered in the trade forever. Spielberg, Tarantino and Redford can throw away the Queensberry Rules and grapple and gouge at each other in the street where I live, the bloody victor given leave to pay me hugely in return for permission to make the Oscar-scooping bonanza movie of the year, while I quietly and with dignity relieve the wholesale grocer,

Booker McConnell, of however many thousand it is, these days (pitiful, really, against what I've earned already, but the prestige is undeniable), and if the beer people, Whitbread, are inclined to follow suit (and I think it would be seen to be perverse not to) then who am I to block their impulse? *That* sort of plotting I find quite remarkably easy; it's just the bloody book itself I simply can't fathom – just don't know what to do with it – and I certainly don't want to sit down for months and months on end and actually *write* the fucking thing, Christ let's face it. All I want, all I want is a way out of wherever it is I currently am. Is all. And I stupidly thought a book might do it.

Actually completely sick of even the *word* book, now (where has Tara put the bottle? Peace and crates of booze, she promised me, and here I am, just dry and jangled); she seemed to have just thousands of books in this flat of hers, Tara – stacks of contemporary fiction along with all the requisite Proust and Freud and Gibbon and Woolf and Hazlitt and Trollope and Milton and Sartre and Swinburne and Lawrence and Huxley and Dryden and Jung and Russell and Joyce and all the rest of the other fucking bores that John had never read and never bloody would. To get her off the subject, he had fucked her on the floor, which had been nice if too brief (John's fault) because now as she got back her wind and untwisted her thong, she'd be bound to get back to the literary thing. And while he had ridden her (Yee-haw!) John had been made aware again of that singular noise she made whenever whatever he did connected. Hoh! she went: Hoh! Hoh! *Hoh!* Not so much arousing as bloody familiar, from somewhere or other. It was only now he pinned it down: it mirrored exactly the response of some hapless Japanese foot soldier, perspiring by the River Kwai – a mingling of shame, fear and unthinking subservience, when admonished by the officer in jodhpurs (and watch out for what he does with the crop).

334

God – the junk that clutters my mind: you'd *think* I'd be good at fiction, wouldn't you, really?

'Who would you say, sweetie, was your muse? Have one?'

'Oh God, Tara – can't we leave all this book stuff, now? I'm not a real writer, am I? Never will be. Where's the bottle – could do with a top-up.'

'But that's just it, sweetie – you don't know till you try, do you? That's why you've got to knuckle under and get the thing written. The whisky's right next to you, what's wrong with your eyes? What about Kingsley Amis? On the face of it, you seem to have something in common.'

'Christ I didn't even see it – thanks, Tara: I thought you'd put it away. Yeah – Amis. Like Amis. The early stuff, anyway. *Lucky*, um . . .'

'*Jim*. Have you read the son?'

'The *Sun*? Oh – you mean the son, son: Amis *fils*. They both hated that père and fils stuff, apparently: their bloody fault for making it run in the family. Yeah – he's good. Again, I've only read one or two. Oh Christ let's face it, Tara – they're *all* good: it's just me who's crap. Do you know, the first hardback book I ever bought as a boy – secondhand, of course, ten bob it was – was called, I'll never forget it – *The Quintessence of Ibsenism*. Shaw. Believe it?'

'What did you think of it? I've not read it.'

'You think *I* did? Christ no. It was just to impress. I carried it around for months. What are you reading, Powers? Oh – GBS's *Quintessence of Ibsenism*, sir: riveting stuff. Didn't even cross my mind to *open* the thing. The only words of the title I understood were "the" and "of". If pushed, I might have guessed that "quintessence" was some sort of damson jam, whereas "Ibsenism" . . . I don't know: maybe a bone disease? But none of this nonsense actually *bothered* me – I wasn't at all curious to find *out*, or anything. I quite got to like Shaw, later – well, you know: *Doctor's Dilemma*, *Pygmalion*, that sort of thing – but I probably think he's a fucking

335

bore, these days. And Ibsen, well – never obviously read Ibsen, but he's just *got* to be a fucking bore, hasn't he?'

'Maybe you should look at more novels by modern, living writers. What about John Fowles? Or William Trevor?'

'But they're ancient, aren't they?'

'Well – William Boyd, then. Ishiguro. Ackroyd. Barnes?'

'No no – too successful. Too literary. I'd be jealous.'

'Rushdie?'

'Joking.'

'Irvine Welsh? Roddy Doyle?'

'Too Celtic. Couldn't give a sod about drunk Scots and Irish. I do quite like Dick Francis. But God – I read one of those Grisham things once – it was terrible, terrible – really dull. Sells in zillions. Can't understand it.'

'If you read some women writers, it might broaden your outlook a bit, you know. You might even know why you send one into a shop, for no good reason.'

'No no: they all write about how vile men are, and how you go about getting one. And they're obsessed with ovaries and birth and bleeding and muck like that – quite repulsive. Iris Murdoch's good.'

'It sounds to me like you haven't read anything at all for absolutely *years*. Are you getting hungry? I got the most gorgeous-looking wild salmon – still almost rigid: smells of the sea.'

'Oh yum. Have you ever cooked salmon in whisky? It's great like that. So are prawns. I *don't* actually read much any more, you're quite right. Don't read. Don't write. Just drink and moan and . . . oh . . .'

'And what? What else?'

'. . . oh God. Nothing. Miss my *wife*.'

'Any chance, do you think? Getting her back?'

'Well . . . there's always a . . . I mean there's just *got* to be a chance, hasn't there? *Hasn't* there? Funny – talking of books, Lulu said to me one time that she'd decided she hates *all* novels, now, because of the endings.'

'The *endings*? But – '

'Well *exactly* – that's what *I* said: but Lulu, I said, they've all got different endings, haven't they? I mean that's the whole *point* of them, isn't it? And she said No no – I don't mean the *actual* endings, but knowing you're *getting* to the end, is what I mean, she said. You always know it's nearly over when there aren't many pages left to strum – and so if someone's old and ill, or something, you know they've just got time to die. And if some other character says he's emigrating to Canada, or somewhere, you know he's just going to vanish because the author's just aching to be shot of him – you can't actually follow him to Canada: there just aren't that many pages left.'

'Hm. I *sort* of see what she means, I think. Bit of an odd way of looking at it, though, isn't it?'

'Praps,' allowed John – not really listening to either of them, any more. It was his simply saying the big word 'Lulu' that had done it: bugger *books* – Christ, what do books matter when the love of your life is walking away? But she cannot – no, she mustn't. I have just worked it out – and it all seems so beautifully simple: what finally about me did Lulu decide she just couldn't bear? Well two things, I think (two *major* things, anyway): the jealousy – the mad and mouth-frothing, unreasoned and blaze-eyed jealousy and, more latterly, all the drink. So what I must do (yes yes – this is it, this is it – why did I not think of it sooner?) is stay with Tara not actually over Christmas, no, but right up to the very brink of it. Then I must go where Lulu will be: there she will see me in quite a new light. Will I be overbearing, eaten alive by emerald devils? No I shall not. I shall stand idly by, like a husband who is sure of the love of his beautiful wife. And nor will my walk any longer resemble a perpetually arrested headlong fall: I shall be upright and sober – decent and kind (even witty, and certainly deft). Then she will come to care for me all over again; we can curl up warm and shut out the cold of the last few days and nights of the year – and nobly in love, face the new one: together.

✳

'Elizabeth – this is Emil.'

And of course Elizabeth was all politeness: not in any way odd, was it, that Melody should have picked up merely the latest in her seemingly endless string of *men* friends (none of whom ever seemed to linger long enough to form the nucleus of anything approaching a stable, I note). *Timing* was rather annoying, however, because Elizabeth had now been sitting in the hotel bar (quite nice and cosy – bit cramped, yes it was, but on the whole really perfectly agreeable) for very nearly an hour, now. Had they said they would rendezvous at eight? Yes indeed – and of course Elizabeth was hardly surprised when nine was fast approaching and still Melody had failed to put in an appearance; but it was vexing, in truth, because Elizabeth had quite a while ago ventured a pastis – something she tended to do when in Paris, please don't ask her why – and without at all wanting to drink another, nonetheless found herself ordering one because – well look, call her old-fashioned if you must, but Elizabeth did not actually think it *seemly*, for want of a better word, for a lady to be sitting on her own in a bar, but if that was the inevitable situation, then a drink to play with was surely de rigueur. And she'd also made far too many forays into all these little dishes of nuts and pretzels (just *too* fattening – please someone stop me or else take them all away) when what she actually needed was quite possibly an omelette fines herbes – breast of chicken, maybe: rather think steak frites is a bit heavy, this far on into the evening. Something *hot* is the point – and so I very much hope that this *Emil*, did she say his name was, will not be hanging about for a drink, or anything, because I for one have drunk my fill, quite frankly; I'm tired out from shopping and it's food I need. Why on earth

338

couldn't Melody have contented herself with toying with the boy (and he hardly seemed more) among all the Mickey Mouses and whatever other foolishness it is they have at Disneyland, and not drag him all the way back here to parade before me. Was Melody, do you suppose, *addicted* to the presence of men? Sometimes it could certainly seem so.

'I've asked Emil to stay for dinner,' said Melody – smirking at the lad, in that singular way she had: almost as if she'd invented him. He, in turn, had a large proprietorial hand clamped to Melody's hip: his property, now (it was like he had bought the pair cheap, and here is just a sample, proudly fondled).

Even for Elizabeth, the smile of welcome was a big, big effort – and, unusually for her, she maybe didn't even mind if some of that showed.

'That's nice,' she said. And you will, of course, won't you Melody, allow me to pay for this dinner for a presumably impecunious Emil – won't you, my sweet? (Just look at that shirt – hasn't been changed for days.) And then she glanced at him quizzically, possibly to ascertain that he wasn't, in fact, as surely appeared to date, fashioned from wax and wheeled along – but was actually a Frenchman composed of the usual sullen sinew: the customarily sluggish blood stirring in his veins.

'Allo,' he said brightly – seemingly as pleased as an infant with a recorder who had finally honked his way to the end of a dire assemblage of missed notes and fumbled pacing and, quite unaware, now anticipated the awesome deluge of rapture due to him from Nan and Granpa.

'Yes . . .' agreed Elizabeth slowly, to nothing whatever. 'You do remember, Melody, we have to make a fairly early start in the morning, yes?'

'Oh that's all right – Emil's coming with us, actually – aren't you, Emil?'

'Allo!' he said again, with even a touch more animation.

'His English isn't *great*,' admitted Melody, ruefully. 'He sort of said – he's pretty hard to make out – but he's always wanted to see London and he's no one to stay with at Christmas so I thought Oh gosh how sad and I said he could come over and stay with me.'

'I see,' said Elizabeth. 'Well – isn't that nice?'

And some hours later, back in her suite (Melody was somewhere else, no doubt sharing yet another bottle of red wine with this apparently rather stupid young man), Elizabeth was screeching down the line to Howard not so much edited as magnified highlights of a good deal of this – and she noticed herself, too, very fleetingly wondering what he would make of it (oh dear, oh dear – I really do think a seed has been sown); but now she needed to swiftly move on, and talk of other things – and Howard, I don't know what it is but you seem rather uncommunicative this evening, darling, but what I have to say really won't take two minutes and tomorrow I'll be home – and I'll be pleased to be back, yes I will as a matter of fact – and then I can get stuck into seeing to things.

'And how are Brian and Dotty, Howard? Hm? I mean they are going to be all *right*, aren't they? Don't want them moping and *spoiling* things.'

And before Howard responded, he thought Oh God – it's me who's moping, but there's little left to spoil.

'Well,' he said slowly, 'Dotty seems pretty OK – came home this evening with an enormous pile of shopping, God knows where all the money came from. And she's got Dawn, of course. Extraordinary, with Dawn: haven't even been aware there's a baby in the house.'

'I know: it's uncanny. And Brian? Do you know, Howard, Melody's *still* not back and it's nearly twelve, here; that girl – she really *is*, isn't she?'

'I daresay she'll be in soon. No – Brian is a bit of a worry, really. Tried to – you know – *talk* to him and everything – get him to have a drink, sort of thing, but he just sits there and *stares*. It's not so much unnerving as bloody boring, if I'm honest, but Christ knows what he's feeling. All he said was that he wouldn't be a burden for longer than he can help, or something: that sort of *thing*, anyway.'

'Poor Brian. He really does come in for it, doesn't he?'

'Yes,' Howard agreed. Yes, yes – I suppose he does, but it is *I* who came in for it this morning, but here is not, believe me, something I can talk about. Even more than wanting Laa-Laa's neck between my thumbs (why, Laa-Laa – *why*? I'll never understand it) and yes, still missing her now-spoiled body – I really need Furnish's face to connect hard with my fucking fist, so then I can kick him, when he's down. At least, by the end, she went away quietly; it just shows you, doesn't it? People like that – they always have somewhere to go. Hurry and say whatever else you want to, Elizabeth, because I really need to fix another drink.

'And Nelligan? Please tell me he's gone.'

'Gone. He's gone. Took my million and went.'

'Oh *Howard*! And does it look just too perfectly lovely?'

'It looks ... just lovely enough. It's fine. You'll be pleased.'

'*Sweet*, Howard. Can't *wait* to get back, now. And are you looking forward to all the festives? I just simply can't *wait*: I'm going to make this one the very best *ever*.'

'I'm sure,' said Howard – and then as Katie wandered out of the kitchen clutching all sorts of food and a bottle, Howard latched on to her and already was on his way to that litre of Macallan. 'Ah look – Katie's here: Katie, have a quick word with your mother.'

'Hi,' said Katie, into the phone. 'I'm just more or less in – just had to get some *sleep* tonight, you know?' And if that caused Elizabeth fairly strenuous palpitations, it was nothing compared with what Katie did next: 'Oh and yeah – don't have too much of a shock when you see me, OK?'

'Shock? Shock? Why should I have a shock? What?'

341

'It's just that I've shaved all my hair off – been meaning to for ages. Bye, Mum – see you tomorrow, yeh?'

'You've –! Katie! *Katie!* Katie –?'

Elizabeth lowered the dead receiver and put a cold hand to her brow – just at the very second, back at home, Katie cackled deliriously and ran all her fingers through her thick and shaggy highlighted mane. Elizabeth practically suffered a seizure when the phone now set up its shrill and insistent squawking.

'Katie?! Oh *Lulu* – Lulu, it's *you*. I called and called – '

'Yes,' said Lulu. 'I couldn't face home. I'm staying with Pippa Bramley, pro tem. How's everything? Melody still with you?'

'Yes – well no, not now: out with some man.'

'*Good.*' And then (why not?) Lulu simply let it go: 'I *hate* to think of her there with you. She should be with Howard.'

Elizabeth was electrified, briefly – and still she tingled:

'Howard? With *Howard*? Why should she – why did you say that?'

'Oh nothing – I didn't mean anything. *I* don't know why I said that – all I mean is, she shouldn't be with you. *I* should. Oh but listen, Lizzie – this'll make you laugh: Pippa was telling me she met a load of what she describes as "truly rude children" in the street this afternoon, and one of them called out to her, Hey, you – Look at me, look at me – I'm picking my bloody nose! Did you pick your bloody nose when you was a little gal?'

'How perfectly revolting,' breathed Elizabeth, more or less on autopilot. Why on earth had Lulu *said* that? Why Howard? How did Howard come into any of this? Why should Melody be with Howard?

'*And,*' ploughed on Lulu, stifling back chortles over what was to come, 'do you know what Pippa said back to them? Of *course* not, she said – don't be so disgusting. When *I* was a little girl we had servants to do absolutely bloody *everything*. God oh God – she's really hysterical, and I don't even know if she knows it.' But she certainly knows something, dear Pippa Bramley, Lulu reflected with tenderness: the only reason I say all these things, she had last night blurted, is solely to appear to you *interesting*, dear Lulu; and now you're here, you won't go away again, will you? Tell me you won't. I am so very lonely. 'I've got you the most fabulous present, Lizzie: can't wait to see you. What time are you getting in?'

'Hm? Oh – just after lunch, I should think. Lots to do.'

'I'll come round and welcome you back. Missed you.'

Elizabeth was forming her mouth into some sort of reciprocal response when suddenly the door to the room imploded and a very drunk and bright-eyed Melody half fell in, sort of righted herself, and started to stumble veeringly towards and then into Elizabeth, laughing wildly as the two of them fell chaotically across the bed. Elizabeth heard only faintly Lulu's muffled exclamation as the phone was knocked away from her – but now she had it back:

'Oh God – *sorry*, Lulu – that was Melody – get *off* me, Melody – she just knocked me on to the bed! Lulu? Lulu? What's wrong? Are you there?' And then Elizabeth glanced across at Melody and said quite simply: She's hung up. Only then did she become aware of the deep drone of sleep from the back of Melody's throat: her lipstick was a mess, and her face in repose was puffy and white. Elizabeth suddenly felt terribly tired.

The magic of Christmas will make everything special – nothing must be allowed to stand in the path of its glittering trajectory. This one I'm going to make the very best *ever* – just you watch: just you wait and see.

PART FOUR

Snowballing

CHAPTER SIXTEEN

How many times now had Dotty squealingly called on
Dawn to look, see, take in, devour – oh, be like me and
enraptured by this, your very first taste of the shimmer
and sparkle of Christmas lights and dark blue London skies:
little twinkling red and white pinpoints entwined around
lampposts, the entire and still – after all these years –
enticing length of Oxford Street. And yes – Oxford Street is
precisely where Dotty had deliberately chosen to take her
angel Dawn, determined to feel nothing else but all this,
with her. Not Regent Street, no – although it was garlanded
with the larger and glitzy neon and flashes that older
children would still come and gasp at, or at least let out a
semi-grudging and uncool Wooooo. Here was much more
the Christmassy feel that Dotty recalled from, oh, so long
ago as to maybe never even – not really – have existed; only
the spark that she felt when she saw it again brought back
to Dotty whatever it was she had been filled with as a child.
She remembered her father crouching low and pointing –
urging her to look, Dorothy, *look* – see, take in, devour – be
like me and *enraptured* by this (and he surely did look it: the
lights made his eyes bright-glassy and adoring as he gazed
at it all, seemingly sated yet alight with nearly lust). Even
Dotty's mother's perpetual thin-lipped resentment
appeared to be momentarily suspended: she sipped at the
excitement of this annual outing, but unlike her husband –
his uneasy breathing forced out in heavy bursts from his
mortally collapsed insides – whatever chains she had in
place would never let her gorge.

And it was good that they were crowded and jostled on the pavement and sometimes into the kerb; all the bustle made it happen for Dotty – and she had no difficulty at all in swallowing the conviction that the scowling and harassed, occasionally even ferocious expressions welded to the faces of practically everyone scuttling and barging by were actually no more than a demonstration of serious determination to gratify by close of play even the most frivolous whims of their dear friends and family – leavened by maybe an overlay of unsmiling dignity, as befitted the coming and crowning glory of another year on earth. It excited Dotty that knots of typists and shop assistants were so eager to pass over their ten-pound notes into the palm of a hoarsely barking man, squatting on a crate before a suitcase – and with his eyes settling nowhere, keenly thrusting back cellophane and lushly-packed fragrances, no one at all concerned that the price might be over-low: it's Christmastime, isn't it? And this nice man is giving us the first of our presents. When the snow began to fall – large and soapy flakes – the man said Fuck, once, but Dotty well knew that the young people there saw it as fairy gold, and they raised up their faces to be sure that its cold kiss couldn't pass them by – so that their hair too would be flecked by the fresh, white and tingling proof that it wasn't just on cards and calendars that all this soft stuff fell and touched you: *Christmas* is coming – practically here – and despite all else but baby Dawn, Dotty kept discovering that inside herself she was soundly thrilled. At each new sight or exclamation, angel Dawn – strapped up safely into a brand-new sling, barely bouncing at Dotty's breast – she would glance up, and when their eyes were fusing (Dotty beaming into her the assurance that here was good, here was secure and also splendid) Dawn would happily chuckle and Dotty became again flooded by a love that buoyed her up and made her weak.

And pay no mind to the queue: it doesn't remotely matter

that it trails and snakes through looks like four very dull and unrelated departments. They had seen and cooed at all the Selfridges windows devoted to the magic of Alice (look, Dawn – the Mad Hatter in his funny grey topper? Have you ever seen such a huge big teapot? I'll read to you all about Alice's fabulous journeys, when you are a little bit older) – and now it was time for Dawn to meet Santa. Uncle Holly, it seemed, didn't live here any more; Dotty had loved him, with his big red cheeks and his bright green coat – and he gave you a very special badge, and Dotty had kept all of hers for years and years: and then one day, like so much else, they were suddenly gone.

As the queue inched forwards, almost in a trudging parody of slowness, Dotty carefully explained to Dawn – are you listening? You are? – that Uncle Holly had probably by now become so fine and famous that he lived in a grotto all of his own, in some dreamy wonderland or other, and that on Christmas Day he had the biggest and most wonderful lunch with Santa and his elves and *Rudolph*, of course – and when he and Uncle Holly stretched out in front of a roaring fire, suddenly dear old Santa was no longer tired from his endless night's flight through enchanted skies, delivering toys to all the good girls and boys. A lad in huge and lettered sports clothes a few places up was whining at his hot and practically hysterical mother, near buried under carriers, that this was a real *drag* and he wanted a burger and anyway he doesn't even *exist*, this bloke, and it's just for *kids* – and Dotty was more pleased than she could say that little Dawn, blissful in her lack of understanding, continued to laugh with her wet eyes, as her lips went on burbling at Dotty their bubbly and secret message.

They had moved maybe twenty feet on, now – largely as a result of grizzling children forcing their parents to abandon the whole caper, one or two of these putting up a token show of outrage (But Jesus, Harry, we're nearly *there*, now – Christ we've been waiting for a bloody hour: can't

349

you just last out a little bit longer? No? Well to hell with you, then – and don't be surprised if Santa doesn't bring *you* anything this year, you ungrateful little sod. I'll tell him, when I see him, yes I will – and it's no good *crying*, Harry – we're out of the queue, now, aren't we? No you *can't* change your mind – you've just spoiled it for *everyone*). Other times it was the father who snapped: Right – that's it. Enough. Can't – just can't bloody *stand* here any more – need a drink. Oh do stop *whingeing*, can't you? You saw him *last* year, didn't you? It's not as if he's *changed*.

But Dotty was content to wend her way; she dipped her little finger into a jar of Mexican honey she had bought earlier in the Food Hall, and she and baby Dawn took yum-yum turns in sucking on that. And in between asking Dawn Who her ickle baby girl was, then (and coming up trumps with the answer: It's *oo*, izzunt it? Yes it is – yes it is), Dotty was belatedly compiling a Christmas list. What on earth shall I get for Elizabeth, though? How does one ever buy Elizabeth anything? She'd already seen to Colin and Brian at Marks & Spencer, over the road. For Colin she had bought just piles and piles of anything trendy: awful, mainly, but he's bound to love them, Dotty was sure (he was still coming to terms with his home having been reduced from the you would think irreducible, to dossing down with Howard and Elizabeth: boy deserved *something*, don't you think?); and of course he can always change them, if anything's not twice as large as it needs to be. And she had also got him a beautiful blue and green marbled Waterman pen; it might momentarily stun into silence one or two of the baying hyenas at the awful school the poor boy goes to – probably one of them will offer not to kill him if he just hands it over (maybe just nick it). For Brian she had gone for a mid-grey V-neck – largely because M & S didn't run to gift-wrapped arsenic; had toyed with something very lovely to the touch – pure cashmere and quite feather-light – but in the end had come down on the side of lambswool.

It wasn't the money – it was just, well look – it's *Brian*, isn't it? What, in fact, would be the *point*?

No – it wasn't the money. Money, at the moment, was quite OK. The very morning after the accident, Dotty had triumphantly ushered in Dawn to her little cubicle on the top floor of the store where she did all this, and of course the baby had spun her magic (Hullo, Dotty – thought you'd gone on holiday; oh – what an absolutely *gorgeous* baby! What's her name? Dawn? Ah – lovely). One girl – Sue Fletcher, don't much care for her – had said God, Dotty, I'm amazed: is it *yours*? And Dotty had smiled and said Yes, oh yes.

She had cheerily volunteered for all the overtime going, and quite apart from her legitimate pay and not-too-stingy Christmas bonus, Dotty's haul over just those two long evenings had been prodigious. She had spent the whole of the next day with Dawn, travelling a meticulously scheduled if serpentine journey through every single branch of the store in central and outer London, and even one in Richmond. All the rushed and overworked staff fell in love with the baby, and eagerly supplied Dotty with bales of cash in exchange for her perfectly collated fistful of receipts; some even apologized for the unsuitability of the goods returned. So they were fine till New Year, and then Dotty would have to think very seriously again: a different job, almost certainly – if she could get one – because her stretch of gut-tearing luck, as well as her nerve, just couldn't hold. Head Office must have *some* form of checks, mustn't they? A procedure they go by? And when it swung into action, Dotty – and she knew it – was facing not just the shame of exposure, but also prison (baby or no).

When they got to Santa, he cradled little Dawn in his arms, and his great white and wavy beard moved up and down as he pronounced her beautiful – and no surprise either, he twinkled at Dotty, with so very lovely a mother.

Dotty felt herself blush and simper – and then she just cried with joy.

※

Cyril could hardly believe his luck – an actual reason (not a great one, admittedly, but a reason nonetheless) to pop round briefly to Howard and Elizabeth's on the very day that he knew that Elizabeth would be up to her eyes in it, and Howard – if he had any sense at all – would assuredly be elsewhere. Certainly on the morning of Christmas Eve, given the choice, Cyril would have preferred to be just anywhere but home, but there were so few excuses, weren't there – when the rest of the world had more or less closed. Edna had been preparing some sort of decorative surprise for simply days and nights, now: half the morning room had been screened off by sheets suspended from track lights on the ceiling, and every time he had ventured in there he had been pursued by shrieks and admonitions, raucously underlining the truth that Edna would not so much as countenance anything approaching *peeking*; stupid woman – as if Cyril cared a jot one way or the other what new awfulness was lurking behind her bloody sheeting.

So Cyril was ringing the doorbell, now, attempting some show of eagerness for the message he had for young *Colin*, of all people on earth – that was his name, wasn't it? Brian and Dotty's boy? How it had come about was like this: Edna had been poking around in the loft, she told him (can't leave well alone, that's her bloody trouble – one of the many, anyway), because next year, as discussed, we just must see about having it converted. Oh yes – *got* to do that, haven't we? Bloody vital. Then – in return for no more than quite fantastic cost and even more upheaval – we gain in time yet another vast and tarted-up room to add to the maybe eight or so others they had lavished more fortunes on, and never even so much as stepped into. But the upshot of her exploratory foray was a clearly long-forgotten and cobwebby, big

old cardboard box crammed full of rather scabby old toys
and board games – school exercise books, things rolled up
and pens and badges. You know who these must belong to,
don't you, Cyril, she had said. No of *course* I don't, Cyril
had responded rather irritably (don't know and don't
bloody care – it's a load of junk: heave it out). They must be
Colin's, she averred – with all the cockiness of The Great
Detective (yes – that *was* his name, Brian and Dotty's boy) –
and the poor little mite, he's lost simply everything lately,
hasn't he? I think he'd just love to have these back. Cyril
had just nodded in his customary and utterly desultory
manner – and then he practically heard and felt the reson-
ance of the word *Bingo* detonating at the forefront of his
brain. He had for ages – ever since Lulu had kicked and
bundled him away – been trying to think of just *anything*
that would get him back there and past that door again
(couldn't just stroll round for a casual word with Howard –
they weren't really, in truth, that pally). Had eventually
determined on some nonsense concerning a non-existent
overhanging tree that badly needed lopping – but this old
toy business was a vast improvement, having at least truth
on its side, for starters, not to say (at this so tender time of
year) the element of *caring*.

But never mind Colin and his box of sodding crap – was
it just possible that the divine Lulu *hadn't*, in fact, crept
away and stalked off home? Maybe all talk of going had
been no more than that – idle talk; possibly by now she will
have seen the error of her ways, do we think? Could she
have come to realize how I would truly be the *making* of the
woman, and all she may be now is just shy and hesitant to
reopen the approach? She could, indeed – couldn't she? – be
simply *pining* for his arrival. Soon find out (one way or the
other).

Colin himself had opened the door – grateful, in truth, to
have just anything to do: his mother was with Dawn – what
a bloody surprise – and whenever he approached he was

hustled out and away with insistence (Don't come in! Don't come in! You'll spoil all of the surprises!). Huh. I've had enough, too many, surprises just lately: enough to last me the rest of my life. My face still hurts so much: I said I walked into a door, and nobody argued because nobody cared. And God knows where Dad is (doesn't much matter). And yeh – I know that Elizabeth is terribly busy, and everything (Jesus – all the stuff she's doing: it's like the Queen's expected) – but even so, she doesn't seem to have any time at all for me, these days. Offered to help – do something – but the only person she seems to want around her is that weirdo kid Peter: truly pervy, he is; and she calls him *Zoo-Zoo* – I mean, Christ. And Katie's off with her bloke. Lucky Katie. I was, till not too long ago, with my girlfriend, you know. In a flat. But I'm not, now, no – and won't ever be again. And never mind for now the sheer and awful *loss* of her (there's all night every night to weep and dab around the worst of that) – what I know I will never forget and always loathe myself for doing is *running*, like that. There hadn't been a bus, predictably: spent the whole night in the wet and freezing shelter – thinking what? Thinking Carol oh Carol oh Carol oh Carol – just that, on the one side, and alternating all of it with only this: why is Terry Terry? And why, oh God, must I be me? And who the hell is *Tony*? Whoever he is, she's with him now, bound to be (I wonder if she might be wrapping up for him, as I stand cold and stupidly at the open door, staring blankly at Doctor Cyril Davies, a Christmas gift she had maybe bought for me?). I bought for her a handbag, red and white shoulder-bag thing – and inside I put a book of actually pretty yuck and crappy poems, but probably the sort of thing she would've loved; and a myrrh and frankincense candle. Maybe give it to Elizabeth; Elizabeth probably, on the whole, deserves it – she does tend to keep on saving our lives.

'Ah Colin!' Cyril greeted him with vigour (a Ho Ho Ho would maybe have overdone it, but comparable gusto was there, as he ostentatiously stamped his feet and blew into the cupped ball of his hands). 'The very person I wanted to see.'

Elizabeth at that point fairly cantered across the hall, hair amok and bearing with care something tinselly and alive with silver stars.

'Cyril! Hallo! Can't stop – see you tomorrow! Love to Edna.'

'Me?' said Colin, dumbly. 'Why me?'

Well *not* you, obviously, thought Cyril ungraciously; ask yourself, you arrogant little twerp – why in God's name should *I* want to talk to *you*? Is *Lulu* here, is all I care about. Is she? Is she? She's not, is she? If she were here I'd feel it and I don't. I am now quite crushed – so I'll quickly tell you of your box of garbage, and then you can do what you bloody well like. What's that you say? Would it be OK if you come round and have a look? Be my guest, be my guest – I'll maybe even give you an éclair, if there are more than four in the larder: 'tis *Christmas*, after all. (Tomorrow, then: not till tomorrow will I be able to see my Lulu again – just must get her on her own, somehow.)

This was the first time Colin had been in the old house – since long ago last summer when Cyril and Edna had moved on in and torn it up; it was so odd to see – never mind all the new lushness and colour, even the *walls* didn't seem to be in the same places any more (though, to be fair, a good deal of them weren't). And there – look there: there used to be that ghastly old brown and dingy hall-table thing there, with the wonky drawer and the knob that kept on coming off (The knob! The *knob*, Brian – Dotty had gone, oh – how many hundreds of times? You keep on sodding around with cat flaps when we don't even have a fucking *cat* and bloody ugly slabs of shelves for your unspeakable *man*hole covers but will you just ever in your life put a spot of glue to that bloody Goddam *knob*?! I will, replied Brian – mildly and invariably – of course I will: it's just a question of *getting* to it). And now there was a huge and looks like marble sort of Grecian urn type thing, like you'd see in the British Museum, or somewhere – and it's all writhing at the top with these jazzy boas and plumes and I think they're peacock tails: Mum would have a fit. Or maybe – dunno – she'd really like it; she never actually had any choice in it, did she? Maybe this is what she'd go for, who's to say? Anyway – bit late now.

'Oh hoy!' said suddenly a friendly girl's voice – and spinning round to trace it, Colin was quick to appreciate that here now was a real live friendly girl that came attached – truly sort of honey brown and slim and loads of golden hair and Christ I really do, gosh, quite like the look of all that. And the voice (and the girl) had more to say:

'Killy,' said Kelly. 'New here. You're Col – yiss? Here's the box of stuff – come on in to the kitchen when you've sorted it, and we'll have a cup o' something, ow-kye?'

'Yes,' agreed Colin eagerly. 'Yes, right – OK.'

There was a bashed-up Monopoly set with all the houses and hotels gone missing (Colin sort of remembered Evo-Stikking them all together, for some long-lost reason or another, and using the resulting thing as a sword, before throwing away the splintered bits of it). And some tedious little relief maps he must have drawn in Geography just absolute centuries ago, all prissily pointed up with thin red biro lines and pencil shading: what the hell had he kept all those for? This was good, though – a scrap-book, full of Concorde and Ferraris. Some *Beano* annuals: quite like to look at those again (I really loved The Bash Street Kids). A Corgi red bus – I'll keep that and stick it on a shelf, if I ever have a shelf. But not all this stuff's mine, though – these aren't: photos. I can't have been born when some of these were taken. God – just look at this one: Mum looks so young, and Dad – despite the lapels on that suit – he seems almost normal. They seem, what? What do they seem to be? Happy, I think.

Most of the rest he chucked – including an old brown envelope with these really naff little tin badges inside: some fat red-faced guy with a stupid green hat – never seen them before in my life. And now I've sorted it, I am very much off to the kitchen for a cup o' something – ow-kye? As Colin passed what used to in his day be a junk room (many were, let's face it) and now seemed to look like a kind of shrunken Roman temple, he glimpsed Cyril Davies – staring quite wide-eyed at a whole wall that appeared to be covered in solid gold and studied with rubies and emeralds and whatever those blue ones are – and diamonds and all stuff like that. A disembodied voice that just had to be Edna's was demanding quite imperiously of him Well? Well? *Speak*, Cyril – you do *like* it, yes?

Cyril nodded and answered her really quietly.

'Remarkable,' he said. 'Quite . . . remarkable.'

All old people are nuts.

❋

And the prime example of the breed – the one of whom Colin had long despaired: yes indeed, Brian, his very own father – was sitting at that moment amid the bright and glitzy, yet deeply unwelcoming interior of an East End pub (and this at lunchtime, Christmas Eve). He had read in an article, one time (and he'd cut it out, as he used to do), that this was rumoured to be one of the haunts you come to, if you want things done (know what I mean?). Certainly Brian had been initially encouraged by the distinctly hostile and tar-drenched eyeballing that had coated him head to toe as he sheepishly – head lowered, don't need eye contact, not yet I don't – made his crab-like way through the acid-etched door and eased across, he hoped quite unassumingly, to the five inches spare at the horseshoe bar. He hadn't bargained on the white and scrawny naked girl, taking round a beer mug and swearing at anyone who plonked into it anything less than a quid (the drunker punters with fivers were wished a Happy Fucking Christmas). Her feet – and it was maybe only Brian who had focused on her feet – seemed quite red and painfully swollen, crammed into a could be too tight pair of chipped white stilettos: maybe she and not just Christmas Eve explained why the bar was so terribly full? In a sane world, Brian could not help but reflect, she would've emptied the place, wouldn't she?

A sane world: now there's an idea. I think it maybe wouldn't catch on: where would be the scope for human behaviour? So anyway, mate – what next? Well – just finish your beer and leave, I think is about the sum total: no sense in hanging about now, is there? Not now that you know that you've wasted your time – again again again (and yet time, rather strangely, is this thing I have left – and all I want is to be shot of it). You were actually rather brave, though, if I may say so, Brian my lad. Think so? Well – it's why I *came*, after all: had to speak up, didn't I? Ah yes – but what if the man had been an undercover policeman, hey? What then? I know, I know – but I reckoned, well – lunchtime Christmas Eve – maybe not too likely; some would be back at the Nick with a porno film show, courtesy of Vice, with Customs & Excise chipping in with refreshments; others might be explaining to a tearful WPC that it was only a few *days*, love – and I've put in for the redeye shift come the day after Boxing Day, haven't I? Hey? So we'll see each other then; yet more could be traipsing round Debenhams, and when asked what they think of this, saying Lovely – and when asked what they think of that, saying Lovely.

Mind you – had the other bloke, the first bloke, not started up the whole thing, I maybe would've lost my nerve: nobody *smiled* here, or anything – even those knots of hard men who seemed to be friends, you'd think – they just glowered into their beer as if it had done them harm. Harm. That was the word the other bloke – the second bloke – had mentioned: that, and 'The Business' – quite scary, once you realized we weren't talking actors on the telly.

'You're a new face.' That's what the first bloke had said.

'Yes, I . . . yes. I don't, er – I haven't, um . . .' That's what Brian had said.

'Bit out of your manor, ain't it? Long way to come for a drink.'

'Yes, I . . . yes. I don't, er – I haven't, um – exactly just come for a drink. I'm actually looking for someone to do a job. Little job.'

'Yeh? You gonna get me one in, or what? What sort of a little job? Going down the chimney and nicking all the stockings?'

'No. No. It's a bit bigger than that.'

'I'll have a word. Why don't you sit yourself nice and cosy in the far corner over there, ay? And I can have a swift word with a mate for you, if you like. What's your name?'

'Brian. No – it's David. Oh Christ – no, it's Brian, actually.'

'Well Brian, I'll tell you what I'll do – you make sure I get a nice little drink out of this – say, give me a score – and I'll drop the right word in the right ear. OK?'

And Brian had gone for all of that: bought drinks, sat himself in the far corner over there – given the man his twenty pounds (earmarked, along with not much more, for some presents, yes – but maybe here was the first step towards the best present he could ever hope to give them: at least it was for keeps). And he just went on sitting there, fooling with beer (and thinking Christ Almighty, I really am aren't I? I really am a gift from heaven to people like that – already he's probably blowing my twenty in another pub altogether, and laughing like a drain at this tosser what give it 'im). And just as Brian was giving himself one more – yet another – ritual going-over (and they were pretty frequent, these days – sometimes even every hour on the hour) a really what they call nasty bit of work sidled over and sat down beside him, staring dead ahead. Brian did the same; it was as if the two of them were engrossed in a movie featuring several of the more senior members of our Royal Family, together with half a farmyard.

'So-o . . .' opened the man.

'Get you a drink?' offered Brian. Do with a whisky, now.

'Drinks come later. What you after, son? You want a bit of harm done, is that it? Someone leaned on?'

'It's – yes, that sort of thing. Bit more so, if you see what I mean.'

'Uh-huh. So we're not talking about a good smacking, then? How heavy, mate? The business? It gets to cost, you know.'

'Well it's the whole hog, really . . .'

'Don't say the word.'

'Right.'

'How urgent?'

'Well – any time at all would suit me, really. Now, if you like.'

'You taking the piss, son? This some sort of wind-up? Cos if you fancy spending Christmas with a couple of broken legs – '

'I want – I just want you to kill me. Oh God – I've said the word.'

'What are you – nuts? Are you a fucking pervert, or summing?'

'The thing is, I haven't any money. I thought you might do it cheap because I promise not to *struggle*, or anything: I won't be hard to find. But I don't want it to hurt, if that's all right. Just do it quickly.'

'You serious?'

'Oh yes. Very.'

'Mm. What insurances I got? I mean – I get someone, right? What insurances he got?'

'Well – we've never met. I never come here. They maybe won't even find me for days . . . of course, that bit's rather up to you. Him.'

'Hell of a way to spend Christmas, my son – dead in an East End alley. You sure about this?'

'Yes – I said yes.'

'How much? How much is cheap?'

'I've got fifty pounds.'

'You've got – ! This *is* a wind-up. Who are you? Are you fucking wired up, or summing? Cos as far as I'm concerned, all this is just funny talk – I don't admit to nothing. You the filth?'

'No. I'm not. I'm no one. I just want to die.'

'For fifty quid.'

'Yes, I – yes, I'm afraid so.'

'Well I'm sorry to disappoint you, my son, but you're just going to have to knuckle dan and get through it like the bleedin' rest of us. Intcha? You can't fucking *afford* to die, mate. Tell you what – I'll send you over a very large brandy: my treat. I reckon you're just some sort of sad old nutter what wants elp. Cheer up, mate – it's bleedin' Christmas. Innit? Ay?'

So. What next? Just finish your beer and leave, I think is about the sum total (I notice the brandy hasn't arrived). Maybe check out that bit of railway track you passed on the way down here – remember? Yes, I do – I might have known that you'd be quick to spot it too: the steep embankment? The broken fence? Could be ideal. Right then – I'll be off. Coming? Right behind you, lad: train to catch, if I'm not mistaken.

CHAPTER SEVENTEEN

The evening was glitteringly dark, and as Elizabeth lit the eight little red and candytwist candles – proud like soldiers marching across their Scandinavian arch on the sill in the bay of the drawing-room window – she almost yelped out with the thrill that kicked her at seeing just lie there so perfect a thick rug of snow – the colour of creamy caramel in the ochre of the welcoming porch lamps – the longer shafts of light showing pale icy blue and shadows, petering away into the black of beyond. Thank you, she thought – Whoever-it-is-you-are-up-there: here is the one sublime finishing touch that only You can handle. But You must admit – I've attended myself to just everything else: people are already saying Oh Elizabeth! How have you made it all so beautiful in so little time? Dotty had said it – dear Lulu too; even Katie seemed vaguely and grudgingly impressed – although of course she'd never actually bring herself to say so – you don't expect it, not with Katie. Melody, I'm sure, will also say lovely things when she comes over tomorrow (and she really did, you know: take that foolish Frenchman home – Emil, is it – and of *course* bringing him along with her, but what can you do?). In a funny way, though, it's Edna Davies's reaction I'm most looking forward to; I really can say that what with everything I've done here, and my utterly wonderful kitchen (it's a dream, a dream – more fabulous than I even dared hope for) – then on top of that and confronted by my famous Christmas Day lunch, she will quite simply be dumbstruck: maybe (hee hee) go right back home and rip everything out and start all over again! Poor Cyril: must be awful, living with a woman like that.

In the next room, people surely did seem to be content to lounge amid the flickering glow of fireside peace (the bow-fronted gunmetal grate well banked up with these wonderful logs mixed together with pine-cones that every Christmas we always have delivered by this terribly useful little man in the country, somewhere: Surrey, or something) – and you know, Elizabeth could have almost convinced herself that the scene before her eyes was quite as mellow and posed as a happy tableau on one of the very many Christmas cards cluttered and crowded on to every shiny surface, peeping from behind Waterford bowls and Coal-port vases and those rather sweet silvergilt half-size carriage clocks that she and Howard used to sort of collect (she would choose, he would pay) until it didn't any more, in frankness, seem even remotely amusing to do so.

That American – the Rick person (haven't really spoken to him properly yet – quite hard to make out the accent – so I don't really know what to think) – he has ensconced himself like a lord, right royally, in poor Howard's arm-chair: Howard is over on the other side, now, just by the tree (and oh! The tree, the tree! In a minute I'm going to gaze at that tree: shimmering in warm pinks and orange – this year's theme – the very marvellous and crinkle-cut lametta making it wink, and all the little lights cloaking it utterly in a twinkling blush, like uncut diamonds; I wouldn't trade you my fresh and towering Christmas tree – and it's *Badedas*, you know: that's that clean and festive aroma, the true smell of excitement that always reminds me of rustling presents – I wouldn't trade you that for all the *real* diamonds in the vaults of de Beers). But he seems happy enough, Howard – sipping his whisky, his eyes appearing glassy and quite unreal now as two white lights leap up within them, as he goes on gazing into the fire. Katie is lounging at the feet of Rick (well – her choice: she does as she likes; and she *didn't* shave her head, thank the Lord – she's such an odd child, Katie). Brian still hasn't come – missed his supper, which I thought rather rude; Dotty says he often wanders off somewhere on Christmas Eve, she's never asked him why. She expects he'll turn up later. And what of Dotty herself? Well – you can all guess what Dotty's up to, can't you? She just had to, she said, give her angel Dawn an early Christmas present – and a big fat plastic yellow teddy was now clamped to a chair leg, each light-up coloured part of him making a different noise: bleep, ping, parp, clunk (none of this, it has to be said, was doing any favours to the latest Sinatra track – Have Yourself A Merry Little Christmas – his mooning baritone at just the right degree of audibility, to Elizabeth's mind – you don't want it to be overpowering, do you? But at the same time it just wouldn't be the same if it wasn't there at all). She always played the old LPs at Christmas – Nat King Cole, Bing Crosby, all the singalong carols, of course (King's College Chapel Choir saved especially for the brightness of Christmas morning itself, when at last that mountain of presents could be carefully investigated – ripped apart, in Katie's case). And God – just look at them: under the tree simply wasn't enough – shining and ribbon-decked avenues of them were stretching away just everywhere (there's a little square one from Howard – tartan paper and a huge gold bow – and I know it's silly and I know I'm just being a little *girl* but I just can't wait to know what's inside: others too, but that one in particular). Lulu's next to me now, on the sofa, and holding my hand just faintly; she won't, I think, say any more till later.

Colin seemed fairly preoccupied (awful bruise on the side of his face, poor love) – and drinking too much champagne, but that I suppose is my fault (and maybe why he's started walking into doors). I still do find him a desperately attractive young man (and I know it's awful to say it, and remember what I've done) – and now, with just that single guilty thought, I'm nudging into the truth that here just isn't, is it, an innocent and traditional Christmas Eve scene? The way I always assumed it was in the past. Because earlier, when I knew that just everything was ready, I pretended it wasn't so that I could escape upstairs with Zoo-Zoo, for maybe half an hour. He bade me no welcome, when he saw me again; his eyes could have widened, as they dwelt upon me for seconds longer. All he had to do was touch me and I quivered and slackened and his hands as they slid up the length of my legs were just cool, then warming, and after – so firelike. All he said to me – and he said it as still I lay there, my eyelids and stomach continuing to flutter – was that his 'people' (he called them people, his family – how odd to think of him having such a thing) had a Christmas Eve ritual of opening presents and so of course, I must understand, he would have to be there; but he would be back for our own big day tomorrow, he promised me: all I said was Thank You.

And soon after – too soon after, I have to say (my cheeks were still hot and my fingers needed taming) – I ran into Lulu, dear Lulu – and Lulu had an urgency about her, I could tell. Where have you *been*, Lizzie? I've been looking for you everywhere. Oh, I said airily – Peter and I had to finish something off. I *hate* him, she said – with a real vehemence that I had not known before (but yes, of course, eternally expected); and Melody too – hate her, hate her: I can't even stand it when Howard's around. *I've* got to be with you, Lizzie – and there was no use in my saying But Lulu, Lulu – you *are*, you *are*, because breathlessness now added energy and need to the whole of her lovely and meaning-it face, and when she backed me into the spare room, when she kissed me, held me by the hips and pulled me to her, I loved it – loved it, like the last time, and tugged just all of her towards me. But Christmas things were calling out, and with an unspoken promise now hanging between us, I came downstairs to melt into what really couldn't, could it – no way in the world – be truly described as a

365

traditional and easy Christmas Eve evening, because I, for one, had my own agenda – and although it is difficult to imagine any such thing for anyone else, you never really knew, did you? You never really could. Not really.

And oh heavens look: it's Mummy! I'd momentarily forgotten all about her – she had nodded off very soon after supper (we always have Cumberland sausage and pureed potatoes with my own very special gravy, on Christmas Eve – and lots of lovely cheeses afterwards: I think it started the year Katie was born – just did it, and it sort of stuck) – and this was quite a relief for *me*, I don't mind telling you, even if it is an awful thing to say about your own mother – and God it is *Christmas*, after all; but heavens – if I'd had to listen to just one more word about how Uncle Jeff had this very fine port decanter and matching glasses – did I remember? (No I didn't – could barely even remember Uncle Jeff.) Yes of *course* I remember, Mummy – what about them? Well it's all very mysterious, her mother had confided (and already Elizabeth was dimly recalling the bones of the storyline – it had several variations – if not the bloody decanter and matching glasses: didn't it use to be a Wedgwood dinner service?), but after we buried him, they totally disappeared! And now the voice narrowed and creaked, as if to point up the denouement of a chilling and other-worldly tale from the crypt: nobody admitted to as much as *seeing* them – not your Auntie Jessie, not Edwin – none of them: all was innocence and silence. *Well* – call me a silly old lady but I *tell* you, Elizabeth – one minute they were there, the next minute they were gone! Didn't vanish into thin *air*, did they? Someone had them – of course they did: and that someone should have been me because I was always closest to your Uncle Jeff, everyone forever said so. And then they could have been yours – and you could have given them to Alice. Alice? Who's Alice, Mummy? Hm? Did I say Alice? Oh no, not Alice – didn't mean Alice – Alice has been dead for years. Who do I mean, Elizabeth? Katie, Mummy – Katie. Ah yes – Katie, dear Katie: of course.

And now – oh Lord – she was risen, and padding across to speak to Howard: their annual little get-together, it seemed, was due to begin. And was it just the sudden aversion of Howard's whole face from the firelight that made his eyes shut down, like those of a frog?

'So, um,' she opened. 'Another Christmas is upon us, hey? I daresay I'll not see the next, um . . .'

'*Howard*, Mother,' sighed Howard, with huge and gritted patience. 'My name is Howard.'

'Well I know *that*. What a thing to say. Of course your name is Howard – I know *that*, don't I?'

Well why don't you ever bloody *say* it, then, Howard was – yes, just about as near to thinking, he supposed, as he was ever going to get – but not really, if at all. He was actually in a semi-trancelike state – had been sitting here for ages, now, vaguely aware of the sound of some sort of electronic toy, must it be, overlaid by the rich rumblings of good old Sinatra, of course; that new American man's voice – deep, and reasonably incomprehensible – punctuated by the odd yelp from Katie; from time to time a bauble on the pendulous tree alongside him would slump, slither and then rush on down through the branches to land with a clink. All this, and the very welcome hot scourge of whisky hurrying along inside of him, all this Howard had more or less registered – but he was now actually moved to wondering whether his impulse of this morning had truly and in fact (bearing in mind how women could be) been as smart and gung-ho an idea as it had appeared at the time. Hadn't, in all honesty, even expected any post (did they deliver on Christmas Eve? Newspapers, yes – but he could never remember if the post came or not). Well evidently it *did* because here on the mat was one of those Jiffy Bag affairs, which had mildly intrigued him – but he straight away stuck that aside when he saw and recognized at once the pretty handwriting on the one single letter that lay there: Laa-Laa.

'It's not, is it,' went on Mummy, 'like the wartime Christmas. Everyone has everything, now.'

'I wouldn't know,' said Howard. 'Wasn't born.'

An address in St John's Wood. She had opened the letter with just the word Howard. Only that. And it was silly, but despite just everything, such distance had hurt him. She was sorry, she wrote, 'about the other day'. Yes – even now she seemed to see it as no more than a clash of timetables – an unfortunate error of timing (how long had she been whoring there, at Howard's expense? And with that bastard *Furnish*, of all bloody people in the world!). She thought, however, that his reactions had been extreme: imagine her plight – eviction at Christmas. Compensation. That was the next big word – followed by just the merest hint of menace, the faintest suggestion that if he paused to consider, he would see that really there was no option. That had fired up Howard to the point where he nearly tore the letter asunder – but instead and suddenly he drew out his pen, scrawled 'Fuck *Off*!' right across the whole of it, got on the phone to his regular team of couriers and in no time had the thing winging its way back to whatever St John's Wood pad she was currently scrounging.

'I think,' sighed Mummy, 'the old days were the best days.'

Howard gave out a grunt: so do bloody I.

'Dad!' called out Katie. 'D'you fancy a film, or something? There's a *Star Trek* on telly, and some Spielberg thing – or we could dig out a video.'

'Well *yes*,' interjected Elizabeth hurriedly, 'a video certainly – but you know it's got to be one of our traditional ones, Katie – the ones we always watch on Christmas Eve. Does anyone want more drinks, by the way? Nibbles?'

'Star Trek,' muttered Mummy. 'Aren't they those little lace-up shoes I used to buy you for school, Elizabeth?'

'Oh *Mum*!' wailed Katie. 'Not *again*! I know that bloody Scrooge thing off by *heart*, now – and as for *It's A Wonderful Life* –! God – that angel Clarence and Bedford bloody Falls – I just can't face all that again. Oh *please*, Mum . . .?'

'It's a *tradition*, Katie,' Elizabeth quite formally reminded her. 'No, Mummy – that's Start-Rite: different. And anyway, Katie – you know we all enjoy them, once they're playing.'

And then a dark and wholly unfamiliar voice broke into all this:

'Zoo-Zoo's petals,' said Rick, with crooked lips and a sort of a lisp.

Both Howard and Elizabeth turned to him as one, as well as if electrified: how could he know of this, they each thought independently – Zoo-Zoo is just for me, me – mine alone! Everyone else just gaped (Dotty, Colin and Mummy more or less simultaneously thinking something along the lines of Who actually *is* this person?).

'Jimmy Shtoo-ert,' illuminated Rick. 'One of the greats. You recall the scene where George Bailey tucks away his little girl's rose petals into his vest?'

No, thought most people – even Katie, who was sure she knew the bloody thing backwards. Elizabeth, though, was thinking Zoo-Zoo – really? His little girl was called Zoo-Zoo? I never ever noticed that; Howard could only think testily Why the fuck did he want to stick petals in his *vest*? Not that it matters to me a damn either way. (Could've actually sworn it was Gary Cooper in that film, but no great surprises there: Christ, my mind.)

Scrooge won. As the opening credits rolled, Elizabeth's mother clapped her hands once and cawed delightedly Oh yes, yes – I remember this one: I've seen it before. You saw it last Christmas Eve, Mummy, said Elizabeth, quietly: we watch it every Christmas Eve, don't we? Just said that. Colin moaned Oh God – it's in black and white: what's it about? It's about, replied Dotty, this very mean man – oh God, Colin: you must know what *Scrooge* is about – don't they

369

teach them anything at school? A very mean man who meets ghosts and spirits, and then at the end he becomes jolly and generous: it's only a *story*, of course. Anyway, Dawn and me are going to watch it, aren't we? Yes we izz – yes we izz. What a shame, murmured Elizabeth, Brian will miss it (though I am actually merely underlining the truth that still he is elsewhere: drunk in a pub, I have no doubt). You guys, intoned Rick – you gotta, like, excuse me while I make a cuppla calls, OK? Mister Street – I'm not getting a signal, here – would you mind too much if I used your phone? Obliged to you. He was already on his way to the one in the hall, Katie close at his heels: Who are you calling, Rick? It's Christmas Eve – who are you calling? Honey – I don't like you should ask: kay? Who a man calls is his personal business – but as it's you, and as I love you, tonight I'll tell: I gotta see my Momma's OK – OK? I then gotta bitter business take care of: take no time.

The film had reached the early stage ('Pour me another Scotch, would you, Katie?' practically pleaded Howard – if I'm going to sit through this lot again, I'll bloody well need it) where Ebenezer had snapped at everyone and been utterly vile and beastly and shouted out that Christmas is *humbug*, I tell you – *humbug*! And now he was in a dingy coffee house on his way back to Marley's old house, in the snow ('We've got snow!' exclaimed Elizabeth) and he rejected more bread on the grounds that it would cost him a ha'penny extra, sir – and Colin was thinking idly What's a ha'penny again? But now he leapt up alert and with hope as the doorbell sounded: Oh great, he thought: oh great. Elizabeth said: 'I'll get it – shall we pause the thing, film, for a bit? Probably only Brian' (hope he's not in any sort of a *state*). Dotty for her part had not even thought of it being only Brian: she simply briefly convulsed with, well – it must be *irrational* and momentary panic: why on earth should she? Would it always be like this, now? As Elizabeth had said – probably only Brian.

'Oh *look*, everyone!' was Elizabeth's latest rallying cry from the hall. '*Come*, all of you – come, listen!'

Most people drifted off and towards this clearly heartfelt summons (I'm not moving, thought Howard – whatever it is, I'm staying put: snug as a bug in a mug. Rug; Rick moved away into a corner, shielding the phone with his arm and shoulder, cutting into whatever he was hearing with Hey – back up, guy: didn't get that – got this broad braying in my ear).

Elizabeth had ushered in the four children – like small, pink-faced and multi-coloured Michelin men in their thick and puffy clothes – the snow was shuddering away from their wellingtons as they stamped them on the doormat. The tallest of them was holding a lantern (not a real candle one, like we used to have, observed Elizabeth: only battery, but the effect was just as lovely) – I recognize her: she's the daughter of those terribly nice people who have the baker's, now; two of the others I know by sight – can't tell you, though, who this little baby boy is, but he's quite enchanting: just like the small one in a beret on the *Star Trek* poster – oh *Start*-Rite, I mean, oh heavens: please don't tell me I'm getting like Mummy.

And they trilled and sighed their way through Silent Night and then they clanged out Jingle Bells – and not till the second refrain of Glaw-aw-aw-aw-aw-aw-*aw*-aw-aw-aw-aw-aw-*aw*-aw-aw-aw-aw-aw-*aw*-ria! did the youngest falter and look decidedly nervous as Rick beat the wall and practically yelled into the telephone Sheeeesh! I just can't *tell* you what I'm dealing with here, man! And Elizabeth – having very much given Katie one of her *looks* (he's *your* friend – and I don't much care for his behaviour) – plied them all with fresh cream Belgian chocolates and some little light-up snowman and Santa keyrings she had bought for no reason whatever just that very morning because they were silly and so perfectly sweet and she couldn't resist them – and Elizabeth just adored the cold and young softness of the baker's girl's hand as she pressed into it a folded ten-pound note.

'Merry *Christmas*, children!' she almost wailed, as she waved them away. 'Oh – wasn't that just *lovely*? I'm *so* pleased they came – they usually do, but last year they missed us and it just wasn't the *same*.'

The doorbell rang again ('Oh Jesus *Christ*,' escaped from Rick – now crouched in the farthest corner, as if under attack – 'they're gonna hit us *again*! Look I'm real sorry, man, but you're gonna have to run that by me just one more time . . .!').

Colin had been quiet and sad through all the singing (Huh! I should've had my very own Christmas Carol, this year – but instead she's with not just *Tony* – who she maybe even loves, oh God – but her *Dad* as well, who she bloody well adores and will probably marry, with shitty Terry as the bloody Best Man – *and* she's got her blissy White Christmas). But suddenly he shrugged all of that away because this second time Elizabeth swung wide the door (and goodness knows what she was expecting this time) – there was at once a girl, deep brown with wet eyes and a wide mouth, who straight away made everyone else around look really quite ill and pasty, to Colin's way of thinking.

'Oh, Elizabeth,' he barged in. 'This is Kelly – come in, Kelly.'

'Thinks,' said Kelly, stepping nippily into the hall. 'Gee – it's sow *cowled*.'

'Kelly,' went on Colin, 'is from next door. She works for the Davieses and she's new in England and she had nowhere to *go*, sort of, this evening, and so I . . .'

'Well you're very *welcome*, Kelly,' beamed Elizabeth. 'Come in, come in – the more the merrier. Everyone – this is *Kelly*.' Just look, she thought, at the eagerness all over Colin's red face: he really wants her. I remember that expression: it's exciting. I wonder what happened to that rather nondescript little girl he vaguely fooled with at the seaside, that time. Probably ended then and there: these summer things do – especially if you're young.

'Oh *Howard*!' Elizabeth was deploring – now that she was back in the room. 'What's happened to *Scrooge*? I thought we were going to *pause* it? I just can't bear this sort of tacky Christmas television – you *know* that, Howard.'

And she really couldn't: the repeats of the old Morecambe & Wise specials, she loved; another Bond film – well all right, if we really must. But it was the presenters in between that made her cringe. I mean – look at this one now: big creepy grin and a ghastly little suit and of course an *amusing* tie (covered in Christmas puddings); and that red-buttoned leather wing armchair – you only *ever* saw those beastly things at this time of year, with someone appalling sitting there. And the cards on the mocked-up Adam mantel behind him – no one sent them, did they? They weren't *real*; and nor were the wrapped-up boxes at the foot of that perfectly dreadful and tasteless tree – just like those light and dusty things that high street banks and building societies still saw fit to pull out year after year and throw underneath a bent wire Dyno-Rod of a so-called '*tree*': tinsel hurled at it by a blind man from a distance, surmounted by a waning star and surrounded by racks of colourful pamphlets advertising *loans*. Too, too depressing – quite as bad as the covers on the tackier TV guides: game show hosts and soap stars and, oh dear God – *hostesses*, amusingly got up in Santa suits and deliberately wonky beards and handing to each other yet more of these flagrantly artificial and suspiciously perfect bow-tied 'presents' – all this the result of a photo studio session back in sweaty August. (Elizabeth always, but always, bought the *Radio Times* at Christmas, because it could at least be relied on to have a painted and unashamedly nostalgic cover depicting – if not Santa himself, cherry-cheeked on a snow-capped roof – then certainly a robin on an equally snowy bright red

373

pillar box or, if all else failed, a grinning bowler-hatted snowman, replete with carroty nose and a football scarf.)

'Well,' explained Howard, 'it *was* pausing' – a terminally frozen Jacob Marley, juddering his cash-box chain, mouth agape, for seemingly hours – 'and then it clicked and whirred a bit and changed over to this. You *know* I don't understand these things, Elizabeth – so I just left it.'

'Well it's *completely* spoiled now,' was the last word Elizabeth had to say on the matter.

'*Good*,' pronounced Katie. 'Sick to death of the thing. Oh Rick – come on in! What can I get you to drink?'

'Honey babe,' he said quietly, holding both her hands and pouring liquid truth right into her eyes (it was rather as if the time had come to finally confess he was really an alien – which, at times like this, he surely did seem). 'Listen – I gotta go.'

'Oh – Rick!'

'Listen, hun, when I talk to you. There's some papers back at the hotel, is all – something I need to fix before Chicago shuts down. I'll be back tomorrow, baby. Miss me.'

An encompassing wave to the rest of the company, and Rick was outta there; the general impression was that, sure – he had 'coptered into 'Nam and entertained the troops big time, but sorry kids – his agent regrets he has no time for autographs.

'It's chestnut time!' announced Elizabeth, brightly (I really do think he's dreadfully rude – and you keep reading that Americans aren't meant to be). 'Who's for roast chestnuts? And marshmallows – yes, everybody?'

There was just about a sufficient rumble of assent, though only the Lord knew where it had come from: Colin was chatting and giggling with Kelly – who seemed to have drunk a great deal of lager: they liked it, didn't they, Australians? Lager – and Dotty was, as usual, lost in Dawn (my baby's getting dozy – izzunt she? I think so. We go bed soon, and wait for Santa to come). Elizabeth looked at Lulu:

never known her so quiet – and yet all she was radiating was palpable, very. And look at Mummy – gorging on all the soft centres: she'll be as sick as a pig in the morning – I'd better try and prise her away.

'Would you like to go up, Mummy? Everything's ready for you.'

'I think maybe I shall, Elizabeth. It's been a lovely Christmas – thank you, dear.'

'No – it's *tomorrow*, Mummy.'

'Is it? Is it really? What – it's tomorrow *already*?'

'No – oh God. No – it's *Christmas* tomorrow, Mummy. This is Christmas *Eve* – we haven't had it yet.'

'Well I'm sure it will be perfectly lovely, whenever it is. Thank you, dear.'

Elizabeth took her up ('Now mind the bottom *step*') and Katie idled over to her Dad.

'So – all right, Daddy? What do you think of him?'

'Mm?' grunted Howard. 'Oh – your American friend, you mean.'

'His name is Rick, Daddy.'

'I daresay.'

'He's asked me to marry him. 'Member I told you he'd said something about it in the summer?'

Howard sipped whisky. 'And what have you told him?'

'Nothing. I've said nothing. I don't really know anything about him. He flies on Concorde – he drives a Ferrari: that's about it.'

Coo, thought Colin – breaking off for just a second with Kelly: just like my scrap-book!

'Not really, is it,' started Howard, with care, 'much of a basis for marriage? Money is important, yes, but . . . God, Katie: you're so terribly *young*.' Yes you are – and I don't suppose for a moment you remember, but when you were even younger yet – years and years ago, now – it was me you were going to marry, Katie my sweet. I don't suppose, no, you remember that at all – why on earth would you? You were only a baby girl. But I do.

'I know. I know I am. We'll see how it goes, hey? Is this going to be a *happy* Christmas, Daddy dearest?'

Howard reached up to kiss her forehead. 'Best ever, my angel.'

'Come on, everyone,' called over Elizabeth. 'Gather round.'

She had already rigged up the racks of chestnuts over and at the sides of the glowing embers – glass bowls full of puffy marshmallows lay at the ready, toasting forks alongside. Only two low table lamps glowed and glistened, and every one of Elizabeth's movements sent long and orange-tinged shadows swooping up and diving. The smells and the excitement of Christmas were beginning to fill out and build, now – Elizabeth could feel it: Howard and Katie, Dotty and Dawn, Lulu, Colin and his new friend Kelly – all were clustered about the fire, kneeling on rugs or slumped against cushions: their faces were tingling with a warmth that she knew they were feeling – for many reasons, maybe, but also simply that of Christmas. And Elizabeth sizzled with utter pleasure as the next Sinatra track – for Ol' Blue Eyes was back – coiled up and around them: Chestnuts Roasting On An Open Fire – oh joy, oh joy – no one could have timed it better! So can anyone imagine how utterly trounced she was feeling the very next second when the jangle of the doorbell sheared through just everything – but Elizabeth manfully and straight away bustled off to deal with it (please don't let the mood be broken!) and calling out to Katie to not let anything *burn*, will you, she swung into the hall quite ready to bundle in and with a bit of luck away a vile and drunken Brian – and she stopped dead only when she saw the policeman.

Back now in the room, Elizabeth was doing her best to gently detach Dotty from the assembly ('Oh I really don't want even to *see* him, Elizabeth – just tell him to sleep it off upstairs') and she was aware that if the atmosphere was now still OK, there was no knowing at all how long it would last, because she had no idea what the policeman had come about – had simply asked politely for Mrs Morgan. What could he be wanting? So late on Christmas Eve.

Dotty reluctantly drew away from Dawn and, summoning bile, grudgingly entered the hall – and she stopped dead only when she saw the policeman. Her heart leapt out of her, as she instantly knew the truth: oh God – dear God – this was just the terrible end.

'Mrs Morgan? Wife of Mister Brian Morgan? We tried telephoning, only your phone seemed to be, um – anyway, er – Mister Morgan is down at the hospital. Accident, I'm afraid.'

'Accident?' breathed Dotty. 'Oh thank God, thank God – what a tremendous relief . . .'

'Both arms broken, otherwise fine. He'll be out of it tomorrow. Sorry to have to break this to you, on er . . . Found him by the railway, half on the track – unable to say how he came to be there. Maybe had a few, ay? Time of year. He was lucky, though – no trains running over the holiday, otherwise he would have had it.'

'Poor, poor man,' said Dotty to Elizabeth, when the policeman had left. 'Fancy having to work over Christmas – and did you see that terribly painful-looking boil, just to the side of his neck? Look, Elizabeth – let's not *tell* anyone about this, hm? It'll only spoil the evening, and Colin will be so embarrassed – oh God oh God, why is Brian such a cackhanded *fool*?'

Elizabeth just shook her head, and went along with that. Dotty followed her back into the room, still palpitating from the shock of it: but what an absolutely *tremendous* relief, though – she had felt sure that he had come for to take her away, so thoroughly covered – so intimately tainted was she, now, both inside and out – with all the depravity of *crime*: I will never (just mustn't) commit it again.

Later yet, and the warm and lazy easiness of Elizabeth's

Christmas Eve had clambered over everyone. Still, the embers of the fire were the absolute focus, the crackle and spark of it joined only by the rustle of Katie's groping at the wrapped-up presents (and how lovely, thought Elizabeth, to see that the child is alive in her still). Howard stood and reached down for the last of his very last whisky.

'Wa-a-all . . .' he yawned. 'Big day tomorrow.'

And yes, it was difficult, so hard, to pull oneself away. All of this – it passed so quickly: but tomorrow (Howard was right) would be bigger and better and more special in every single way – no? Katie had pinned up her ancient woven Christmas stocking – the one with Piglet on one side of it, her name on the other – patched and still unravelling (she snorted derisively as she did it – but she did it). Howard said Christ I've Had It, and with a series of Sleep Wells, he made off for the stairs. Dotty said I'm Coming Too – Ssh Ssh, She's Already Asleep, The Darling Little Angel (is Colin *still* in the hall, saying goodbye to that girl?). Katie paused by the window on her way up to bed (what room am I in? Bloody musical chairs. Have to be up pretty early – buy Mum and Dad something: *somewhere* in London must be open, I hope. I don't quite know what the hell Rick thinks he's doing, but I don't really go for it so much any more).

'Hey!' she called out softly, as she parted the curtains. 'It's just like that Wenceslas song out there – deep and crisp and thing – whatever. Watch out everybody – snowballing tomorrow!'

And as Elizabeth was damping down the last of the fire, Lulu crouched down low to her and whispered sidelong: Sleep With Me. Elizabeth did not look up from her task, and quietly said No. Lulu stayed still, and then she hissed at her *Sleep* With Me – and Elizabeth turned and said No, No I – No. Lulu touched her face and let her eyes say Please, and Elizabeth looked down and away. No, she said. Tomorrow, then, urged Lulu. Tomorrow – yes? Say Yes. No, No I – No.

Lulu kissed her on the lips, and Elizabeth gazed up into the tree and its spangled lights, still and shimmering, and said No, No I – don't know. Maybe.

CHAPTER EIGHTEEN

'Pull!' urged Katie. 'Pull pull *pull*!'

'I'm *trying*!' gasped back Colin. 'God almighty, they're as tough as – '

But he broke off there as laughter and the blam-blam of other people's crackers detonated around him; he almost was tempted to ram his foot against the rim of the dining table to give him just that bit more leverage – never *known* a cracker so reluctant to snap and tear open and spill out its loot. And then it did – Colin was sent spinning back into and over Elizabeth just next to him – she was clapping her hands with real delight at all the sights and sounds of the scene before her.

'Mine! Mine!' shrieked Katie, as Colin made a lunge for the bundled-up goodie that had clunked to the table, and almost immediately became lost amid the fantastic clusters of silver and turquoise, gold and maroon deep-down good and oh-so-special Christmas things littering richly the main white damask drag – and grouted into any spaces left between the layered dishes and the teeming ranks of King's pattern cutlery (the sterling set, instead of the plate – if not today, then when?): the sparkling goblets and fluted beakers, the beribboned linen napkins and placements – each held fast by a metallic snowflake – the festoons and stars and glowing nightlights in red glass shades, all somehow urging the gorged and glittered eye towards (and in no way at all – no not a bit, not by any means suffocating) this truly spectacular creation at the table's centre, alive with mauve and scarlet berries, lush ivy – speckled and

380

golden ears of corn jetting away from intricately sinuous spirals of thick and glossy, dark green holly; here too was a vast and out of season pineapple somehow stuck with twinkly lights that flickered constantly, its stiff crested tufts like those of a perfect palm tree.

Two courses, now, into the Christmas Day lunch (the goose, said Melody, had been just to die for), and the state of the table was truly that of an opulent jumble as everyone held aloft in triumph their bijoux and trophies – the big haul from these extraordinary crackers, puffed out and trimmed with net and brocade, they had been: now they lay broken and scattered as so much gorgeous debris – the sumptuously spoiled and splayed out fallout of more than a dozen little Madame de Pompadours, in the aftermath of a drunken and ravishing orgy.

Dotty, poor Dotty (and Elizabeth had lent her a very dark pink and deeply pleated dress – French cuffs and a perfectly plain neckline – for she seemed to have bought presents for everyone but herself) was particularly pleased with a small gold-plated folding double picture frame, each hinged wing incised with an oval (must take photos of Dawn, she kept on saying). Edna Davies – and Elizabeth had to admire just everything she was wearing (she had expected Escada, she didn't know why, but here was something else, and quite superior; it was true that with her colouring, Edna could maybe not utterly carry off with brio so strident an emerald, but never mind – she's done her best) – Edna seems equally gratified by a pack of plastic-coated playing cards in a snapshut leather case: We used to play cards a lot, one time, she said – didn't we, Cyril? But Cyril was talking to Lulu – had been since the moment he got here, Elizabeth had observed; and whenever he does, she looks at me, Lulu – yearningly. Can it be she doesn't like him?

Melody, of course, is just eating, eating – eating and drinking, as she loves to do; the oafish Frenchman Emil is tight beside her – taking long draughts of one of Howard's rather better oldish burgundies and letting out what might be a howl of approval, or else the evidence of something quite nasty and bronchial, which really has no place at table. He touches her a lot; you can't actually see where his hands are – and this is more or less my point – while his shoulders are often hunched across at a fairly odd angle. Mummy appears to be more or less OK – waving a fork and moving her lips apparently in time to some piece of music she once must have heard at another Christmas altogether, somewhere else and years ago. Zoo-Zoo truly is a very odd young man, you know: even when he opened my presents to him earlier, it was impossible to read so much as a jot of what he was feeling – I think there could be something on his mind, yes I do; but still – it's Christmas: I really do think we all must make the effort.

And then there's Rick – Katie's Rick. He's not actually at the head of the table (amazing he didn't simply march up and usurp the position as his God-given right, because that is rather how Rick seems to be) but he certainly nonetheless has that *air* about him: wrists perched and poised just at the edges of the place mat, his wide eyes and tight mouth at once savouring and overseeing the scene before him – quite as if here is the result of his total endeavour. I do hope Katie's not too *too* serious about him – it's a different culture, isn't it? America? She might take to it, I daresay, but Howard and I, I feel, would never quite be really *easy*. And look at him, dear Howard – content, as ever; if everyone's happy, then that's fine by Howard. I once or twice tried to see if he ever glances over to Melody, but he doesn't seem to. (Just look out of the window – the snow, it's still falling: oh – the fun people had with it this morning! Simply can't remember the last time it snowed on Christmas Day.)

And have I mentioned Brian? Oh God yes – he's here now, Brian. Arrived quite early, just as we were settling down to the presents. This alone seemed to unnerve him (he clearly hadn't *bought* any, or anything, but what can you expect: it's Brian). But again – once again – you couldn't *not* feel sorry for him, could you? Each of his arms was caught in a starch-white sling, tied with bows like rabbit ears – his forearms meeting in a cross against his chest, fists coming close to slugging him with a left, and then a right: it was as if he was about to bestow a sacrament or, less likely still, break out on the beat into a spirited bout of go-go dancing.

'Oh my *God*, Brian!' Melody had exploded – fizzing with laughter, and nudging Emil. 'What have you done to yourself *this* time?'

'Come and sit down, Brian,' said Dotty, curtly, as Colin very visibly cowered in shame, and did not even try to meet his father's eye. (On the one hand, though, he wanted to go up to him and say: You OK, Dad? But the other hand won – no contest.) Thank God, anyway, that Kelly isn't here to see it – it's always worse, much worse, when your parent is a prat and there's some girl around, watching it. But she's coming round later – Elizabeth said it was OK; not first thing, though, Colin – early Christmas Day is just for family. So how does that explain the loopy Frenchman, the creepy Yank and the nutcase 'Zoo-Zoo'? A sexy Australian could only be a plus, so far as Colin could see (I just can't wait till later, when we're going to do all the things she said we're going to do later. Carol? Who's Carol?).

Katie was passing out presents with one hand (King's College Chapel Choir frankly gets on my tits – I don't know if it's the screaming high notes or the rolling of the Rs that mostly drives me crazy) and with the other fingering the little gold Tigger at the end of a chain around her neck. It was a tradition that every year, her stocking would be crammed with mandarins, and in there somewhere would be something to do with Winnie-the-Pooh: I think I'm kinda fed up with it – I mean, it was OK when I was a kid, yeh sure, but it seems a bit manky, now; but I'd hate it too if it ever ended – if Mummy ever stopped.

Elizabeth was passing around thick-sliced wild smoked

salmon, urging Howard to open more champagne (Melody's glass is empty!) and asking Dotty if she had any idea how the people who lived on the other side of them, can't pronounce their name, ever celebrated Christmas – we've never actually *asked* them to, you know, come round or anything because the man at the deli in Prince Street told me one time that they were terribly orthodox something-or-other and had these rather quaint holidays and dietary laws and all the rest of it, so it wouldn't really *work*, would it?

Howard was protesting that this present couldn't be for him – he had four or five already: you shouldn't waste your money, buying things for *me*. Don't be silly, Howard – you deserve it, doesn't he, everybody?! And this was followed by a good deal of founder-of-the-feast and appreciative rumbling. What's that in your hand, Howard, Elizabeth now enquired, while passing a rather oddly-shaped package to Lulu (looks very *interesting*!). Hm? queried Howard. Oh – some video tape, looks like: came in the post yesterday morning. No idea. Here, Elizabeth – *you* haven't opened anything, yet: this is from me.

'Oh no – not that one yet!' squealed Elizabeth, as Howard passed across to her the little tartan box with the big gold bow. 'I'm saving that one – let me open something else first.'

'Open this,' said Lulu immediately – her beautiful face now dark, as she placed an elegant box, wrapped in pleats, on top of all those from Howard. 'It's from me.'

Amid the tearing open of paper all around her (Colin was ripping into piles of stuff that was really cool – good old Mum; don't much like this dreary old pen, though; Katie was so far best pleased with her black Prada backpack) Elizabeth simpered at Lulu – so sweet, but should you have? Thank you – and unwrapped the present with more care than most people could ever devote to doing it up. Brian said quietly, and to no response whatever, that he liked his grey V-neck, thank you, Dotty. Howard had opened it up for him, poor sod – held the thing out in front of his eyes – God alone knew when he could actually wear it. Plaster a bit itchy, I expect, is it, enquired Howard: fancy a Scotch? 'Tis a bit, answered Brian, close to docile (*why* can't I kill myself? Why *can't* I? Why did I have to slip and fall on my way down to that track? And why couldn't a train have come along and finished me off?) – thanks Howard, yes: a Scotch would be perfect.

Elizabeth gasped at the sheer glossy weight of the superbly cut silk and Chanel shirt that Lulu had bought her: she held it to her face, and just the first kiss of it under her chin made her want to wear it now.

'I had one just like that!' called over Elizabeth's mother. 'They used to be made out of parachutes.'

'Oh *Mummy*,' chided Elizabeth. And then she assumed the expression of a mournful and apologetic mongrel: 'Thank you *so* much, Lulu. It's – well, you know how very lovely it is. Thank you.'

Elizabeth raised herself to briefly nuzzle the side of Lulu's throat, and did not visibly react when Lulu whispered I Want You. Elizabeth (Affecting Not To Hear) now set about opening her present from Dotty – a green melamine and anodized aluminium breakfast tray: she really, thought Elizabeth – while thanking Dotty so very profusely – shouldn't have.

'Has Mummy got anything to open, Howard? Pass one over to Mummy.'

Dotty was quite careless of any gifts for herself ('Look, Dotty, look,' urged Elizabeth: 'all this lot's for you') – too immersed in unwrapping all the things for Dawn that she had spent a good deal of yesterday decking out with care in the brightest coloured paper and ribbons she could find: explaining with patience and love to her bright-eyed baby all the fun they would have with the spotty paddling pool and the wind-up clown and the big floppy bunny – do you see big and floppy Mister Bunny, Dawn, my angel? – and how adorable she would look in all these soft French cotton, primrose and eau-de-nil dresses and smocks.

Elizabeth was now so engrossed in Lulu opening one of hers, while she excitedly tackled another from Lulu, that she only now remembered to look across to where Zoo-Zoo was sitting, slightly away from the party: she had given him the beautiful cashmere, the Charvet scarf and the silk pyjamas much earlier this morning (would've looked a little bit odd otherwise, don't you think?) and so she was not too surprised that he was well this side of rapture over the blue denim shirt – her 'official' present, she had whispered (and why had she thought of denim, now she wondered: never ever seen him in anything rough). Just look at what Katie's given her father – a funny-looking tin with Turtle Wax and shammy leathers and things: she knows he has the car *done*. And for me? CKbe – her favourite, at the moment. And it was Katie's greedy scream that well and truly cut through all the bustle and rustling and tiny conversations: she was holding high a gold Rolex Oyster with a diamond bezel and yelping out the word *Rick* repeatedly as she flung herself at his neck (for Elizabeth he had brought a bouquet of flowers the size of a tree: she had stuck it in a bucket, for now). One or two people were muttering Very Nice, but few had the stomach for more. Elizabeth far preferred the perfectly simple white gold Cartier bangle – the ultimate secret from the little tartan box – and she hugged Howard briefly but firmly, and her lips touched his forehead. I'm glad, he said, you like it. Yes, he thought darkly, as he hoisted in triumph a litre of thirty-year-old Glen Grant and mugged his pleasure to anyone around – probably anyway look better on you than it would've on Laa-Laa.

And after the presents (My God! deplored Elizabeth, in big-eyed and mock horror: I am simply up to my *knees* in waste paper – no no don't be *silly*, Lulu, just joking: have all this cleared up in next to no time) Katie was urging everyone into the garden: prizes all round for the biggest

386

and best snowman in fifteen minutes, everyone! And Colin said Oh great – and went next door to get Kelly. Rick joined Katie ('We can't let these other people *win*') and Melody and Emil swiftly followed (he kept on shouting 'Allo!') – and soon the shrieks and barks as snowballs flew were scything through the white and ice-cold air, and seeping into the warmth of the house. Elizabeth was serving hot chocolates – laced with cognac and piped with cream – jumping and flinching each time the odd snowball thudded dully against one of the windowpanes. Elizabeth's mother, gazing critically, said That doesn't look anything *like* a snowman – goodness, Elizabeth, the snowmen we used to build, when I was young: like the Guys on November the, um – Guy Fawkes. Not nowadays, they don't – everyone has everything, these days, and no one makes the effort. Remind me, Elizabeth – have we had Christmas lunch or not yet? Only I won't have a biscuit if we've not eaten, else it'll spoil it. (Lunch is coming, Mummy – lunch is coming soon.) Brian was momentarily lifted by the yelps of revelry – the hot breath of the leaping flames in the grate and the young people outside, alive and cavorting, my poor bloody unfortunate son among them. He went to freeze by the back door and watch them, inhaling sharply as the first gust of cold rushed in to him. He looked on, really quite fondly, until one fat snowball caught him full in the face, whereupon he cuffed at his cheeks with trussed-up elbows, banged shut the door with his bottom, and wandered off anywhere, again.

When they all fell over each other to be back in the warm – red-faced and batting clotted lumps of snow from out of their hair, scooping up more from under their collars – Elizabeth eyed with elaborate care the malformed, greyish and teetering stumps on the lawn and declared the Grand Snowman Contest a brilliant success and a three-way draw, and prizes were coming to all. Katie let out a donkey noise of exhilaration more at home in a rodeo, while Melody tried unsuccessfully to explain to Emil even the gist of what Elizabeth had said, and Colin was burned by the icy collision of his and Kelly's faces as she hugged him close. Rick muttered to Katie that theirs was way ahead of the other two, you just gotta look – but yeh, I guess: it's no big deal. Elizabeth felt so elated as she served out to everyone a frothy mixture of advocaat and lemonade in tall striped glasses – it's a *snowball*, she trilled excitedly: that's the name of the *drink*. And nor was she done yet: the lid came off what looked like a shoebox, and tightly packed inside were a dozen big and fluffy clouds of cotton wool, each surmounted by a shiny sprig of paper holly. These she hurled with quite un-Elizabeth-like abandon around the room – because now we can *all* go snowballing, even *you*, Mummy! Catch! Catch! And quietly to Zoo-Zoo (who had not gone outside – it would have amazed her had he done so): You're not trying, Zoo-Zoo – catch one, catch it: they've all got presents inside; I'm not, he said evenly, into games.

Cyril and Edna had arrived then for lunch – Welcome, welcome, cried Elizabeth: oh you are so *naughty* – you shouldn't have brought *presents*! Look, Howard – *presents*! (And yes indeed – when she saw the kitchen, Edna had practically *died*.) Each of them pretended to enjoy the hurling of the cotton wool snowballs, Cyril ducking rather than catching any that whistled close. Then everyone crowed over the gifts inside as they tore them all up – Brian just loved his set of miniature screwdrivers (very handy for minor electrics – if, of course, you have a house). Dotty swapped with Katie her blue plastic earrings for the mummy duck and ducklings for little baby Dawn, and Colin studied closely Kelly's left eyeball with his brand-new tiny magnifying glass. Even Rick seemed pleased with his Disneyland keyring (Yeh – reminds me of the time I had a condo in Florida) – but the true wonder came when Elizabeth threw back the double doors to the dining room, so that all could marvel at the Christmas table to end them all.

And nor had she been disappointed by the wall of sheer admiration, spiked by appetite (the aromas coming from the kitchen were unmistakably both Christmassy and fabulous). And now they had reached the stage where Elizabeth had tugged shut the curtains, and amid only the throb and sparkle of all the little lights the length of the table, she bore in high and on a bright red platter the blazing pudding – and this was met with practically applause. I actually, thought Brian, don't think I could squeeze in even one more thing – which is just as well, because I didn't at all enjoy the brick-like resentment all over Dotty's face during the first three courses when she had reluctantly set aside Dawn, cut my food and thrust it down me.

And again the table was alive with not just chatter, but sluicing and gorging. But a few were quiet, and one of them was Edna. Since we have stepped from next door and into this house, Cyril has lost no time in detaching himself from me but utterly and talking so very animatedly to that woman, Lulu Powers. I can't understand it. I *could* understand it, yes, if it was Elizabeth he was lavishing all this attention upon: Elizabeth is, yes I suppose (have you *seen* that kitchen?) all that I aspire to – and one day, maybe, I might have made it. But I can never be Lulu. Lulu just sits there, and is beautiful. I can never just sit there: I can never be beautiful.

Elizabeth was now saying it was time for Charades, which meant it was also time for Howard to refresh his latest whisky, and chuck up his eyes to heaven; from Katie there came her signature whine – 'Oh *Mum* . . .! Not *that* again – we do that *every* year . . .!' And now Elizabeth was saying You really don't see it, do you Katie? That's the whole *point* of the thing: it's a *tradition*, isn't it? And Elizabeth had all the Christmassy words and phrases there and at the ready (of course she did – she even had a real silk black top-hat to pick them from, for there must be nothing less than quite perfect here, you know).

Katie, anyway, flat refused to go first ('It's not fair – I *always* do') – Colin was practically in hiding, praying he wouldn't be called on, and Brian was excused on the grounds that you need a good four limbs in this game (although in Brian's case, as most people tacitly acknowledged, a combined and implicit understanding of tic-tac, semaphore and deaf-dumb sign language would hardly have helped him). So Rick was first up – and while he was rummaging around in the depths of the top-hat – willing a winner to come to his hand – so he suddenly announced in a voice that he maybe imagined to be half-posh English (half very much not):

'Oh – Choody, Choody, Choody!'

Which was greeted, as ever, with dumbfoundedness tinged at the edges with unease, if not outright apprehension (so odd, aren't they? Americans).

'Cary Grant – yes?' he offered. 'He was in the movie Sha-Raid, yeah? With Oddrey Hepburn?'

Elizabeth affected her gently encouraging smile (I think he's touched, but fundamentally harmless) and then Rick was frowning over his challenge – and now he was sagging at the knees and rolling his eyes and pointing at his head with one revolving finger.

'Idiot,' volunteered Howard. And then more quickly, 'He's miming "idiot", yes?'

'Idiot isn't a *Christmas* word, is it Howard?' admonished Elizabeth.

'Drunk!' called Katie. 'No? Pissed, then – red nose: Rudolph!'

Rick indicated No no no, and then let his tongue sag out of the corner of his mouth as he wagged his head this way and that.

'Psychiatric Case,' put in Cyril. 'Oh no – that's not Christmassy either, is it? Nutcase – Brazil nuts! No? What do you think, Lulu?'

'Oh Christ's *sake*,' hissed Lulu. 'Will you bloody stop *talking* to me? How many times? How many *times*?' And then, very quietly: 'I think you're *disgusting*.'

'Crackpot,' offered Brian, at the same time thinking Don't, anyone, please turn and look at me.

And Rick was going More! More! Beckoning with all his hunched-over fingers as if urging a nervous motorist into a far-too-small space. *Fucking* crackpot, grunted Howard – more or less inaudibly; and then two or three people blurted out at once: *Crackers*! Oh yes – *crackers*, of course, brilliant – well done, Rick. And as all of that gently subsided, the sound of the doorbell was vibrant enough, and Colin jumped up saying That'll be Kelly (because Kelly, it had been made plain, had not been welcome to stay for lunch: you do *understand*, don't you?). Colin scampered off to the hall, and it was indeed Kelly – and he kissed her and he wanted her (she was magic, like that) but before he got the door shut a man strode up the drive and said Hi there, Colin – remember me? And Colin knew who he was, and so he let him in.

It would be overstating the case to suggest that Lulu was actually *pleased*, when John walked into the room (Elizabeth most certainly was not – last time she had seen him he had utterly wrecked her summer party by attacking Melody's then so-called boyfriend with a champagne bottle, God help us; what on earth is *he* doing here?) – but at least he could be depended upon to finally rid her of fucking Cyril, in his own inimitable way.

'Elizabeth,' John opened, really quite meekly. 'Howard. Sorry to, um . . . Merry Christmas, everyone! Just thought I'd, er . . .'

'Have a drink,' called over Howard. Always best, he'd found, just saying that: covered a multitude. 'We're playing Charades – John's go!'

It was a welcome of sorts – couldn't really argue, could he? John was still in fact catching his breath, so floored had he been by that first sight of Lulu; God – oh *God*, she's so lovely, my wife, my wife: what can I do to make her want me again? You never *will*, Tara had sniped at him, when he had said he was leaving: Why would a woman like that ever come back to a dismal little nobody like you? Hey? A talentless no-hoper like you – *huh*?! Yes, that's what she had said – then hurling the half-stuffed turkey at his head (it missed, but he slithered on it) just before she fired him from the magazine, *sweetie*.

John gazed at the massed array of drink, and yearned for it. 'I won't, thanks Howard,' he had managed to say (if I start in on that, I'm finished before I begin). As he was miming his phrase – Robin Redbreast, how the hell? – he was very aware of Cyril in huge and earnest discussion with Lulu, sometimes touching her hand (her hand!) and sometimes even patting her shoulder (her shoulder!). But he tamped and then crammed right down deep inside of him the boiling stir of jealousy – and when Lulu caught his eye and widened hers, he pulled off the nearest to a devil-may-care grin, and even a little just-you-see-how-cool-I-am wavelet. Meanwhile, he had a Charade to do: he pointed out a bowlful of large glass and cherry-coloured baubles, to denote the red bit, but everyone just shouted out *Balls*, so that was no good; and Robin Hood with his bow and arrow got simply nowhere, so in the end he was forced to tell them just what in hell he'd been banging on about, and the general consensus was that absolutely nothing he'd attempted even had so much as a *bearing* – and the second John was officially released from this pitiless drubbing, Lulu was on to him:

'John – do something about Cyril. Now, please.'

And Cyril was alongside as John urged everything within him not to rip the bastard's head from his shoulders.

Instead, he arched his brows into a big show of insouciance and said My dear Lulu – whatever can you mean?

'I *mean*,' stressed Lulu (and her voice was rising – Elizabeth caught it, anyway), 'do what you *do* – hit him or kill him, or something. He's driving me *crazy*.'

John gritted his teeth. This is a test, right? Got to be. 'I'm sure he's just – being friendly.'

Cyril nodded and smiled. 'Of course,' he agreed. 'No more.'

Elizabeth decided that they were in urgent need of another Charade – no good asking Howard (doubt if he can stand) – and as for Colin and Kelly, well! (Odd, though, to think that one time not long ago it was we two who could barely keep our hands to ourselves.) Melody and Emil were hardly any better – Mummy was asleep, thank the Lord, and Dotty had pottered off to see to little Dawn; Zoo-Zoo, I simply don't dare. There was only Edna left – and the way she'd been eyeing Cyril for just ages, this could maybe only be a good thing.

Edna dipped her hand into the topper, gazed at her selection and said to Elizabeth, I must just quickly go and powder my nose, which will also give me time to think – and so as Lulu continued to fume (John was now pouring for Cyril a large glass of claret, without taking one for himself) Elizabeth went about the business of giving the fire a damn good poking, while calling over her shoulder for Katie to do the rounds with trays and trays of just everything – briefly told Howard he was drinking too quickly, and then she paused to check that Mummy was indeed still breathing (she was – and rather too audibly, for Elizabeth's liking).

It was Colin and Kelly's braying honks and hootings of near-hysterical disbelief, allied then with the quite drunk and too high-pitched cackling and mumming from Melody ('I knew it! I knew she was nuts!'), that first alerted the rest of the party to exactly what, dear God, could be happening now: the softly collapsed and pink and whitely naked Edna padded quite delicately across the carpet as voices and even two glasses were dropped around her. Cyril barely whispered 'Edna . . .!' as everyone else fell uneasily silent. Elizabeth – more concerned than she could say – took off her cardigan and approached with care, saying *Edna*, dear . . .?

Edna, quite proudly, and apparently heedless of how she appeared (she came over as simply Edna: no more and no less), announced to the company that she had *won*, then, hadn't she? *Christ*, Edna, muttered Cyril, darkly: Jesus, Elizabeth, I'm so sorry – textbook case – Look, I'll . . . But as he reached out for her, she batted him aside, and now quite loudly she called out the word Turkey! Yes, *Turkey*! That's the word I chose. *You* should have seen it, Cyril – you're so good at games . . .

'Elizabeth!' exclaimed Howard. 'God's sake – can't you – ?!'

Edna smoothed her palms down over the tops of her legs, and around the greyish tangle between them.

'Thighs,' she explained. And then, fingering a near-inverted nipple ('*Right* – that's it!' thundered Cyril – moving in fast). 'Breast!' she managed to stutter, as he bundled her up in his jacket, and started to grapple her away and towards the door, yelling out his blind and utter hatred of the woman, and mixing this with quite plaintive apology to just anyone who further shamed him by looking. Elizabeth rushed out with them to the hall, and supplementing Cyril's jacket with a raincoat of her own, she looked with real sorrow into Edna's eyes – tried and failed to say something.

'But alas,' concluded Edna, quite mildly, as Cyril heaved her out of the house and back to the hell of their own, 'alas, alas, Elizabeth – no wings, you see.'

And despite the still falling snow and quite shocking cold, Elizabeth followed solicitously into the porch, and even a little way beyond – watching as if mesmerized the retreating form of Cyril, trudging off with a firm and unforgiving arm around his trussed-up wife, poor dear Edna's half-dragged feet (what *can* she be going through?) leaving drunken ruts behind her. And then – how odd – some young woman climbed out of a car (hadn't even registered the car) and clutching a piece of paper appeared to make some sort of enquiry of Cyril; Elizabeth could not hear his reaction, but she saw the angry shrug and hugely dismissive wave as he plodded on up his driveway. The woman watched them go, and then to Elizabeth's even greater surprise and then annoyance, she glanced across and caught Elizabeth's eye – and immediately began to come on over. Oh God, thought Elizabeth – how can anyone be wanting directions on Christmas Day! And *now*, of all times. But I can't just go back in, because she's clearly seen me, and one doesn't want to appear in any way *rude*; anyway – she'd only ring the bell (even now I can see she's that determined).

'Hello!' Laa-Laa greeted her warmly. 'Isn't it *freezing*? Look, I do realize that this is the most awful moment, but I wonder if I might just have a quick word with Mister Street?'

Elizabeth was amazed. 'Howard doesn't do business on Christmas Day,' she said, with a degree of hauteur – though already something ugly was lurking at the borders: this woman wasn't a fool, was she? She must know that; so if not business . . . 'Whatever it is, I am sure it can wait.'

'No, believe me,' said Laa-Laa – now quite acid – 'it can't.'

She pushed past Elizabeth and into the house – Elizabeth momentarily paralysed by not just this action, but also her embittered comment as she did it: 'You're the wife, aren't you? Yes you are – you've just got to be.' But Elizabeth was racing now – all she knew was that she must reach Howard in advance of this woman: no one must see whatever will happen.

But too late: all Laa-Laa had done was stand firm in the hall and repeatedly scream out at the very top of her voice

Howard! Howard! Howard! Howard! – until Elizabeth –
blunted by dizziness – thought she might be close to losing
her senses: she hissed and spat at Laa-Laa – Get out! Get out
of my house, you mad bitch! Get out – get out – get *out* of
here, you madwoman! She yearned to be able to attack her,
but she couldn't, she couldn't – she just knew she couldn't.
And now there arrived – alive with surprise and anxiety –
not just Howard, but more or less everyone else as well (oh
God, oh God – I simply can't face this). And now, as Laa-
Laa subsided, they formed themselves unconsciously into
excited clusters. Elizabeth could not bring herself to look
over at Howard, and was therefore spared any interpre-
tation of his bulbous and wide-eyed staring out at what
quite simply just couldn't be happening.

'Oh there you are, Howard,' smiled Laa-Laa. 'Having a
good Christmas? I'm sorry, everyone, to mess up your day
but –'

'Get *out*,' said Howard, heavily, the words just making it
past his teeth (Christian Dior's Poison, he automatically
recognized).

Elizabeth husked out, 'Who *is* she, Howard? What does
she –?'

'Never seen her before in my life. She must be mental.'

'Oh *no*!' rejoined Laa-Laa, roundly. '*Not* mental, oh no
Howard. I am the woman you have been keeping in a cosy
little flat, aren't I, Howard?' She turned to Elizabeth. 'Sorry
about this – it's not *personal*. I didn't ever mean to hurt you.'

'Oh Christ,' blustered Howard. 'Call the police, someone – she's mad, I tell you – crazy. Never even *seen* the
woman –'

And now Elizabeth raised her eyes to him. 'Howard . . .?'
was all she managed.

'Never *seen* her, I tell you!' (Not like this, I haven't: what
has become of her prettiness? Why does neither eye say *Laa*,
or *Laa*?)

'Now look, everyone . . .' tried Brian, feeling he owed it to

Howard to say something or other, here – but he was damned if he could think of a follow-up: just wouldn't come.

'He fucked me,' went on Laa-Laa, 'whenever he could' – and she went right on talking through the frisson that rippled around her – 'but now I am apparently surplus to requirements.'

The doorbell rang like a shriek, which caused Lulu to practically leap as if stung.

'Anyway,' concluded Laa-Laa. 'I'm about done here. I'll go.'

'*Look!*' bellowed Howard, 'Miss whoever-you-are – you're clearly sick – she's *sick*, I tell you. Raving. I have never before seen this woman in my *life*, I tell you. Elizabeth – believe me. How many *times*!'

The doorbell rang again – a prolonged and shrill addition to the electric feeling all around them.

'Someone at the door,' said Elizabeth, stupidly.

'Leave it,' snapped Howard.

'Could be Cyril,' said Lulu. 'For Edna's clothes.'

'I'm off,' was Laa-Laa's brief and parting shot – and she had the door open before anyone else had thought of stirring.

Two men stood there, one of whom goggled at Laa-Laa and blurted out as he stepped in:

'My God! *Sophina*! What are *you* doing here?'

Laa-Laa laughed out loud. 'Oh Christ – *you*. What a happy reunion. Well Howard? Still mad, am I?'

Howard moved quickly over to Norman Furnish, intending to kill him, once and for all. Elizabeth had automatically closed the door against the swirling snow, and now Melody came forward with the light of hope alive in her eyes.

'Miles! Oh Miles, thank God! I've missed you so much!'

'Huh?' grunted Miles – off-guard and sweeping the assembly in search of Katie.

'Please!' screamed Norman, as Howard grabbed him roughly by the throat. 'Please don't hit me, Howard – Mister Street, Mister Street! – I swear to you, oh God I didn't know she was your *mistress* or I never would've gone round there! It was only because I knew the address because it's one we used to manage, and – ' And then, dully: 'Oh Christ. Sorry.'

Melody was tugging at Miles, desperate for his attention. 'Miles – thank God you've come back. I love you – love you. Look – I lied to you about the baby, you maybe found out – but I'm giving her away, I swear it!'

Miles just stared at her. 'Where's Catherine?'

'Do you really *mean* that?' Dotty gabbled excitedly to Melody. 'You *mean* it, yes? Really?'

Norman had only time to gasp out to Miles: 'Catherine? *Katie*? What do you want *Katie* for?' because now he was down on his knees, and Howard was purple in his efforts to strangle the bloody life out of him. But when Katie stepped forward ('Christ's *sake*, Daddy – God's sake – you'll *kill* him!') Norman found and drew on some reserve of nearly strength and wrested his way out of Howard's appalling grip and wriggled on his belly right up to her – just at the moment that Miles had her by the shoulders, and was drawing her towards him. Norman had Miles by the ankles, now (both Elizabeth and Katie were dragging at Howard, so desperate were his efforts to get to Furnish and rip him up), and as Norman hauled himself up by way of the man's trousers, Miles kicked out at him and launched into his impassioned babble to Katie. John Powers was lurking at the back, and clutching hard a side-chair – he just had to restrain himself from pitching hard into that Miles bastard himself (he's the fucker who fucked my wife! At least it's not her he's come for – what would I do then? Let him?) because he knew that if he lashed out now then Lulu would see that he was just the same old jealous John and that he hadn't *changed* – and then he'd fail the *test* and she'd leave him for ever.

'Catherine!' panted Miles – and he accompanied it with a mighty flexing of his whole left leg that had Norman sprawling, but gamely crawling back for more. 'Listen, girl – I've left them, right? You didn't think I would, but I have. Sheil, the kids – the lot. Come away with me now!'

'Get off her! Get off her!' cried out Norman. '*Me*, Katie – *me*! I can't live without you! I've tried – stop hitting me, bastard! – but I can't.'

And if everyone was looking at just anyone around at each of these gasped out utterances, no two were doing so more intently and with more amazement than Norman and Miles at that briefest of instants. Both of them – and Katie too – opened their mouths to say something urgent, but no sound came from any of them because at that moment a fist like a jackhammer came from nowhere and practically bent Miles's face in half, so jarringly powerful was the total collision – and as Miles staggered as if broken across the hall and into Dotty and Dawn – the three of them pitching over into a squealing heap – Melody, Lulu, and Elizabeth screamed out horrifyingly and all set about pounding with fists the American Rick, who had silently delivered this most massive of stunners – but he seemed barely to notice as he turned calmly to face Norman – now near incontinent with fright – and it is possible that Norman fainted just before the big and juddering blow had even connected. And now as Miles and Norman lay entwined and more or less in bits on the floor, Rick – brushing away women – reached into his jacket and pulled out the gun. As his steady finger squeezed into the trigger, just one figure broke free of the suddenly stricken and quite frozen tableau: Dotty had raised talons and a vast and unappeasable outrage was ablaze in her eyes.

'You *swine*!' she bellowed, as she pitched herself into him. 'You could have hurt my *baby*, you – !'

Rick was knocked sideways as the shot that boomed dully had some people roaring briefly, and others struck by a new and even deeper silence. Howard jerked, and with Katie and Elizabeth screaming as he did it, slowly pitched forward, and fell as if demolished.

CHAPTER NINETEEN

The wait for the ambulance had been interminable; Elizabeth's nerves – thoroughly frayed – now grew so ragged as to be effectively beyond her command. She was having the greatest difficulty, yes, in patching together in her storming mind quite what had happened next. That perfectly terrible *villainous* man Rick – yes, she certainly remembered this – had lost little time in leaving. But he had been in no hurry in the sense of *bustle*, you understand – Katie's venom was having little effect (she had been crying, *wailing* for her father and screaming at Rick – came that close to pitching the bloody Rolex right back in his face). At the mention of police, though, he simply walked out of the house, with seemingly practised ease. (He had a gun! He had a gun! The man had a gun and he actually fired it!) And that awful, awful woman – the one that Howard . . . oh God, oh God – I just can't think anything of Howard, just now: and still he's lying there, conscious and watching me. When will it come, this bloody ambulance? Why was it taking so long? Anyway – she went with him.

The relief that rushed over me when I knew he hadn't been shot – was it Brian who noticed the splintered table? – that had been blessed, just as they say it can be. But he was white and in pain and clutching his sides: it hurt, he whispered, even to speak. Before this impending stupor had time to descend on me (I knew it was there – I felt its hover) I hustled Norman Furnish out and away; his eye would be a terrible colour and no doubt he was in awful pain, but just his presence was edging Howard ever closer to a seizure – if, indeed, he was not already in the grip of one.

Katie had not looked at Norman – he tried desperately to tell her as he was being edged through the door that the only reason he had come was not *just* to see her – that yes, of course – but mainly to get back the video before Howard could have a chance to see it; I didn't, on reflection, want to *hurt* him. And it had been a terrible walk, in the freezing cold and snow. Miles had been sitting in his car outside – waiting, apparently. We'd become really quite matey – clearly we had a similar problem: Jesus – we even *laughed* together about it. He said it just had to be today, he came – and I knew just what he meant because that's exactly why I was there too; but Christ – I thought he'd come for Melody – or that other one, what's she called, Lulu. Not *you*, Katie – I'd no idea he was here for *you*. So where is it, Katie? The video? I don't, she said coldly, have the faintest idea what you're talking about: go now, please. (In fact, at that moment, it had just been viewed in its entirety by Kelly and Colin – he had found it just lying around; they had watched it upstairs – Colin had breathlessly slid himself into a hot keen Kelly as they lay sprawled across Howard and Elizabeth's king-size divan, and he came quite glitteringly and well within seconds just as Katie, on film, was demonstrating just what could be done with the imposing aid of a still closed magnum of Bollinger. Did *you*, he had panted to Kelly: did you come too? 'Now,' she answered, quite honestly – adding on rather generously, 'but prick-tickly.')

Miles's jaw was clearly at the very least broken, if not utterly shattered; Katie ignored him and so, although it killed her, did Melody too. He would have to go along with them in the ambulance, if ever the bloody thing got here. And so Elizabeth continued to sit there, just next to Howard in the hall on the spot where he had fallen; she held his hand and he stared around him. She was beset by yet more confusion as suddenly Lulu – bright-eyed and urgent –

402

rushed up to her and with both hands snatched her fingers away from Howard's. Elizabeth could only look up in maybe puzzled enquiry.

'Leave him,' Lulu insisted. 'Let him go. He's no good.'

'But,' protested Elizabeth, wearily, 'he's *Howard* . . .'

'And what about that woman? Hm? They're all the same, men – they're all disgusting.' And then Lulu breathed hard and hurtled down the trump she had been hoarding: 'And don't think she's the only one – I suppose you know he's had an on-off affair with *Melody* for absolutely *years*?'

Howard's eyes sprang wider and his mouth opened – but was closed down quickly by a shudder of agony. Melody had heard that, and she spoke up boldly, if only to douse a little of her own deep hurt and disillusionment – just sitting here amid it all, next to this prat of a fucking Frenchman.

'Well so bloody *what*!' she roared. 'We don't *all* hate men, you know, Lulu! Why do you think she's saying all this, Elizabeth? It's only because she's bloody in *love* with you – Christ Almighty, anyone can see that.'

Howard was fighting the pain and trying to speak, but the pain was winning easily.

'Yes I *do* love Lizzie – I *do* I *do* I *do*. At least she's *clean* – clean and beautiful, unlike your strings of *men*, Melody – Christ, look where they got you: a kid you don't want and *alone.*'

'Oh fuck off, Lulu,' snarled Melody. Too hurt – too damned hurt to say any more.

'The baby *is* wanted,' said Dotty. 'Wanted desperately.'

'Have her,' snapped Melody. 'Yeh – I really do mean it, this time. I love you for loving her. I just can't. Hah!' She grinned with mischief at this one: 'But you might as well know that the father's that bloody idiot Norman Furnish! Still want her?'

'Christ,' said Katie, in a low and wondering tone.

'Lulu!' burst out John – can't, just can't keep quiet a single moment longer. '*Lulu*, Godsake – what's all this Elizabeth nonsense? It's me – *me*, Lulu: I'm your husband – I *love* you.'

'Oh Christ shut up shut up shut *up!*' screamed back Lulu. 'You love *you*, you bastard, John! You wouldn't even lift a finger today when I was being practically raped by that fucking creep *Cyril* – that's how much I mean to you, John. We're *over* – if we ever *were*.'

John was left there, mouth struck open in pain and amazement, as Elizabeth – held now by awesome fascination – turned her head to another still voice:

'She's not, you know,' said Zoo-Zoo, easily. 'Clean. Not really, Lulu. I know because up till today I had an ongoing and very physical relationship with Elizabeth myself – which is why I resent you so very much, Lulu, because I know you love her, I know it.'

Before anyone else could respond, Colin – by now at the foot of the stairs – put in quite cheekily: 'No, he's right – she's not that clean' – but couldn't, even had he wanted to, say any more: Mum was there, and looking.

The letterbox rattled and a voice was heard:

'Hallo? Hallo? Ambulance. Hallo?'

Only when Howard was bound on to the stretcher did Elizabeth see the silvery glaze of tight and drying tears across his face.

'Take care of him,' Zoo-Zoo said quietly to her. 'Because I have loved him too with passion, and I know how he must feel – to be in this state. You, Elizabeth, are softer. Goodbye.'

Elizabeth, practically borne up into the clouds, walked alongside the stretcher and towards the door, looking forward to getting away from here. Her mother had emerged from the drawing room, scratching at her forearms.

'I think I dozed off, you know. Have I missed anything? Oh – poor, um . . . not well, is he? I must say, Elizabeth – lunch was quite wonderful – thank you, dear. We have *had* lunch, yes?'

'Howard, Mummy,' said Elizabeth, softly. 'His name is Howard.' And then, more generally to the sea of eyes that gazed at her: 'Help yourselves to everything, won't you, everyone? What a shame . . . we didn't get round to playing Consequences . . .'

Lulu held her arm. 'Must you go with him?'

Elizabeth regarded her. 'Yes,' she said.

'But you'll come back? Will you? To me?'

Elizabeth regarded her.

CHAPTER TWENTY

It was a hell of a squeeze in the ambulance – Howard and
Miles just lying there, and between them a totally silent
and seemingly dreamy Elizabeth. Katie too was there, alternating her constant enquiries as to how her Daddy was
feeling now with crabby asides to one of the paramedics
about how much damn space he was taking up (Sorry, he
kept on repeating, Sorry, love, sorry – Katie responding
tartly with I'm not your *love*, am I?). This acted as the cue for
bloody Miles to start in again on some large protestation,
his yelps of pain following each incoherent syllable making
Elizabeth wince and Katie bark out And I'm not bloody *your*
love either – just shut *up*, Miles, you utter creep: it's *Daddy*
I'm here for, it's my Daddy I care about – how *are* you,
Daddy, hm? But God, she was thinking, I can't help but look
at him oddly, now – and Mummy too, Mummy too. Parents
aren't meant to *be* like that, are they? Particularly not when
they're so dull and boring and old like my two. But you've
got to just go on *loving* them, and everything, I suppose, yes
you do – because no matter how awful they turn out to be,
they've just always got to be better news than scumbags like
Miles and losers like Norman and out-and-out psychos
like American Rick: if I ever see *him* again, I'll spit right in
his face. I think I had a lucky escape with that bloke. *God*,
though – I've only just this second twigged to what that prat
Norman was drivelling on about: the *video*, oh Christ of
course! Got to get hold of that before anyone else does – it
was simply *filthy*, pretty sure. Jesus; what a bloody funny
Christmas Day.

Brian also had come along for the ride, the crush of bodies forcing his bent and plastered arms up to and across his throat, each jolt of the road more or less obliging him to cuff his own nose. What on earth do *you* want to go for, Dotty had demanded: they don't want *you* going, do they, Brian? What in God's name makes you imagine that they'd want *you* along, hm? And Dotty was still alive with the tingle of delight, the true certainty, now, that Dawn was finally to be her Maria – and tingling too, she supposed, due to the nature of so rapid a succession of unthinkable revelations. One thing Brian and I always did have was fidelity; but that, of course, is never really enough on its own, and ultimately, it would seem, counts for little. I do not know if any more pretensions to Christmas will now be attempted by Lulu and Co, but I for one have had more than enough: I shall say good-night to Colin – and just look at him, will you? Nearly all grown up – and I've never even seen it before. There he is by the fire, laughingly assuring that Australian girl (quite pretty, I suppose, in a rather obvious way) that Christmas in England isn't, honestly, *always* like this. (And what on earth could he have meant about Elizabeth? She has always seemed terribly clean to me.) My angel Maria is asleep, and very soon I shall be too. Now where's Lulu? Oh – oh dear, that very strange husband of hers is over there with her; I think what I'll do is just quietly creep away.

John – stunned by sobriety – just kept on uttering Lulu's name, time and time again, while his eyes beseeched her – and all he could do was absorb her bout of temper as she hissed at him to, oh God, *go* John, can't you? Just go back to wherever it is you came from. But *Jesus,* Lulu, he tried again – but quite in vain, and of course he knew it. He turned away bleakly, two thoughts only now tugging within him: I wonder if Tara cooked the turkey, after she threw it at me? And my God, you know, I've spent all my years with Lulu being gnawed alive by jealousy of *men*: nothing else had even occurred to me.

And as John, wild-eyed and amazed, walked off and out of there, stiff-legged and uncertainly, so Melody (eyeing it) made her move – but she backed away again swiftly when she saw that young Peter person – the one Elizabeth used to call some other thing altogether, can't quite remember – sidling across to Lulu; and now he was there and next he was speaking:

'What I shall not now have to say to Elizabeth, Lulu, is that my people are moving on, at the beginning of the year. They do this. I think it is looking good for you, Lulu – I think you might get what you want. Goodbye.'

'Your presents . . .' said Lulu, indicating his special tousle of luxury, selected by Elizabeth.

He smiled, and shook his head. 'I won't need them. They won't be me. Whenever I find myself somewhere new, I become something else entirely.'

Lulu just watched him go, sensing rather than seeing the approach of yet another.

'I think,' opened Melody, 'you should not have told Elizabeth about me and Howard – she might now hate me. But I know how love can be – the things it makes you do and say. Lulu – what is it about you and Katie? Why does everyone want you? How on earth is it *done*?'

Lulu wearily half closed her eyes. 'I think now I have to get Lizzie's mother to bed.'

And as she set about doing just that ('So much excitement, so much excitement,' is what Mummy was muttering now) Lulu was thinking I tell you what, though, dearest Lizzie, you were quite wrong about us not having had time to play Consequences: we've all been doing it for simply ages.

❄

The doctor is talking to me, yes, thought Howard, but I must be careful not to hear too much: there is always, I think in these things, a limit, don't you? It's a nice room – quite restful, despite the silly bits of tinsel: all those years of BUPA are finally paying off. And talking of BUPA, apparently that twelve-year-old kid who gave me the check-up, that time, was not entirely wrong: spot of trouble with the old liver, it truly would appear. Also some other thing renal – that's kidneys, I think, isn't it? Mild heart attack thrown in for good measure: bloody well fells you, you know, this sort of thing. Not fatal, is the message I'm getting – but quite clearly rather far from being good news. He's telling me more right now, the doctor, but as I say – enough is enough. Cut out the booze, seems to be the bottom line – which is a bit of a bugger, actually, because all the way here in the ambulance (and Christ: could barely hear myself think – that bastard with the broken jaw was setting up a fearful racket) what I was thinking was Christ, you know, that's about all I've got left, the drink. But not even that, apparently. Elizabeth said – she's just left: not here now – that when I'm quite well again, she wants to go away alone. To think, apparently. Christ Almighty – you don't have to go away to do that: I'm still here and I can't bloody stop. Could even, while I was just lying in the hall, there – however long ago that was – could even have voiced a bit of what I was thinking, but what, in fact, could one usefully say?

So what all this means, I really couldn't tell you: everything seems to have rather snowballed out of all control. Katie was looking at me terribly oddly, as well she might: not every day, is it, both your parents are exposed as a pair of bisexual philanderers. Oh dear. Anyway – told Brian (Brian was in, short while back) that there's a flat going begging he might as well have: somewhere for the baby, somewhere for young Colin. Terribly grateful. Even tried to demonstrate his early New Year Resolution to finally stop concentrating on topping himself and knuckle down instead to getting a decent job. Poor sod – tried to tear up before me the latest of his suicide notes, but you get nowhere, do you, with two broken arms. Dotty's leaving him, but I don't think she's said so, yet.

And me? Well – more or less as you see: bit of a lame, er . . . lame thing. Whatever that lame thing is. You know my mind.

'So,' wound up the doctor, 'that's about it, Mister Street. Questions?'

'Duck!' said Howard.

The doctor flinched and looked about him. 'I'm sorry?'

'No – nothing. Just something that came to me. I'm dying for a whisky . . .'

'Well,' opined the doctor, 'in a very real sense, of course, you *are*, Mister Street. But that's what we're here to deal with. Right, well – I'll be popping in to see you over the next couple of days. Anything you want – just ring for a nurse: button right there. So – apart from all this, though – how did you enjoy what Christmas you had? Any good?'

'Hm?' grunted Howard, before sliding with ease into his stock response. 'Oh – the usual.' And then he shut tight his eyes. 'Family . . . few friends – *quiet*, you know . . .'